"Black/on/black!" All around him, the chant began again, softly at first, then louder, building into an ear-splitting litany he could not shout down. "Black/on/black!"

Heyoka stared at the people he had crossed a galaxy to find. The fire of fanaticism was written across their furred faces. He wanted them to stand with him because they understood the danger, not because of a chance-generated genetic combination that made him resemble an old legend.

But moments before, they had been ready to tear out his throat because he was born of Levv. Now that they had caught him up high on the wave of their expectations, they were his because he had taken command in the only way they understood.

A few feet away, Nisk lifted his gaze from the charred form of the priest, speaking to Heyoka with searing ebony eyes: the Black/on/black was a weapon forged to their own hands. If he would be what they expected, the Hrinn would follow him and fight the Flek with every life and resource they possessed. But if he insisted on being merely Heyoka Blackeagle, an outcast Levv male, he would share Levv's, as well as Anktan's, death.

He threw back his head, and with a roar that shook him down to the depths of his soul, thrust his fist high into the air.

Black on Black

K.D. WENTWORTH

A Baen Books Original

Baen Publishing Enterprises
P.O. Box 1403
Riverdale, NY 10471

ISBN: 0-671-57788-3

Cover art by Patrick Turner

First printing, February 1999

Distributed by Simon & Schuster
1230 Avenue of the Americas
New York, NY 10020

Typeset by Windhaven Press, Auburn, NH
Printed in the United States of America

For Clay,
who listened to my stories
long before anyone else

Chapter One

Heyoka Blackeagle stepped out of the shuttle's conditioned air into a hot buffeting wind. Airborne sand ticked against the metal transport and Anktan's arid, red-orange landscape swept before him out into a series of low, green-carpeted mountains in the distance. In the foreground, a shallow, meandering river bordered the rudimentary landing pad which was all the Danzig Research Station needed. The river evidently changed course in times of flood and a nearby dry channel was choked with rust-colored sand. More sand extended back from the river's current banks, then trailed off into desert hardpan.

The dry air was thinner than humans liked, redolent of sun-baked rock and dust and sand. A faint road of sorts led from the landing pad to the station in the distance, both recent developments. Although Heyoka had viewed innumerable pictures and holos of this region without ever being able to recognize anything, he had hoped a smell, or perhaps some long-forgotten sound, such as the shrill of the wind, or the murmur of the river against its banks, would invoke a buried sense-memory and bring his lost past back to him.

But he had no sense that he had walked here before, as the wind ruffled his fur, only the same emptiness he had known all his life. His earliest memories were still the stink of flek slave pens and the throb of the neuronic whip burns across his emaciated ribs. Of the mother who had borne him, or the species to which he belonged, he remembered nothing.

His partner, Mitsu, emerged from the shuttle, blinking against the light, and touched his arm, the pink of her human fingers contrasting sharply with the silken black of his outer coat. "So—what do you think?" She studied the sand-dusted tarmac. "Anything look familiar?"

His nostrils flared as he drank in the hot dry breeze, rich with the scent of a thousand mysterious things he had never smelled before. "No." He shaped the human word without difficulty on his narrow hrinnti tongue, although the skill had cost him many hours of practice in his youth.

Releasing his arm, the wiry black-haired woman trudged heavily down the sloping walkway in the 1.12 Standard gravity, bowed under the weight of her duffel bag. "It doesn't make sense—why would a pilot risk his license just to steal a single juvenile from a Grade Seven Culture?"

Grade Seven—too primitive and aggressive for assimilation into Confederation culture. He brushed a strand of mane out of his face, then flexed his claws, studying the savage three-inch points that gave him a fierce edge in hand-to-hand combat. He had struggled his whole life against the wild, unnamed *otherness* within him, a being too violent to live among humans, who had only found expression on the battlefields of the Confederation's enemies. He had crossed the stars to understand these claws.

A group of mounted figures approached across the cracked hardpan. Mitsu dragged a sleeve across her damp forehead. "What do you suppose they want?"

"What I want." He watched as the riders drew close enough to be seen as six distinct figures, each clad in a different color. "To know who and what I am." He hooked his top thumbs in the loops of his empty weapons belt and stepped off the walkway. His right leg still moved stiffly, a lingering legacy of the wound he had taken in his last action back on Enjas Two. He breathed deeply of the unfamiliar air. Certainly this barren landscape held no sense of home. He had a sudden pang for the rich air of Earth and the Lakota hills of his youth.

Behind them, the walkway shimmered, then disappeared as its generating field terminated. The small automated shuttle that had ferried them down from the supply ship in orbit hummed into life and lifted on antigravs back into the hazy amber sky.

Mitsu grimaced. "Too late to change your mind now," she murmured, shading her eyes.

Heyoka shifted uneasily in the hot sun as the memory of Enjas Two swept back: *the sandy green beach, the hot white dwarf star dominating a silver-blue sky, the brittle silence that seemed to go on forever after it was all over* . . .

He thrust the memory away. Even if he recovered fully from his injury, Bill Rajman, his captain and superior, would not allow him to return to duty until he could explain what had happened that day. Perhaps here on Anktan, he could find some answers.

"I still say you shouldn't have come," he said to Mitsu. He felt excitement overlaid with uneasiness as the six hrinn slowed their burly mounts to a ground-covering walk. Five of them had fur ranging from yellow to gray to dark red, but the one who held his gaze was black with a spectacular white throat.

"Hey, it's my leave." Mitsu slid a sonic blade out

of the sheath in her boot and casually thumbed it on. "I can spend it anywhere I damn well please."

The natives were closing fast, riding their hump-backed steeds with apparent ease. Heyoka drew in the deep musk of hrinnti fur, subtly like and yet unlike his own, and blood began to pound in his ears. He felt flushed, as though all his capillaries had suddenly dilated, tasted cinnamon on the back of his tongue, the richness of melted butter in his throat. Pheromones, he told himself, resisting the urge to pant away the excess heat he was generating. He had never been exposed to scent molecules from his own species before.

The waves of heat beating down from the red sun made the colorfully robed bodies shimmer. Their beasts' feet crunched over the last few feet of sand-littered ground and the breath caught in his throat; they were all so *tall*. Something indigenous to this world, perhaps the greater gravity, or a nutrient in the soil or vegetation, had given them more height than he had and, no doubt, more strength as well. They carried their maned heads high, magnificent and proud, clearly savage.

Stopping a short distance away, the six sat their beasts for a long stretched-out moment as the breeze whipped their lengthy plumes of mane. The black-coated hrinn's mane was bound with green cord to match its loose overtunic and breeches, and swept nearly to its feet. Heyoka had never let his grow half so long.

The gray-coated hrinn drew its thin, large-boned body up proudly and threw a single sentence in guttural Hrinnti at him.

It was female, he realized suddenly, although he could not say how he knew. If anything, her voice had more resonance than his own. And, although he had studied under hours of deepsleep during the journey to this planet, he had difficulty with her accent. Then the fur on the back of his shoulders stood on end as he grasped her meaning: "Stand up." The inner nictitating membranes of his eyes spasmed shut for a second. This strange female had told him to stand up—in the superior-to-inferior mode of the native tongue.

His lips drew back over double rows of gleaming white teeth as he suppressed a deep rumbling growl. He felt the nameless *other* he had fought all his life stir, and shuddered. "I am standing!" he spat back at her in Hrinnti.

"If you are hrinnti"—the old female's nostrils widened as she urged her beast closer—"why were you riding in that Dead shell of the Outsiders?"

The tone of her voice was insulting. Heyoka's claws sprang free, then he sheathed them again. "I have lived among the Outsiders all of my life," he said, adopting her term for humans. "They raised me after I was stolen from my own people."

Her black eyes narrowed. "Then you can never have a place here. Everyone knows Outsiders have no purpose in life. Not one of them has ever been reported to fit into a *pattern/in/progress* of any kind."

The term had not occurred in any of the language lessons. "I have come to find my—" He paused, unable to find the comparable word for family among the vocabulary provided by the tapes. "—my people." The old female edged her shaggy beast closer. "I intend to learn how and why I was taken from this world."

"An Outsider who lives in the Dead place prophesied such a one was coming. We did not believe it." With jerky, painful movements which rattled the many metallic bracelets around her ankle, the old female slid down the side of her mount. The breeze ruffled her gray fur, revealing the white of her denser undercoat. She circled his black-uniformed body one time, then stopped before him, so close that her scent was

overwhelming. "You smell like *them*." Her nose
wrinkled back, exposing shards of broken yellow teeth.
"No Line would claim such a dreadful scent, even
if they wanted to. And no one would want a Dead
thing like you anyway."

Heyoka's claws sprang free again. He felt his breath
coming in short, hard pants.

"You have no males' house and certainly no Line."
Her eyes glittered like black diamonds in her sunken
old face. "Go back to the Dead where you belong."

"He has the *Black/on/black* coloring." The black-
coated hrinn spoke suddenly, revealing himself to be
male. "That cannot be denied."

The gray female aimed a vicious raking blow at
him, but the white-throated male dodged his mount
to one side.

"If you refuse to smell it, I will." He leaned
forward, black nose quivering. "Underneath all that
Dead stink, there is something familiar."

Mitsu edged toward him, the shimmering green
sonic blade extended in her right hand. "I can't make
all of this out," she whispered to Heyoka. "Are they
discussing whether to eat us?"

"They're saying I smell bad." Suddenly the ridi-
culousness of that washed over him, and he felt a rare,
almost human amusement simmering inside him.

"Well, I could have told you that, fuzzface." Mitsu
straightened, still gripping the blade. "We didn't have
to come all the way to this All-Father-forsaken place
for that."

"He is not Black/on/black!" The female remounted,
her ears flattening again. "It is well known the
Outsiders can change their appearance, even the color
of their fur. I have seen it myself. No doubt, tomorrow this creature of the Dead will be some other
color, although it will still smell just as bad."

Heyoka shifted his weight as his weak right leg
cramped in the extra gravity. "What Line do you

represent?" he asked, trying hard to capture the native inflection of speaking to an equal.

The gray female snarled and clawed her beast into a loping run back in the direction from which she had come. The remaining hrinn flattened their ears, the backs of their necks bristling. The male coughed low in his throat. "This —— represents the five Lines of this region, as well as all the males' houses."

"This—what?" Mitsu glanced over her shoulder at Heyoka, but he shook his head, unable to translate the term himself.

"How can I find my people, my—Line?" Heyoka addressed the male, who seemed the most receptive of the lot. "Where should I start?"

Four of the remaining hrinn hissed, claws bared, then whirled their shaggy mounts and followed the gray matriarch. The male rode a step closer, bone-white teeth bared. "I realize you have not been properly brought up, but you should try not to be insulting."

Heyoka held very still.

The male turned his head one way, then another, examining Heyoka with feral black eyes, as bottomless as the deepest space Heyoka had ever seen while journeying between the stars. "When Ankt rests below the horizon, come to the males' house by the river." His black nose twitched above his white throat. "It would be helpful if you would take a proper sandbath first. You cannot expect civilized people to deal with the Dead."

Then he too turned his beast and rode after the other five back across the tarmac, heading toward red sandstone cliffs that rose like a barrier in the distance.

Mitsu deactivated the sonic blade and eased it back into her boot. "What in the Thirty-eight Systems was all that about?"

"I'm not sure." Heyoka rubbed his aching knee.

"Do you really want to mess with this bunch?" Mitsu hoisted her duffle bag and shifted it to her shoulder, grunting a little with the extra weight this gravity imposed upon her. "They're so primitive. I don't see that you'll ever find much in common with them."

"We don't have to love each other." Heyoka hefted his own bag with the double-flash Ranger insignia on the side. "Besides, I don't have any choice. I have to understand what happened to me, or—" He shaded his eyes, studying the stubby white buildings of Danzig Research Station in the distance. "Or it could happen again."

Seska prowled her quarters, not caring how her extruded feetclaws shredded the Vvok-red mat Nintk had just finished. Underneath the stink, that creature had smelled of *Levv*! The scent-memory rose in the back of her mind, savagely sharp, bloodied torn bodies cooling in the chill dankness of a mountain night, the mingled scents of the five other Lines working in rare concert to stamp out a madness that, left unchecked, could have destroyed them all.

She shook herself. Leave it to that uppity male, Nisk, to give voice to the notion of Levv though. Why Jafft had sponsored a witless brute like that for ascendancy in the males' house still baffled her unless he had sniffed out one of the elusive sacred *purposes/in/motion*. Life was not random, so there was obviously some subtle interplay of opportunity and leverage here leading toward a goal she had missed. Her ears flattened as she cursed herself for being unable to divine it.

Or, she told herself, as she turned at the far end of the room and stalked back, it was possible no pattern was emerging and Jafft had just been trying to make her crazy. It would have been just like an earless, no-good male—

A scratch at the door broke her train of thought. She snarled. "Enter at your own risk!"

A gray-and-white form edged in, then prostrated herself on the red carpet. Seska's nose twitched at the scent of her direct-granddaughter, Khea. "A message from the Jhii, Line Mother," the prone figure whispered.

Seska flexed her handclaws. The subservience of this child almost provoked her into attacking. How her birth-daughter, Akea, had ever bred such a disappointing cubling was entirely beyond her. Young as she was, Khea's black eyes should glare up at her from the floor, scheming for the chance to send the old female through the Gates of Death. Instead, she was cowering like a frightened yirn, sure to be culled in the next gleaning.

"The stink of your fear defiles this house." Seska turned her back on the child. "Get out and send someone to attend me who can behave as befits Vvok."

"Jhii asks what you will do, Line Mother."

Seska whirled around to glare at the young face. One eye regarded her from a background of gray and the other from a field of white, a mischance of coloring which lent the child a perpetual half-surprised look. "Do about what?"

"About the Outsider, and the questions he is asking." The fringes around Khea's ears betrayed her trembling, but the cubling remained within reach, a point in her favor. Seska knew she was shedding pungent anger-scent, thick as rain, through the room.

"What concern is that to Vvok?" She hobbled to the corner and eased her aching body onto the pile of soft cushions. Her weight crushed the gynth leaves within and released a soothing menthol aroma. "Nothing which smells like that could come from Vvok, so why should we do anything?"

"Beshha says he is Levv." Khea's black eyes narrowed, then her gaze returned to the floor.

Seska's lips wrinkled back over her broken teeth. "Tell Jhii not even a Levv smells that bad." She stretched her arthritic arms over her head and hissed. "After the message is sent, return to massage my legs and arms, and see you are quick about it."

Ears flattened, young Khea slunk out the door.

Seska rubbed her cheek against the velvety herb-scented cushions. The aromatic scent threaded through her brain, relaxing the knotted muscles in her jaw and shoulders. Such a spineless youngster, she thought. No wonder Mevva had assigned this particular cubling to be overseen by her personally. No doubt, the cub-trainer was counting on her to put some fight into this one before the next gleaning. Squirming onto her back, she stretched luxuriously on the soft mound of pillows.

Well, if it could be done, she would do it. At her age, it went against the lay of her coat to see Vvok breeding more than its share of culls.

The Director of Danzig Station, Eeal Eldrich, was a balding, soft-jowled man in his mid-forties who looked as though he couldn't hike around the compound, much less volunteer for years of privation on a primitive backwater world like Anktan. He retreated behind his desk as Heyoka and Mitsu entered his office, then fixed his pale gray eyes pointedly on her human face. "We cannot guarantee your safety."

Heyoka took the chair on the left without being asked, Mitsu the right. She pulled aside the collar of her black uniform to reveal a white patchwork of shiny laser scars. "I'm a three-year Ranger veteran." Eldrich blanched and turned his eyes away. "And Sergeant Blackeagle has served the Confederation for over ten years. We guarantee our own damn safety."

Eldrich changed position, then shifted again, as if his skin didn't fit. "Sergeant, you are obviously an educated man. Whatever your beginnings, I think you will find you have nothing in common with these natives at this point in your life. They have very little we recognize as culture, no written language, no code of laws, the barest framework of a religion, no sense of progress, or desire to make each succeeding generation's life better."

He leaned forward and spread his hands across his shining desk. "You must realize hrinn—" He glanced at Heyoka. "Or at least, *native* hrinn don't have feelings like humans, no sense of regret or mercy, no concept of familial love, or of heterosexual bonding between mates. The only cognates we've found to human motivations are rage and revenge. If you cross them, they'll kill you without a second thought."

Heyoka's nostrils twitched at the annoyingly sweet odor. Humans, with their lesser sense of smell, drenched themselves in artificial scents that tormented his sensitive nose. This compound was based upon some variety of flower—violet, actually—and animal musk, and one of the aldehydes, and the combination was cloying. He longed to escape. "Corporal Jensen will not be going with me this evening."

His leg ached and he shifted uneasily in the chair which was too small for his bulk by at least a third. "I have been invited to the males' house, whatever that is. All I require from the station are the directions, and perhaps the proper clothing."

Eldrich grimaced. "Four years ago, several anthropologists were severely mauled for venturing near one of those places. I couldn't possibly allow you to go."

Heyoka rose, relishing the height advantage conferred by his seven-foot-four-inch frame. "They were, I assume, human anthropologists?" His handclaws flexed into visibility.

Eldrich folded his hands in the precise center of his desk. "As a matter of fact, only one of them was human. The other was gervaa'se, the only one who ever signed on here and, after he was patched up, the poor fellow had the sense to resign. However, I fail to see what difference that makes."

Spreading his hands across the desk's black surface, Heyoka leaned forward. "The difference is they weren't hrinn with legitimate business on this world."

Eldrich stared back stonily.

Heyoka hooked his underthumbs into his belt. "Thirty-six years ago, someone stole me from this world, Director, and then sold me as a slave."

"I still insist that's impossible." Eldrich's face twisted as though he'd tasted something bitter. "This world has been under Interdiction for over forty years, and we are quite assiduous in our monitoring. No one is allowed to take natives off-planet."

Mitsu stood, adding her small frame to Heyoka's mass. "Someone did anyway, Director, and Sergeant Blackeagle has every right to find out why."

"Very well." A muscle twitched in the man's face. "I'll grant temporary permits, but regulations forbid modern weapons outside the compound." He drew out a scented sani-chief and wiped his forehead. "You will have to check your weapons with Security and sign a release."

Heyoka caught Mitsu's eye and they turned as one to leave.

"Two weeks!" Eldrich called after them. "That's all I can give you. I don't care who you are—I have my research permit to protect and this is still an Interdicted world."

The flames, though little more than banked embers, cast shadows which stretched up the curved wall, as though they would escape through the narrow smoke hole high overhead. The chamber was thick with the musk of a dozen males, all of them mature, and the air was pleasantly mellow with the smoke of gynth, which made it comfortable for them to share such close quarters. Nisk scratched absently at one ear with half-flexed handclaws, ignoring the weight of the priest's fervid eyes on his unprotected back.

"I tell you, it's impossible!" A deep snarl escaped the priest's massive dark gray chest. "More than that, it's blasphemy!"

"But he was there." Nisk felt the notch of a long-past fight in his right ear and combed his ear fringes to cover it. "And, unless his clothing hid some off-color marking, this one is black from the tip of his nose to the ends of his feetclaws. *Black/on/black*, just as—"

A claw-sheathed blow sent him reeling against the far wall. Nisk sprawled against the whitestone, the side of his head gone numb. He scrambled up to face Rakshal, claws extended, as the dark-gray prowled restlessly through the shadows beyond the fire.

"Do you really think you're ready for this, priest?" Nisk's controlled voice was barely audible above the other's breathing. He felt a shape emerging in this moment, perhaps even the elusive *patience/in/illusion*, which he had never encountered, said to be a harbinger of wonders. Life brimmed with patterns within patterns, each one a map that could be followed to a different destiny. The key was to sniff them out and then let their structure dictate every subsequent action, every decision so that he was always in the sacred center, always in control and dominant. His pulse bounded and a wild singing joy burned through his veins—it had been so long since he had detected something new. "Challenging me will not send this Outsider back, nor alter his color, but do come at me again while I am looking!"

Rakshal flicked an ear, signifying he understood: if he approached Nisk again this night, he would have his fill of combat and perhaps more.

Perhaps—death.

"He comes to us after Ankt rests." Nisk's lips wrinkled back in challenge to the remaining males lounging around the central fire. They each looked away, indicating assent. "Since he is male, I claim this as the business of the males' house." His ears, notched with the aftermath of numerous challenges, flattened. "Will anyone speak against it?"

The crackling of the flames sounded his only answer.

Chapter Two

The temperature down in the Stores section had been set cooler than the rest of the station to preserve both outgoing artifacts and incoming electronics. Bins and cabinets and shelves occupied every millimeter of space, floor to ceiling, and the air was redolent of sheets of plas packing protectors. Allenby, the manager, grudgingly allotted Heyoka a set of black hrinnti robes, originally acquired by station anthropologists to be shipped to off-world institutions for display and study. Under no circumstances, though, could Heyoka get the nervous middle-aged human to agree to a different color.

"You don't understand, Sergeant." He shoved the material across the stainless steel counter and turned back to straighten the pile of robes he'd sorted through. "Color is almighty important to these brutes." Then, looking up, he met Heyoka's hrinnti eyes and blushed a fiery red. "Begging your pardon, sir. I didn't mean anything."

Of course not, Heyoka thought. They never did, but it was the same everywhere he went—it wasn't *their* fault he looked like an animal. The long-suppressed nameless *other* snarled inside his head and he had to concentrate to quiet it. He was not a dangerous, unthinking savage, no matter what anyone thought.

He smoothed his overthumbs across the tightly woven cloth, noting both the fineness of weave and the silkiness of thread. The material still bore just the slightest tang of hrinn. He glanced sideways at Mitsu who had busied herself in the far corner, digging through robes cut in the female style.

Allenby shrugged. "I would rethink this, if I were you. You have no idea how violent they can be."

"Strange that they wear so many clothes here," Mitsu said. "It's so hot, what with their fur and all, I would have thought they'd wear very little, or nothing."

"They wear this style precisely because of the heat." Allenby slid a folded pile in the cupboard and closed the door. "Desert cultures favor long flowing robes that create cool air pockets and protect them from the sun."

"I'll take these." Mitsu held up a set of elegantly cut robes, dyed in a startling crimson which matched Anktan's fiercely red sun.

"No, no, no!" Allenby seized the material out of her hands. "That color is the sole property of one particular outfit. You go out dressed in that, meet up with the wrong bunch, and the first thing you know, we're shipping your remaining bits back to your next of kin!"

Mitsu's slanted blue eyes radiated a calculated iciness with which Heyoka had become very familiar on battlefields ranging across a dozen worlds. She slipped her thumbs through her belt and squared her shoulders, never taking her stony gaze off Allenby's face. He clutched the crimson robes to his chest and backed out of reach.

Heyoka headed for the door, trying not to favor his stiff leg. "We've already settled this. You weren't invited. I'm going to the *males'* house, and the last time I had any reason to check, you were not equipped as either a male or a hrinn."

"All-Father blast it!" Sinking back into her home-world dialect, Mitsu turned back to Allenby. "Then give me some black ones too. They'll blend with the shadows better anyway."

Allenby surrendered the first set that came to hand, then retreated again, his uneasy eyes fixed on her face. Wadding the material under one arm, Mitsu followed Heyoka to the door.

"This is not a social occasion, Mitsu." Heyoka studied her set expression as they walked the long corridors, matching each other stride for stride. "You heard what Eldrich said. You could be mauled if they catch you prowling around where you don't belong. And even though you think you're good enough that they won't hear or see you, these are *hrinn*. They'll *smell* you."

Mitsu measured the length of the black outer robe against her body; it was much too long. "They didn't care much for the way you smelled either, if I recall."

Heyoka's ears flattened at the memory of the old female's insults. "Get some rest. This is supposed to be your vacation."

"And who's going to watch your back?" Mitsu shadowed him to the brink of the outside lock. "You don't know what those sodders are capable of."

Heyoka flashed his yellow pass at the security guard. Actually, he figured his fellow hrinn were capable of roughly the same amount of mayhem he could commit himself. The thought was not comforting.

The security guard cycled the airtight door open, managing to never quite meet Heyoka's gaze during the process. Heyoka stepped across the threshold and lifted his face into the rapidly cooling evening air. The red sun had dipped behind towering cliffs to the west. The wind was out of the east, sweeping down from the mountains, rich with promising scents after weeks of sterile, recycled air on the old merchanter. He had studied the map earlier, so all that remained now was to change clothes and be on his way, except for the "sandbath." Folding the black robes over his arm, he set out toward the cliffs.

His nightsight was far superior to that of a human, and the darkness rested pleasantly on his eyes. Mitsu was forced to use dark-filter lenses when they drew night patrol, like that last battle on Enjas Two. He recalled the acrid stench of drones from the flek warrior caste lying in wait just above the green beach, eager to burn the flesh from his bones, then transform the pristine green and white of Enjas Two into another flek hellworld. A gust of wind sifted grains of sand against his face and his inner nictitating membrane eyelids closed. Sand . . .

Blinking, he cast about, locating it as much by smell as by sight, ten or so feet to the left, the dry rockiness of a shallow layer of sand trapped on the windward side of a small rise. He angled toward it, letting the soft sounds of the night wash over him . . . the beat of small wings . . . tiny claws scrabbling across hard-baked desert soil . . . wind sighing against stone, all soothing, natural sounds, so different from the mind-numbing bedlam of battle.

At the edge of the sand patch, he stripped off the black duraweave Ranger uniform he had tailored to make him appear more human and realized that once he donned native robes, he would be indistinguishable from the native population, a prospect more daunting than he had expected.

Even in the darkness, he could make out the long ropy scar of the flek laser burn that snaked around from ankle to knee. The Meds had said the damaged nerves would never heal properly without a series of grafts; he would always have weakness and pain. As he was not human, though, grafts were not an option. Meds were not set up for hrinnti biology and no one was going to finance that kind of research for a singleton like himself.

Holding the leg out stiffly before him, he eased down onto the grittiness of still-warm sand. Now—what? Exactly how did one go about a *sand*bath? He sifted a handful of sand over the fur on his left arm. In the cool evening air, the sun-baked grains were pleasantly warm. He worked them into the finer dense fur of his undercoat, then brushed the sand out and sniffed. The scent was different somehow, cleaner . . . wilder.

Scooping up another handful, he began with his mane and worked downwards. As a primitive custom, this really wasn't too bad. He thought back to the first time he'd been forced into a water bath after the old trader, Ben Blackeagle, had bought him out of the flek slave pens. Sporting a long bloody scratch from his attempt to immerse the feral hrinn cubling in the soapy water, the old man had calmly donned the gloves from his emergency evacuation space suit. Then he returned and scrubbed Heyoka from "stem to stern," as Ben put it.

Of course, his name hadn't been Heyoka then. Slaves awaiting sale had no need of names. The tall, spindly flek, with their red eyes and punched-in faces, called for him with blows and kicks and neuronic whips . . . Heyoka scrubbed harder, frustrated he could remember the pens and their pervasive stink so clearly, but nothing before. He couldn't help feeling something inside him should recognize this red-orange, windswept place. Ben had been dead for over twelve years now and Heyoka longed for some sense of roots.

Finishing with his feet, he stood and shook himself

in the cool evening wind. His body felt alive and glowing, as though he'd had a first-rate massage. He scooped up the discarded uniform and sniffed. Its scent was clearly different than his now. It smelled of humans and synthetic building materials, like plas and durallinium, and the beef stew simmering in the station's kitchen before he left.

It smelled of home.

As Chytt urged the reluctant yirn across the ford on the slow-flowing Mish River, she was glad the beast was exhausted. Otherwise it would have made its usual fuss, balking and squalling at the sight of so much water until she was forced to use her feetclaws to make it cross. Up above the river's high-water marks, the tiny lights of Qartt Hold glimmered through the night. Leaning over the yirn's hump, she snarled into its drooping ear, then clung to the riding harness with her claws as the weary beast quickened its rough pace.

By the time she reached the outside pens, she could see a delegation of daughters holding waxy gyb torches high to light the end of her long journey home. The beast stopped of its own accord before the wide gate and hung its weary head. Chytt gazed down at her progeny's faces, ranging in hue from pale amber to deepest red. Events were forming a pattern; it was up to her to interpret it correctly. She hesitated, trying to gauge its shape . . . the coming of the strange male . . . the involvement of Outsiders in hrinnti affairs and Qartt in theirs . . . it was something large, dank, ominous, *fire/in/water* perhaps, one of the most ancient, signifying bitterest deception.

Her daughters knew something of the smell of things already, what with the messenger jit she had released after the meeting this morning. Swinging down from the yirn's harness, her hip popped and she winced. Getting old, she thought, trying not to favor that side as she turned to face the waiting females.

Someday soon, an elder daughter would present challenge and, after that, her successor could worry about all of this and welcome to it!

At any rate, the stranger was a male; they could thank the Voice for that much. If a female had come asking the same questions, there was no knowing where things would have ended out on the sand this morning under Ankt's unblinking red eye. A male, though, would never dare come sniffing around the Lines. No doubt one of the males' houses would take care of the matter in a fashion that honored everyone.

A hand slipped under her elbow and Chytt's ears flattened as she turned to see which daughter dared acknowledge her weariness: Fik's impudent pale-orange face returned her stare, breath for breath. Interesting, she thought. This one smelled of trouble. Her tongue flicked out across her lips. Very interesting. She looked around at the circle of waiting faces. "Children—" She delivered that insult in an oh-so-casual voice as she watched to see whose ears twitched and whose did not. "A peculiar sort of trouble has descended upon us from the sky. If you know anything about it, now is the time to speak."

It was for this she had ridden her nerves to shreds, the need to see their expressions when she broached this matter. The glyph for *fire/in/water* burned behind her eyes. At some point, a lie had been told, and so, when the pattern was whole, someone would have to stand responsible. The circle of waiting Qartt faces shifted uneasily, pairs of black eyes glancing sideways at each other. After a few blinks, it was obvious the younger generations had little idea of what she was talking about, but some of the older ones, several of the *breeders*, by all that was holy, *their* eyes had gone suspiciously opaque and the acrid scent of worry permeated the air.

Shoving aside Fik's arm, Chytt turned toward the familiar whitestone hold, the names that went with those faces clawed into her mind with broad, deep strokes. Someone here at Qartt had nipped into this in the past, had actually interfered in the business of another Line.

Unfortunately, now they would all have to stand good for it.

Heyoka spotted a primitive one-legged ladder propped inside a hole, then recognized the sheer sandstone cliff rising just beyond the river, as described on the map. This must be the males' house then, not built above the ground like human habitations, as he had expected, but dug into the earth like the den of an animal, dark and secret. A circle of cleared earth marked its dimensions, and a hundred meters or so beyond, a wisp of pungent wood smoke curled up through a second hole.

He rolled his uniform into a ball, then stuffed it behind a scrubby treelike growth, keeping only the yellow security pass, which he secreted in a pocket of the new robes. He felt strangely undressed in the flowing shirtlike garment and loose trousers after so many years in the tight-fitting uniform of the Rangers.

His nose twitched at the strong concentration of hrinn-scent mingled with the smoke and he heard an almost musical chant from below, two distinct rhythms sliding across each other, then merging at odd intervals only to separate again.

The ladder was a single pole with alternating rungs on either side, an unstable arrangement. Grasping the pole with both hands, he began the long descent. His bad leg, weakened by the unaccustomed higher gravity, slipped halfway down and the ladder listed dangerously to the right as he hung by his handclaws, legs dangling. He bared his teeth in a silent curse until his groping feet found the rung again, then shifted his weight to steady the ladder.

He willed the damn leg to bear his weight, but the

widely spaced rungs seemed to go on forever and the ladder rocked back and forth with each step. He could see a faint reddish glow of a low fire, burned down nearly to the coals, laid in a shallow pit in the center of a huge circular room. His breath was coming in hard pants as rows of chanting hrinn, all robed in green, watched his painful descent.

Finally his right foot touched the floor and the chant trailed away. He stood there, gripping the ladder until he was sure the leg would not give way. The floor of the subterranean chamber was earthen, but compressed over the years to a rocklike hardness. The walls had been constructed of a white, fine-grained stone that reflected the firelight. The smoke was much thicker inside, strangely aromatic and not at all unpleasant. The mingled scents threaded through his brain, like keys turning in unsuspected locks. He became conscious of a vast array of feelings and emotions of which he had never before been aware, urges without any human name.

"We invite you to join this night's pattern and see where it leads." A black figure with a white throat spoke to him through a blue haze. "I am Nisk, Leader of Mish River Males' House."

Heyoka followed the other toward the fire, managing not to limp, but his gait was stiff, unnatural. As he passed the concentric circles of seated figures, the murmuring stilled, but not the restless rustling of robes, the feel of eyes on his unprotected back. Gods, he told himself, but this room was stuffy and hot! How did they all stand it? The heat and the scent of so many hrinn crowded together made him feel like his nerves were crawling with fire. He felt on the edge of something immense and unknowable, a path that might lead anywhere but home.

The heady smoke swirled thickest above the smoldering coals, overriding the musk of so many hrinn. He had a sudden, intense flash of another place, dark like this and pungent with smoke, furry shapes that towered above him, speaking in guttural whispers. He hesitated, but it dissipated as quickly as it had arisen. Wary, he lowered himself to the hard-packed floor, wondering if the smoke were some sort of narcotic.

"You posed a question today." The white-throated male sat on the other side of the fire, resplendent in green, gazing over Heyoka's shoulder.

"Yes." Heyoka stared into the red coals until he could see them with his eyes closed. "I wish to know my Line. Is that an improper question?"

Snarls rumbled through the dark room behind him. The black-coated male stared down the assemblage of seated figures, then turned back to him with glittering onyx eyes. "Since you are only an ignorant Outsider, you do not know this, but Lineage is a female preoccupation. For males, Line is beneath notice, nothing more than a fading memory from cubhood."

"Look at his coloring." An old gray with heavy dark stripes across his face stood up in one of the back rows. "He is Black/on/black—he has a right to know."

"He is not!" A shadowed gray-furred figure, dressed in gray rather than green, sprang up and prowled closer to Heyoka, his eyes reflecting the red glow of the fire.

"Black/on/black?" Heyoka turned to Nisk. "You called me that earlier. What does it mean?"

The gray male snarled from the shadows. "This creature is not part of any pattern, now, or in the past. It's not even a hrinn, much less the Black/on/black! No Line has ever reported losing a cubling to Outsiders, not even a male!"

Even through the smoke-induced mental fog, Heyoka felt the fur on his shoulders rise. His long-suppressed *other* surfaced again, frighteningly angry. Scent molecules danced through his brain, shunting off logical responses, feeding his anger. He jerked to his feet, ignoring the fierce jab in his leg. Dropping into a loose fighting stance, he circled the gray, keeping his sound leg forward. "So this is how you welcome your kin after he crosses the vastness of space to be with his own?" A white-hot rage burned along his nerves, fueled by disappointment. "Are you afraid I have come to take something from you, or is it your guilt speaking? What do you know about a child stolen thirty-six winters ago?"

"I know an imposter when I smell one!" The gray's bared teeth gleamed palely through the dimness.

The white-throated male, Nisk, interposed his body between the two. "If we are going to speak of *smell*, Rakshal, then you know what will have to be said."

Heyoka heard a murmur of assent echo through the vast chamber.

The other male's dark-gray ears flattened. "Say it then!" Rakshal whirled and shoved his way through the hrinn seated on the floor. "And may this creature have much joy of the knowledge!" He disappeared into a side tunnel.

"Tell me what?" Heyoka forced his tone to remain level.

"Very little." Nisk glanced around the restless circles of males. Their black eyes glinted with reflected light. He threw another branch, tiny blue leaves and all, onto the fire. The flames leapt up again, curling blackly along the edges of the leaves first and then thickening the haze of smoke.

The circular earthen room seemed to wander in and out of focus as he attempted to concentrate on Nisk's black-furred features.

"This is not a male matter." Nisk squatted before the fire, gazing into the flames which were already dying down. "It is inappropriate for males to concern themselves with such female nonsense as Lineage."

Shifting his weight onto his good leg, Heyoka tried

to understand, but the sense of the other's words was growing more remote every second.

"But—if we had to guess your Line—which you understand, we are not." Nisk stirred the fire with a long stick. "If we guessed, it would be Levv."

Blast his fur-bound hide! Mitsu confined her scathing comments to the inside of her head as she eased past the station's left wing and made her way silently across the sandy ground. In combat, one muffled curse could cost a whole unit its life. Of course, she told herself, this wasn't a combat situation, but then why the hell did it feel so much like one?

How could he just go off and leave her to twiddle her thumbs among noncoms? Reaching up, she jerked the dark, overlarge hood down lower over her face. They'd smell her, indeed! These were genuine hrinnti robes. If the sodding beasts smelled anything, it would only be another hrinn, of which there certainly seemed to be no shortage.

After operating as Blackeagle's partner for almost three years, she knew he had too much pride to ask for help. That oversized body of his was strong, as well as hypersensitive to sounds and odors beyond the human threshold of awareness, but he hadn't regained his full strength since the injury. His leg was still weak, and they both knew it. She had been born to a world where children were raised in common by trained professionals. The notion of "family," as other human societies understood it, did not exist. Heyoka was the only friend she'd had, since leaving her birthmates, and she wasn't about to lose him to a bunch of primitives.

Unfortunately, she'd had to hang behind far enough that he wouldn't sense her following, but she'd pried the same set of directions out of the database he'd used, and she intended to be at his back before there was any real action. Using heat-filter lenses, she tracked his thermal trail across the desert, stopping to study the heat signature in a shallow depression of sand where he'd lingered at one point. What had that been all about? Rot him, was he already going native on her? If he decided to stay here, she would lose the best partner in the unit, in fact, probably in the whole bloody corps.

She left the sand and struck out across the desert, heading for a series of cliffs that reared above the horizon like irregular towers, black against the star-filled night sky. Every so often, she dropped to a crouch, fingers spread across the warm ground, and strained to catch the sound of something beyond the soft whisper of the night breeze.

Finally, she caught the sonorous rumble of voices somewhere out of sight. She crept toward the sound. Where could the sodders be? How could this scrubby stretch of earth hide so many of them? Closer in, she caught a faint glow and the outline of something protruding out of the ground. Some sort of pole perhaps? Just as she reached out to touch it, a snarl split the darkness behind her.

Chapter Three

"Levv?" Heyoka blinked through the haze, trying to focus on Nisk's face. He felt dull-witted and inert, an effect of the smoke, no doubt, but he could still smell the secondary pungence of unease and disapproval permeating the subterranean chamber.

A sharp snarl filtered down from the surface and every head swiveled as one toward the ladder hole. Nisk spat a phrase that Heyoka could not make out as they all scrambled to their feet and sprinted either toward the ladder or several shadowy side passages. Heyoka stood too, his leg aching, and balanced awkwardly by the fire pit, bewildered. His head felt like it had been stuffed with cotton. Up on the surface, someone snarled again, and then he heard an angry human voice, female, cursing in Standard. Gods! That had to be Mitsu!

Flattening his ears, he bulled through the crowd. When a burly brown male snarled and raked his ribs with open claws, the angry *other* within him surfaced, striking back with a ferocity that made the brown flinch and give way. "Leave her alone!" he shouted up the ladder. "I know her!"

"Come any closer, you big sod—" He could make out Mitsu's words clearly now. "—and I'll cut those sorry ears off and stuff them down your flea-bitten thr—"

With a curse of his own, Heyoka vaulted up the ladder, frantic with worry, the pole rocking back and forth and his weak leg slipping on every other rung. He should have known Mitsu had too little experience of alien cultures to really understand the risk she took by coming here like this. She was so young, she thought just because she was a skilled soldier, she owned the universe, and he *knew* that. He should have been paying more attention! He had a sudden intense memory of being small and helpless amidst a savage onslaught of teeth and claws, blood soaking the ground, the rocks, his fur.

His arms burned with the strain of Anktan's higher gravity as he climbed. Just when he thought his lungs would burst, his head surfaced. He pulled himself onto the still-warm ground, collapsing like a dying sea creature. The cool night air began to clear his head. Dark hrinnti shapes poured from a hole in the cliff behind him, spreading out to quarter the area. Heyoka forced himself onto his feet, then joined the search, limping. He could feel the blood seeping into his fur and robes, and the deeper slashes along his ribs burned. Mitsu's familiar scent was scattered about the barren circle of earth, as well as that of innumerable other hrinn. "Where is she?" he demanded of the nearest. "Where would they take her?"

The dark-brown male sampled the wind, then wrinkled his nose. "Bah! It was one of those Dead-smelling Outsiders, not even good eating." He shook himself, then, ears up, trotted off toward the dark, rolling river.

A murmur of surprise rose from several other

nearby hrinn. "First it wants to know its *Line*, by the Voice," one said, "and now it is chasing after Outsiders! Name that pattern, if you can."

The pain of his numerous claw marks and slashes fueled his anger as he started the spiral of a standard search pattern, orienting on the ladder hole as his center. As he searched, the other males drifted away. His bad leg slowed him, making the spiral take much longer than it should have, and by the time his circle finally widened enough to take him back to the bank of the murmuring river, all he found were spots of dark blood soaking into the sandy bank and a few shreds of red cloth. Kneeling, he picked it up and sniffed at the stain.

The smell was of hrinnti blood mixed with human.

Eldrich studied the traffic monitor, noting the incoming green blip's perfect arc. The ship seemed to be on course for a change, as well as on time, although the landing would be visible from several males' houses, blast his luck. Earlier, Allenby had reported to him that both the hrinnti sergeant and his human partner had left the station this evening, although separately, a rather interesting development.

A smile seeped across his face. Those big hrinnti males were sensitive about their territory. If those two overstepped their bounds, the savages would eliminate this problem for him. Lacing fingers across his stomach, he leaned back in his chair and propped his shoes up on the desk.

And no one could say he hadn't warned them either.

Dark . . . laced with blinding flashes of light that pierced the depths of her brain. Pain . . . time seemed to . . . jump around as she struggled to think . . .

Worry . . . that thought came back to harry her

. . . there was something . . . something to worry about . . . she must . . . do something . . .

Then a smooth, beguiling blackness drew her into a vast silence where there was neither pain nor worry nor time.

Aching from a dozen claw marks, Heyoka punched the yellow pass into the access slot, then braced his head against the station monitor and tried to think. Would anyone be on duty this late, or would the system be shunted over to automatics? And if he did manage to get access before dawn, would anyone help him search for Mitsu? They had both signed that damned release; the station was under no responsibility to provide aid.

The door slid aside, revealing a rumpled staff member. The man's face went blank with shock at the sight of him. He jerked back and keyed the door shut again.

Damnation! Heyoka remembered too late that he wore the face of a violent, unpredictable savage. Wearily he raised his arm to punch in the pass again and left a smear of red-orange blood across the sand-pitted building.

"Voice identification?" the monitor demanded.

Heyoka's lips wrinkled back from his teeth in a half-snarl, but he knew one furred hrinnti face must look much the same to the human staff as another. He told himself to be patient. "Sergeant Heyoka Blackeagle, Confederated Ranger Corps." Standing away from the door, he waited for it to open again, and as the minutes slipped by, a smoldering rage brewed behind his eyes. What in the name of all the gods who ever existed were they doing in there! Calling in the Rangers from twelve systems away?

At length, the heavy door slid open again. "How did your visit go, Sergeant?"

Heyoka stepped inside and stared down into the

pasty features of Eldrich. Claws flexed, he bit back the angriest of his thoughts. "I need access to a medkit," he said, keeping his voice smoothly neutral, "and then I'll need more maps printed out, as well as information on the local native populations."

Eldrich's pale-gray eyes dropped pointedly to the white station floor where Heyoka's clawed arm was dripping red-orange blood on the smooth tile. He shook his head. "I did warn you, Sergeant. The natives are a rather . . . rough bunch."

Heyoka's anger increased another notch. One of his ears twitched. "The medkit?" he asked coldly.

"Oh—yes." A look of distaste flitted across Eldrich's face. "Billings, escort the sergeant down to Sickbay." He straightened his collar. "And have this mess cleaned up. The staff would have a heart attack if they saw it in the morning."

"Yes, sir." Billings nodded at Heyoka. "If you'll just come with me, Sergeant."

Heyoka drew himself up straight, trying to ignore the slashes across his ribs and the shredded condition of his clothing. The security guard took him several halls down, keyed a door open and stood aside. "Sickbay, sir. If you'll step in here."

"I just need a medkit." Heyoka stepped inside, his nostrils closing at the strong medicinal smells. "I have a few scratches, nothing serious."

At the far end of the room, a sleepy-looking dark-haired woman in blue coveralls knotted a fall of dark hair at the nape of her neck. "I'm Dr. Alvarez. If you'll sit down, we'll have a look at those wounds."

The door slid shut. Heyoka whirled to stare at it, feeling terribly *closed-in* for some reason he couldn't explain. Picking up a medscanner, the woman walked toward him, a crease between her eyes adding to the lines in her middle-aged face. He heard the faint hum of the medscan as a wave of dizziness washed over him. When it receded, he found himself leaning against the Sickbay wall.

"Shock is nasty, isn't it?" She raised an eyebrow. "Now, would you like to sit on the examining table, or would you prefer to just fall over on the floor?"

Heyoka tried to focus on the tan oval of her face, but it seemed to be curiously fluid. Bracing a shoulder under his arm, she levered him up from the wall. "Not that Sickbay's floor isn't a perfectly respectable place, I'll have you understand. We clean it once a week, whether it needs it or not."

He settled heavily onto a low white-covered table in the middle of the room. "Just seal up these scratches with some liquid bandage." He ran weary fingers back through his matted mane. "I have to go back out."

"It looks to me as if you've had quite enough for one night." Her knotted hair fell over her shoulder as she bent to examine his wounds.

Heyoka's eyes focused on that length of hair; it reminded him of the style affected by the natives, except that— Gods! He groaned and rubbed his eyes. He couldn't let his mind wander when he had so much to do.

"At any rate," Dr. Alvarez said, laying aside the scanner and selecting a silver tube from the medicine cabinet, "you seem to have tangled with the local equivalent of a bear."

"It was the hrinn." He swallowed, tension easing from his body as she applied a cool, soothing gel to his clawed back and sides. "They took my partner. I found—blood."

Working her way around to the deeper gashes along his ribs, her brown eyes glanced up at him. "Is she hrinnti too?"

"No." His eyelids sagged as the gel quieted the sting of his wounds. "Human."

"Well, you're not in any shape to go after her

tonight. You couldn't defend yourself against a butterfly." Clicking the cap back onto the silver tube, she discarded it on the counter. "I suggest you rest here the remainder of the night, not that there's much left of it, then take a search party out after her tomorrow."

"No." Heyoka suddenly felt like a wet towel; now that his pain had eased, it seemed it had been all that held him together. "The station won't help. We signed a . . ." What had they signed?

"A release?"

He nodded.

Hands pushed him back against the table's yielding surface. "Oh, everybody has to sign those damn things when they're assigned here, but plenty of folks will be willing to help you search—*tomorrow*."

"No . . . tonight." Unexpectedly, he found his head resting on a pillow, undoubtedly the softest thing he had ever felt. Ben . . . his mind drifted . . . Ben Blackeagle hadn't believed in pillows.

"Oh, you won't be fit for anything before the morning." Her voice came from the door. "According to my records, the sedative in that gel should be effective even on a hrinnti metabolism. Sleep well, Sergeant."

Heyoka strained to open his eyelids, but they seemed to be weighed down with a million gees, a billion incredibly . . . heavy . . .

"You brought it here—to Vvok?"

Khea pressed her back to the wall outside the Line Mother's quarters, ears flattened, unable to shut out the angry words flooding from the next room.

"How could you endanger Vvok like this?" The wall thumped with the weight of something thrown against it. "This creature is worthless, random, outside all patterns. Nothing it does can affect us, so if it saw you, why not just slash its throat and heave the carcass into the sand? It would have made no difference to the long-term flow of things."

Khea peered at the pale-skinned, motionless heap on the red carpet just outside Seska's quarters. It had not moved since Fitila had dropped it there and hissed at her in passing to watch it. She shivered. Perhaps it was already dead and all this fuss was pointless. She crept to the open doorway and saw the light tan of Fitila's coat moving near the far wall. The scout was still alive, anyway. The Line Mother had not been angry enough to kill her—yet.

The black-robed heap on the rug stirred. Hunching over it, Khea's nose wrinkled at the strange odor. So this was the "Dead" smell of which the older ones had spoken. She peeled aside a fold of the black servant's robes with the tip of one claw and then sat back on her heels to study the delicate-boned creature. By the Voice, its pinkish skin was nearly hairless; it had only a bit of black mane on its small head and nothing more in the way of fur that she could see, except for a brief tracing above each small eye. And its fingers were so strange—blunt-ended with no real claws and only *one* thumb on each hand! No wonder the creatures were forever outside all patterns.

She rubbed at the short fur on her forehead in amazement. How was it they were so clever then, making all sorts of wonders like ships that fell from the sky and then jumped back into it again and that strange white hold out in the hottest part of the drylands where the hunting was terrible?

"Khea!"

The young hrinn's gray-and-white body stiffened. Her eyes turned toward the Line Mother's quarters. On the floor beside her, the Outsider moaned, its small head rolling weakly from side to side. Khea darted through the Line Mother's door to prostrate herself on the thick red mat.

Seska, present Line Mother to Vvok, was prowling

restlessly around the confines of the large room, the numerous silver bracelets around her thin gray ankles jingling at every step. Fitila, a Vvok scout two generations ahead of Khea, waited with twitching ears at the far side of the room, well out of the old female's reach. A damp streak of blood marred her coat.

Waiting for the Line Mother to speak, Khea watched both females out of the corners of her eyes, uncertain what to expect. Several breaths passed while the Line Mother quartered the room. Fur bristled across her shoulders and Khea's ears flinched with remembered blows each time the old female passed. Finally, Seska stopped and stared at Fitila's tan face.

"We will have to salvage what we can from what this—*nurseling*—has done." She spat the words out as though they tasted bad, then whirled on Khea, black eyes enormous above her yellowed teeth. "Take the creature down into the servants' quarters and see to its hurts. If it dies, its value will be on your head. You are excused from further duties."

A tremor ran through Khea's body. She was not sure she'd heard the Line Mother correctly. Take charge of the thing lying out there like a heap of rags? Touch that disgusting pale skin?

Seska snarled and cuffed her against the wall. Stunned, Khea sprawled on the thick red mat. The Line Mother was speaking, but she couldn't make out the old matriarch's words through the ringing in her head. She staggered to her feet and hoped the Line Mother's words required no answer.

Outside Seska's quarters, Khea leaned against the cool stone wall and took a long shuddering breath. Mevva, Vvok's ancient, one-eared cub-trainer, still loved to freeze the hearts of newly emerged nurselings with the story of how Seska had killed two successive cublings in the same afternoon when they failed to respond appropriately to direct orders. Each time the Line Mother beat her, no matter how much she had deserved it, Khea feared that was where it would end, and fear was the worst disgrace of all. It meant she would not pass the next gleaning, or ever serve as a breeder, never do Vvok any sort of honor at all.

However, she would certainly die now if she neglected her new duty. Bending over the pile of pale alien limbs and black robes soaked with strange fiery-red blood, Khea closed her nostrils to the creature's smell and gathered it into her arms.

Standing before the wall of fine-grained white-stone that enclosed the meeting chamber, Nisk dipped an extended foreclaw into the small pot of indelible scent and retraced the ancient *mountain/over/stars* scent-glyph, used to signify wonder. When hrinn appeared from the sky, that was wonder indeed. What tales could this male tell, what incredible sights had he seen up there in the very presence of Ankt? It was almost enough to make one give credence to the words of priests.

Feet scuffled behind him and he recognized Bral's youthful scent as he began the next glyph, a complex series of perpendicular and oblique lines symbolizing *undue/transformations*.

"As you thought," Bral's voice spoke from over his shoulder, "the Outsider returned to the white hold."

"He is hrinnti, not Outsider, with his own part to play in the great patterns yet to emerge." Nisk finished the last difficult stroke, then leaned closer to sniff out the next portion of the ancient frieze.

"He may be dead," Bral continued. "His blood fed the land all the way back."

Nisk's nostrils flared, studying the faint uplifted curves of the next glyph, *patience/in/illusion.* "I think not. I sensed a great strength in that one."

"Strength for what?" Bral fidgeted behind him. "If he really is a person, then why does he not just apply to a males' house and take his rightful place? Why

all this nonsense about Lines and patterns that were
complete such a long time ago?"

"He was raised by Outsiders." Nisk dipped his
foreclaw and traced the sinuous shape of *death/in/
longing*. "Outsiders have no sense of the sacred. He
has no idea yet of the forces that shape existence,
or what it means to be hrinnti."

Bral sidled closer. "Then why did you tell him
about Levv?"

"Why not?" Nisk's ear twitched. "It is the truth."

"When he learns of Levv's disgrace, he will not
thank you."

Nisk whirled and struck the younger male to the
floor. Claws flexed, he loomed over the buff-colored
body. "Truth is for telling." His eyes bore down on
Bral and the younger male looked away, unwilling to
challenge. "Not for being thanked." Then, turning
back to the frieze, he contemplated the subtle dotted
pattern of *balance/in/flow*.

Chapter Four

Heyoka's adoptive father, Ben Blackeagle, faced the east and the glory of Earth's rising yellow sun. "The grass and the water remember." The old man blinked, his eyes full of grief. "Only people forget."

Warmed by the morning sun on his black fur, Heyoka panted, his narrow hrinnti tongue lolling out of his mouth in a most unhumanlike way.

Almost buried in wrinkles, the old man's eyes were as bright as brown beads polished to a sunlike radiance. "The Oglala have forgotten what it cost to regain this land and make the old ways live again." The gray-haired head nodded slowly. "They forget they are brothers to all who live under the sky of the Six Grandfathers." The old man's voice dropped to a whisper. "If they had not forgotten, they would see that you are their brother too."

"Nothing like me was ever born under the sky of the Six Grandfathers." Heyoka rolled a slick green stem of grass between his double set of thumbs. "I'm alien to this world, and they have never once let me forget that."

39

"Perhaps I should not have brought you back to the Oglala Nation after I sold the jumpship." Ben stared at his gnarled hands. *"But from the second I blundered into that gervaa'se market and saw you being beaten in the slave pens, I knew you were a person, not a mindless beast. I wanted you to grow up free and this was a good place to live when I was a boy."*

"A good place for humans." Heyoka shrugged his mane back out of his eyes. *"When they look at me though, they only see that I'm not like them, not even of Earth, much less human."*

"They fear you." Ben's classic Oglala face was etched in sadness. *"They think you are more than human, not less, and that fear makes them forget they are relatives to all living things, Terran or not."*

In the village below, the Oglala were preparing for another day, but Heyoka had long ago accepted the reality that this life—their life—did not belong to him. They did not want him. He would always be an outsider.

"We are all related. See that you do not forget." Ben touched Heyoka's face with trembling fingers, then the breeze blew him away as though he were only a gray-haired wisp of smoke curling up into the clear blue field of the morning sky . . .

"No, Father, wait!" Heyoka leaped to his feet, Ben's beloved scent still thick in his nostrils.

"Sergeant!" Someone shook his shoulders. "Sergeant, wake up!"

Opening his eyes, Heyoka blinked into the concerned face of the station doctor. Alvarez clicked on the medscanner. "I was beginning to think I'd misread the drug compatibility records on your species last night."

Heyoka tried to sit up, but his muscles ached. His stomach was queasy, too, his mouth dry, and his head felt like it was going to explode. "If you had *asked* me, Dr. Alvarez . . ." Each word had to journey from far away. "I would have told you that my metabolism processes drugs of any sort poorly." He sat up, then doubled over as a wave of nausea gripped him. "*If you had bothered to ask.*"

Her tan face paled. "I'm sorry. You'd lost a fair amount of blood last night and were slipping into shock. You were in no shape to make decisions." Her knuckles were white where she gripped the scanner. "Shall I give you something for the side effects?"

"No!" The word escaped him with a ferocity he rarely allowed humans to glimpse, then he cursed himself as she flinched. "Sorry." He braced his head between his hands. The savage *other* within him prowled perilously near the surface, waiting for its chance to explode. "Water would help. I'm probably dehydrated. I ran all the way back last night."

She let out a breath. "Sure." She filled a glass from the tap at the sink and handed it to him, retreating, he noticed, out of reach.

Tipping his head back, Heyoka managed to drink the whole glass without spilling a drop. How many hours of practice had *that* skill cost him? He tried to remember, but the pounding centered behind his eyes concealed the answer. He held the glass out for more.

Alvarez turned back to the sink and refilled it. How did his fellow hrinn manage water, he wondered. Did they lap it up from pans as he had done when Ben had first rescued him, or did they teach their young to drink in a civilized manner as Ben had taken the care and patience to do?

"Thanks." He accepted the glass from her trembling hand and drained it too. The pounding receded to a dull ache. Gods, he did feel a bit better. "What time is it?" He glanced at his wrist, then remembered leaving his chronometer with his uniform behind some scrubby excuse for a tree last night.

"Almost noon." Her brown eyes watched him uneasily.

"Noon!" The word burst out of him, loud enough to make his head pound again. "Then she's been out there for hours, unless—"

"No." Alverez's voice was low. "She hasn't returned."

Heyoka slid off the examining table, fixing his eyes on the door until the dizziness eased. "I have to find her. You said the staff would help."

She nodded and turned to her screen. "I'll punch in a request and see who's available."

Watching her long tan fingers key in the information, Heyoka cursed himself for trusting these people. They were all noncoms, as well as strangers who saw him as less than human. They didn't understand. He should have known better, should have relied only on himself, no matter what Ben had told him all those years ago.

The sacred pool chamber was as still as the deepest blue-black silences of the night. Moisture condensed on the limestone cavern walls and trickled down into a hot-spring pool as old as the world itself. Rakshal paused at the entrance, inhaling the redolence of heated rock, overlaid with the acridness of sulfur mingled with aging jit droppings. All was as it should be. There was no recent scent trace of any male, save himself. He wedged his torch into a sconce carved into the wall by unknown hands, then ran his fingers over markings etched around it, ancient sight-glyphs for which no one knew the meanings anymore.

"The tellers say doing this so often is dangerous." Buff-colored Bral edged inside, ears down, his long face distraught. His voice, oddly hollow, echoed from the damp walls as the torchlight danced over the pool's surface. "They say you could die."

"Of course the Old Ways are dangerous, that's the

source of their power." Rakshal savored the sulfurous steam swirling above the mineral-rich thermal pool. He heard the soft pop of mud pots simmering further back in the cave system and smelled their fierce molten-earth odor. Already his fur reeked of it, and would, no doubt, for days to come. "The most vigorous patterns always begin with risk, but bring the greatest reward. If you lack the courage to enter, you will be left behind, always single and alone, forever outside events and acted upon, rather than in control." He shed his threadbare gray robes onto the rocky cavern floor, then gazed down into the mysterious blue-green depths of the steaming sacred pool.

"But what if this traveler is hrinnti?" Bral's words spilled out, reckless as a thief. "If he was stolen as a cubling, it was not his fault. Should we not make a place for him?"

Rakshal's hackles rose. "If he were truly hrinn, he would make a place for himself! Since when do we welcome the weak, or the foolish? Is every cubling who applies accepted into the males' house?" The newcomer's face floated before his inner vision. Black/on/black, Nisk had said. Rakshal's lips curled back from his teeth. "No Black/on/black has been born for generations. And if one of the sacred color pattern had been given to us, it would not have been through traitorous Levv!"

With a snarl, he splashed into the steaming water and anchored his handclaws on the rock. If he slipped into the dark-blue hole at the bottom of the pool, said to end at the sacred wild fire of the earth's core, he would be lost forever in fiery torment. Out of the corner of his eye, he saw Bral retreat to stand the traditional watch at the chamber's entrance so the power-drawing ritual would not be disturbed.

Rakshal lay back in the sweltering water's embrace to draw power in the oldest of ways, the sacred ritual which few practiced in this age of Dead-smelling creatures who fell out of the sky and wrought unasked-for miracles. The long muscles in his arms and legs tingled, then burned as the torrid heat triggered the special receptors.

He closed his eyes. It was bad enough the Council permitted these creatures to build on worthless land at the edge of the Mish River Males' House territory, where they attempted to converse and trade with the more reckless of the Lines. Outsiders were random, their actions fitting no pattern ever named, clearly without honor or purpose of any sort, and now they had presented this fake hrinn in an effort to disrupt ongoing patterns! There had to be an end to such affront, or the world would dissolve once again into chaos.

His lips drew back in a fierce baring of teeth. This must be a test by the Voice, perhaps even the trial of courage known as *undue/transformations* in which monsters walked the world in the guise of everyday creatures. He could smell it, if no one else could. He would hunt this blasphemous creature, so cunningly transformed by Outsiders into a false likeness, and tear it hide from bone. Then all would join him in scouring the Dead-smelling Outsiders from the face of this world so that events could once again flow in their time-honored fashion and blessed order would reign.

When he thought he could take no more of the water's power, he forced himself to remain, knowing full well he was skirting death with each breath. He had never taken in half so much before, and yet he remained in the steaming water until his ears sagged like wet cloth and he thought he would burst. Only then did he heave out of the pool's basin and sprawl across the rocks, limp and breathless, barely able to pant the killing excess heat from his body. When he finally recovered enough to sit up, the fierce strength of the earth's core hummed through him in such measure as it had never before. Stretching one gray-furred forefinger toward the other, he watched a sacred blue spark arch from claw to claw.

Heyoka limped through Eldrich's open door into the spacious office furnished with leather chairs and antique bound books, the nest of a civilian comfortable with luxuries. Conditioned air whispered through a ceiling vent, cool and carefully neutral.

"Sergeant Blackeagle?" Eldrich glanced up from his monitor. "I didn't know you had been released from Sickbay."

In a flek's eye, Heyoka thought. Eldrich's strong cologne made his nose twitch and he fought the urge to sneeze. Violets again, laced with something spicy, and beneath that, an acrid base note. Heyoka stood at parade-rest, arms clasped behind his back, his weight subtly shifted off his aching right leg. The hike last night out to the males' house and then his subsequent run back across the desert had strained the damaged muscles. Not only was he limping again, but the blasted leg threatened to give way altogether.

"Please take a seat." Eldrich indicated a chair before his desk. "You don't look at all well."

"My partner is missing." Heyoka limped to the chair and sat down heavily. "The doctor said the staff would help me search."

Eldrich made a triangle with his forefingers and thumbs. "A search party, Sergeant?" A puzzled look crossed his face. "But surely you remember the release you and Corporal Jensen signed. Danzig Station can provide no help."

Heyoka's ear twitched. "Not officially, of course. I'm only asking for volunteers."

"Under normal conditions, yes, I would permit volunteers." Eldrich leaned back and folded his arms. "However, I'm afraid your unusual—appearance—has excited the natives. They are especially active right now, therefore I can't, in good conscience, allow my personnel to risk themselves in nonstation-approved excursions at this time."

Heyoka rose to his full height to glare down at the soft-skinned human. The savage *other* within him clamored to be heard, claws extended, hair bristling. His voice roughened as he fought to contain its thirst for violence. "You are going to let her just die?"

Eldrich gestured with empty hands. "The young woman is most likely already dead. I read the doctor's report on your condition last night. With your hrinnti physiology, you had at least some chance of surviving an attack, and yet here you are, after only a few hours among them, badly slashed, weak from loss of blood, barely on your feet again after spending a night in Sickbay. A human could hardly have survived similar abuse."

Heyoka had a sudden vision of Eldrich sprawled across the floor, his throat torn out. He could smell the hot blood, taste the coppery richness in the back of his throat. With an effort, he sheathed his claws. "She is not dead."

"Why don't you return to your unit, Sergeant?" Eldrich picked up a pile of reports and squared their edges against the desk. "We'll work with our hrinnti contacts and try to recover the body. We'll send word as soon as we know anything."

Heyoka repressed an unhumanlike snarl. "I have no intention of leaving without Corporal Jensen."

Eldrich smiled thinly. "Well, check back with me in a few days then, and let me know how your search is progressing."

Heyoka turned to go, cold fury pumping through his veins. They both knew Mitsu did not have "a few days."

Whisperings, like the rustle of dried flowers . . . darkness . . . a familiar musky scent. Mitsu shifted,

then gasped as pain stabbed through her right arm
and side. Had she screwed up and landed in the
sodding treatment tank again? No, there was never
any pain in the tank. The pain came after the Meds
broke you out and you saw what you were left with.

Confused, she tried to remember what planet they
were on . . . Beckman Seven? . . . Giriz? . . . Enjas
Two? So many planets, so many actions, dead and
dying at her feet, weapons shrilling.

A faint light worked toward her. She lay on a pile
of cushions, limp as a boiled noodle, until it finally
resolved itself into a torch carried by a—

Memory flooded back . . . Outside the males'
house, a hrinn dressed in red had motioned to her
as though it wanted her to join it, but she'd scrambled
back the other way. It had leaped after her then,
across the sandy soil, faster than she would have
thought a bloody fur-face could run. The stronger
Anktan gravity had made lead weights of her feet and
she'd fallen under its claws, cursing.

A small gray-and-white hrinn wedged its torch into
a wall socket, then squatted gracefully on the earthen
floor beside her, cradling a small pottery basin in the
crook of one arm. It was dressed in red too, like the
one who had attacked her, but seemed younger. She
thought of Blackeagle's savage teeth. Did these
creatures eat human flesh? With an odd tenderness,
it lifted her mangled arm, and the resulting agony
cast her into a soundless dark well . . .

When she came to herself again, the creature was
laving her clawed arm and side in herb-scented water,
its touch amazingly gentle. When it saw her looking
up at it, the half-gray, half-white nose wrinkled, baring
double rows of wickedly sharp white teeth. "Lie
quiet," it said in Hrinnti accented very differently
from the deepsleep tape she had studied. "You ——
bleeding ——"

Mitsu tried to shape a question in Hrinnti, but

could not remember even how to begin. She sagged back, aching and exhausted.

The hrinn finished bathing her wounds, then wrapped her arm in clean undyed cloth and laid it back across her chest. Supporting her head with one hand, it held a wide-mouthed flagon of water to her lips so she could drink. Its mismatched ears trembled as it blinked down at her with huge black eyes that reflected her ashen face, then it took the torch and left her alone again in the vibrating dark.

So. For some reason, the hrinn had taken her prisoner instead of killing her outright. She asked herself why, as her eyelids sagged, but the darkness gave no answer.

Stores was cool and quiet, the lights dimmed. Electronics hummed below the threshold of human ears. Heyoka drummed his claws on the front counter, waiting for Allenby but, after the passing minutes added up into the tens, and still no one came, he circled the counter and examined a large shipping crate shoved against the wall that was almost as tall as he was.

"You can't open that!"

Balanced on his sound leg, Heyoka turned to Allenby's startled eyes. "Why not?"

"It contains native artifacts being shipped to a university research program." Allenby was pale. "I've already transmitted the manifest."

Heyoka's nose wrinkled in a fierce scowl. "Then help me find supplies for a search-and-rescue mission."

Allenby scuttled behind a pile of boxes in the corner. "I'm afraid I'm very busy at the moment, but please feel free to help yourself, Sergeant," he said in a quavering voice. "You're quite welcome to anything that's not already packed."

Then, without a doubt, everything he needed was

packed. Heyoka's ears flattened. Why was no one in this blasted station the least bit concerned that a *human* was missing? If it had been him, he could have understood this apathy.

Allenby's scrunched-up face peered out from behind a unit of shelving, then disappeared again. Heyoka's claws flexed. Very well, he would help himself to what he needed, and he didn't care where he found it.

Bending over the shipping crate, he worked a claw into the locking mechanism and fiddled with it until it opened with a click. Easing the top off, he stared down in surprise at com-units, still sealed in colorful plas casings from the factory. Com-units . . . sent to a university *from* Anktan? Baffled, he reached for one.

"Begging your pardon, sir!" Allenby pushed the lid back down and relocked it. "I seem—to have more time this afternoon than I thought. If you'll just give me your list, I'll find what you need."

Heyoka appraised the little man and read fear in the tense lines around his mouth and the sweat sheening his pinched-up face. He took a short list scribbled on a scrap of plas out of his pocket and handed it to him.

Allenby scanned it. "No problem at all, sir. You just wait here. I'll be right back!" He scurried off into the labyrinth of boxes and shelves that filled the enormous room.

Heyoka sat on a crate, thinking about the com-units, then turned as the door slid open behind him.

"You haven't gone yet." The doctor's face was relieved as she hurried into the room, arms full. "I'm glad I caught you."

"Volunteering for the search, Dr. Alvarez?" Heyoka scratched his ear.

"Call me Sanyha, please." Her tan face fell. "Eldrich has issued an order forbidding anyone to go."

"Yes." Heyoka stood up and limped over to a table

of unsorted hrinnti robes. "Interesting, isn't it? You thought everyone would be willing to help."

"They are." She bit her lip. "At least they would be, but Eldrich has threatened to terminate anyone who goes." She looked away. "No one will risk losing their job."

"Not even you."

She flushed. "Not even me, Sergeant. My real work here is as an anthropologist who just happens to be a doctor as well. A lot of us are double-certified to cut down on the overhead. I've spent the last six years working out hrinnti patterns of kinship. I'm not going to throw that away!"

"I'm not asking you to go." Heyoka selected a set of green robes, the same shade most of the males had worn the night before. "I wouldn't trust you, or anyone else here, at my back anyway." He shrugged his arms out of the spare uniform he'd donned earlier and then pulled on the loose outer garment.

She laid down the items in her arms. "I brought you a medkit and a power brace for your leg. With an injury like that, I imagine you've used one before."

Heyoka stared at the black plas leg brace. His ear twitched. He'd used one all right, had cursed and strained for weeks to get his leg working in one just like it, weeks when he hadn't known if he would ever walk again under his own power.

"I thought it might help." She looked away as he shucked his pants. "You were pretty crippled up when you left Sickbay."

He hitched up the flowing hrinnti trousers, then made himself pick up the slick, cool plas without flinching. "Thank you," he said in a tone that made it mean something else entirely. Then he turned away and adjusted the settings along the length of the brace so it would fit his hrinnti leg.

At least it was black, he thought. It matched his fur. Maybe it wouldn't be so noticeable outside in the sun. But even if they didn't see it, he knew full well they would smell it.

Behind him, the door slid open, then shut.

Chapter Five

Seska heard a scratch, then glimpsed a gray-and-white face at her threshold. Vvok had bred basketfuls of daughters colored so, but the mismatched fields around these eyes could only be Khea. She lolled back on her cushions and flicked a disinterested ear. "Speak."

Padding more softly than any self-respecting youngster ought, Khea approached, then folded her body into a hesitant bow, black eyes blinking at the floor in obvious distress.

A scowl wrinkled Seska's nose. "You have not allowed the creature to die?"

"No, Line Mother!" Ears down, the cubling gulped a breath. "But it is badly hurt and I do not know how much longer it will survive. It is so . . . delicate."

"Do not be ridiculous, child." Seska smoothed the gray overfur on her forearm, covering the white undercoat. "Nothing that hideous could be delicate." She picked up the list of the woven goods which Ghita had requested for trade.

"I think we should call in the Restorers' Guild."

"We?" Seska glanced down sharply at the youngster. The young eyes, still cast properly at the floor, watched her from their corners. So, she thought, a little spirit appears in this one at last. She scowled. "Then summon Mela."

Khea's breast heaved. "Th-the creature is injured, not sick," she forced out. "Mela treats disharmonies of the body." Her ears trembled. "We need a wound restorer."

"I suppose then you are referring to Vexk," she said acidly. "Well, despite her vows, even an honorless creature like Vexk would not lower herself to touch one of those loathsome Outsiders."

"She would not have to touch it." In her anxiety, the cubling looked directly at Seska. "If she could just tell me what to do . . ." Khea hurriedly returned her gaze to the floor. "I would care for it."

The fur rose on the back of Seska's neck but, intrigued in spite of herself, she allowed the brazen liberty to pass for now. This child had never spoken up even once since she'd been assigned to her as a trainee. She stretched an arm above her head until the bones popped in her spine and shoulders. "Such services are not free." Her ears flattened at the thought of debts incurred and payments which would only be named later as she weighed the potential cost against the advantages conferred by possessing this creature, and its knowledge, alive. It was somehow connected to the strange hrinn that had fallen out of the sky yesterday, perhaps even part of a new, as-yet-unnamed pattern that was emerging far wider and more powerful than any in untold seasons. And if Outsiders were involved in the sacred *purposes/in/ motion* which governed all life, then they were clearly more than the foolish prey-animals she had previously considered them to be. The information she might gain from this one could be invaluable.

Khea's eyes were squeezed shut; obviously the child

had run dry of arguments. "Very well." Seska leaned over and seized a handful of gray-and-white ruff, letting her handclaws prick as she pulled the cubling close to her muzzle. "But remember that when the price for this service is named, you will have to be involved in the payment."

The cubling hung in her hands without flicking so much as an ear, displaying more composure than Seska had thought she would ever develop. The old matriarch flung her to the floor. "Tell Ghita to attend me. I do not like the looks of this list." Then she fussed with the trade goods manifest until the cubling collected herself and crept away.

Fik allowed the messenger jit's leathery brown body to crawl onto her pale-ginger arm. The sinuous flyer's eyes, no larger than scarlet pinpoints, glittered up at her. Too bad that small triangular head had no room for sense. She would have liked to discuss this dire mistake returned unexpectedly from the past, but there was no safe place in Qartt Hold to talk, even if she could find a sympathetic listener. Although the Line Mother seemed to suspect many at Qartt had been involved, what Fik had done for Qartt, and Anktan, so long ago, she had done alone.

Shaking the jit's tiny claws off her arm, she pushed the creature back into its wooden cage and fastened the top. This was her fault. They were all supposed to be dead, every last daughter and cubling of oh-so-proper Levv. She'd heard occasional rumors of a few Levv outcasts back up in the mountains, and whispers that some had been taken in as nonbreeding servants among the plains Lines who ranged far away from this river valley. Those might or might not be true, but she knew by the evidence of her own eyes that the majority of Levv were dead.

Her handclaws flexed in frustration. Why had it fallen to her to be the one to come across the ancient color pattern on that fateful day? Staring at the toddling handful of Black/on/black fur amid the bloody destruction of Levv, knowing full well the Line was innocent of wrongdoing, she had not been able to dash its brains out against the nearest rock as she should have. Though she had never really believed in the power of the Voice, or the great *purposes/in/ motion* from the old tales, the appearance of the sacred coloration after so many generations had seemed the portent of an emerging dark pattern. Superstition had overwhelmed her, even as she reached for the cubling, and she found herself turning aside, allowing him to flee into the brush toward the plainsward side of the mountain, a moment of supreme foolishness for which now they would all pay.

But not if she found him first, a distant portion of her mind whispered. Not if this supposedly powerful Black/on/black died before he could ask more questions. The jit clung to its cage with all four clawed feet, its long tail curled around a wooden bar. A message, she thought, reaching through the bars to stroke the tiny head with one finger. She must communicate with her fellow conspirators. If they could overtake the Black/on/ black while he was alone, they could tear his throat out and still be safe. No one ever had to know who had set the other Lines against conservative, old-fashioned Levv.

She reached underneath her cushions and brought out the rectangular talker-box. She still marveled at the strange black metal, so different from anything a hrinn had ever produced. She and the others had been right to make a deal with these Outsiders, who knew so much more about the way the world worked than hrinn were ever likely to discover alone. As the Line Mothers were gradually defeated by the original conspirators in lawful challenge, they would use such devices and many more to make life easier and more interesting, and no one ever had to know such progress had been bought with the blood of Levv.

Rakshal sauntered into the subterranean chamber and his bristling, disapproving presence immediately crowded Nisk, even though the two of them were still separated by a fair amount of space. Several younger males gave way without protest as he approached, but Nisk turned his back, both to avoid a direct confrontation and to demonstrate disdain. There were all too few priests left among the people these days, and he failed to understand why this one was so abrasive. He should be spreading the wisdom of the Voice to males' houses up and down the river, creating structure and strengthening association, not sowing dissention among those already bonded.

He squatted before the fire, feeding gynth leaves into its glimmering red heart and studying the shifting flames. The soothing scent filtered through the air, settling his nerves and making it possible to consider all aspects of the emerging pattern carefully, even the seemingly erratic influence of Rakshal, who might have his own part to play. Were events shaping into *patience/in/illusion*, as he suspected, or something darker and altogether less malleable to the desires of hrinn? He feared the latter, having encountered occasional patterns so destructive, one could only pin one's ears back and endure until they dissipated.

Rakshal loomed behind him and Nisk's nostrils flared at his altered scent; he stank of *power*. He had been to the pool. Fury kindled within Nisk. Rakshal was clearly spoiling for a fight, but something immense and far-reaching was developing and this was not the time. "Don't interfere with what you obviously lack the ability to understand," he said. "This pattern is an old and slow-growing one that began back with the demise of Levv, and I have always felt the true

name of that day has never been known." Nisk rose
to face the dark-gray priest.

"The Council named it *death/in/longing*." Rakshal
prowled around Nisk, heedless of where he placed
his feet or whose path he crossed, forcing the other
males to give way. They backed off with rumbling
growls. "It could be nothing else. Levv had to know
how it would end when they slew without trespass,
or blood-debt, or even challenge."

Taking a life outside established rituals was the
worst of transgressions, cutting across all patterns,
large and small, sowing chaos in the midst of order.
Nisk's stomach turned at the very thought. The desire
to rend and slay simmered just below the surface of
every waking moment, indeed, burned through him
now with the same urgency with which his heart
sought to beat, his lungs to breathe. That need had
to be controlled and channeled, made to serve order,
rather than destroy it. If not, the old times would
return when every hrinn's claws were turned against
all others. Chaos would again rule and civilized
cooperation would be but a fool's dream. He stared
into the fire. "I never saw any evidence that Levv slew
without reason. Did you?"

Rakshal's ears flattened. "You know very well I had
not yet drawn breath then. I am part of this new day,
which calls for younger, stronger teeth."

Nisk shifted his weight onto the balls of his feet
and sheathed his handclaws only by sheer exertion
of will. The smell of Rakshal's insolence battered at
him until it was all he could do to hold onto rational
thought and not leap at that dark-gray throat. "I was
quite young, but had already been accepted into the
males' house." Nisk forced reasonableness into his
own voice. "I never saw Levv to be less than honorable. This house accepted many males born of that
Line before—"

"'Before.'" Rakshal's eyes glittered. "Before they

slaughtered, before they fell, before they betrayed us all! *Before!*"

For the first time, Nisk felt his age pressing in, whispering he might not win in an all-out fight with this brash youngster. He glanced uneasily around the circular chamber, the sound of his own breathing loud.

"If this Outsider insists on knowing his Line, then he aligns himself with Levv and all that means." Rakshal stalked back to the whitestone wall and stopped before the frieze of painstakingly maintained scent-glyphs. "Either he drops this matter and applies for membership in a males' house, or shares Levv's end." Extending a foreclaw, he retraced the winding shape of *death/in/longing* with a line of brilliant blue sacred fire.

A hint of light approached around a corner in the blacker-than-black darkness. Mitsu shifted, then stiffened as pain shot through her right side. All-Father, she was thirsty, and it was so damnably cold in this hole. Hadn't these fur-faces ever heard of blankets? Then a weak laugh shook her, bringing even more pain. What need had hrinn for blankets? Black-eagle had slept unprotected through every kind of weather their unit had encountered.

Helplessly watching the faint light grow brighter, she wondered what had happened to him. Had the beasts in that underground pit killed him? The breath caught in her throat, turned into an agonizing tickle, then a wracking cough that jarred her wounds and enveloped her in pain.

The light turned one last corner, then two hrinn entered her small chamber, the solemn gray-and-white which had tended her earlier, and another, whose white fur was edged with just a hint of gray.

Mitsu blinked up at the fierce long-muzzled faces through the tears brought on by the coughing. "Why don't you just kill me and be done with it?" she whispered hoarsely in Standard.

The white hrinn's lips pulled back over huge teeth, then it leaned down and sniffed at her. The smaller gray-and-white, with its almost comical one gray eye and one white, wedged itself in the corner, cocking its head to one side as Mitsu had seen Blackeagle do many times. Blackeagle . . . Her eyes fluttered closed. He had told her not to go to the males' house, warned her they would smell her out. It was so irritating that he was always right.

A finger brushed her cheek. She tried to open her eyes again, but could not.

"You have —— waited —— long. It is ——," a voice said in Hrinnti. "—— body —— smells quite different —— ours. I cannot —— our —— work —— its blood."

Damnation, despite the deepsleep course, she was getting only one word in every two or three. A deep chill seeped through her and she fought the urge to cough again.

"Then —— die?" a second voice said from very far away.

"Perhaps." The first voice was calm. "Perhaps not. We ——. I —— do what —— can here."

Leave me alone! Mitsu wanted to tell them. Let me die in peace! But she could not find the energy. She felt the sting of bandages being eased away from her arm and side.

"Perhaps —— help?" the first voice asked. "Healing —— strong in Vvok ——"

The second hrinn did not answer. Mitsu heard the crackle of flames, smelled smoke, then drifted, seeing Blackeagle's black-furred face in her mind as he watched her with his ears pricked forward, ready to tell her what a stupid, wet-behind-the-ears boot she was.

"I'm sorry," she whispered.

"What —— say?" one of the hrinn asked.

"Nothing," the other answered. "Very —— this —— hurt. Hold —— still —— soak —— a Restoring —— and watch —— teeth."

A fiery liquid drenched Mitsu's clawed side and arm, burning the raw flesh. She gasped, trying not to cry out, then darkness swept her away.

The fat red sun glimmered down through the unfamiliar pale-amber sky as Heyoka trudged across the hard-baked desert floor, skirting occasional patches of sand. Although the brace stiffened his gait, he found he could walk without limping for the moment. The extra gravity dragged at him though, making every movement, no matter how small, more strenuous.

In a black duraplas backpack, he carried concentrates for two weeks and what little information he had been able to pry out of the research station's database—a few sketchy maps and details on local kin-groups, surprisingly sparse for a study that had been in progress for over forty Standard Years. He suspected someone had locked out the more pertinent information. Still, he had the maps and the scrap of red cloth he had found. According to the database, that shade of red dye designated a local, mostly female kin-grouping known as Vvok. The map had indicated a stream just ahead which he needed to cross and then climb to the higher ground overlooking the eastern shore of the river. Vvok Hold was located in the middle of that plateau. With luck, he would reach it soon after nightfall.

Falling rock rattled down the hillside. Heyoka listened, his body rigid with concentration. Unhealed claw marks stung along his ribs. Listening intently, he heard it again, the click of a dislodged rock somewhere behind him. Someone was back there, perhaps even trailing him. He abandoned the boulder and waded across the stream.

On the opposite bank, he sniffed the breeze for a clue as to who was following him, but the wind was out of the west and brought no answers. The ground ahead of him rose sharply now, strewn with broken sandstone boulders. He wove upward, using the rocks for cover, gritting his teeth against the renewed ache in his leg. Finally, he reached down and thumbed the power brace to a higher setting, then pushed on as fast as he could manage.

To his disgust, he found himself panting. Too much time on Med-leave, he told himself. Using a broken chunk of sandstone for cover, he studied the drylands below, finally spotting a band of tiny figures retracing the route he had just taken, mounted on the hump-backed riding beasts called yirns.

The fur rose across his shoulders. Sliding back behind the boulder, he tried to think. His best clue indicated Vvok had taken Mitsu, but this group rode from another direction. Who were they and what did they want?

Glancing down at his aching leg, he realized he had few options, since he could not outrun mounted trackers. Seething at the loss of time it entailed, he worked his way back down the hillside, angling downstream of the spot where he had crossed before and hugging the lengthening shadows.

Several of the hrinn urged their mounts into the water, then plodded up the hillside, following his scent with apparent ease, while two remained on this side of the stream. Trapped, Heyoka listened with growing frustration as the broad flat feet of the yirn picked their way up the hill. Why in the bloody hell weren't they all going on? Just as he decided to risk crossing the stream again, he heard the faintest brush of softness against rock—from *behind*.

Flek! his combat reflexes shouted, and his hand-claws flexed automatically before he got hold of himself. This was not Enjas Two. His lips wrinkled back over his teeth. He drew the steel-bladed knife from the sheath at his waist, whirling to face the rocks. Without warning, a tawny streak leaped onto his shoulders and swept him to the ground.

Chapter Six

Heyoka sprawled on the rocks, the air hammered out of his lungs and his bad leg wrenched back underneath his body. His nostrils flared: his assailant was both hrinnti and female! While he was still struggling for breath, she scrambled up and clawed his throat from behind. His combat reflexes took over and he leaned into the punishment instead of fighting. Thrown off balance, she stumbled, then squalled as Heyoka's full weight crashed back to pin her against a boulder.

Whirling, he faced a lean tawny-furred female, at least as tall as he was. She pinned her ears and bared double rows of white teeth at him, naked hatred written in the lines of her scarred face. In response, the savage *other* within him roared for release.

"Who are you?" The blood pounded in his ears as he grappled with her writhing body, which was as sinuous as a snake, and barely avoided the slashing claws. "What do you want?"

Instead of answering, she broke his grip and leaped again at his throat with both teeth and claws. He struggled to hold her off, his heart racing, and then the—world—shifted—to— *blue*—just as it had done that bizarre day on Enjas Two. Like a recording shunted into slow motion, her blue muzzle oozed toward him. He parried with a blue elbow to her blue eye, then with leisurely precision, rammed a fist into an unprotected nerve center at the base of her blue throat.

It took forever for her body to drift to the blue ground. Then she lay there, crumpled and unmoving, while his mind cried flek! Not here! he told himself, his breath coming hard and fast. He stood over his blue attacker, teeth involuntarily bared, fighting the overpowering urge to tear her limb from blue limb. The *other* would have, he was quite sure, but this fight was already decided and she was not his enemy in the same brutal sense the flek were; it was not necessary for her to die.

Gradually, his vision shifted from the ominous shades of blue back into the normal range of colors. He could perceive the tawniness of the unconscious hrinn's fur again, the red of her robes. Weariness swept over him with a suddenness that was sickening and he felt ravenously hungry. He sheathed his claws and knelt beside her, wincing when his bad leg took weight. She wore red, Vvok-red, he realized, the Line which had probably taken Mitsu.

Something splashed upstream; he peered around the boulder and saw the remaining two hrinn urge their yirn through the cold water and follow the others up the boulder-strewn hill. He thought one of them wore blue, but in the rapidly fading light, he wasn't sure. He dropped back and searched the unconscious female's robes. Her thick scent stirred an emotion within him, neither attraction, nor hatred, but something else wide and deep, ice-hot, frighteningly intense. His fingers grazed her luxuriant fur, and he trembled, realizing he had never before touched a female of his own species. Hardly ideal circumstances, he told himself, his ears flattening.

He found packets of dried meat, and then a sonic blade, of all things, and a com-unit. Sitting back on his haunches, he studied the blade. Mitsu's name was etched on the hilt. He put it aside to examine the black metallic com-unit. It was Confederation-made, tunable to a range of frequencies, scratched and dented as though used for a long time. Even the labels on the front were in Standard, but neither he nor Mitsu had brought such a unit along and he couldn't imagine the less-than-helpful station personnel issuing her one last night. This hrinn must have obtained it from Danzig Station, but how and what for? Who in the Thirty-eight Systems would she call on it?

Her arm scraped across the red-orange soil. Quickly, he ripped strips from her robes to bind her feet and hands, and then her muzzle, leaving the gag only loose enough for her to breathe. He needed time to lose himself before the others trailed him back down the hill.

He stowed the dried meat, the blade, and the com-unit in his pack, then slipped into the stream to hide his scent and waded downstream around the cliffs. His stomach demanded food and his body rest, but he had no time for either now.

The Director was lost in thought when Allenby signalled for admittance. The Stores manager had to buzz again before Eldrich looked up from his desk. "What?" He scowled. "Oh, it's you—finally."

Allenby's stomach tightened as he slid into a chair before the ostentatious desk. "I came as fast as I could."

Eldrich picked up a plas printout from his desk. "I see you filled the sergeant's supply list before he left."

He tried to swallow around the lump in his throat. "I—I know you said not to be too helpful, but—" He dabbed at the sweat beading up on his forehead.

"But—what, Mr. Allenby? You are wasting my time!"

"But—" Allenby's shoulders hunched, feeling the weight of the Director's displeasure. "But Blackeagle started digging through the shipping crates, the *locked* ones. He even opened one. I had to distract him."

Leaning back in his chair, Eldrich studied him with those awful gray eyes that made Allenby think of dirty snow. "Why didn't you just call Security?"

"You said not to make him suspicious." Allenby's fingers knotted. "He is a Ranger, after all, and trained to notice incongruities. I didn't want to make a fuss."

"Yes, the Rangers." The gray eyes, alligator-cold, blinked. "Little more than a pack of assassins and hotheads, by all repute." He crossed his arms. "For someone who has been on Anktan for little more than a day, Sergeant Blackeagle has certainly made himself felt." Rising from his chair, he thrust his hands into the pockets of his crisp blue station uniform and stared at the large map on the opposite wall. "Did you also violate my orders about issuing them modern weapons?"

"Oh, no, sir!" Allenby's eyes widened. "I even supervised when Security checked him at the door lock. He only took an ordinary steel knife."

Staring at the bands of orange, red, blue, and green on the map, Eldrich shook his head. "Still, with all that combat training and experience, he could pose a problem, even for our magnificently savage friends out there." He traced the band of blue with one finger. "I wonder what the sergeant is really after."

"After, sir?" Allenby couldn't keep the surprise out of his voice. "I thought he just wanted to come home."

"Don't be an idiot." Eldrich turned back to him.

"Who in their right mind would settle for a backwater dive like this when he had the run of civilized space?"

"He said he wanted to find his family."

Eldrich's lip curled. "Don't make me laugh. You know very well these brutes have no concept of real family." He picked up a plas printout and studied it. "No, my bet is the sergeant is after something else." A thin smile curved his lips. "Are you really so dense that it has not occurred to you the sergeant and his young friend are government spies?"

All-Father rot them all straight to hell! Mitsu thought crossly. She tried to sit up and failed again. Hot and dizzy, she sagged against the thin pile of cushions. She must be feeling a little better, or she wouldn't be letting the eternal lack of light in this sodding place bother her so much. She'd always hated the dark, even back on Miramem when she was just a creche-brat. Turning her head, she strained to see something, anything, but there was only the hole-black darkness, almost as bad as the night she'd been assigned to Blackeagle's outfit for her first action back on Beckman Two.

All-Father, she had been so scared when they'd landed, hadn't even seen a flek at that point, except on the vid, of course, which couldn't do justice to their stomach-churning faces or their sodding *stink*.

That night had been a soulless black, too, with low-hanging clouds so there were no stars, not that seeing them would have made her feel better; strange constellations only emphasized how really far from home she had come. Along with the rest of the replacements, she stumbled still red-eyed from deepsleep into camp, dumped out a scant ten minutes before by an automated shuttle and only two weeks' subjective time out of boot camp.

Trying to report to their commanding officer, they had taken plenty of ribbing, the usual sort of

comments and whistles and other dumb-ass stuff that
boots had to endure—and then some wit had thought
to send them to Sergeant Blackeagle.

Walking up from behind at the mess tent, with him
all dressed out in that black Ranger uniform and
helmet, she couldn't tell right away there was something—different—about him.

"Sergeant Blackeagle?" She waited, smelling the
fresh-brewed coffee and thinking she would kill for
a cup herself.

"Yes?" he said without turning around.

"Replacements, sir. We're here to report in."

He pulled off the black combat helmet and twisted
around in his seat. "How many did we get?" a long-
muzzled, large-eared face asked.

After a moment, Mitsu swallowed, unable to take
her eyes off his seven-foot, black-furred form.

The creature flicked an ear at her. "Well, Private?
They are still teaching boots to count?"

She could feel her fellow boots frozen in place
behind her as a low chuckle rippled around the mess
table. She flushed. No one, not even a bunch of
sodding officers, was going to laugh at Mitsu Jensen!
"Ten," she said stiffly, her face as hot as a goddamned
torch.

Blackeagle nodded at her, then turned back to his
dinner. "Half of what we requested, as usual. I guess
it will have to do." And, of course, he'd known all
along what the first sight of him did to people. He
loved a joke as much as the next guy; it just never
showed on that hairy face of his.

She swallowed suddenly. All-Father, but would he
ever razz her for getting into such a bloody mess!
She'd be hearing about this one for the next twenty
years.

Hrinnti feet whispered in the dark passage outside
the room. They made almost no noise, she thought,
remembering how the hrinn had surprised her outside

the males' house. Her hand crept to the empty sheath in her boot where she had hidden a sonic blade when she left Danzig Station . . . how long ago?

She caught the guttural murmur of voices, then a dim glow that grew steadily larger. They were coming back, no doubt to finish her off. Unable to move, she cursed her weakness. The light rounded the final corner and entered the small chamber where she lay, borne by the gray-and-white that had come before, as well as several unfamiliar, small dull-grays. Their arms were full of cloths and bottles as they squatted on the floor beside her, their black eyes unreadable.

"You are ——." The gray-and-white hrinn blinked down at her, then passed Mitsu a shallow bowl. "That is —— since the Line Mother —— look ——."

Mitsu lifted her head to sniff at the bowl. It was only water, as near as she could tell and, All-Father, she was thirsty! Tipping the bowl, she let a long tepid swallow roll down her throat. "Who Line— Mother?" she asked in Hrinnti, her tongue having a great deal of trouble twisting itself around the guttural syllables.

The two smaller hrinn shifted uneasily, glancing at each other with their dark eyes. One whined deep in its throat. The gray-and-white flattened its ears and then the other was silent.

"Since you —— our language, that —— matters ——," the gray-and-white hrinn said. "I —— Khea, a —— Vvok. These —— nonbreeding servants —— no importance. You will not —— them."

"Kee—uh." Mitsu made an attempt at the name. "Not—ser—vant?"

The two smaller hrinn shrank back, hiding their long-muzzled faces against the wall. The gray-and-white's ears flattened again. "I —— direct-daughter —— Line!" Her black eyes narrowed to slits.

Fuzzily, Mitsu tried to recall what she had learned of hrinnti society from the deepsleep tapes, but very

little had been implicit in the basic structure of the
language, and the effort of this conversation had
already sapped what energy she had. Her arm and
shoulder throbbed and her head felt as though it was
stuffed with the mush served for breakfast at the
creche, a million years ago on Miramem.

The long gray-and-white face studied her a moment
longer, then the hrinn brushed a strand of mane back
out of its eyes. "If you —— that —— Line Mother
—— dead."

Mitsu closed her eyes. Too much of this conversation was eluding her. There was no telling what
it was really saying, and even worse, it thought she
understood. On the surface, these creatures resembled
Blackeagle, but they were nothing like him, and the
deep weariness seeping through her brain would not
let her think what to do.

"You —— dead." The voice seemed to come from
far away. "These servants —— wash and —— to
come —— Line Mother."

When Mitsu managed to open her eyes again, she
saw only the two servants pouring water into a low
basin and laying out clean cloths, as well as black
robes that matched their own.

The water's chill seeped into Heyoka's bones,
making his bad leg ache as he waded downstream in
the eel-gray dusk. He kept slipping on submerged
rocks and his feet were scraped and bruised. While
there was still enough light, he had used the map to
plot an alternate route. Now, after passing the foot
of the red-orange cliffs that marked the initial rise
of the plateau above the river, he finally abandoned
the stream. The cooling air carried the dry, pungent
scent of low, scrubby brush that covered the ground,
and he could smell the river just out of sight. On the
western horizon, mountains glimmered fiery red in
the setting sun, while behind him, sandstone cliffs

stood like sentinels, dark against the night sky. And somewhere beyond those cliffs lay Vvok Hold and Mitsu.

He caught a thread of the same aromatic smoke he'd encountered at the males' house the night before, as well as the musk of other hrinn. The fur prickled along his shoulders and he drew upon his Ranger training to move silently. He hadn't planned to come this way, but had no option now.

He was at a loss as how to interpret last night's events in the circular underground room. What did all that rambling about Levv and Black/on/black mean? He'd searched for Levv on the map of local kin-groupings, but found nothing. Perhaps Levv was farther away, beyond the mountains even, a hostile tribe.

Thin gray smoke marked the hole in the cleared ground, just as it had the night before. He spotted the dark irregular openings of caves in the cliffs and remembered waves of hrinn pouring out in search of the intruder. This whole area must be honeycombed with underground chambers.

He became intensely conscious of the reek of the artificial materials in his pack and the brace on his leg. He'd been a fool to bring them. His own scent and that of his native robes might fade into the background, but off-world materials stood out like a torch at midnight. Guttural whispering drifted up from the underground chamber, the rough syllables louder one moment, then fading the next. He spotted the central pole of the ladder protruding from the hole.

A dark shape walked within twenty feet of him to the right and disappeared into one of the caves. His ear twitched, but he forced himself to continue at a nonchalant pace, hoping these hrinn were all too busy with their own concerns to notice him. He passed the smoke hole on the left and the voices faded. A few more feet, he told himself, and he would angle back to the cliffs and continue walking until either the sun rose or he found a place where a one-legged soldier could climb the plateau.

Then, for no reason he could discern, claws scrabbled as hrinn bounded out of the caves and surged up the ladder. He froze as dozens of natives surrounded him, black eyes glittering. Their mingled scents were heady, evocative. Half-shaped images formed in the shadowy recesses of his mind, as though he had stood here before, experienced the electric scent and feel and taste of this particular night. The savage *other* surged back into his awareness; his claws sprang free and his breathing deepened, ready for something, he knew not what.

Someone snarled in the back ranks, then hrinn gave way as a black-furred male with a white throat cuffed his way to the front. Heyoka's nostrils flared at the remembered scent. "Nisk."

Broad-shouldered and tall, Nisk stood with his head held high, staring back at Heyoka with black eyes that disappeared in the background of his black face. Heyoka suddenly knew *he* must look much the same to humans: dark, enigmatic, unreadable.

Nisk flicked an ear at him. "Black/on/black."

Heyoka glanced at the wall of hrinnti bodies surrounding him, almost every one of them taller and built more heavily than himself. "Why do you call me that?"

"It is an acknowledgment of the obvious." Nisk's black-furred arm gestured and Heyoka was gripped by the strange feeling that he was observing himself. "Return to the males' house and we will discuss its implications."

Curiosity warred with the need to find Mitsu, and there was the additional problem of what they would do if he refused. Would it be a deadly insult, or only of passing interest?

Before he could reply, another male pushed his way

to the center of the circle, a stocky dark-gray robed in gray. "He cannot enter that sacred place again!" the newcomer said. "This matter must be settled between this creature of the Dead and me."

Chapter Seven

"I lead this house, Priest." A deadly silkiness threaded the voice of the powerfully built, black-furred hrinn as he stepped in front of Heyoka and faced the dark-gray. "Or have you forgotten?"

Heyoka studied the newcomer over Nisk's shoulder. It was Rakshal, the dark-gray male who had labeled him "imposter" the night before. He wondered if he would have to fight his way out. Rakshal was in his prime, no older than himself in all likelihood, and had the advantage of developing on this world, so that he was taller than Heyoka, topping a good eight feet at least, and better muscled, with a broader, denser frame. And—he wasn't lame.

Rakshal flattened his ears and snarled. "Come closer, Dead-thing. Let us settle the truth of this ridiculous lie of yours once and for all!"

The fur bristled along Heyoka's spine and his lips wrinkled back in a fierce display of his double rows of bone-white teeth, a savage expression he had always fought to suppress. His breathing deepened and his senses sharpened to almost unbearable clarity. He could detect the aromatic smoke from the underground room that saturated the others' fur, the faint bloody tang of their last meal on their breath, hear the least sigh or mutter of the onlookers, feel each separate grain of gritty sand on the ground beneath his bare feet and how the evening wind riffled the individual strands of his mane.

Several older males, lean as sticks and scarred from head to toe from past fights, pushed through the circle of watching hrinn to wedge two torches deep into the sandy ground. Their black eyes seemed grimly joyful. The onlookers crowded around them, jostling for position and clawing to maintain their place. Heyoka heard the puzzling phrases *mountain/over/stars* and *death/in/longing* repeated from hrinn to hrinn.

Rakshal seized one of the torches and defiantly thrust it into the air so that the flames danced above his head. "Speak to us of *Levv*, Dead-thing!"

Heyoka's breath quickened. "That is for you to tell me. I know nothing about Levv." The violent *other* within him raged to be set free—this foolish gray had no right to speak to him so! Everything about Rakshal, even the tone of his voice, was the deadliest sort of insult, well worth dying to avenge. The gray's scent was more acrid now, inciting Heyoka to mayhem somehow, as though strong emotion had altered the gray's pheromones and called up an involuntary response in himself. An unbidden growl rose in his throat.

A wave of expectancy beat at him from the watching faces. The sharp angle of their heads and the narrow focus of their gaze indicated they were waiting for him to make the proper move, to do—something. The air was thick with hrinn musk as he tried to infer the correct response. The dark-gray's eyes glittered as he stared up at the torch flames above his head, then Heyoka understood—*he* was supposed to take up the remaining torch.

He set his jaw and stepped around Nisk, trying not to limp, steadied himself on his good leg before the second torch, which leaned crazily to one side, reached to—

Without warning, Nisk blocked his hand with an outstretched arm. "I invoke the right of sponsorship!"

Surprise rumbled through the watching hrinn as Heyoka wavered, then recovered his balance. The torch flickered just beyond his reach in the rapidly cooling night breeze, a fierce beacon of yellow-orange so bright, he could see the afterimage when he blinked. Blood pounded in his ears in a wild rhythm which knew nothing of soft-skinned humans or their tentative ways. "What do you mean—sponsorship?"

"Come now, Outsider." The dark-gray tossed his torch easily from hand to hand. The shadows shifted across his muzzle. "Surely even a wretched thing like yourself can appreciate the honor of being sponsored by the legendary Leader of the Mish River Males' House." He glided closer, each lithe movement a study in hrinnti grace and strength which Heyoka's damaged leg would never again be able to match. "But sponsorship or not, my challenge still stands."

"*I* accept challenge in his place, Rakshal." A deep-throated growl underlay Nisk's words. "As sponsor, I have that right. You have been sniffing around my shadow far too long. Come ahead and fight me, if you dare!"

"No, he challenged *me*." The cool night breeze whipped Heyoka's unbound mane across his face.

Nisk whirled, arm outstretched, and struck him to the ground. He sprawled at Nisk's feet, dazed, nose pressed into the sandy soil, the dry scent of sun-baked ground overwhelming all other odors.

"That was your first lesson." Nisk breathed heavily as he stepped over Heyoka's twitching, outstretched body and snatched up the remaining torch. "You will obey me in all things, or I will tear your throat out where you lie! There is a pattern arising here that you do not yet perceive."

Head high, ears pricked, the dark-gray sidled closer. "You are a fool, Nisk! That creature is outside all patterns, large or small, no matter what he looks like. His existence means nothing and I will prove it by feeding his blood to the earth, after which the *pattern/in/progress* will still complete itself, just as it is meant to."

"Are you saying you actually Heard that from the Voice?" Nisk asked. The wind gusted, bending the torch flames double. "I think not!"

Ears still ringing from Nisk's blow, Heyoka pried his head off the ground and saw him step into the cleared circle, the torch held high above his head. The black-furred Leader of the males' house appeared to have experience on his side, but Rakshal was obviously younger and stronger. The whole scene shimmered with an air of unreality in the uncertain light.

Crouching low, Rakshal circled smoothly to the left as the spectators drew back to give the pair more room. Heyoka struggled up to his hands and knees, trying not to be sick, then several males caught his arms and dragged him out of the way. He twisted to break their grip and one of them clubbed the back of his head with a fist, turning his thoughts into fog and his legs into sand. As if in a dream, he saw Nisk close with the younger male, heard the fury of their snarls and growls, saw the ivory flash of teeth and dark adamantine claws that caught the light, the garish red-orange of hrinnti blood as it splattered and soaked their fur, smelled the hot exciting richness of opened wounds.

The ear-splitting fight continued, neither male giving nor gaining any quarter. Only half-conscious, Heyoka sagged against the silently watching hrinn, aware the outcome of this fight had some meaning beyond his personal survival, but unable to sort it out. Then a new note of desperation entered Nisk's snarls and Heyoka seemed to see a halo of blue fire crackling around the two struggling bodies. For the first time, the onlookers glanced at each other and commented in low tones.

The two torn and bloodied hrinn wrenched apart and stood glaring at each other with molten black eyes across the barren circle of ground, each still holding his torch high in the air. Blood matted their coats and the acrid odor of singed fur permeated the cool night air.

Rakshal stretched out a dark-gray arm toward Nisk, concentration outlined in every inch of his massive body. Moving slowly to his right, Nisk's breath came in great heavy pants, but he never took his eyes off the other male. Suddenly the dark-gray lunged forward, blue fire streaming from his outstretched fingertips toward Nisk's broad chest. For a moment, it seemed Nisk would withstand the attack, then his knees buckled, his body sagged to the ground. The torch slipped from his fingers and guttered in the sand.

The dark-gray kept his feet for another few seconds, then stumbled backwards and sat down heavily. Across the circle, Nisk's muzzle scraped weakly across the sand, but no one moved to help him.

Still constrained by the other males, Heyoka trembled with rage. This had been his fight! The sight of Nisk's beaten body there on the ground filled him with fury and shame at the same time, and worst of all was the whisper in the back of his mind that under these circumstances, and on this particular night, he himself would not have lasted half so long.

"Let—me—go!" He wrenched at his arms, still dizzy. "Or is it required that I watch him bleed to death in my place as well?"

The brown hrinn holding Heyoka threw him to the
ground. "Outsiders!" he said with obvious contempt.
"You wouldn't know a pattern if it nipped at your
heels!" He turned away.

Heyoka sprawled there for a moment, feeling every
inch that had been beaten, clawed, or bruised in the
last twenty or so hours. Then he pushed himself up
to his feet and limped over to Nisk's prone body.
Putting a hand on one shoulder, he rolled the black
male onto his back.

Nisk's eyes slitted open and his narrow hrinnti
tongue lolled to the side. "We must—leave—this
place." His voice was only a harsh whisper.

Heyoka looped Nisk's arm over his shoulder and
braced his good leg until the other hrinn regained
his feet. Then they limped out of the shifting circle
of light cast by the torch which, even while sitting
on the ground and half-conscious, Rakshal continued
to hold high overhead.

The claw wounds on the creature's damaged side
and arm still possessed an angry redness and were
seeping a disgusting milky fluid. Its smell had grown
even worse, a terrible rankness that burned her nose.
She ran a finger over its delicate skin: hot as the
ground at midday and even drier than before. Of
course, she had no idea of what its normal body
temperature was, but such terrible heat was a sign
of infection among hrinn and boded for the worst.
Khea dispatched a servant back up to her quarters
on the main level for the salve which the Restorer,
Vexk, had left yesterday.

The fragile Outsider lay on a few worn cushions,
its strange blue eyes following her every movement
until she longed to swat the helpless creature for its
audacity. How had it survived this long with such
terrible manners? She was surprised Fitila had not
killed it when she had the chance. "When you go

before the Line Mother, it would be unwise to stare at her like that." Khea rolled up the soiled bandages and placed them in the passageway for the servants.

A faint scrabbling of feetclaws in the passage signalled the return of the servant with the salve. The Outsider turned its head restlessly toward the door, murmuring in its high-pitched alien babble. Khea sat back on her haunches as the servant entered the chamber and passed the small pot of herb-laced grease into her hands, then waited as though it wanted something, black eyes covertly studying her. Did it suspect she was a weakling, bound to be culled in the next gleaning? Were even the idiot servants gloating behind her back? She flattened her ears. "Dismissed!"

It pressed its face to the earthen floor and fled.

Covering her fingers with salve, she coated the claw marks with soothing aromatic medicine. Beneath her touch, the creature lay quieter, only muttering in its strange tongue from time to time.

An ear twitched as she considered summoning the Restorer again, which would cause an angry scene with the Line Mother she would have to bluff her way through. Seska would be angry at the accumulating expense, but not as much as if this apparently valuable captive died. Her ears drooped in distress. The older she got, the more hazardous the path between duty and self-preservation became.

On the day when she had finally fought her way out of the nursery up into the light of Ankt, she had stood in the warm sunshine, foolishly thinking life would be easier, that she would at last have enough to eat without fighting for every scrap, a place of her own in which to sleep, proper clothing like an adult. Those things had come to pass, but now her existence was suspended on the weak thread of the Line Mother's approval, and she was painfully aware she lacked the strength of spirit that would let her achieve the revered rank of breeder some day. In this hold, she would always be an underling, only one step above an unnamed servant, nothing more.

Eyelids pressed tightly closed, the Outsider loosed a string of alien syllables. Khea shook herself, then covered its wounds with clean cloths. Vexk would have to be called back. Let the Line Mother take it out of her hide. She wasn't some half-witted servant to sit and do nothing while a creature placed in her care died.

Heyoka was still walking when dawn crept across the broken terrain on either side of the river, thin and gray, colder than a flek's heart—assuming flek had hearts. He couldn't remember the indoctrination lectures well enough to be sure and laser rifles never left much to examine on the battlefield. He stopped on the top of a knoll overlooking the river, so weary he could hardly hold his aching head up. Because of Nisk, they had made little progress during the remaining hours of darkness. The other male had been close to passing out more than once and they had been forced to rest repeatedly.

Nisk's hand gripped his arm. "Wait." The deposed Leader's tattered ears swiveled, sampling the early morning sounds. His black nose quivered. "I smell the house yirn herd foraging up ahead."

Heyoka sniffed and thought he did detect something hot and rank, animal-like, but had difficulty concentrating. His head still throbbed from the two stiff blows he'd taken, one at Nisk's own hand—stupid, letting himself be caught flatfooted. His reflexes, not to mention training, should have prevented that. Despite the brace, the pain in his bad leg dragged at him. He stared through the dimness at Nisk's blood-matted muzzle and thought of the huge shaggy yirns he had seen at the landing field. "Do you think you *can* ride?"

"I could ride even if I were dead." Nisk squinted at the sun just rising over the red sandstone cliffs on their right. "We have only until Ankt departs the sky this day to leave this males' house's territory."

"What do you mean 'we'?" Heyoka's nostrils flared. "I can't leave until I find my—" He paused, unable to remember a word for friend or partner. "My—companion," he said finally, though the term in Hrinnti meant literally "one who hunts with me" and only applied to a person of the same sex.

Nisk drew himself up. Claw marks and gashes crisscrossed his battered body like roads on a map of some unknown land. "Your Outsider companion behaved in a foolish manner and so must answer for it now. If he lives, he will return to his own kind, no doubt much wiser." He swayed, then caught himself, ears drooping. "As Black/on/black, you cannot concern yourself with those outside the great *purposes/in/motion* anymore. You have far more important matters to which you must attend."

"My name is Heyoka!"

"That is an Outsider's name, merely noise without meaning." Nisk rubbed his forehead wearily. "Black/on/black speaks of what you are, a condition far beyond mere naming."

"Then explain what it means."

"Not here." Nisk's eyes closed as he tilted his nose into the morning breeze. "I will say more after we reach the mountains. Such an explanation requires time, and no interruptions."

"I can't go to the mountains." He tried to focus on the murmuring river, instead of the ghastly wounds and burns Nisk had incurred in his place. "I'm going to Vvok to take back my companion." He walked down the knoll to the bank.

Nisk followed, ears flattened. "A hrinn has but two legs, duty and honor. Even though you were raised among Outsiders, those qualities should be etched into your soul. It is not necessary to be told of them."

Heyoka flicked an ear as something long and black scrabbled away from him over the sand, then slid into the water's green current. The water was smooth as newly molded plas, glimmering in the gray light of dawn. The darkness of wet sand filled his nostrils. He squatted on the sand and palmed the cool water in his cupped hands. Duty and honor. His duty lay to Mitsu who had come to this primitive place because of him. And honor? Whatever Nisk made of that word, it was bound to be something altogether different than a human would have meant.

But, of course, he was no more human than Nisk was.

"Are you content to be nothing more than an unknowing beast?" Nisk demanded. "Something greater than yourself is at work here. I believe the Voice spoke for your life many seasons ago, sparing you and setting something sacred in motion, a *pattern/in/progress*. This one is like a great storm, gathering on the horizon, full of the sky fire that bites. Nothing like it has ever been seen before, and you stand at its center. If I had let Rakshal kill you, it would have spun apart."

"*Slavers*, creatures who believe people can be owned like a yirn or a set of robes, stole me from this planet," Heyoka said, using the Standard word for "slavers" because none existed in Hrinnti. He limped angrily along the river bank. "I would not call that being spared."

Nisk loomed behind his shoulder, breathing heavily. "A deep ravine up ahead leads to the high land above us, and so to Vvok." His voice had gone low and strained. "Rain cascades down it in the wet season, but it is dry now. You should be able to climb it without much trouble."

Heyoka turned back to him. "Then you understand I must go."

"My understanding is not necessary." Nisk faced the rising sun. "If you believe your obligation to the Outsider outweighs your duty to me, you must go to Vvok." He stretched a blood-matted arm above his head, then winced. "I will wait here until you are finished."

"That's ridiculous!" Fur bristled across his shoulders and he flattened his ears with suspicion. "You've admitted you only have until sunset to leave this area, or they will kill you, and I have no idea how long it will take me to find my companion, or even if I can."

"Honor forbids that I save myself and leave you to face Rakshal's wrath." Nisk straightened a fold of his tattered, blood-soaked green robes and sat down heavily. "I have made you my responsibility, therefore it is my duty to wait."

Cold fury snaked down his spine. He felt the presence of his savage *other* again, eager to fight, to punish Nisk's superior attitude and establish dominance over him. Blood pounded in Heyoka's ears, the rich wet scent of the river sharpened, along with the drier sun-baked odor of the nearby desert hardpan. He swallowed and looked away from Nisk's eyes, which seemed to help. "I will not let you wait."

"How will you stop me, youngling?"

Now! the *other* whispered in the back of his mind. *Leap at his throat. Slash the soft hollow beneath his jaws with your teeth. Taste his blood!* He shuddered. "They will kill you."

"Perhaps," Nisk said calmly. "It is possible this pattern will be served by my death."

"If you will not go on alone, then come with me." Heyoka found himself pacing up and down the sand, his aching leg dragging. "Help me find my companion."

"That concerns Vvok." Nisk's eyes narrowed. "A *female* matter. I realize you are extremely ignorant for a male of your status, but surely even up in the sky, in the house of Ankt, males do not interfere in the business of females."

Heyoka's jaw tightened. "What if I just kill you here then and save Rakshal the trouble? Would that satisfy your honor?"

Nisk's lips wrinkled back from his teeth. "That is one way to end the obligations of sponsorship."

Heyoka stared at him as he stood in the shadow of the sandstone cliffs, painfully aware of the males' house just a few miles back upriver and the red sun edging ever higher in the sky like a great eye. "I can't just leave you here to die."

"Of course not." Nisk lurched back onto his feet and looked up at the sun, sand sticking to the blood matted in his black fur. "After we catch the yirn, you and I will cross the river together." Turning, he hobbled downriver.

Heyoka grimaced, then followed. As soon as he lured the stubborn old male into the hills, he would lose him and return for Mitsu. There seemed no other way at the moment.

Chapter Eight

When Seska saw the pallid, soft-skinned thing lying in Khea's arms, she snarled in frustration. The cubling had not exaggerated; if the creature wasn't dead already, it was only a breath away. She was furious with the child for not making her understand there would have to be another visit from the Restorers Guild. "Send for that wretch, Vexk, at once!" The thin silver bracelets on her arm jangled as she gestured toward the door. "In fact, do not send a messenger jit—it might stray, and due to your bungling, we have no time to waste. Put that creature down and go yourself."

Khea's black eyes glittered angrily up at Seska, then the cubling gazed down again. "Yes, Line Mother." Her voice was little more than a hoarse whisper, but Seska caught the undercurrents. *I told you*, Khea's stiffened young body said, as well as the reckless tilt of her ears. *I warned you that it would die.*

And so she had, again and again, and still it remained the cubling's fault. It was her duty to keep at Seska until she made the Line Mother understand.

If this creature died before Seska pried the truth out of its disgusting pink hide, Khea would bear the full brunt of her displeasure.

The gray-and-white cubling rose and stalked from the room, her gaze still focused on the red mat underfoot. Seska watched the tall, well-muscled form with calculating eyes. Khea was nearly full grown. Decisions would have to be made about her by the next gleaning. Only yesterday, Seska had been certain this cubling, with that unfortunate color pattern and meek manner, would be culled from the candidates for breeders, but now . . .

Flicking an ear, she realized Khea might be a late developer, one of the latent strains that sometimes appeared in the Vvok breeding pool. Such latents were easy to overlook in early gleanings, but when detected and brought on as breeders, they often were among the best of their generation, bigger and stronger, longer-lived, producing many fine daughters. If Khea were such a one, they could not afford to lose her.

Abandoned in an awkward heap on the mat, the Outsider rolled its black-fringed, round-eared head and muttered a string of alien sounds. Seska eased off her thick pile of cushions and prowled closer, the fur standing straight up along her spine. The ears were the worst, she decided, stiff, hairless knobs of flesh that apparently did not move at all. At least the creature had been washed and dressed in clean robes; its awful smell was almost bearable.

Standing over it, handclaws fully flexed, she glared at the pale, bizarrely naked skin, willing the creature to open its eyes and speak before it passed beyond anyone's claws. "Why have you come?" she demanded. "How much does this Black/on/black know about what we did? And what does he mean to do about it now?"

The creature's eyes opened to slits. Most of them were a sickening white, but the middlemost portion

was a startling ice-shrouded blue which seemed to
slice into her innermost thoughts. A snarl shaped
Seska's lips, then the strange eyes sagged shut again.

Chytt smoothed a fold of Qartt-blue robes across
the dark-red fur of her arm, admiring the contrast.
The fine cloth, woven by the westernmost hold of
Kennd, was a luxury in which she rarely indulged.
There were so many necessities to trade for, so many
smaller pleasures, that she rarely allowed herself
something this dear.

The shift in her weight wrung the coolness of
crushed gynth from the cushions, and the aromatic
scent threaded through her brain, summoning memories of hunting up among the blue-leaved gynth trees
in the elevations where rain fell regularly so that the
vegetation was lush and air always refreshingly brisk.
She longed for such excitement now, but she had far
too much to do.

No further word had come to her yet concerning
the troublesome Levv male, but she could not get that
eerie Black/on/black face out of her mind, nor the
telling angle of certain ears when she had spoken of
him upon her return. By all that was holy, what sort
of pattern linked Qartt Hold with the return of this
Levv?

It was apparent one or more of her daughters knew
something about this business, but that did not make
sense. None of the Lines had contracted blood-debt
of any sort against Levv in those long-ago days, so
why would any daughter of hers have risked both
herself and Qartt's honor to bring them down?

Killing outside established venues recalled the
ancient taint of genocide, long purged from civilized
hrinnti behavior. Such madness threatened them all,
and it was for that Levv had been destroyed. But what
if Levv had been innocent and the other Lines had
been incited to execution without cause? She had

never dared ask herself that question before, and now, when the emerging pattern was at hand and little could be done but follow where it led, she found she did not want to know the answer.

Someone scratched outside her door, asking for admission. She lounged back on her cushions. No doubt it was that wretch, Fik, for whom she had sent a good long time ago. There were always caves within caves with that one. She stretched one arm languidly, and then the other. Fik only came to bow her disrespectful pale-ginger head when she was good and ready, so now she could wait until the Line Mother condescended to gaze upon that insolent face.

She speared a mottled-green mizb fruit with a flexed handclaw, then scored the thick rind from top to bottom. Fik's familiar scent drifted into her quarters as the female edged almost into sight. *So, daughter, you push me.* Chytt bit into the sweet flesh of the fruit. Not a wise decision on Fik's part, though due in some measure, no doubt, to the fact that Fik had been birthed by one of Chytt's younger cousins, not Chytt, herself. Theoretically, all female children of Qartt Hold had become her daughters when she vanquished the previous Line Mother, but the reality of hold life never lived up to that ideal. The birth-daughters of her rivals always seemed a bit hungrier and more wary than her direct descendants—just as *she* had been in the time of her predecessor, old Hallat.

After finishing the fruit, she said, "Enter."

Fik prowled into her quarters, her squat muscularity typical of a less desirable body type that cropped up in Qartt descendents from time to time. Chytt much preferred the taller, more graceful build—like her own—that had come to characterize Qartt bloodlines in the past seasons.

Anger was written into the stance of every pale-ginger hair on Fik's body. She sank stiffly to her knees before Chytt's cushions. "You sent for me, Line Mother?"

Laying her ears back, Chytt tossed the tough mizb core into a dish. "I sent for you some time ago."

Fik did not look up. "Mimki is near delivering."

The tension between them charged the air with electricity. Chytt felt her own fur stir with its intensity, and she wrinkled her nose at the sharpening odor of Fik's coat which was not the acridness of fear exactly, nor the hot rawness of unbridled aggression either, but a muddle somewhere in between. "I often question my wisdom in allowing you to head the breeders." Her eyes narrowed. "I wonder what was on my mind that day for me to make such a mistake."

"It was your decision, Line Mother." Fik's pale-orange ears lowered just a hair, the large well-shaped ears over which she had always been so vain.

"It is also a decision I can rescind at the blink of an eye—for the good of the Line." *Just I could shred those lovely ears and no one in this entire hold would twitch so much as a single eyehair.* Leaning forward, Chytt wiped the sticky mizb juice from her handclaws on Fik's robes. She and Fik understood each other— most of the time, but, by the Voice, there had been increasing undercurrents of disrespect and resentment from her for at least a season now. This child of her cousin was preparing to challenge.

Chytt rose. "Ghitil is quite skilled—and well regarded by the other breeders as well." She let that nip sink in. Fik was competent, but popular with her hold-sisters, she had never been.

The pale-ginger ears flattened. "Ghitil is an empty-headed little yirn who has yet to bear a living child!"

"Yes, a great tragedy, is it not?" Chytt lifted a straying strand of mane on Fik's neck with a flexed handclaw. "I wonder if poor Ghitil has always received the best of care?"

The pale-orange form stiffened and Chytt waved

away Fik's unvoiced protest. "I am only wondering, you understand, not asking." Sinking back onto her cushions with an ease and grace that she knew belied her age, she allowed a fierce grimace to wrinkle her muzzle. "Not yet, anyway." She reached for another mizb fruit. "What can you tell me about Levv?"

Fik stopped breathing, every muscle in her powerful frame locked into absolute stillness.

"What have you done?" Chytt leaned forward, bringing her teeth close to the pale-orange ears. "For what foolishness of yours must Qartt stand good when the pattern is complete?"

The female kneeling at her feet might as well been made of sand for all the sign Fik gave of hearing. Trembling with fury, Chytt slashed parallel trails of red-orange blood across a pale-ginger cheek and ear. "You reek of insolence!" she spat at the dazed figure at her feet. "Go and groom yourself before someone else smells it too."

Fik pulled herself up from the carpet, blood dripping down her muzzle, then, for one chilling breath, gazed straight into Chytt's eyes before stalking out the door. Hair still on end, Chytt stared after the younger female. Trouble had only been postponed. A reckoning would come between them. For the sake of Qartt and all her daughters, she hoped the truth about Levv signified less than she feared.

The shaggy liver-brown herd had strayed farther than Nisk expected. When he found the yirn at last, clumped on the river to graze on the wiry low brush that dotted the bank, he was winded and aching and hollow as an empty bowl. He had used a great deal of energy the night before, fighting the much younger priest, and had not had either strength or leisure to look for food since. With the coming of the day, Ankt's crimson eye glared down from the sky, calling heat up out of the ground as flames are drawn from wood, and he knew neither he, nor the failing Black/on/ black, could go much farther on foot.

His nose wrinkled at the yirn's scent; the herd was ranker than usual. This lot had not been worked lately in the hunts, and a few wild beasts must have strayed into it, which would make them edgy and harder to catch than usual. He dropped into a half-crouch, meaning to prowl closer, then snarled at a hot flash of pain as several of his scabbed-over slashes broke open. The feeding yirn froze, stared up with hot yellow eyes, radiating a peeved wariness.

Nisk sat back on his heels and conserved his strength while he waited for them to settle back down. They fell back to grazing, with snuffles and whuffs, still watching him out of the corners of their eyes. He had directed the Black/on/black to hide just beyond the last bend, so as not to alarm the beasts more than necessary. The Black/on/black had complied without argument. He obviously intended to travel only a short distance with Nisk, and then slip away to return for his Outsider companion. He had not said as much in words, but it was written in the slant of his ears and the uneasy lay of his fur and his frequent glances back at the red-orange cliffs guarding the plateau.

But Nisk could not permit that. He was now more sure than ever that the pattern shaping events was the legendary *patience/in/illusion*, never before perceived in living memory, but said to be unimaginably large, reaching into the skies and the lands beyond Anktan itself. The Black/on/black himself was part of its illusion—he had seemed to be dead, along with the rest of his Line, and yet was not. He also appeared deceptively ignorant, forever looking directly into Nisk's eyes until the blood pounded in his ears and his claws ached for the other's throat, yet this same male had hunted the stars themselves, where no hrinn had ever ventured before, had seen wonders which the eyes of earthbound hrinn like himself were forever denied. Being in his presence was like touching another plane of existence, one beyond all imagination, overpowering and unsettling and utterly unfamiliar.

The herd gradually grew careless of him and Nisk schooled his breathing to evenness, waiting for his chance. When one beast finally strayed within reach, he leaped and locked his fingers around its dangling ear. The yirn squealed and bucked as he dug his heels into the sandy ground and held on as though picking a ripe piece of fruit. With a deft twist, he avoided its horns and scrambled up to leap onto the broad back, clinging to the matted fur of its hump with his clawtips.

The Black/on/black darted around the bend and stared up at him. The whole process had taken less than two blinks of the eye. Nisk reached down an arm, beckoning him to come forward and mount.

He hesitated. "Can this beast carry the weight of two?"

Nisk bared his teeth in exasperation, but then thought of the pattern looming below the surface. *Patience/in/illusion*—nothing was what it seemed. He would have to wait until all participants abandoned illusion for reality, taking on their real forms, and events made themselves known. He leaned back. "Do you wish to catch your own yirn?"

The Black/on/black scowled, then took the offered hand and leaped. His weak right leg buckled, making him fall short against the yirn's side, then slide to the ground. The beast squalled and bolted sideways, halted only by the judicious application of Nisk's claws. He gripped its huge barrel with his knees and stared into the distant green-capped mountains. The Black/on/black was said to possess the strength of the molten core of the earth itself, stronger than all others of his kind, male or female, regardless of size. This

apparent weakness of body was only another part of
the illusion.

The Black/on/black picked himself up out of the
sand, then stepped up on a flat rock. His fur was
matted and he was panting as though he had run
since last night. He flung himself upward, grabbing
the yirn for purchase, started to slip back, then flexed
handclaws into the matted fur long enough to swing
his leg over the wide back. Pricked by a claw gone
too deep, the yirn leaped forward as he settled into
place behind Nisk.

Nisk kept his seat easily, moving with the beast,
watching the whole procedure over his shoulder
without flicking an ear. When the other settled into
place behind him, breathing heavily, Nisk heeled the
yirn into the river. "Not a promising beginning."

Drained and aching, Rakshal waded into the river
until the cold green water swirled up to his breast-
bone. He braced himself against the throb of the
current, letting the water numb the gashes written
across his ribs like mysterious glyphs. Despite his
age, Nisk had been far fiercer and more agile than
he had expected. Without the foresight to draw
power beforehand, events might have ended very
differently.

He sank lower in the cold current until the water
swirled around his throat and muzzle, redolent of the
soil and sand it carried, almost brackish in this season
from high mineral content. The taste lingered on his
tongue, whispering of other, more verdant lands
upstream, other, less sacred ways to live. He shuddered. Last night's challenge had strayed far beyond
his intent. He'd meant to slay the false Black/on/black,
revealing him for the falsehood he must surely be and
thereby gain additional status for himself.

Instead, Nisk had stepped into the center of events
and taken control, obviously discerning a different

pattern in this situation than *death/in/longing*, the one Rakshal had glimpsed, something potent he could exploit to his own advantage. Now Rakshal found himself mired within this unnamed *pattern/in/progress*, forced to make decisions he had not planned, to act in ways he had not forseen. He had meant to wait until Nisk was older before he challenged. Now he was Leader in Nisk's place, a rise in status, but subject to challenge himself with all that implied, while the Outsider male was wandering free in the company of wily old Nisk, benefitting, no doubt, from his counsel, and all the while following the dictates of a pattern Rakshal could not divine.

Deep in thought, he waded toward the shore, then stopped, still knee-deep in the shallows. The water sluiced from his dark-gray fur in rivulets. At least half the males currently in residence, including most of the older ones, were watching him from the shore. Silhouetted by the rest of the group, Jikin's pale-gray form blocked Rakshal's path, so still he might have been carved from whitestone.

Jikin? Rakshal stared. The wiry old Teller who never harassed anyone, not even cublings just accepted for training, who just told the old tales and let them be? He emerged from the water as though nothing were out of the ordinary. "What do you want, Teller?" he asked, edging his tone with the superior-to-inferior inflection.

"I am serving you notice." The breeze ruffled Jikin's green robes around his tough old body, revealing muscle and bone under the pale fur, and very little else. "After the required ten days, I intend to challenge."

Jikin was a head shorter than Rakshal, and more than twice his age. The old male would never survive. Rakshal took a deep breath that made his open gashes sting. "That is your right."

Jikin glanced at the males fanned out behind him.

"Each of these others intends to challenge in turn, if I fail."

So. Snatching up his gray priest's robes from the sand, Rakshal thrust dripping arms into one sleeve, then the other, feeling the burning weight of all those eyes. Last night, they must have seen something in him that they could not respect, and so now he would face challenge after challenge, each spaced only the minimum ten days apart, until he fell, as he must, and another took his place.

He buckled the leather straps across his aching chest, then glanced up into their silent faces. "I shall be waiting."

Forcing the obstinate yirn along the faint path with flexed handclaws, Khea squinted, trying to mark the edge of the plateau, somewhere beyond the scrubby gray-green brush ahead. The sunbaked ground smelled like the inside of one of the immense ovens outside the hold, hot and closed, fused. Panting against the terrible heat, she wondered why the Line Mother had bid her travel in the hottest portion of Ankt's midmorning gaze instead of sending a messenger jit. Was this yet another of the endless tests a cubling was subjected to between gleanings?

If she were culled this next time, she might be relegated to the nursery, one of the lesser responsibilities, or even worse, sent to the fields to sow and reap, activities at which even unnamed servants took a turn. Her ears trembled. She did not know how she could bear the shame of that. Far better to die than to fail, better to leave this life altogether than live the rest of her days, a worthless shadow among her superiors.

The yirn trotted up a small rise, grunting with the effort, and then she saw the tumbled redstone rocks that signalled the plateau's abrupt edge. She tethered her mount, then slid down the steep sandy descent, dodging boulders and loose chaff all the way. At the bottom, bruised and scraped, she paused to catch her breath and look at the Guildhouse. Someone actually seemed to be sitting on the whitestone roof under the sweltering morning glare of Ankt. How strange, she thought, hurrying down the well-worn path, but then Restorers were reputed to be an odd lot, even pale-gray Vexk, who had been born of Vvok and was a cousin of hers out of her birth-mother's generation.

Vexk emerged from the hold as she approached. "I bear a summons from the Line Mother," she said, making an effort not to pant.

"So." Vexk's ears flicked. "It is as I feared."

"Will you come?"

"I can do nothing more for this creature at Vvok." Vexk studied her face. "Tell the Line Mother it must be brought here—by you, no one else." Her lips wrinkled back from bone-white teeth. "Otherwise, we shall refuse the honor of this service."

Khea forgot herself and stared at Vexk's pale face in wordless, undignified surprise.

Her expression was strange, unreadable. "Now, come into the hold and rest. There is time enough for that."

Khea's ears pricked forward, then she thought of the Outsider, how it had stirred in her arms when she laid it at the Line Mother's feet. What if it woke and stared directly into Seska's eyes, as it often did hers? Seska would kill it out of pure reflex.

Her ears sagged. "No," she said hastily. "I must return."

Chapter Nine

Heyoka found riding double with Nisk difficult to endure. The beast, sturdy as a buffalo crossed with an elephant, took no notice of the extra weight, but the ascending trail forced him to hold onto Nisk or fall off. The other male's scent triggered something in the deepest recesses of his brain, making him twitchy and irritable. He began fantasizing about killing Nisk. *It would be so easy to break his neck from behind, just one quick twist,* and then he was even angrier, both at himself and the older male, for creating this pointless and idiotic situation.

When, for the tenth time in the last hour, Heyoka had to forcibly resheathe his claws, he glanced over Nisk's bobbing head up into gradually rising green-topped hills to distract himself. After Ben's death, he had left the Oglala hills and Earth behind forever to train as a soldier. The alien flek were making deadly incursions into Confederated Space and soldiers, of any description, were desperately needed. Fortunately, the long-repressed vicious *other* within him made such a splendid soldier that his military unit did not quibble about his appearance, or what appallingly primitive race had birthed him.

It was only after his injury on Enjas Two, when soldiering was no longer an option, that he contemplated a life outside the military. Surely, he had told himself, during those long, difficult days of rehabilitation, there was more to him than just a frighteningly efficient killing machine. If he could find his own kind, they would know thousands of ways to make life meaningful, and one of those ways would be right for him.

But now that he had at last met the hrinn, he was more lost than ever. The vicious *other*, whom he had struggled against all his life, seemed the foundation of their culture, a veritable ideal, and unpracticed as he was at giving in to that aspect of himself, he was not nearly ferocious enough to suit them. He had no desire to live like that.

The yirn's broad hooves beat a steady rhythm as it plodded up the winding trail, and every step wasted valuable time by taking him farther from Mitsu. His skin itched from the inside with the need to act until he couldn't sit still. He had to get back, and soon— if he weren't already too late.

"Where are we headed?" he asked finally. Not that it really mattered, he told himself. He and Nisk would part company at the first opportunity.

Nisk flicked an ear back at Heyoka. "Levv Hold."

The path forked and he flinched at the sight of Nisk's claws urging the yirn onto the steeper of the two tracks. Blood dribbled down the beast's matted coat, and Heyoka held on as its muscles bunched beneath them to navigate a steep rock jumble. His fingers tightened over Nisk's arms and the iron bands of muscle beneath; blood pounded in his ears. He felt dizzy and hot, sick with a sudden, overwhelming desire to slash the other's throat. "Levv—you mean my Line?" he forced out.

"Levv birthed you." Nisk leaned over the yirn's hump as though to examine the trail, casually breaking the physical contact between them. He snagged a handful of tiny blue leaves as they passed a tree and stuffed them into an inner pocket of his robes. "No one with half a nose could mistake that."

Heyoka wiped his hands on his robes. It must be male pheromones, he thought. He wasn't used to them, and they were making him crazy. How did hrinn share the males' houses without killing each other? He swallowed hard. "What is Levv like?"

"I cannot say, Black/on/black."

"Heyoka!" he blurted. "I told you before—I have a name."

Nisk stared ahead. "Not a Hrinnti name."

"An *Oglala* name, given by my—" He broke off, unable to find a name for the relationship of "father," much less "adoptive father," in his Hrinnti vocabulary— "by the Outsider who rescued me from the *flek*."

"You were not of his kind and yet he cared for you?"

Heyoka thought of the wizened Oglala trader, the only family he had ever known. "It did not matter to him. He considered himself to be related to everything that lived, as well as rocks and earth and water. It was an ancient belief of his people."

"H-a-oo-kka." Nisk tried the name out on his narrow hrinnti tongue. "This name has a meaning?"

"It means 'sacred fool,' someone who has had a—special seeing—something important for the people to know, and who does everything differently from that time on."

Nisk's ears flattened. "These Outsiders thought you a fool?"

"Most were afraid of me." Heyoka remembered the startled faces of the Oglala when Ben had emerged that first day from the shuttle towing a snarling, half-wild, sharp-toothed cub.

Nisk's ears lifted again. "It was proper for them to be afraid. But why then should they name you 'fool'?"

Heyoka understood Nisk's confusion. It had taken years for him to understand, not that he was certain he had ever completely understood Ben's Oglala people, or they, him. "The man who cared for me gave me that name. It means someone different, touched by the—the Voice, as you would say; someone who does not do things the same as everyone else—but for a special reason."

"Outsiders honor these 'sacred fools'?"

That was a harder question for Heyoka to answer. The Oglala did honor their own heyokas, but their feelings about raising an alien cub among their own sons and daughters had never been better than mixed. "A few of them honored me, but most were afraid. They felt I represented something outside their world, a sacred presence made flesh. They were uncomfortable when I walked among them."

"So now you walk among us again."

"It has taken me many seasons to find Anktan." Heyoka thought of the database sweeps, the DNA studies, the comparison of dentition patterns he had authorized with his back pay. "Few Outsiders have heard of this world, or the hrinn."

Nisk glanced back at the black power brace encasing Heyoka's right leg from the knee down. "Were you born imperfect?"

The emerald beaches of Enjas Two flashed back into Heyoka's mind, prickling every hair along his spine. "No, it was an injury."

"Then perhaps a Restorer can do something for you."

A solid sheet of flek fire pinning them down on every side, green laser bursts blindingly brilliant against the pale blue of the sky. Heyoka shook his head. "The damage is—permanent."

Nisk glanced at him sharply. "Do not be so certain. Even though Outsiders were unable to heal your flesh, you know little of your own kind or our abilities."

Waves crashing against the shore as his vision shifted to blue, time slowed to a crawl—

Heyoka shivered, the remembered tang of alien seas thick in his nostrils. After the severity of that injury, he was lucky to walk at all. He glanced up at the red sun, now high overhead in the pale amber sky.

Nisk's unfathomable black eyes turned away and Heyoka felt he had failed in some important way.

A couple of servants accompanied the gray-and-white cubling to help carry the litter. Vexk watched them struggle down the steep path from the plateau, while she herself prowled the red-orange rocks at the bottom with a restlessness born more of excitement than worry. This Outsider was important to old Seska. If the Guild could restore its life, they could rightfully name a great price, and she had just the sum in mind.

The two undersized servants, their legs stumpy and their coats an unfortunate grayish-brown, had likely been culled at birth, but the young gray-and-white, there was a prize. Vexk had sensed great depths in that one on her previous visits to Vvok. Khea had the tensile strength of one often bent, but never broken, yet she retained a sensitivity to others in the face of all the hardening an upbringing in the Lines imposed. Such empathy was regarded as "weakness" among the older breeders who supervised the Line's genotype, and was discouraged at every turn. Cublings like Khea usually died young, far below the ground in the nursery at the claws of their age-mates, never to look upon the eye of Ankt, or sniff the rising wind. The Line Mother doubtless only saw another potential breeder to be beaten into a preordained form as she had once attempted to beat Vexk.

Even young Khea, with her greater height and strength, was panting hard by the time she reached the bottom of the ravine. The two servants were staggering under the weight of the litter, their black tongues lolling. Vexk peered down at the still form bundled onto the litter. The pale hairless skin was curiously red and patchy on the creature's face, and it breathed so shallowly she could hardly tell if the fragile chest were moving at all. She took Khea's pole. "We must take it into the hold."

Khea's ears flicked nervously forward, then back. She looked away.

Vexk wanted to sigh. *What have they told you— that we slaughter cublings for our food, and grind medicines from their bones?* Khea must be the progeny of one of Vexk's age-mates, perhaps Cyka or Akke; her graceful build was very like both of them. Vexk thought back to her youth before she had fled Vvok, remembering the many times she had nearly died in some pointless squabble. It was tradition that only the strongest ever left the nursery, and yet it seemed such a waste. Who knew what talents died in the teeth of some spitting cubling each season?

One of the servants stumbled over a gnarled root protruding from the hard-baked ground. "Just a little farther." She laid a hand on the weary creature's shoulder and met its eyes. "Look, you can see the roof."

Khea's mismatched ears, one gray and the other white, flattened. Behind the cubling's back, Vexk took a deep breath. *You will see much more shocking things than touching an unnamed servant here, young one. May you have the strength to understand that there are many patterns and those you choose must fit your own nature.*

The servants paused outside the door, clearly

expecting the worst from the expressions on their
bedraggled faces. Of course, at Vvok, they were only
property, of no more account than a bowl or a rug.
Just inside the doorway, Siga and Jind, two of her
older hold-sisters, waited in the cool shade. Vexk
motioned to them. "Please take this poor creature
inside."

The two yellow-robed females accepted the poles
and bore the litter into the cool, shadowy interior of
the large whitestone hold. Vexk watched them go,
worried. The creature had not moved or made one
sound all the way back from the cliffs. At best, this
would be a difficult *restoration/to/balance*, if indeed
hrinnti craft had any chance at all to cure something
born of another world. She turned to the two
exhausted servants. "Please rest here before you begin
your return journey. Food and water will be brought
to you shortly."

The servants' black eyes glanced up at her furtively,
then at each other. For her to take notice of their
needs was unheard of, even disturbing. They looked
away, unable to respond. Khea thrust her body
between Vexk and the servants. "The Line Mother
said they are to stay until I return with the Outsider."

"That will not be possible."

Khea bowed her head, fear apparent in every line
of her young body. "The Line Mother said they are
to wait!" Her ear fringes trembled.

"They cannot." Vexk put a hand on Khea's soft
thick fur, but she flinched from her touch.
"Restoration is a difficult process, requiring great
concentration, and their presence would disturb the
harmony we seek to reestablish. Seska knew
this when she sent you." Still, she understood
the cubling's distress. If old Seska had ordered the
servants to stay with the cubling, knowing all
the while the Restorers would not permit it, Khea
would nonetheless bear the blame for not forcing

through her bluff. That was the way of the Lines. Vexk still bore the scars to prove it.

The incoming supply ship was a green blip on the screen as it descended through the western skies. Eldrich checked the chronocrystal on his wrist. It was right on time, and the glare from the afternoon sun should keep it from attracting unwelcome attention. Two more Standard weeks, he thought, and it would be finished. This worthless planet could finally start earning its keep, as humans liked to phrase it. He found the wording amusing, but then he found a lot of things about this species entertaining, which was just as well, since he had spent the last twenty-seven Standard years on this abominably frigid rock. It was only right he should be able to squeeze an occasional dab of amusement out of the situation.

Clearing the ship's trajectory from his screen, he turned his mind back to the problem of the two military personnel who had descended upon him without warning—spies, no doubt, sent by some suspicious official who detected something out of the ordinary on Anktan. He had no current word on the sergeant's exact location, but hrinnti informants reported the Jensen woman being held by Vvok. It would be quite interesting to talk to Corporal Jensen and determine exactly what she knew. He would have a word with that old she-devil, Seska, and have her captive returned to the station. Then he would learn exactly why she and the sergeant had intruded at such an inopportune moment.

The sun hung like a swollen red eye above the mountaintops to the west by the time they stopped beside a rushing stream and drank their fill. Then, while Nisk fashioned a hobble for the yirn, Heyoka eased his claw-marked back against a stubby trunk and stared down across green hillsides that had taken the whole day to climb. The air was noticeably cooler up this high and had an alien tang, a subtle acridness nothing like the rolling plains of the Restored Oglala Nation back on Earth where Ben had raised him. Even now, when he closed his eyes, he could smell the richness of damp earth just after a summer shower.

Nisk left the hobbled yirn to graze and stretched out on the grass, grimacing at the pain from his unhealed slashes. "We have come far enough now to rest here until dusk and then hunt in the early evening." His eyes closed.

How long since he had last eaten? Heyoka couldn't remember. Hollow with hunger, he stared up into the amber sky, waiting for Nisk to fall asleep. Despite his own weariness, he was too edgy to sleep, even if that had been his intention, which it was not. How did hrinnti males live in such close company? He couldn't take much more of this. Constant exposure to Nisk's scent was jumbling his thoughts and making him increasingly reckless and irritable. It was hard to believe now that he had been foolish enough to seek this experience out.

Once Nisk's breathing deepened into the evenness of sleep, Heyoka eased to his feet and limped back down the path. He had considered attempting to hide his tracks, but knew all too well that Nisk could trail his scent and there was no way up here to disguise that. His only chance was to get enough of a head start before Nisk woke that he couldn't catch him before Heyoka passed back into the males' house's territory.

His leg was stiff and he found his progress much slower than he had anticipated. Just as he rounded yet another switchback, foliage rustled on the hillside above him. He hesitated, then Nisk burst from cover with a suddenness that belied his injuries. Before he could think, the *other* within him swept to the surface, seizing control in the blink of an eye so that the lust for Nisk's blood seared through his veins, burning away all hope of rational thought. He lunged for Nisk's throat, but his opponent dodged and kicked his bad leg out from under him.

He fell heavily onto his side, twisting the damaged leg. Nisk straddled his body, a fist knotted in his robes, claws a scant breath away from slashing Heyoka's exposed throat. His scent was hot and heavy and his eyes smoldered down at him, fierce black moons that absorbed all light. "Yield!"

His whole life, Heyoka had been bigger, stronger, more ferocious than any of his companions. He had never been afraid among humans, except that he might give into his savage *other* and hurt someone, never forced to admit defeat in a purely physical fight. Blood thrummed in his ears and he found he could not breathe while Nisk looked at him so, could not make his heart beat, his mind think. The unbearable black gaze swallowed him, compelling him to—what? Some shadowed corner of his brain whispered the answer, and then without volition or understanding, he looked away.

Nisk released him and lurched back onto his feet, panting hard. "Fool!" he spat, hackles still standing on end. Several of his gashes had broken open again and orange blood seeped into his matted fur. "You cannot even begin to fight me, or anyone else, with that useless leg. If I had not taken your place last night, Rakshal would have ripped your throat out before you were two breaths into that fight."

Heyoka rolled over and lay on his back, struggling for breath. The pain in his wrenched leg rolled over him in waves.

"I am not ready to speak of Levv," Nisk said. "But I see now you do not possess the strength or wit to wait for the proper moment. I either have to kill you to keep you from running back to certain death or tell you now." His eyes were narrowed as he hunkered down to draw a map in the dirt with a twig. "Levv was once a respected Line, breeding more than its share of the Black/on/black down through the generations, holding the difficult westernmost territory—here"—he indicated a place on his crude map—"which bounds the savage nomads of the plains who do not share our language. My birth-mother's mate was bred out of Levv." He held out his arm and brushed back his black overcoat to reveal the dense undercoat, also black. "Save for the white patch on my throat, I have the Black/on/black coloring myself."

He cast the twig aside. "Near what must have been the time of your birth, scouts found dead hrinn with terrible burns, both up here in the hills and down along the river, and even out in the drylands where no Lines hold land. At first, Outsiders were thought responsible and watchers were set to kill any of the disgusting furless things who ventured out.

"But, even after they were contained, the bizarre killings continued until a wounded Qartt female survived to name her attacker—Levv." He stared off into the greenery. "In the forgotten days before the great tales of the Tellers, hrinn killed one another in great wantonness, without any reason other than the burning fierceness which lives within us all, until finally there were almost no hrinn left. The yirn and kikinti herds ranged fat and reckless, with no one to hunt them. Patterns emerged unnoticed and passed hrinn by. Chaos ruled our lives and we were almost at an end, but then the Priests arose and brought us the wisdom of the Voice, beginning with this precept: Killing without purpose is the worst crime a hrinn can commit. The young must cull the weak, of course. Adults have to satisfy insult and blood-debt, and resolve challenges to leadership, but always death is part of the sacred patterns of life and full of meaning. We could not survive another such time of darkness.

"Both Lines and males' houses banded together to search Levv Hold, where they discovered a cache of Outsider weapons. On that day, Levv was exterminated down to the last nurseling, lest their madness be allowed to breed and sow chaos. The strange weapons were destroyed." Nisk paused. "Even males of Levv descent who had been accepted into males' houses were examined by the Council, which was, of course, a fearful insult. Males leave Line behind forever once they enter a males' house." His lips wrinkled back in a fierce grimace. "No further trace of insanity, however, was ever found, so the Council concluded the madness had run only through the females and the matter was considered at an end."

An iciness crept into Heyoka's bones. He managed, despite the pain, to sit up. "Then they are all dead."

Nisk did not look at him. "Yes."

"What is the point of going there?"

"That whole business never smelled right to me." Nisk smoothed the fur on his arm back down so the black undercoat was again hidden. "The Council labeled the pattern of that terrible day *death/in/longing*, but I think it was never truly named and goes unrecognized still."

Leaning forward, he tapped Heyoka on the chest with an extended claw. "Now you walk among us, proving that in some way, Outsiders did have a claw in this. No Levv, or any other hrinn for that matter, could have taken you off this world. Somehow, your life is the thread that weaves this pattern together. It is for you to name it."

Nisk's black-furred hrinnti face, so like his own, studied Heyoka, waiting. He glanced aside, unable to meet those black eyes directly. Nisk was apparently kin to him to some degree. It was a strange feeling. And stranger still was the knowledge that, even though he must have seen that carnage, he could not remember.

The wind whipped Seska's face, hot with the scent of frightened kikinti. She glanced sideways at her age-mates, then raked her yirn's neck to send it loping ahead. If she were quick, she might draw the first blood. She pulled even with the first straggler and leaned out with open claws—

A thin wail broke into her dream. Heart pounding, Seska bolted upright on her thick pile of pillows, then dug to stop the noise before the Outsider box brought the rest of the hold down upon her.

"Line Mother!" Khea's replacement, a smallish black-and-white cubling, raced through the open door.

"Get out!" Groping beneath the cushions, Seska finally found the box's hard outline and pressed the button to still its insistent voice. Then, glancing over her shoulder, she realized the cubling was still there, eyes turned to the floor, trembling.

Sitting up, she swatted at the black-and-white nose. "Leave me!"

The young female, Rhys, went rigid with pain, then obeyed. Seska growled low in her throat. Now she would have to keep an eye on that one; Rhys had heard more than was good for her. She pulled the traitorous black box out and punched the button.

"Seska?" the box said.

"What do you want, box?" She turned the small shiny thing over. Although in the beginning some had said the Voice itself spoke through the box, she had never believed it, but she had always been puzzled as to how the Outsiders had managed to imprison a living being in something so small.

"Vvok has taken an Outsider."

"So?" Seska bared her teeth in irritation. The box had never cared what she or any of the others did with Outsiders before.

"Bring it to the white hold."

"No!" Fur bristled on the back of Seska's neck. "I have not finished with it."

"Bring it, or I will turn the Lines against Vvok, just as I once did against Levv."

She thought of Levv as she had seen it last, a scorched and empty mountain warren, its ancient whitestone walls smeared red-orange with the blood of its daughters. "The Outsider is dead."

"Then bring me its body or suffer Levv's fate." The box clicked off.

She flattened her ears. There was little time. She would have to retrieve the Outsider from the Restorers, tear what it knew of the Black/on/black out of that disgusting pink hide, then deliver the remains to the Outsider hold.

Unless she were willing to put Vvok at the same risk as late unlamented Levv.

Chapter Ten

The sand chamber where Vexk left Khea was spacious by Vvok standards, filled with light to a degree only the presence of the Line Mother herself should have warranted, and pleasantly scented with an herbal concoction which Khea did not recognize. The fragrance had an astringent greenness to it, vaguely sweet, summoning visions of cool highland forests, running beneath trees with sunlight filtering down, crushed leaves beneath her feet.

The deep inviting body-length pit had been filled with fresh red-orange sand warmed with hot stones, then stirred to distribute the heat. She stepped inside and stooped to sift a handful of sand through her fur. Her skin tingled and she sighed; it was blissful to feel clean again.

After scrubbing thoroughly, she picked up the yellow robes Vexk had laid on the rim; the cloth was of an exceptional weave, soft and smooth. She speculated even Vvok's finest weaver, old Nnenk, could have done no better.

Claws scratched at the door. Her nostrils flared,

but she didn't recognize the inquirer's scent. "Come."

A young female stood in the doorway, in all probability no older than she. The newcomer was slight, an unusual build for one who had passed sufficient gleanings to reach this age, but her fur was deep red, shading to pale cream on the throat and chest, then overlaid with black stripes on her back and arms, the most striking color pattern Khea had ever seen.

She forgot herself in an unmitigated stare, then looked away. "Please excuse my boldness." Her ears drooped with shame as she scrambled out of the sand pit. If the cub-trainer or, Voice forbid, old Seska herself had seen her behave so, her ears would have been hanging in shreds.

"Boldness?" The dark-red female hesitated in the middle of reaching for the travel-stained robes lying on the floor, regarding her so unflinchingly that Khea knew she must have a high position in this hold.

Her insides turned to sand, just as they always did when she blundered before her elders at Vvok. She tried to make some sort of response, but could think of nothing to say.

"Was the sand stale?" the other said. "I thought Yrb stirred it this morning, but perhaps she was called away."

Khea's claws tightened. She raised her gaze just enough to look at the other for a half-breath. "The sand—was—perfect."

"Oh." The female's large dark eyes studied her. "Is there something else you require then? You seem . . . distressed."

Khea's eyes closed; if only she could start over. Now she seemed to have implied this hold's hospitality was lacking. Would she never stop making mistakes? "Everything was wonderful," she managed finally. "I require—nothing."

"Well, if you will get dressed, Vexk is waiting for you to go with her to the caves."

In her surprise, Khea raised her eyes again. "The caves?"

"Yes, and you should hurry. The creature you brought is quite ill." The dark-red head cocked to one side. "She says it may slip beyond our reach before morning without your help."

"My help?" Khea fumbled the clean yellow robes over her head. "But Vexk said it was beyond Vvok's skill."

"Well, I know nothing about that." The youngster reached again for the robes in Khea's hands. "But Vexk understands the intricacies of *harmony/through/balance* better than anyone. She is seldom wrong about these matters."

Khea hastily bound her mane back with a length of soft yellow cord. She must be crazy, she told herself angrily as she worked the knot; she had only just arrived and already she was arguing with her betters. If anyone back at Vvok got even a sniff of this, they would cull her on the spot without waiting for the next gleaning.

"Vexk says you are called Khea." The red female glanced over her shoulder at Khea as she turned back toward the door. "I am Cimmi."

"You honor me," Khea said breathlessly as she hurried to follow.

"I do?" Cimmi turned to stare breathtakingly straight into Khea's eyes again, then led her along the passageway up toward the surface.

Confused, Khea focused on Cimmi's feet. The wide corridors were dim and still as they made their way upward. In fact, the atmosphere of the entire hold filled Khea with a sense of something so quiet and restful that she could find no name for it, knowing only that it was something she had never encountered at Vvok—and never would.

The young female paused finally outside a large

chamber which Khea had not seen before. "Vexk waits for you inside." She studied Khea's face. "I would like to say I am also honored to have heard your name, but I do not know you that well yet." Then, with a flick of her ear, she turned and disappeared down the passageway.

Unable to escape the feeling she had piled mistake on top of mistake, Khea hesitated outside the doorway.

"Come in, child." Vexk's voice floated to her from within. "We must hurry."

Trying not to tremble, Khea lowered her eyes and entered. On the far side of the room, the Outsider lay propped on a pile of cushions with Vexk's pale-gray form kneeling at its side.

"Is it going to die?" she asked.

"All things die." Ears at half-cant, Vexk looked up. "For all we know about this species, it may be old for its kind and this may be its time. I cannot say for sure. Still, we will do what we can." She rose gracefully and walked to the door.

Khea lowered her gaze. "Shall I watch over it then while you prepare?"

Vexk paused. "Has your watching been of any use so far?"

"No." Over by the wall, the creature moaned, then murmured something in its strange high-pitched voice. Khea shivered. It seemed very near death.

"Come with me to the caves where I will show you what will be of benefit." The tall, nearly-white-furred Restorer walked out the door and Khea hastened to follow.

As they emerged outside, she saw Ankt had passed behind the far mountains and the early evening sky now had a faint greenish cast to it. A messenger jit flitted past them overhead and landed on the white-stone roof of the hold. Someone else must be ill, she thought. Perhaps one of the others would be leaving before they even returned.

Vexk followed a dim trail which wove around patches of sand and tumbled rock. She never looked back. What did the Restorer want from her, Khea wondered as she hurried after her. She was only a worthless youngling, not clever or strong, and certainly not fierce. Rumors about the Guild came back to her, strange bits of gossip and innuendo that floated around the halls of Vvok from time to time . . . something about a terrible price that had to be paid for the Restorer's gift . . . some sort of . . . sacrifice.

Her eyes adjusted to the lack of light and she could make out dark irregular openings just ahead, leading inside the red cliffs that bordered the plateau—and home.

Pausing just outside the biggest entrance, Vexk waited as Khea followed her up the loose rock. The pale-gray reached down to her and clasped her arm firmly. The touch of her palm was warmer than anything she had ever felt before. "Now you will experience something very few females of the Lines ever witness."

As the yirn topped the wooded hill, Heyoka gazed over Nisk's shoulder down into a small curving valley where a large whitestone compound sprawled. Torches gleamed around the building's perimeter and the dark shaggy shapes of yirn were penned nearby. One bawled and their own beast answered. Nisk pointed with his muzzle. "Jhii."

The air was cool, filled with the heaviness of chilled rock and rotting wood, thick leaf mold disturbed by the yirn's broad hooves. Something chittered nearby in the rocks and then was still. Heyoka caught the hot flash of its scent which caused his stomach to rumble with hunger. Nisk had never mentioned hunting again after Heyoka's ill-omened break for freedom and he could not make himself bring it up. He felt foolish and angry over

his failure, and some other more alien sentiment
which he could not describe. A human might have
labelled it "chastened," or perhaps "humbled," but
justly so, as though he should have known better,
or been better prepared. This emotion, though, was
both more than either of those and less, and
decidedly hrinnti and he could not work it out
clearly enough to give it a name. He straightened
his weary back, careful not to brush Nisk. The touch
of the older male's fur made his nerves crawl. He
cleared his throat. "Is it a males' house?"

"Jhii is one of the five remaining Great Lines." Nisk
thumped a leg against the yirn's shaggy barrel to turn
it aside where the trail forked along the ridge. "Jhii's
lands lay nearest to Levv."

Heyoka eyed the ominous black clouds gathering
overhead to blot out the stars. "Could we shelter there
for the night?"

Nisk snarled. "Males do not go running to females
when they need a place to sleep or food to fill their
bellies!"

His tone was caustic and Heyoka wished heartily
he had not asked. Then his nostrils flared at a whiff
of unexpected scent just as a silent, sharp-toothed
shape launched itself onto his back. Reflexes took over
and, without thinking, he fell with the attacker, letting
momentum sweep them both to the ground. *Flek!* his
mind insisted as the thing beneath him writhed and
snapped, trapped by his weight. He shook its teeth
off, then rolled aside and leaped to his feet in a
defensive stance, but pain seared through his bad leg.
He transferred his weight onto the other, breathing
hard, claws flexed. As his attacker scrambled up and
leaped for his throat, he caught a brief glimpse of
Nisk's black outline atop the yirn, a few feet away,
quietly observing. He backed up, stumbled again as
his bad leg would not hold him—then his vision
shifted—to *blue*. His opponent now only inched

closer, seeming to barely move. Limping aside, he shoved it with almost leisurely precision.

The creature thumped into the rocks in slow motion, then drifted to the ground. Heyoka snatched it up with one hand and raised the other to tear out its throat, but stayed his claws at the last second. It was not a beast, but a young hrinn—and female. His instincts screamed *flek!*, even though he knew better. The green beach flashed back into his mind, the hot-oven stench of sand fused by laser rifles, the screaming of wounded. For an instant, he was there again, trapped in a cross fire, bewildered, overwhelmed by the reek of his own burned fur. With an effort, he wrenched himself back into the present.

Two pairs of eyes glittered down at him from the rocky ledge, both hrinnti. He retracted his claws with a convulsive shiver and dropped the female.

"E-x-c-e-l-l-e-n-t—r-e-f-l-e-x-e-s." A dark-furred hrinn leaped down, taking long seconds to land, according to his distorted senses. She brandished a spear with a gleaming metal point at him. "F-o-r—a—m-e-r-e—m-a-l-e."

The remaining hrinn made no move in his direction. Heyoka backed away, willing his staccato heartbeat to slow, the blood to stop thrumming in his ears. He felt dizzy and sick as his vision gradually shifted, allowing green to show through the stubby foliage, dark brown to creep back into the jumper's fur.

Nisk leaned over the yirn's hump, the cant of his ears casual. "Good hunting tonight?"

"Good hunting, my eyes and nose too!" The dark-brown female aimed a vicious kick at the crumpled youngster on the ground, who didn't move. "What are you two misbegotten males doing on Jhii land?"

As the blue faded, Heyoka sagged back against the face of the rock, shivering, much colder than the temperature of the air warranted. Claws scraped against stone from above as a second youngster peered down.

"And you!" The dark-brown hrinn gestured angrily. "*You* are no better than this empty-head at my feet! If you had backed up Clea, the two of you could have taken this undersized misfit. There are only two of them, both males, at that. If it were up to you, these scruffy outcasts could enter the hold unchallenged and make off with anything or anyone they choose."

Nisk dismounted. "Actually, we were only skirting the edges of Jhii land."

"The edges! Since when have males worried about where they walk?" She glanced in disgust at the fallen youngster. "Get up, Clea. Running trail as long as I have, I certainly know shamming when I see it."

The young female rolled over on her back, then sat up and hunched over, her eyes scrunched in obvious misery. Heyoka saw streaks of blood matting the fur of her shoulders and back through her torn purple tunic.

I could have killed that child, he thought numbly, *and to what purpose?* These three had every right to be here.

"Well, at least Clea may have learned something she will not quickly forget." The older hrinn jerked the youngster to her feet. "Perhaps next time, she will *wait* for her hunt-mates."

Ears down and blood trickling across her muzzle, the youngster took a deep breath and gazed up at Heyoka. "The way you fell off and pinned me, did you plan that?"

Heyoka stared back at the cubling wordlessly.

"At any rate, this one"—the dark-brown pointed to Heyoka—"has earned the Line Mother's attention. As for you . . ." She studied Nisk. "I can imagine what the Line Mother will have to say about stray males defiling Jhii land."

The evening fire was already blazing in the great circular communal room of the males' house when

Rakshal entered from a side tunnel. Although it was past the usual time, only a few of those currently in residence had gathered to enjoy the soothing fragrance of burning gynth leaves. Beside the fire, Jikin, who had given him notice of challenge, conversed with old Jafft in low tones. Rakshal's nose twitched at the smell of that pairing: Jafft had been Nisk's sponsor long before Rakshal had been birthed.

Settling in the shadowy outer circle, he watched the two old males out of the corner of his eye. Although they possessed a great deal of knowledge and experience between them, neither had ever professed to hear the Voice. That was, no doubt, why the Leadership of this house had fallen under his claws now and not theirs.

His ears pricked as feet padded along a side tunnel, then a group of cublings, who had not even received their greens yet, burst into the communal chamber, their black eyes wide with the honor of being allowed into this adult setting.

"Is this where the males meet every night?" one large-eared cubling asked the oldster, Fihht, who had charge of them all.

Fihht's spotted ears flattened. "If you close your mouth, you may learn something." Then he glared until they huddled together and fell silent. "Now, approach the wall and see what you can sniff out."

Rakshal watched the youngsters spread along the curving whitestone wall. These cublings were so young, they had most likely never even seen an adult male before a few days ago. Where had this lot come in from? Rebban, perhaps, or far Kendd? It was late in the year to be receiving cublings, but perhaps these had been born out of season.

None of them were tall enough to smell out the top rows of scent-glyphs, but several got the idea. "They are—shapes." A small light-gray youngster looked back over his shoulder at Fihht's scarred old face for confirmation. "All sorts of shapes marked out in—smells."

"The expression is 'written,' not marked out." Fihht blinked at the cubling in a pleased manner. "Each one signifies one of the sacred patterns that shape existence, and for each, there is a story."

"A story?" a large-boned brown cubling said. "The mothers told us that we would get no more stories once we came here."

"Do you see any mothers here?" Rakshal asked from behind. "This is the *males'* house." He walked over to the wall, his shadow preceding him. "No mother, or daughter, or even Line Mother has ever set foot here, or has any idea of what is written upon this sacred wall. All of this is males' business. Females can only guess at how we live."

The smallish light-gray, braver than the rest, traced the curving shape of one of the scent-glyphs with a clawtip. "Could we have a story then?"

The other cublings, no more than a few days out of the nursery, looked to Fihht hopefully with bright black eyes.

Fihht wrinkled his nose. "None of the Tellers is in residence right now, and I am not practiced at Telling, but perhaps in a few days, Dyuu will be back from the hunt and—"

"I know a story or two." Rakshal met the old male's eyes defiantly, then walked along the wall until he found the scent-glyph he wanted. "Perhaps you would like to hear the tale of 'Uwn First-male and the Voice'?" Although he did not look around, he heard the scuffle of small claws as the cublings pressed up close behind him to get a better sniff. "This is one of the greatest patterns, *wisdom/through/silence*." With an extended claw, he traced the three curving lines interspersed with four dots. "After the Voice had uttered the first word, which brought into being both Ankt and Anktan, the land was barren. Nothing spoke but the wind shrieking through the rocks and, as I am sure you know, that is a very lonely sound. After a time, the Voice wished for someone to talk to, so three more words were spoken over the land, creating Uwn, the first male, and the first two females.

"Now that there were ears to listen, the Voice spoke of many things, how to make fire to stay warm in the cold seasons and how to burn gynth leaves, which soothe the urge to fight, how to hunt striped kikinti and stubby-legged zzil and preserve the meat against times of want, how to dig homes deep into the earth to stay warm in the cold and cool in the hot, and how to find water when the earth is determined to hide it.

"Everything a hrinn needed to know to live a good life, the Voice explained, but soon the two females began to speak to each other and, liking the sound, ceased to listen to anything else. Distressed, the male bid them be quiet so he could continue to hear the Voice's wisdom, but they only snarled and bared their teeth at him."

"Then what?" The brown cubling edged closer. "What did Uwn do?"

"So Uwn went apart from the two females and sat on the highest hill he could find, so high that it poked through the clouds into the night sky and the tiny star points hung close enough that he could reach out and hold their cold white fire in his hand.

"'Why have you come to the top of the world, so near my true home?' the Voice demanded. 'And what has become of the two females I made for you?'

"Ashamed, Uwn said nothing and only bowed his head until his nose pressed against the cold rocky ground.

"The Voice saw how Uwn remained there in the windblown cold, his ears pricked for anything the Voice might say. Then the Voice looked down to the lowlands and saw how the two females talked on and on to each other without a moment of silence for listening to anything else. Filled with anger, the Voice turned back to Uwn. 'You are wise indeed, Uwn, to understand that when the mouth is closed, knowledge can find the ears. In order that it may always remain so, you and your male progeny must live apart from females, coming together with them only once a year so there will always be hrinn.

"'Since they prefer each other's words to wisdom, females shall always abide with females and go on filling each other's heads with nonsense.'"

Rakshal paused to retrace the three-barred glyph with its dots. "And that is why, since almost the beginning of the world, males and females have lived apart, so males may have quiet in which to hear the Voice. Now that you have come among your brother males, your duty is to be silent and learn as much as you can." Rakshal stepped away from the wall. "Go with Fihht and always remember to close your mouths so you can truly hear."

Fihht's spotted old face wore a new expression as he gathered up his charges and ushered them back through the side tunnel. Rakshal had seen other males look at each other like that many times, but no one had ever looked at him so before.

The emotion on Fihht's face was that of respect.

Chapter Eleven

Nisk's ears flattened as they rode down into the valley toward Jhii Hold. Two granite towers reached up into the night sky like huge blunt-tipped claws. Unlike the traditional structure of a males' house, much of this hold extended aboveground, rendering it vulnerable to attack. It was a reckless, foolish way to live, but then he had always found Jhii to be a boastful, swaggering sort of Line, far more attendant to appearance than substance.

As they descended, the night air grew warmer, filled with the richness of newly turned ground from a series of fields and the aroma of ripening grain. When they reached the well-lit main entrance flanked by the two towers, the taciturn cub-trainer gestured for them to dismount. Nisk and the Black/on/black surrendered their footsore yirn to an old scarred female, who bared her broken teeth and hissed at the unheard-of sight of two adult males in such a place. Their captor muttered an aside to the two cublings in the flickering torchlight and sent them running ahead into the hold, then motioned with her spear for Nisk and the silent Black/on/black standing behind him to enter as well.

Fur bristled along Nisk's neck and shoulders. From earliest memory, all cublings were taught no adult male ever returned to the female territory of the Lines. Forcing males to enter the very heart of Jhii was an insult of the gravest sort to all concerned. Any scout worth her meat would have questioned males found this close to the hold, but then let them go on their way. They had committed no offense, crossed no boundaries, nor approached females out of season. They had not even brought down Jhii game, though their stomachs were hollowed out with hunger. He found it insufferable to be treated with such wanton disrespect. If it had been only himself involved, he might well have fought to the death, rather than bear such an insult, but the emerging pattern he sensed here was too big for any ordinary individual to understand or control. The Black/on/black must survive to assume his role once all elements were in place, and so Nisk stayed his temper, though it grieved him sorely to be shamed in this way.

He glanced back at the Black/on/black's glazed, exhausted eyes; it was obvious he had drawn upon the Old Power with no idea of how to control or replenish it. He needed rest and food now, and then training in the near future, or he might well die in his next attempt.

The twisting stone passages were only dimly lit, interrupted by frequent doorways. The hold was scented with mountain herbs, and Nisk caught glimpses of females hunched over small tables, often with the gleam of gold, copper, or silver in their hands. Jhii had long been preeminent among the Lines for skill with metals.

A small yellowish-gray servant cowered aside at their approach, averting its face as was entirely proper. The cub-trainer passed it without a glance, but Nisk

caught a flicker of dismay in the Black/on/black's
weary eyes as he was forced to step around it.
Following the winding hall downward, they passed
room after room, taking first one fork and then
another until Nisk worried that he was quite lost.
Finally, the cub-trainer stopped and scratched the
outside of a large arched doorway.

Something rustled within. "Come."

She looked back at them, curling her lips over
teeth that gleamed in the half-light. "If you value your
worthless male hides, think before you speak."

Nisk shouldered past her, mindful of his bloodstained robes hanging in shreds. In the middle of a
lushly appointed room crouched the same two chastened cublings they had encountered on the ridge.
The one with whom the Black/on/black had fought
had not yet had her wounds tended and blood still
matted her dark-brown fur.

The room possessed an air of great antiquity with
its rough-hewn wooden posts and whitestone walls.
Lit by sweet-smelling gyb torches, it was elegant and
well ventilated, but cluttered with heaped-up carpets
and piles of richly worked cushions, as well as
overflowing platters of meat, fruit and breads. The
aroma of freshly killed zzil tormented Nisk's empty
stomach, and he saw the Black/on/black's ears twitch.
At the far end of the chamber, a plump dark-brown
female, robed in the rich dark purple of Jhii,
reclined on a mound of pillows. An atmosphere of
indolence permeated the scene, at odds with the
studied industry of the other Jhii they had just
passed.

Nisk recognized the scent of Beshha, present Line
Mother to Jhii, although she rarely attended the
Council of Lines in person. Strangely inactive to hold
such a position, she preferred to send one of her
direct-daughters rather than travel herself. Everyone
had been shocked a handful of seasons before when

she had somehow ousted the feisty old Line Mother, Menn, and taken Jhii under her claws.

Shifting her position, Beshha studied the Black/on/black with narrowed eyes. "Two lone males broaching Jhii land." She laced her fingers across her stomach and blinked thoughtfully at them. "Well, you will find no wantons among the daughters of Jhii. None *here* mate out of season."

Nisk stepped forward. "We had no intention of approaching your daughters. We were skirting your boundary, nothing more."

She flicked an ear at him, then picked up a handful of blue-shelled cedt nuts from the copper dish at her side. "You smell vaguely familiar."

"We met in Council," Nisk said, "some time ago."

"Oh, yes—one of the male Leaders, Mimsk—or Ninnk."

"Nisk." He longed to cuff the impudence off her smug brown face. She obviously remembered him. Why pretend otherwise? "I no longer lead, but have accepted the sponsorship of this male. I am taking him into the high country for training."

"I no longer bother with Council meetings since I became Line Mother and discovered what a dreadful bore they are." She heaved to her feet and prowled closer, studying the exhausted Black/on/black. "At any rate, this one is far too old for sponsorship."

Nisk assumed a stance of readiness, muscles tensed, ears up, signalling his willingness to fight should the need arise. Why was she behaving in this way? He was no ordinary unaligned male. She knew him and he had still retained a great deal of status, despite his loss of the Leadership, and the Black/on/black deserved a certain amount of consideration simply for being what he was. "He came to maturity without the benefit of other males and so has special need of training."

Her nostrils flared. She seized hold of the other's

arm and brushed his overcoat back, paying no attention as he stiffened at her touch. "Black/on/black!"
Her tiny eyes stared at his undercoat. "Syll spoke of
such a one after she returned from the Council, but
I did not believe her." She glanced at the two
cublings. "Get out!"

Ears down, they fled without looking back.

"He reeks of Levv!" Beshha released the Black/on/
black's arm and wiped her hands on her purple robes.
Nisk watched as she settled heavily back down onto her
cushions with a trace of fear in those small dark eyes.
"That problem was supposed to have been solved a long
time ago." Her narrow tongue ran across her lips as she
turned back to Nisk. "Is that why you have placed him
under sponsorship, because of the risk of madness?"

"No." Nisk met her gaze without blinking, but an
unbidden snarl rattled in his throat. "This is unpar-
donable! We have done nothing wrong and you have
no reason to detain us."

"A bad business, Levv. Hard to forget." Bracelets
clinked as she ran a hand over her ears. "I really can't
allow you to go until I think about what pattern may
be forming here. Skett?"

The thin dark-brown muzzle of the cub-trainer
poked back into the room. "Line Mother?"

"Shut this pair up down in the servants' warrens."
Beshha reached for a half-gnawed haunch. "And have
more of this freshly killed zzil sent up. I may be up
all night considering this matter."

Skett fingered her spear. "You two, come with me
and no male tricks."

Nisk's ears flattened, but the Black/on/black was
in no shape to fight, and as for himself, he was very
curious as to what all this meant. Beshha had some
part in this pattern as well, it seemed. The implications made the fur prickle on his back. He motioned
for the Black/on/black to follow Skett's wiry dark-
brown body out into the passageway.

✧   ✧   ✧

The cave's entrance was overgrown with gyb bushes. Vexk paused outside to cut a branch for a torch, then struck a spark. The waxy bark gave off a pleasant, herbal scent that brought to mind the long evenings spent soaking in preparation to practice her craft, listening to the quiet slap of water against stone. Behind, she heard the gray-and-white cubling's labored breathing as she struggled up the talus-clogged incline. Vexk glanced back at the young face, noting the drooping ears, the downcast eyes. Despite the brief rest, Khea was exhausted. Seska must have been displeased indeed to dispatch her on two grueling trips between Vvok and the Restorers' Hold in a single day.

A faint hopefulness crinkled the corners of Vexk's eyes. She'd sensed great depth in Khea the first time she had seen her down in the stuffy Vvok servants' warrens, tending to an ailing, almost hairless, pink-skinned alien with no more fuss than if it were one of her own age-mates. But that same depth would also be her undoing. Vexk knew all too well how the empathic sensitivity required of a Restorer made life in the Lines an unending misery.

She ducked her head and led Khea inside, following the sinuous curves and branchings now as familiar to her as her own heartbeat. The sulfuric smell of the pool permeated the air as they walked and she lifted her ears, remembering her first time in this sacred place, an experience both exhilarating and profoundly terrifying. It had taught her not only what she was, but also what she might be if she left Vvok, thereby altering her life forever.

She glanced over her shoulder. "Not much farther now." The gray-and-white ears stirred, but the cubling made no answer. Vexk studied her surreptitiously; Khea might have been her child, if she had taken breeder status. The cubling was beautiful, not just in

the natural grace and strength so often possessed by
the young, but in the sense of potential she wore like
a garment. Like her guild-sisters, Vexk would never
bear a cub and had understood that from the beginning, though she had not truly felt the white-hot ache
of that sacrifice until much later. *Restoration/to/balance*
was a pattern of the highest order, but demanded far
more than most females of her rank would ever
willingly surrender.

A heavy, gold-worked tapestry hung across the final
opening, depicting scenes from the old tale of "Hallda
Third-child," the first Restorer. Holding the flickering
torch high, Vexk lifted the edge and motioned to the
cubling. Ears flat, Khea slid along the wall into the
chamber. The brush of her fur against the stone was
overloud in the stillness. Careful of the torch, Vexk
allowed the tapestry to fall, sealing them into a large
roughly oval chamber. At their feet, the sacred pool
stretched from wall to wall. The mineral-rich water
steamed up, and the sense of quiescent *power* was
overwhelming.

Vexk lit three more torches from the supply kept
in the cave, set them in sconces carved into the gray
rock, then wedged the one she carried into another.
She gazed into the pool, at her own shimmering
paleness reflected beside the cubling's frightened gray-
and-white, then knelt and let the strength of this place
seep through her, the immensity of it, the trueness,
until she was as still within as the surrounding stone.

"Restoration requires more than knowledge," she
said quietly. "Herbs and potions and splints could be
learned by any early-culled servant." Her eyes roamed
the pool's jewellike colors: the white mineral deposits
coating the outermost edges, the pale blue of the
shallows shading to the startling, deep blue-green of
the central hole, which led down into the earth's
womb where all such steaming waters were born.
"True Restoration requires power."

Trembling, Khea sank to her knees and closed her eyes. "Why are you telling me this? I was not born into your guild." Her voice, strained and thin, reverberated against the curving walls.

"*No one* is born to the Restorers." Vexk felt the deep ache of that truth, then took a slow, purposeful breath and willed herself back to the calmness of mind and spirit this task required. "Be still. If you listen in this sacred place . . . you can hear the Voice itself." She stepped into the steaming water, then lay back, feeling the tingle of power as the heat penetrated her skin. Her eyes closed and she lost all sense of place and time, no longer aware of the torrid water, or the breath in her chest . . . and it came, as it always did, building without a clear beginning as though it were always there, just waiting to be heard, a wordless strength which became louder and louder until it finally broke like a wave and swept her away to a plane where words and thoughts had no meaning.

It left as it had come, receding imperceptibly, leaving her in the hot embrace of the pool, her body vibrating with power, girded for the coming struggle against death. She opened her eyes and saw the cubling curled up into a tight ball on the rock.

A shudder ran through the gray-and-white body. "Wh-what was—that?" Khea's eyes did not open.

"The Voice." Vexk drew her knees up to her chest, the glorious sound still vibrating through her. "You have been honored. Few experience the power like that, even after many seasons."

"It was terrible—" Khea shuddered again, then opened her eyes just a crack. "And wonderful, both at the same time."

"You were born to be a Restorer." Vexk stood up in the shallows and let water stream from her fur. "I felt it the first time I saw you." She gazed down at her distorted reflection in the pool. "But *restoration/to/balance* is both a gift and a heavy responsibility. You will have to decide whether to take it up."

Khea rolled up to her knees. "I cannot join the guild—I was born to Vvok!"

"I too was born to Vvok." Vexk thought of the age-mates she had left behind, the cublings she would never bear. "In the end, it makes no difference. We are what we must be, no more, but certainly never any less."

Mimki's red-and-white sides heaved again as Fik watched dispassionately from the other side of the Bearing Chamber. It was too late in the warm season for the young female to be delivering this child. Too late, that is, if she had truly bred during the last Gathering, as she had said. Not late at all, however, if she had disgraced herself, and all of Qartt, by mating after the appointed time.

At any rate, the cub would be born this night, and then, after examining it, Fik would know everything. If the truth were as damaging as she suspected, she would finally have her chance to name a new pattern for Qartt, one of daring and progress and unprecedented reward. She combed the pale-ginger strands of her unbound mane with flexed handclaws, satisfaction crinkling the corners of her eyes.

Mimki, so meek and quiet that she had barely managed to fight her way out of the nursery, happened to be a direct-granddaughter of Chytt, Qartt's very proper Line Mother. Under any other circumstances, she would have been a late cull, assigned to one of the hold crafts which required nothing more than quick hands and average intelligence, but because of her lineage, she had survived every gleaning to finally enter the coveted ranks of the breeders.

Mimki writhed again, raking claws deep into the birthing pallet as the birth pains twisted her insides.

Fik prowled the sparely furnished room restlessly, remembering the agony of her own birthings. She had given five living cublings to Qartt, as well as two more who had not drawn breath. This year though, she had purposefully remained barren, resisting the Call of Gathering in order to be ready to seize Qartt, should the opportunity present itself.

Gasping louder this time, Mimki struggled with her pain. Well, Fik told herself, Mimki had sought the rank of breeder, and for such, the season either began in the pain of denial, or ended in the pain of birth, there was no escaping that. Her own trial had come this past season when her body had seethed and burned, demanding that which she was determined to resist. But now, she would seize the first opportunity to take Qartt in her own claws and give the Line over to another more potent pattern, one which would bring them honor and recognition, not the weak, ineffectual one recognized by Chytt.

Mimki cried out in a long shuddering wail. Fik's ears flattened. No doubt Chytt had heard *that*, even in the middle of the night on another level! Her lips curled over her teeth. Such weakness was too shameful, even if this was Mimki's first time. But even more shameful was the knowledge that Chytt had spared her when other, better females had been culled, never to leave their more deserving mark on the coming generations.

Feet scraped in the passageway, then Gitl poked her yellow-furred head into the room. "What's wrong?"

"Nothing." Without taking her eyes off Mimki, Fik wrinkled her nose. "Everything goes just as it should."

Gitl hesitated, then crossed to the pallet, her graceful height contrasting with Fik's more compact build. Mimki's eyes clenched shut as another violent contraction wracked her swollen belly. She hung on for several seconds, then released another echoing wail.

If this continued, Fik thought, they would have half
the Line down here. This soft-head sounded as though
she were dying instead of simply bearing a child!

"Not much longer now." Gitl's yellow-furred hand
rested on Mimki's great belly. "Try to be silent so the
rest of the hold will not worry." Mimki stared at her
with pain-glazed eyes, then tensed as another spasm
came. "Good," Gitl said. "Hold on."

Fik watched sourly as Mimki struggled through the
contraction without a sound this time. No one had
needed to soothe *her* when her cublings came.

"Almost!" Gitl cried. "Once more and then you will
be done!"

Mimki's claws ripped the pallet through another
long contraction, then Gitl took the circle of Qartt-
blue cloth from Fik's hands and wrapped a tiny red
cubling in it. "Solid red!" Her voice was jubilant.
"Small, but red as Ankt above, and perfect! No danger
of this one being an early cull."

Fik took the bundle into her own hands. As
Head Breeder, it fell to her to determine if each
cubling was fit to receive its first feeding of warmed
blood-and-meat paste, already prepared in a small
bowl. Looking down into the tiny pushed-in face,
she checked its features: all there. Then she
unwrapped the cloth to count limbs and fingers and
toes and check proportions. Everything seemed to
be in its proper place. Unfortunately, there was no
way to tell if it were male or female yet, but a few
seasons of the proper diet would resolve that. Just
as she was about to wrap it back up, she leaned
closer and sniffed, recognizing the familiar musk
of Qartt and . . .

Fur rose along her spine as she sniffed again, then
whirled upon Mimki with narrowed eyes. "Fool!" She
set the tiny cubling on the floor and tried to force
Mimki to meet her eyes. "What did you think you
were doing? You had to know!"

Exhausted, Mimki only gazed at the wall. Gitl picked the cubling up and folded it to her own body. "What are you talking about? Even if it was bred out of season, it is still a perfect child for Qartt."

Fik sneered at Gitl's stupid yellow face. "Smell it."

Gitl dropped her head and sniffed the cub, then sniffed again, finally raising a stricken face. "Mimki!"

Mimki huddled on the birthing pallet, arms wrapped around her empty belly, straw stuck in her claws.

Fik snarled. "How could you even consider accepting a *Qartt* male!"

Laying the infant beside its mother, Gitl studied it with shocked eyes. "Our own Line, Mimki, double Qartt! That's—abomination."

"I didn't know," Mimki said softly to the wall, "not at first. I was so ashamed I hadn't conceived at the Gathering, and then later, when I saw him hunting up in our hills, and he was so big and red, the Call came upon me again. I decided it would be better to bear late, than not at all." She closed her eyes. "I was not thinking clearly, and didn't recognize his scent until—after."

Fik scowled. "Take this *mistake* and dispose of it at once!"

Mimki tried to sit up, but her inner nictitating eye membranes closed and she slumped back.

"Just as I thought." Fik's ears flattened. "Useless in every way. I will do it, and then the Line Mother must be told."

Drawing a forefinger along the cubling's tiny red jaw, Gitl gazed at Fik with naked sorrow. "Why not wait until dawn?"

"You were taught better than that." Fik took the child and thrust it under her arm like a piece of firewood. "The presence of abomination in this hold shames us all."

Well, she told herself, as she followed the maze

of corridors up to the outside, Mimki had certainly played into her hands far better than she'd had any right to expect. She had suspected an out of season birth, but not one bred by a male of their own Line as well. Chytt would never recover from the shame.

The cubling whimpered under her arm. Fik stared stonily ahead. The sooner she finished this, the better.

Her free hand stole up to the tender claw tracks across her cheek and ear. She couldn't wait to see Chytt's face upon her return.

Chapter Twelve

Mitsu fled down the narrow green beach, the merciless white sun burning her pale skin and skeletal flek everywhere, grasping at her with chitinous dead-white fingers, their mad chitter the only sound left in her universe. She threw herself against a hillock of spiny gray grass hard enough to knock the air out of her lungs and lay there gasping. Where was the rest of her unit? Where were Benny and Sej and where—rot his soul—was Blackeagle? How could he just abandon her to die like this?

Beyond the hill, she heard the rustle of flek. If she didn't move on, they would sniff her out. She tried to take a deep breath so she could run, but the pain in her chest constricted her lungs. Standing, she tried to run anyway, but slipped and stumbled as the flek crept through the grass, reaching . . .

Someone was crying out in a raw, hoarse voice, but the sound was very far away . . . Moving restlessly, Mitsu longed for it to stop. Her head hurt so much already . . . A hand supported her neck; she felt cool water at her cracked lips and drank, but swallowing hurt her raw throat and did nothing to quench the burning that consumed her. She gagged and turned away. Water would not put out this fire. She needed a Med, but some distant part of her understood that in this terrible, unrelenting place of fur and claws and sand, there would be no such thing.

The so-called "room" was no better than an irregular hole scratched into the ground by a wounded animal. A scruffy, lop-eared servant gestured for them to enter and Heyoka dropped to his knees, reflecting it would've had to be a damned small animal at that. The air was musty down here; the only light was shed by a single guttering torch carried by the servant.

Despite the pulsing headache centered behind his eyes, he considered balking and fighting his way back out into the blessed open air, rather than allowing himself to be trapped. These Jhii were just noncoms, he told himself. They had nothing but brute force on their side, and the first duty of any prisoner *was* to escape, but Nisk was between him and the servant, and he had no room to maneuver in the narrow passageway.

He crawled in until his shoulder fetched up against a rough wall as Nisk followed him into the darkness without protest. Cursing, he turned and wedged himself in the corner. Anger swelled inside him. His leg ached and he found local politics utterly bewildering. Beshha's professed concerns were patently ridiculous. What did she think the two of them were going to do—ravish an entire hold of hrinnti females? He kneaded his aching forehead, still trying to plan a way out of this mess. "What is this level for?"

"It was probably constructed for early-culled servants who will never be fed enough to differentiate sexually, or grow to any size." Nisk squirmed around until he could poke his nose out the small doorway.

"Bring us food and water," he ordered the servant squatting just outside.

A small buff-colored face appeared in the square of light. "Skett, she say naught of food."

"If this male does not eat, he will die!" Nisk's voice rang with authority. "If the Line Mother intends him no harm, you must bring food." The buff-colored nose quivered, then, ears waggling, the guard settled back into place. A growl rumbled in Nisk's chest.

Heyoka leaned over Nisk, his voice low. "Let's take it and get out now while we can."

"Do not be foolish." Nisk kneed him in the chest. He fell back and brought down a shower of dust from the ceiling that made them both cough. "If we leave now, every Jhii daughter and half-grown cubling will be on our trail within the flick of an ear." His black eyes glittered through the dimness. "And look at yourself—you're in no condition to fight. In fact, you will most likely die if you go on like you did this afternoon."

Heyoka settled his aching head against the dirt wall. "I've fought for days in much worse shape than this."

"Fool! You still have no grasp of this pattern," Nisk said irritably. "How do you expect to be in control unless you can see it for what it is?"

Patterns again. From language tapes, Heyoka knew Hrinnti religion did invoke "patterns" of some sort as a prophetic device, but their significance had not been clear. He sighed. How had he let things get so far out of hand? He'd just meant to accompany Nisk a short distance, then slip away. How had he wound up shut up in the bottom level of one of the Lines?

"Sleep while you can." Nisk's voice sounded distant. "I must try to work out what it is Beshha really wants, but I will wake you if they honor their obligations and bring food."

He did feel bone-weary and more than a little

dizzy, but that was from too much action and no sleep in this higher gravity. He could go on, if he had to. As for food, he didn't think he could eat, even if something were brought. His throat was dry and food sounded, well, sickening. His eyelids felt like lead weights, but he had too much to . . .

With a start, he realized his muzzle had shifted down to his chest. He couldn't remember what it was he had to do, but it was important . . .

Caught in an outgoing tide of sleep, he drifted away.

Levv! Beshha kicked a fat purple cushion aside as she prowled the crowded confines of her chamber. Fur bristled along her shoulders and she could not help snarling under her breath. How could that name find a voice again after so many seasons?

Her direct-daughter, Syll, hung back in the doorway, watching her with enigmatic black eyes that were almost invisible in her black face. "I tried to tell you."

"Shut up!" Beshha whirled, but Syll held her ground even as Beshha's gold-dipped claws hovered within a whisper of her throat. The cant of her daughter's ears was a shade higher than this situation warranted, portending a coming confrontation. Beshha turned and preened the fine dark-brown fur along her throat. Violence and force had never been her way. Let others claw their way to the top; she had always found the subtle intricacies of *stealth/in/intent* a much more effective pattern than any of the more brutal ones which other Lines followed, as well as more likely to leave one's hide intact at the end of matters.

She settled back against her cushions. "They both have to die."

"The black one too?" Syll's tone bordered upon fearful. "What if he *is*—"

Beshha closed her fingers over a cedt nut. "You don't actually give any credence to that Black/on/black nonsense, do you? It's nothing but tales passed down by toothless old Tellers. No one has ever actually seen such a creature, and in case you didn't notice, he looked remarkably unwell tonight—for a legend."

"I will have Skett kill them then." Syll turned to go.

"It cannot been done here, you wet-ears!" Beshha cracked a nut thoughtfully between her back teeth. "That is just what we would need, for the whole hold to know we killed this pair against whom we had no legitimate grievance. Your idiocy would put us all at risk."

"But if it were an accident—"

Beshha dashed the empty shells in her daughter's face. "Fool! All of Jhii down to the scruffiest servant knows they are here. Claiming an accident would only bring to mind Levv's madness." She crunched the pale nutmeat, savoring its mellowness. "No, it must be done somewhere else, where no one can ever connect it to us."

Syll hunched in the doorway and watched Beshha crack another nut. Beshha found herself amused; she herself had never been allowed to taste anything as savory as a cedt nut until, with the help of the Outsider weapons, she had ambushed her predecessor, old Menn, and taken her place. Cedt bushes grew best on the other side of Kendd where the soil and moisture were just right. They were a delicacy here in the mountains.

She picked up another nut and rolled the rough shell between her thumbs. "Tomorrow, we will send them on their way. Have Skett and several of her trainees follow at a discrete distance until they leave Jhii land." She flung the uncracked nut at Syll's head, missing by only a hair. "Now, find Skett and see that everything is arranged for tomorrow."

Almost surreptitiously, Syll snatched up the nut from the carpet as she passed. Beshha's ears caught a sharp crack from the hall before Syll had gone three paces. A hint of satisfaction wrinkled her nose.

No, she told herself, it would never do to deprive her daughter as old Menn had once deprived her. Let Syll sample a few tidbits every now and again to blunt her hunger for the Line Mother's place. Syll was sharp-nosed enough to know it would come to her in time. In the meantime, Beshha meant to enjoy her days without having to watch for *that* sort of trouble nipping at her heels.

Vexk and the cubling made slow progress back from the caves. The youngster, pushed far beyond her limits, was stumbling from weariness. But Khea made no complaint, nor did Vexk expect any from a youngster born of such a rugged Line. Above, Ankt monitored them like a stern red eye, hovering just above the eastern horizon. By the time they reached the sprawling hold's outer doorway, the fire of its gaze played over her face; another scorching day was being made.

Cimmi met them in the shadow of the threshold, her muzzle creased with concern, her posture uncertain.

Vexk's breath caught. "It has not died?"

"No, but it is so—hot." Shame written in her eyes, Cimmi lowered her head. "I did all I could, but to no avail. I never knew flesh could burn so and still live."

Behind her, Khea sagged against the wall, ears limp as Vexk brushed her fingers along Cimmi's cheek. "I know you have done your best. It was at the point of death before it arrived."

Cimmi's uneasy eyes met hers again. "A message arrived by jik last night after you left. Vvok ordered the Outsider returned immediately—dead or alive, it does not matter which."

Khea straightened as though she had been struck,

her jaws agape with surprise and Vexk felt an unaccustomed snarl rumbling in her throat. This made no sense. Where was the advantage in letting the creature die now, after guarantee of payment and constant attendance on her part? What bizarre pattern was Seska chasing after now? She bristled. "It matters to *me*!" She stalked past Cimmi in a fog of anger, fighting to regain control. Anger defiled the sacredness of *harmony/through/balance*, the great pattern that gave shape to her life and that of all Restorers.

The Outsider lay propped on a pile of cushions in a darkened room at the back of the upper level, which was reserved for those most ill. Vexk squatted beside the small, fever-wracked body and removed bandages soaked with healing herbs from the creature's damaged arm and side. The aromatic scent filled the air, overriding the foreign rankness. "I am pleased with your growing skill, young one," she said.

Cimmi bowed her head modestly, then knelt on the other side of the dying creature. Vexk heard a rustle near the door. "Enter," she said without looking at Khea, then closed her eyes and summoned the inner quiet required for Restoration, especially in this case. The power involved was going to be great and had an equal capacity for good and bad. It could easily destroy, rather than restore, so her control had to be perfect. She stretched her hands out above the frail body and felt the abnormal heat radiating from it. She stiffened; the creature's skin had not even been this hot last night and that had been the worst so far. Little time remained. Her eyes closed as she summoned the wordless, singing vibration of the Voice into her hands, then added the steaming strength of the sacred pool.

In her heightened state of awareness, the infection in the clawed arm and shoulder shone like a torch in the night. Spreading her fingers, she traced the first angry red line with sacred blue fire, controlling the flow with a concentration so intense that she was aware of little else. At her touch, the creature cried out and tried to rise. Cimmi scrambled to pin it down. After she had traced the length of each wound, Vexk rested, musing that a hrinn would have bitten its own tongue through rather than fight her, but then Outsiders were clearly another breed, with their own strengths and weaknesses.

The infection ran deep, so she retraced each claw trail with a measured discharge of power, attempting the impossibly delicate job of burning the infection out bit by bit without further damaging the creature's fragile skin and muscle. After a short struggle, the alien lay pale and limp as she went over each wound again and again. Dead or alive, indeed! Her lips curled away from her teeth in a fierce grimace. Strange though this creature was, it was still Life and, like every Restorer since the Beginning, she had forfeited her unborn in order to wield the sacred power to bind Life to this earth whenever possible.

When she had expended her last glimmer of power, Vexk hunched over the creature, gasping, her tongue lolling in what she knew was a most undignified fashion. The creature lay quiet now, its pallid, flat face still. Vexk touched its skin and found it cooler. Its breathing seemed easier too. She could sense no more infection lingering in the claw marks, although sometimes it hid deep within the body and came back later. Still, she had hollowed herself out with giving; never before had she used so much in a single session.

Khea crept forward, her ears trembling with fatigue. "Will it live?"

"Perhaps." Vexk ran a trembling hand back over her ears. "It has a chance now, if the shock has not been too much for it. Their bodies are not as sturdy as ours."

Cimmi gripped Vexk's shoulder. "Go and rest. I will keep watch."

Vexk thought longingly of her own pile of soft, gynth-stuffed cushions several levels below, but decided against leaving. "No, its condition is too uncertain. I will curl up here beside it."

"Is there a problem, Dr. Alvarez?" Allenby peered anxiously at her as Sanyha checked box labels in the storeroom.

Sanyha paused. "No, I just want to examine some of these garments for differences between the clothing of direct-daughters and other females in a Line."

The stores manager blinked nervously. "I have some unpacked specimens on the sorting tables in the back."

"Thanks, but—" She struggled with the catch on one likely looking box. "—I remember seeing nice specimens last month in the shipment we got in from Kendd and I have good charts on that Line." Breaking a fingernail, she sighed and turned to him. "I think they're in this box. Would you open it for me?"

A grimace crossed Allenby's thin face. "The Director wants these shipped on the next run. I can't break up the manifest."

"The ship won't be here for over two months." Sanyha watched his eyes. "I promise I'll pack everything back myself and double-check against the packing list. You won't have to lift a finger."

"Just let me ask the Director." Allenby sidled toward his com. "Then you can—"

"Allenby?" Eldrich's voice barked from the com before Allenby could touch it. "Any sign of that Jensen woman yet?"

The Adam's apple bobbed in Allenby's throat. "Not yet, sir."

"Well, keep an eye on the main door. She should be here any time now."

Sanyha moved toward the com. "How do you know that?"

"What was that, Allenby? Have you got someone there with you?"

"That's Dr. Alvarez, Director." Allenby glanced up at her. "She'd like permission to go through some of the packed shipment boxes for her research."

"Permission denied!" The com was silent for a moment. "We have enough work to do around here without undoing any of it." The com clicked off.

"Sorry, Doctor." Allenby didn't look at her. "Why don't you check some of these unprocessed specimens?"

"No, thanks." Sanyha drummed her fingers on the locked crate, thinking. "Is Sergeant Blackeagle bringing in the Jensen woman?"

"I don't know." Allenby walked to the back of the room toward the sorting tables. "You'll have to ask the—"

"—Director," Sanyha finished for him. There was no safer answer, she thought sourly. No one ever wanted to talk to the Director. "Never mind." She gathered up her notes. "I have something else to take care of first."

Like coding the defense system to buzz her when someone came in from the outside.

"Out! Out!"

A high-pitched voice in the outer passageway jerked Heyoka awake. He started and hit his head against the wall as a buff-colored muzzle thrust into the claustrophobic earthen chamber. "The Line Mother, she say go now!"

Ears ringing, Heyoka blinked in confusion at the dirt walls, unsure for the moment where he was. Somebody was between him and the faint light beyond. The air was stale, and his tongue felt three sizes too big for his head. "W-what?"

"Out now!" The servant jabbed his ribs with a sharpened stake. "Stay away from Jhii mothers and daughters!"

The stick tore through his already tattered robes and pierced the skin beneath. Anger blazed through Heyoka and he lunged at his tormenter, but Nisk grasped the stick and shoved the servant back out into the passageway. "Have care, nameless one!" His lips curled in a fierce grimace. "I doubt Beshha would miss a witless cull-face like you!"

The servant fell back into the far wall and squealed. Then it scrambled out of reach, wielding the stake. "Out! Out!"

Nisk gripped Heyoka's shoulder. "Once we leave, we will find something to eat."

Food? Heyoka shook his matted mane out of his eyes. That was absolutely the last thing he wanted. His insides felt like rats had been tunneling through them all night. He took a deep breath and then crawled after Nisk out into the passageway.

"Out!" The servant waved the stake at them. "Leave good Jhii mothers and daughters alone!"

"Gods!" Heyoka muttered to himself in Standard. "What I wouldn't give to have a blaster just long enough to blow this little bugger to atoms!" Lurching to his feet, he staggered after Nisk as they followed the sloping floor upward, lighted only by the servant's torch behind them.

The walls seemed out of focus to Heyoka as they walked the endless passageways, bearing right or left at each fork according to orders shouted from behind. He told himself they had to have been crazy to let themselves be trapped in a rabbit maze like this.

Finally, he sniffed fresh air again, but the fierce rush of accompanying smells turned his stomach. Sagging against the wall, he hung his head and waited for the wave of nausea to pass.

"Out!" The servant prodded him in the back with its stick. "Jhii daughters not want you here!"

The servant's angry face rippled as though seen underwater. Heyoka seized its wiry neck, but even as he tightened his fingers, he thought the hrinn had a curiously unreal feeling to it, as though he held nothing but air.

"Do not dirty your claws with that thing," Nisk said calmly from over his shoulder. "Jhii will reap the harvest of this disgraceful lack of propriety at the proper time."

Heyoka tried to let go, but his hands ignored him, as though they had become independent creatures with a will of their own, and went on with the business of throttling the servant while he merely looked on. Its handclaws gouged his chest as it struggled, but he felt—nothing.

Nisk grasped Heyoka's wrist and flexed his own handclaws into his forearm. "Do not soil your hands on this groveling, nameless thing, Black/on/black. Much as it deserves to die, killing it would take too much of your energy and we have far to go."

Under the sting of Nisk's claws, Heyoka could suddenly feel his hands again. He took a deep convulsive breath and loosened his grip, allowing the buff-colored servant to fall to the floor.

"Just what I would expect from a *male*!"

Heyoka turned around and saw the sharp-nosed face of the cub-trainer, Skett. She seemed both near and incredibly distant at the same time. The hallway slanted suddenly beneath his feet and he fell against Nisk.

Bracing him against the wall, Nisk glared at the cub-trainer. "What did you expect when you abused him like this? I sent for food and water last night, and yet he had none. You saw the manner in which he fought; you had to know he would require it, so do not speak to me of proprieties in this hold!"

Skett's ears flattened. "Get out and take this pile of Levv droppings with you."

"All debts will be reckoned in their proper time!" Nisk levered Heyoka past the cub-trainer. "A day will come when you have cause to remember this one's name."

Chapter Thirteen

The rumor reached Chytt as soon as she rose, but not before it had permeated down to even the stupidest servant in the lowest levels of Qartt Hold. Scratching a persistent itch behind her ear, she tried to persuade herself that Gitl had been mistaken. Mimki might well have bred out of season—it was no great secret that she was on the simple side, and if she had erred, no doubt it was Chytt's own fault for wanting Mimki's spectacular red-and-white spotted coat pattern passed on to Qartt's future generations.

Chytt ran a hand back through the long red mane lying loose on her neck and shoulders, feeling how much thinner it had become. And she didn't have to see herself to know she had lost a full hand-width of height in the past few seasons. Her ability to hold Qartt was weakening, and this breakdown in order was symptomatic of that fact.

But she could not picture Mimki actually being stupid enough to mate with a Qartt male. There was, of course, no telling what a *male* might do, even one bred out of Qartt. Once the male cublings were sent off to a males' house, the Voice alone knew what nonsense they were taught. But no daughter of hers would ever be wanton enough to do such a thing! Everyone knew such behavior invited disease and deformity, endangering the Line. And from the scruffiest nameless servant to the Line Mother herself, the Line was held sacred. Nothing came before its welfare, including the urges of the body. Nothing!

Someone scratched at the threshold. Chytt whirled, handclaws half-flexed, but met only Gitl's sorrowful yellow-furred face. "What?"

"Fik has returned." Gitl lingered uneasily in the doorway, eyes cast down to the deep-blue carpet.

Chytt flicked an ear at her and turned away. If the news were indeed as bad as the whispers said, then nothing would keep Fik's impudent face away. If it were good, then nothing would bring that insolent ginger-colored female here to face Chytt ahead of her own designs.

"I see you have heard," an arrogant voice said behind her back.

Chytt braced one hand against the curving wall of her chamber and told herself that she would *not* tremble before this creature. "Since you are the Head Breeder, I would rather hear it from you."

"Mimki bred out of season." She heard the whisper of fur against the wall as Fik moved about the room behind her. "The child was born last night, although surely you must have heard her caterwauling. She was not at all quiet about it."

"Is it perfect?" Chytt wondered at the calmness of her own voice.

"Yes, perfect." Fik yawned. "You will have to forgive me. I had a full night."

Chytt turned and saw to her amazement that Fik had curled up in the far corner on *her* cushions, the very best ones worked with gold thread. Her ears flattened. "You forget yourself!"

"On the contrary . . ." Fik stretched a pale-ginger arm over her head and lounged back on the soft dark-blue cushions. "You are the one who forgot herself—on the day when you passed that sand-brain, Mimki, at her final gleaning." Flexing her handclaws, she preened the white patch of fur on her chest. "Everyone knows that silly creature would never have risen higher than a non-breeding tender down in the nursery, if it were not for you. She has neither wit, nor courage on her side. In fact, she has nothing that makes her fit to breed Qartt's future generations." She yawned again, but her dark eyes, ice-bright and dangerous, glittered across the chamber at Chytt. "Nothing, but her direct descent from you."

Freeing her handclaws, Chytt glared at the insolent female. "Get out!"

"You thrust that stupid, foolish creature into the heart of this shameful pattern." Fik's eyes followed Chytt from her own cushions. "You invited this degradation into our hold."

"I do not believe she did more than breed out of season." Chytt forced her voice to remain calm. "If she mated with a Qartt male, then show me the child."

"Oh, I can do much better than that." Fik's lips drew back over her large white teeth and she flipped a bloodstained piece of blue birthing cloth in Chytt's direction. "Take a careful whiff of the stench of double-Qartt blood—because in this hold, as long as I am Line Mother, such will never be bred again."

Chytt flinched from the cloth that fluttered to her feet, then picked it up between the tips of two claws. The taint of wrongness in the dried blood sent a chill through her body. Qartt breeding with Qartt—who would have thought she would live to see such a thing? Added to the extinction of Levv, it seemed chaos crept closer with every breath. She had thought the current pattern ruling Qartt was *river/in/fire*, one that twisted and turned, yes, difficult and full of change, but these events indicated a shape far more sinister than any she had ever perceived. And, if she had mistaken the pattern, then this was her fault. How could she have been so wrong?

Fik rose in a fluidly powerful move, muscles rippling under her ginger coat. "Do you think you are strong enough now to box my ears, Line Mother?" Her voice was pitched in the inflection of an adult speaking to a cubling. "How many gleanings did *you* survive because you were Hallat's direct-daughter?"

Chytt's claws were at the pale-ginger throat before she even knew she had sprung. Fik whirled and pinned her to the floor, one arm across her throat. Chytt rolled and threw her off. Scrambling back onto her feet, she faced Fik again, ears flattened to her skull and the breath painfully short in her chest. Maturity had brought her wisdom and a broad knowledge of tricks that could be employed in a fight, but youth had its brute strength. For a bewildering second, she had a flash of old Hallat's surprised yellow-furred face when, all those seasons ago, Chytt had torn out her throat in this very same room.

Had she only been stronger than Hallat then, and nothing else? Not wiser, more fit to take this hold under her claws? Fik lunged and she retreated, catching a heel on a cushion and slipping. Her arms flailed as Fik fastened both hands in her mane and forced her head back, going for her throat with savage bared teeth.

As her head cracked against the exposed stone floor between the edge of the carpet and the wall, she knew it was already too late. Hotness bubbled at her throat as Fik drew back a triumphant, bloodstained muzzle, then tossed her aside like a soiled robe.

How strange that she felt no pain. Her muzzle was pressed hard against the cold stone of the wall, but aside from that, she only felt the spreading warmth of blood as it spurted down her chest onto the floor and soaked into her prized blue carpet, just a stride away. For herself, she could find no grief. From the day she had seized Hallat's place, she had known this would come; Line Mothers passed the Gates of Death in no other way.

But she was overwhelmed with the pain of Qartt passing under Fik's savage, quick-tempered claws. What would happen to the Line, all the daughters and the cublings and even the servants? What dark pattern would Fik give them over to? Fur rustled at the door; Gitl and perhaps a number of others had been there all along, but none would interfere. In the ancient way of things, power passed into only the sharpest of claws so that they would always breed from strength; that was the heritage of the Lines.

Grayness clouded the edges of her vision, then deepened to singing blackness which ate inwards toward the center and finally bore her away.

A tall indistinct shape loomed over Mitsu in the dimness. She took a shallow breath and closed her eyes again. It was too early, she told herself. Blast his fur-bound hide, Blackeagle was always eager to start their run before dawn, but she couldn't see in the darkness like he could.

"Just a few more minutes," she murmured. Every inch of her body felt like lead and the universe wouldn't end if she slept a little longer.

There was a harsh mutter of words close to her ear, and then someone touched her face. "I said, give me a few more sodding minutes!" She pushed at the hand, then curled up at the pain in her right arm and shoulder.

"Lie ——" The guttural voice penetrated her haze of pain, speaking in some other tongue than Standard.

She dimly remembered learning that language at some point, but when? Forcing her eyes open, she made out a sharp-nosed face leaning over her, covered in pale-gray fur though, not black.

Placing a hand under her good shoulder, the hrinn eased her back into the thick pile of cushions. "The —— has fled —— do not burn —— did before. Still, you must —— and allow —— heal."

Mitsu thought she had seen this hrinn before, but not this place. Even though the light was very low, there was a feeling of space in the room and the air smelled fresh. "Water?" she asked, then coughed at the harshness of Hrinnti syllables on her parched throat.

The light-furred hrinn picked up a yellow pottery bowl, then raised Mitsu's head to drink from it. The cool water slid down her dry throat, but moving her head made her arm and side throb.

"Sleep now." The hrinn brushed the hair out of her eyes in a curiously gentle manner. "No one —— you here."

Mitsu's eyes sagged shut, her thoughts evaporating like raindrops under the noonday sun.

His head felt so light as they labored up and down the increasingly rugged hills that Heyoka found himself surprised it didn't just float off into the cloudless amber sky. Down below and incredibly far away, his abused body struggled painfully over the rocky trails. Once in a while, Nisk spoke to him and he answered, but what either of them said, he had no idea.

When they reached a shallow mountain stream cascading over rounded rocks, Nisk motioned for him to drink, but he just stared stupidly at the water, no longer able to feel his thirst, or much of anything else, for that matter. Nisk seized his ruff and forced him to his knees, the water rushing inches away, and splashed water on his face. Heyoka licked the drops off his muzzle, then lowered his head to drink from cupped hands.

Nisk released him and studied the clear water until he finally scooped out a creature with bluish scales and wriggling tentacles. Turning back to Heyoka, he held it out and spoke sharply.

Looking down from his faraway place, Heyoka tried to make sense of that command.

"—take it!" Impatiently, Nisk tore the creature in two and pushed a still-writhing half into Heyoka's hand. "If you do not eat, you will die."

Heyoka brought the handful to his mouth, but the smell was rank and bitter.

Nisk's ears flattened. "Eat, or I will tear your throat out and leave you here for the dako to scavenge so at least something somewhere will have some use of you!"

Nisk's anger penetrated the haze inside Heyoka's head and he pushed the handful into his mouth, trying not to think about the off-taste or the squishiness of it between his teeth.

Nisk handed him the other half. "Now eat the rest and be quick! We cannot stay here."

Heyoka's stomach rolled as the first mouthful went down, but he crunched the second half, then rinsed his hands in the cool stream to wash away the smell. If anything, he felt worse.

They reached the crest of the first hill by the time the red sun was nearly overhead. Nisk knelt, using some low bushes for a screen and pointed back the way they had come. Four hrinn on yirnback were following their trail. "We will wait for them here."

Heyoka stared at him dully. "Why does Beshha want us dead?"

Nisk looked back down the hillside again. "I saw fear in her eyes last night when she looked at you. She knows something about the ending of Levv that would call the honor of Jhii into question."

The world seemed a little more real to him now. Heyoka began to feel the heat of the sun on his shoulders as though he were part of his body once more.

"When we fight these Jhii, you must not draw power." Nisk put a hand on Heyoka's shoulder, flexing his handclaws so that the tips pricked through Heyoka's tunic and fur for emphasis. "If you draw power again while you are this weak, you will die. Do you understand?"

"Draw—power?"

"As you did yesterday, on the hill when the young Jhii attacked you." Ears flattened, Nisk shook him. "That was wasteful. You should have been able to handle a mere youngling like that without even breathing hard."

Heyoka tried to think back to the fight. Drawing power—on the hillside? He replayed the memory, the cubling's sudden leap onto his shoulders . . . his vision shifting to blue, the world moving in slow motion. "You mean—things slowing down and turning blue?"

"Yes." Nisk peered over the edge of the hill.

"But—" Heyoka rubbed the sides of his head; it was still so hard to think. "—that just happens. I have no control over it."

Nisk stared at him, black eyes glittering. "If you cannot control it, you will die."

Yirn hooves clicked against the rocks as the Jhii trackers worked their way up the hillside. The warm afternoon wind blew into the males' faces, carrying their scent away from their trackers and allowing them at least some measure of surprise. Heyoka's ears pricked at the mutter of low voices. Although the four females were still hidden by the trees and bushes below, they had to be very near now.

Nisk flexed his handclaws, ears flat with concentration. "I will take the leader, who should be the most experienced." He spoke in a low, measured voice as though speaking of the chance of rain or some other equally mundane subject. "You must wait and take the third rider, so the yirn behind her will panic and render its rider useless for a breath or two."

Before Heyoka could argue, the first yirn's horned head bobbed just below the ledge where they were hiding. Nisk waited until it passed, then followed it through the brush, so the next riders would come on through. Then, as the third yirn's nose appeared, Nisk flung himself without a sound onto the cub-trainer's back and wrestled her to the ground.

Heyoka let the second rider pass, then launched himself at a nearly grown cubling who turned, teeth bared, and met him halfway. In a second, they tumbled together into the tough branches of the scrub.

With a savage snarl, the dark-brown cubling scrabbled out of the broken bushes and leapt for his throat. Using every combat trick he knew, Heyoka fought the snarling, spitting female off, all the while dreading the telltale slowing that signalled "drawing power."

Feeling a sudden hot breath on his shoulders, he whirled to face the fourth yirn crowding his heels. Without thinking, he clawed its nose and sent the bloodied beast squealing back down the trail. In that split second of inattention though, the cubling broke through his guard, ripping at his throat with razor-edged teeth. As he struggled to fight her off, the amber sky shifted toward blue.

No! He tried to catch his breath. *He did not even have the right to die in this forsaken place!* If he were killed, then Mitsu would never be rescued and she had only come to Anktan to aid him! With an effort he tried to slow his breathing, still prying at the fierce jaws clamped on his throat. Suddenly he threw himself forward against the stone ledge, crushing his adversary against the rock with his weight. The jaws loosened and he ripped at her body with his handclaws, all the while fighting the dislocating blueness which threatened to overwhelm him.

When the cubling's body went limp, he heaved it into the bushes. The savage scratches along his throat throbbed as he looked for the other two cublings, but the fourth rider had stayed with her yirn as it panicked back down the trail and the other sprawled, motionless and bloody, at Nisk's feet.

Nisk disappeared around the rocks, then reappeared, trailing two reluctant yirn by the ears, his face and neck red-orange with blood. As he dragged the second yirn toward Heyoka, the cubling in the bushes whimpered.

Nisk gave him a hard look. "Finish it."

Hovering on the edge of blueness, Heyoka stared back at Nisk's alien black-furred face over the white blood-streaked throat. The pulse drummed in his ears. Kill an injured prisoner in cold blood? A hoarse snarl rose up in his throat. By all the gods, that was a flek trick; it was the *flek* who took no prisoners. No *human* would ever—

A muscle twitched over his eye. He suddenly felt more kinship with the meanest, scruffiest human soldier back in his ranger outfit than this black-eyed mirror of himself—*humans* did not kill unarmed prisoners!

Nisk leaned into the bushes and yanked the limp, unresisting body out by the heel, then Heyoka watched in shock as Nisk's handclaws descended in a leisurely arc toward the cubling's unprotected throat. A shimmering curtain of intense *blue* fell over the world, as though he were gazing through sheer cloth of the most expensive weave. No longer resisting, Heyoka embraced the blueness, then watched his own hand, moving at normal speed, rise to catch the slowing falling arm before it could strike.

Nisk met his eyes without moving a hair. Heyoka could feel Nisk's superior muscles contract; even without blueshift speed, the older male could over-power him and kill the cubling if he wished. Heyoka lacked the strength to prevent him.

"She—will—come—after—us—again." Speaking in a drawn-out manner that was difficult to understand, the older male twisted his arm out of Heyoka's grip. "We—will—only—have—to—kill—her—later."

Blue everywhere, staining the world in a million shades of indigo, drowning him in a chill sea the color of Mitsu's eyes. Suddenly cold, Heyoka shivered convulsively. "Let it be later then!" he gasped and fell to his knees beside the cubling.

Nisk stared down at him, then stepped in slow motion over the cubling's prone body to pull Heyoka to his feet. Dizzy, Heyoka swayed against the rock ledge and tried to shunt the deadly blueness aside. Nisk took his leg and boosted him over the yirn's shaggy warm side. Heyoka groped for the leather harness and settled just behind the beast's hump. Then, huddled there in misery, he watched as Nisk mounted the other beast and rode around the bend, driving Heyoka's own beast before him.

Though still very weak, the creature was no longer ill. Nibbling a crumbly handful of sweet yellow-cake to restore her energy, Vexk watched its chest rise and fall in the evenness of healing sleep. If she could just keep it here, even for a few days, it would regain some measure of strength again, perhaps even be able to walk.

But not if she sent it back to Vvok now, as Seska continued to demand in an unending stream of messenger jits. And, oddly enough, there was some-thing in the spiteful, threatening tone of those messages that spoke to Vexk of the old female's fear. She leaned over and smoothed a lock of the short black mane out of the creature's pale face. What had

Seska, Line Mother of Vvok, to fear from this soft-skinned, hairless thing?

Over in the far corner, Khea stirred in her sleep and Vexk glanced at her. She had hoped for more time to awaken the talents hidden in Khea's nature and to tempt her with a different, more satisfying way of life other than that offered by the Lines.

Still, she had no right to keep either the cubling or the Outsider here past the time the creature could travel. Perhaps tomorrow morning, she told herself, they could not possibly go until then. Finishing the last crumb of yellow-cake, she rose and went to find Siga so a jit could be sent back with that message.

Chapter Fourteen

From time to time Nisk spoke, but the words were so drawn out, Heyoka could make no sense of them. He could feel nothing but his heart racing in his chest, smell nothing, nor perceive normal color. Everything was remote, hidden behind a cold, imprisoning curtain of shimmering blue, distant and unreal. From the disapproving narrowness of the other male's eyes, it was plain Nisk thought he would die, and perhaps he was right. He would probably be dead already if Nisk weren't pressing food on him whenever possible.

His entire body vibrated with the deadly electric blueness he could not dismiss any more than he had summoned it. Though Nisk insisted he should be able to control it, the bizarre blueshift came when it would, departed in the same fashion, and this time seemed determined to stay, even at the cost of his life. It was a powerful enemy, even more cunning than the flek, leaching his life away while he could do nothing to fight back. He longed to tear into the icy blueness, rend it shred from shred, and find his way back into the realm of the living, but he had no idea of how to begin.

The first time it had touched him, back on Enjas Two, he hadn't had the leisure to think about it or try to understand. Just after dawn, he and Mitsu had been sweeping the beach for flek that might have moved up on their unit's position during the night. Heyoka ranged ahead and kept his head low as he hugged the slope up to higher ground. The breeze shifted and he caught the faint scrabble of flek feet in the sand as well as their nose-burning stink. He dropped behind a hillock of spiny grass and listened; they were out there all right. His fingers tightened around the stock of his laser rifle.

Twenty feet back, he heard Mitsu hit the sand too. On his right, waves hissed against the green beach, creeping gradually closer as high tide came in. His ears twitched as everything stilled. Then, a hundred feet down the beach, a wall of pasty-white bodies erupted over the hill, laying down a deadly sheet of laser fire before them.

Trapped, he called to Mitsu to fall back while he covered her. Almost casually, one of the forwardmost flek glanced his way and fired a bolt of green that seared his right leg from ankle to knee. For a baffling second, he felt nothing, then pain exploded through his brain. The damaged leg gave way, pitching him nose-first, gasping, into the coarse sand. Through a red haze, he heard Mitsu call out that she was coming back for him.

"No!" he shouted hoarsely, trying to wrestle the muzzle of his laser rifle up out of the sand. "Retreat, dammit! That's an order!" The flek fired again, this time missing just by inches to watch him jump. Heyoka crawled toward the rise to his left, dragging his smoking leg behind him.

The flek were almost upon him now, the white sun of Enjas Two mirrored in their stomach-turning red eyes. Laser bolts sizzled over his head from behind as Mitsu tried to back the flek off, but they held their pattern of fire, taking aim with deliberate slowness, playing the sick flek game of blowing an enemy apart one bit at a time. He hoped they would finish him quickly, but that was not the flek way and he knew it.

Green fire flared again. He tensed, but the bolt of energy aimed at his shoulder *slowed* . . . He wrenched himself aside and saw it splash over the space he had just vacated, fusing the sand into a glassy patch. The line of flek took on a ghostly blue cast, drifting down the beach in an eerie slow motion. Gaps appeared in their pattern of fire.

Dragging himself up on his good knee, he fired through one of the gaps and saw a flek float backwards into the sand, slowly kicking. The line edged closer as he shot through another hole, taking out a second flek. When they returned fire, the bolts oozed toward him like cold tree sap and, even lamed, he was able to hop out of their way. One by one, he took sight on the remaining dozen or so and burned each of them down until he and Mitsu were the only living creatures left on the beach.

Blood thundered in his ears as he balanced there on one leg under the pale-blue sky, the silence around him cold and brittle, the pain in his leg devouring him like a living thing. Mitsu finally reached him, her face as blue as her eyes. Then suddenly without remembering how he had gotten there, he was on his face, snout-down in the sand and the world was normal colored again.

Captain Rajman came to him that evening in the Med unit, demanding to know how he had managed to penetrate a flek firing pattern that efficiently, but Heyoka's tale of blueness that slowed the world down had been dismissed as a side effect of the shock accompanying his injury. In the end, suspecting him of battle fatigue or personality dysfunction, Rajman suspended him, which turned out to be irrelevant, because the Meds said he would never be fit for duty again anyway.

Heyoka glanced down at his bad leg, dangling against the side of the yirn, still encased in the power brace. How long ago had the doctor back at the station given the brace to him? Two days . . . three? Without recharging, the power supply would last only a day or two more.

His yirn plodded to a halt and Nisk twisted around on his mount, motioning with maddening slowness for him to dismount. Heyoka slid down the yirn's shaggy side and hung there as the world spun and his legs threatened to buckle. Nisk disappeared languidly into the brush, then returned some time later and piled an armful of leaves on the ground.

Sleep. Heyoka walked stiffly over to the makeshift bed, then sank onto the pungent blue-tinged leaves and closed his eyes.

Wading into the current, Rakshal dipped cool water from the living heart of the river and bathed the half-healed wounds on his chest. The water sheared around his legs, full of its own confident power. He watched it, musing that in nine more days he would face Jikin's lawful challenge. Since the old male had never shown the slightest inclination toward Leadership previously, this turn of events could only be explained in terms of an arising pattern, not *death/ in/longing*, as he had originally thought, after the appearance of the false Black/on/black, but something bolder, a testing to draw forth the brave and resourceful, *storm/against/stone* perhaps, or even something else never before named and all the more powerful for it.

Shouts erupted and he glanced downriver at cublings running along the shore, playing at "Dako and Zzil," a youthful game of predator and prey, healthy activity to strengthen their muscles and teach them to hunt as a unit. Because he had been called by the Voice quite young, he'd had little of such games before devoting himself to training with Isen, the old priest who had heard the Voice in this area before him.

Born just after the Outsiders arrived, he had watched his whole life as those around him ignored the patterns that should have shaped their lives. It was a scandalous and well-known fact Outsiders never heard the Voice, nor knew anything of the great patterns, and yet—look at their wealth. They came and went as they pleased from this planet and boasted they held countless other worlds in their clawless fingers. Now the younger males asked why any hrinn should pay heed to the ways of the Voice since it had made no difference in the fortunes of Outsiders. It was obvious the Outsiders had to be scoured from the land so there was no trace they had ever existed. Only then could the people return to their pious ways and avoid the shattering chaos of the before times.

Suddenly the shouts from the game shrilled into alarm. Rakshal splashed toward them as agitated cublings in the shallows pointed downriver. Already several older males were searching the current.

Ears down, a wild-eyed cubling met Rakshal's gaze. "Tama slipped and fell under the water!"

Rakshal appraised the searching males as they waded into the deeper currents without success. They would never find the lost cubling that way. He dropped to his knees on the sand and threw his head back, eyes closed. "Greatness," he whispered, "show these disbelievers the power of your patterns from which they have turned away. Speak of where I may find this child."

Ankt's rays danced hotly on his face as he waited, acutely conscious of the lost cubling, no doubt already drowning. Then suddenly he saw the place clearly in his mind and leaped to his feet, pushing through the searching cublings and older males, struggling to reach the snag of driftwood at the far end of the slippery rocks. He probed under the jammed logs and brushed water-soaked fur. Unable to get a firm grip, he ducked under the clear green water and began to work the cubling's leg out from between the two rocks. Just when he thought his lungs would burst, the leg came free and he surfaced with the youngling's limp body in his arms.

Two males rushed to take the cubling from him and lay the small body on the warm sand, leaving Rakshal to struggle back to shore alone. The other cublings crowded close as old Fihht pressed the water out of the youngster's lungs.

Long blinks later, the cubling coughed, then spit up more water. Wet and breathless himself, Rakshal crouched on the sand, watching as the cubling opened his eyes and blinked weakly up at him. "Never forget," he said, staring down at the cubling's frightened face, "how this day the Voice spoke to save your life." Then he looked up and accepted the weight of the astonished eyes all around him.

The blood-soaked blue carpet had been removed and the flagstone floor scrubbed with fresh sand, but the fragrance of Chytt's blood lingered. Fik punched the thick pile of cushions, rearranging them over and over, fur still on end, unable to settle. The elimination of Chytt had been but the beginning. Now that her blood was up, she burned for the satisfying release of more action, but it was important to choose her battles, as she thrashed this ragtag hold into obedience and eliminated everyone, from the breeders on down, who did not offer bared throats to her.

With her ascension, she and her fellows had achieved a long-awaited majority in the Council of

Lines. Soon they would be free to openly accept all the Outsiders offered—boxes that spoke over great distances, machines which carried one over land and even through the air, strange metal things that could heal the body or plant grain, the list was endless. Why should the Lines be forced to chase after obscure, elusive patterns for guidance and hunt their food like simple-minded animals when Outsiders knew more efficient ways? Fik stretched a pale-ginger arm behind her head, remembering how foolishly terrified she had been on that day when she had stumbled into the Outsider's trap.

The red eye of Ankt had hung low in the sky as she rode her weary yirn back from a solitary hunt, one half-starved kikinti, more a heap of bones than meat, tied over the beast's hump in front of her. If the hunting didn't improve, Qartt would have to abandon its ancient hold by the river and move up into the mountains in search of more game, and of course, Jhii and Levv would protest, if it came to that. Fik, with several gleanings yet to pass, feared to return with so little, even though she had ridden halfway to Kendd on her search.

A sudden twist in the breeze brought the scent of zzil. Her nose twitched as she pinpointed it up ahead, under a stand of dense blue-black bushes well back from the river. Sliding down the yirn's side, she flexed her handclaws and crept toward the scent, using the rocks and foliage for cover.

As she squeezed through thickly interlocked branches, leaving behind strands of pale-ginger fur, she glimpsed a fresh haunch lying on the ground. A few iridescent-green meat-nits buzzed around it. She brushed them away, then sat back on her heels, puzzled. Who could have been foolish enough to leave this here? In this exceptionally lean year, no Line or males' house had food to spare. She grasped the shank and lifted and the air came alive with an eerie, buzzing redness that stood her fur on end. Dropping the bone, she whirled to face her enemy and met instead a wall of glimmering, transparent red.

Panicking, she ran straight into it, hardly comprehending when it *bit* and threw her back to the ground, dazed. She lay there for a few breaths, her nose burning and head whirling, then rose and examined it more carefully. The angry redness enclosed her on all sides, extending even over her head.

Ears flattened, Fik broke off a branch and poked it into the shining redness. She heard the same snapping buzz as before, accompanied by the stench of burning. When she drew back the branch, the leaves were black and smoking. This was obviously a trap, complete with bait. Retreating as far from the meat as she could, Fik began digging, but no matter how deep she dug, the redness was always waiting, biting her claws when she ventured too close. Ears limp with exhaustion, she finally stretched out on the displaced sand and closed her eyes. The rest of the afternoon and then the night passed in a weary haze. The river maddened her thirst; she could both hear and smell the water flowing just out of reach. The sight of the meat so close was another sort of torment, but ravenous as she was, she feared to touch it again.

Sometime before morning, she heard a soft whirring, which ended finally with a whump somewhere out of sight. Fur prickling along her shoulders, she flexed her handclaws. Footsteps crunched across the sand, then she heard the rattle of someone pushing through the stiff-branched bushes. There was a smell, too, strange and unidentifiable . . . acrid.

"What this?" Speaking in strangely accented Hrinnti, an upright two-legged creature holding a small light in its hand stood just outside the red field and studied her with bizarre gray eyes.

Fik snarled. Even though she had never actually

seen one before, she knew this flat-faced thing had to be an Outsider. The Council of Lines had decreed such creatures dangerous and ordered them killed on sight.

"Regret no before come." The creature had a nasty pushed-in, naked face and soft pale skin. Bending over, it dug into the sand, then lifted out a small silver box.

With a pop, the redness died away. Fik's head swiveled as she took a deep breath of night air untainted by the field's peculiar odor. Then she stood, towering over the Outsider, which was not as tall as her chest, though she was not yet fully grown.

It wrinkled its disgusting face at her. "Blue—good. Need Qartt contact." Then it pointed a slim silver tube at her—

—she and the Outsider sat on the sand, with Ankt just peering over the horizon in the east and the river gurgling over the rocks only a few steps away. She glanced around wildly; what had happened to the bushes . . . the haunch of meat . . . the trap? She felt disoriented, dizzy.

"Now . . ." The Outsider placed a small metal box into her hand.

Her ears flattened, then she realized the creature was quite friendly, indeed, that it could be extremely useful to a young female who still faced several gleanings in the coming seasons. Her fingers tightened around the box.

"You no have trouble," the Outsider said. "Simple." It showed her the box's functions, which ranged from summoning the strange white hold in the drylands, to calling the females of other Lines who apparently wanted the same miracles for Anktan that she now did. Holding the box, she had been overcome by a sudden sense of comradeship with this creature. She and it might well have been hunt-mates or even Gathering companions to sit so close and talk in that way.

That had been but the first of many meetings. Nestling deeper into Chytt's plump warm cushions, Fik closed her eyes. There was still so much to do. Tonight, when the hold was shrouded in sleep, she would speak through the box to her allies among the other Lines and they would at last make final plans.

When Khea reentered the shadowy dimness of the guest chamber, steaming bowl in hand, the Outsider was able to turn its head and look at her. "Food?" it said in mangled Hrinnti, then tried weakly to sit up.

"Yes, food." Khea pushed it back gently as she had seen Vexk do. Its oddly jointed bones felt fragile beneath her hand, the skin wasted and thin beneath the overlarge robe in which they had wrapped it, but sense gleamed now in those strange eyes. It was much improved. She studied the smooth gleam of its cheek, no longer flushed with fever, the tousled short dark mane, marveling at the renewal of life in a body where there had been almost certain death before. This was a miracle, part of some wondrously buoyant pattern never before pointed out to her. She had known in a vague way that Restorers drove out sickness and mended bodies, spending their lives in the pursuit of *return/to/balance*, but had not understood the reality of it, that they actually restored life to that which would otherwise perish. Restorers possessed power over death itself, a heady concept. And headier still was the fact Vexk seemed to think she had some potential for Restoration herself.

She knelt at the creature's side with the bowl of warm mash, then dipped a clean cloth in the thick meat-and-grain concoction and raised it to the creature's mouth to feed it as the youngest cublings were fed. It reached up and took the cloth in its own oddly made hand, piercing her with those unnerving eyes that were the same color as the very center of the sacred pool. She averted her gaze and tried not to shudder. How could these creatures allow such an unnatural trait in their breeders? Didn't they have the sense to cull themselves?

It licked the mash from the cloth, bared its teeth and passed the cloth back to Khea. "Good." It gazed at the steaming bowl. "More?"

Khea dipped the cloth again into the warm golden-brown mixture, then passed it back.

The creature ate another mouthful and sank back, closing its eyes. When Khea eased the cloth from its small hand though, it looked at her again. "You?"

The word was very strange in its flat mouth, as though that short pink tongue couldn't make the sounds properly. Khea glanced at the bowl. "More?"

"No." Its voice was faint. "You. You!" Its undamaged arm pointed at her, then fell back across its chest.

"Me . . ." Khea twisted the cloth in her hands.

"You." The creature moved its head up and down, then put one hand on its own chest. "Mit—su. You?"

Suddenly Khea understood. "Khea." The exchange of names warmed her, as though an age-mate had suddenly deferred to her judgement on a hunt or a full-fledged hunter had stepped aside to let her make the kill. "And you are called Mit-su."

The dark-maned head moved again in the same motion, only more wearily this time. There were dark splotches beneath its eyes.

"Sleep, Mitsu." Khea watched its eyelids descend. "Tomorrow, we must return to Vvok." Suddenly, from the front of this aboveground level, she heard angry voices. She glanced down at the creature, but it seemed to be sleeping now, its breathing even. Laying the cloth aside, she tracked the argument through the dim stone passageways.

"The creature is Vvok's, to do with as the Line

Mother will! If she chooses to rip out its life with her own teeth, that is her right."

Fur rose along Khea's shoulders as she recognized the angry tones: Fitila, the Vvok scout who had dragged the half-dead Outsider back to the hold just a few days before. Dread prickling along her spine, Khea searched until she saw familiar buff-colored fur through a doorway. "Elder-Sister," she murmured.

Fitila scowled as she turned from Vexk and a knot of several other Restorers to face her. "This is as much your fault as theirs. Why are you delaying here? The Line Mother has been commanding your return since yesterday!"

Khea knelt at Fitila's feet, the breath painfully short in her chest. "Forgive me, Elder-Sister, I did not know you had sent for us until this morning, and the creature has been so ill, we had no opportunity to come back."

"Fool!" Fitila's claws sprang free. "Seska no longer cares whether it survives or not! Now go and fetch it!"

Khea hesitated, remembering how hard the pale-furred Restorer had struggled against the Outsider's imminent death this morning. It was a wonder that it might live now. Surely this fragile life, won back with the sacred power of the Voice itself, was to be cherished and preserved? Without thinking, she looked up and gazed directly into Fitila's narrowed black eyes. "Could we wait a bit longer? It has just fallen asleep."

Fitila's claws raked her to the floor. She sprawled at the scout's feet, a strange roaring in her bloodied ears and a dark mist rising behind her eyes.

Someone shoved between them and hovered over her, examined her clawed face before turning back to Fitila. "Enough! Such displays defile this hold and the sacred pattern we follow! Take your temper elsewhere!"

Khea tried to rise from the floor, then slipped back.

"Seska contracted for a Restoration, which we have performed." It was Vexk speaking, she realized, Vexk interposing her own body between herself and Fitila's claws. "Now we shall name our price."

Khea dabbed at the warm blood dripping down her muzzle. Strange to realized the pale-gray Restorer had been bred out of Vvok, the same as Fitila and herself. She'd always thought nothing but anger and claws were bred there.

"Go ahead." Fitila's voice was arrogant and cold. "When has Vvok done other than honor her debts?"

A hand slipped under Khea's arm, braced her to stand. "Fetch the Outsider, youngling," Vexk said quietly in her ear.

Khea stumbled out of the room, then caught herself against the whitestone wall just outside, her vision still fogged.

Vexk's voice followed her into the hall. "Our price is that cubling."

Fitila snarled. "Breed your own cublings!"

"You know we cannot." Vexk's voice was clear and firm. "The Outsider is your property. By law, we may not prevent you from taking it back to Seska's claws, but we name the cubling ours to be trained as a Restorer."

Chapter Fifteen

Rakshal stalked into the great underground room, hackles raised, ready for confrontation from his declared challenger, Jikin, or some other, more impatient male, but the mood of the males' house was much altered from the last time he had assumed the Leader's place of honor by the central fire. The males, seated in concentric rows, shifted as he passed, restive and clearly waiting. The mumbling stilled as Rakshal stepped into place and appraised the assembled black eyes. "I come before you this night to speak of a threat to the very form of our lives."

Most ears pricked toward him, indicating a modest amount of interest, though the ears of some—the older, the most experienced—flattened. He let his gaze skip over those, not deigning to see. "Isen, who sponsored me, said before Outsiders soiled Anktan with their presence, every males' house could boast at least seven or eight who heard the Voice—but who hears the Voice now?" Rakshal waited, but only the fire answered, crackling as a cubling fed gynth branches into the hungry red flames. The soothing aroma wove through the varied scent signatures of the six distinct Lines, binding them into a single aroma quintessentially male, forging them into a unified body with a single will. "I hear the Voice— and no one else. And why not?"

The green-robed males leaned forward as he caught the eyes of each in turn. "Because no one *listens!*" He swelled his chest and allowed a note of triumph to creep into his tone. "Now that we have allowed the Outsiders to build their Dead-smelling hold in our drylands, the cublings talk about flying through the air like jits and speaking through metal boxes and killing with sticks instead of their own claws—and no one seeks out the Voice or the *patterns/in/progress* anymore. Fewer and fewer even understand what the patterns are with each generation. Chaos is but a breath away. We must scourge these Dead-smelling creatures from our land and return to the ways made for us at the Beginning of things before it is too late."

Understanding glimmered in their eyes and he felt encouraged. They were listening, finally, after seasons of disregard and disappointment. Perhaps there was yet a chance to return to order. "The patterns are meant to save us as surely as young Tama was saved from the river's green water this morning." For a blink, he let them relive that instant under the hot eye of Ankt when the Voice had led him to the trapped cubling. "Without direction, we will be swept away again into random, meaningless slaughter, each hrinn's claws set against all others, so that we are no better than the witless beasts we hunt."

Yafft, who had been ancient when Rakshal had first entered the Mish River Males' House as a cubling, stood up in the flickering shadows, his age-thinned body stiff and forbidding. "I agree that these creatures are strange, but being different is not the same as committing a wrong act. They ask many questions, but they never make war upon us or hunt our territories."

Rakshal bared his teeth so they caught the firelight. "They steal the dreams of our younglings with their chaotic, off-world ways. They are randomness incarnate. Is that not war enough for you?"

"Cublings are always foolish when they come to us from the Lines." Yafft's bowed black-furred form was difficult to see in the dim light. "It is our duty to speak sense to them, and our failure if they think of Outsiders and not the Voice."

"Yes!" Rakshal tasted triumph as the older male unwittingly gave him an opening. "It is *our fault* if we let these creatures tempt our younglings from the patterns that should give meaning to existence—*our fault*, if we let Outsiders sit on our land and through their own disordered lives, tempt us to chaos!"

Yafft stiffened. "You speak nonsense!" he said, but a low muttering surged through the large chamber. He glanced at the rows of males. "I, for one, close my ears to such drivel." His nose twitched distastefully as he turned and picked his way through the closely packed rows toward a side tunnel.

"Yes, nonsense . . ." Rakshal drew himself up to his full height, seeking to regain their attention as several of the oldest and most respected males followed Yafft out. "Nonsense like the Outsiders sending an outcast Levv male to us in the guise of the Black/on/black, seeking to fool us with a mere likeness of the sacred coloration." Rakshal's handclaws sprang free as he remembered his fury when gazing at that false black-furred face. "They mock us with this imposter! What will our younglings believe if we allow this creature to live when it cannot possibly have the power of the Voice behind it?"

Young Bral rose and pushed his way to the front, his buff-colored face puzzled. "But what does it matter? The Black/on/black is gone."

Rakshal raised his nose as though sampling the wind. "Yes, he has fled—coward that he is—with Nisk, who used to be an honorable male and a good Leader. You must see how he has disrupted the current *pattern/in/progress*; in the normal flow of things, Nisk should have remained here for many more seasons, sharing his wisdom with younglings yet to be born. Instead, he has gone off on a mad journey to sponsor this fraud, abandoning the males' house to younger, less experienced heads." His lips curled back from his teeth. "We must watch for the return of the false one and then feed its blood to the earth, just as we should tear down the white hold and sow the Outsiders' torn bodies into the lifeless sand. When they are gone, the patterns will be apparent again and we will be spared further abominations like Levv."

All around him, eager black eyes reflected the fire's flames and a chorus of low snarls signalled growing assent.

Thunder cracked, startling Heyoka from a deep and claustrophobic sleep. He bolted up in the darkness, heart pounding. Cold rain spattered his muzzle as he floundered to his feet, thinking he was back on Earth again, then he caught the herbal tang of vegetation characteristic to Anktan and sank back on his heels. For a second, memories flickered through his mind, blurred images, smells, sounds. He had stood on this hillside before, smelled this particular combination of plants. There had been screaming, and blood. He must have been here when Levv fell, as Nisk theorized, and he would never understand himself, what he had been then, and what he was now, until he fully remembered that terrible day.

Earth had never really been his home. When Ben had died, the Oglala people asked him to leave tribal land. For Ben's sake, they had tolerated him, but although some thought him a manifestation of the spirit world, the majority had regarded him as little more than a savage, half-sentient alien beast bought out of the flek slave pens. When they looked at him, they saw an animal, and his greatest fear had always been that they might be right. If he could not find out who he was here, where it had all started, he would spend his life as an outcast, roaming the edges of human society, never really part of anything.

Lightning snaked lazily across the sky, slowed by his distorted senses, still stained with the blueness that overlay everything. Despite his effort to sleep it off, he was still mired in the bewildering blueshift. He made out Nisk's huddled shape, stretched out a few feet away, and beyond him, the dark bulks of the two yirn. Thunder growled, vibrating the ground beneath him as rain pelted down more thickly. Heyoka tilted his head and let the fresh cold drops fall on his tongue. The rain, at least, felt real.

High above, another light flared, small and coherent, obviously artificial, lingering when a falling meteor would have faded. Staring at it, he felt the dim stirrings of having seen something similar before, but he was too tired to remember when or where. When the blue-black storm clouds swallowed it, he checked Nisk, but the older hrinn was so exhausted that even the thunder and rain did not wake him. The wind picked up, driving the rain sideways, filling the air with the odor of wet yirn wool and sodden hrinnti fur. Soaked and miserable, Heyoka turned—

A sharp metallic point jabbed the hollow of his throat. He froze as dark shapes loomed in the blackness, then reflexes took over. He rolled down a small ledge, landing on a jagged boulder that drove the breath out of his claw-marked chest. Feet squished after him in the mud as his attackers no longer took any pains to be silent. One of the yirn snorted, then leaped in slow motion, following him off the same ledge, narrowly missing his head as it drifted past him, careening on down the rock-studded hillside. He crouched in the darkness, gasping for breath and trying to get his bearings. The trackers from Jhii must have found them.

He heard Nisk's voice, still too distorted for him to make out. Heart racing, Heyoka dug his claws into the mud and climbed back up over the ledge. Another bolt of lightning illuminated the hillside, revealing a dozen or more dark-furred hrinn gathered around Nisk's fallen body while, a few feet away, several more strained to anchor the remaining frightened yirn.

One of them turned and spoke to him, slowly brandishing a spear that reflected the blue lightning like a torch. Slow, he thought. Although it would probably kill him shortly, he still had the bewildering advantage of blueshift speed. Diving for Nisk, he shoved the attacker with the spear aside and kicked another over the ledge before any of the attackers even managed to twitch.

As the lightning flash faded, he seized Nisk's slippery wet fur with desperate fingers. Thunder rumbled again and rain sheeted down as the surrounding hrinn moved sluggishly toward him. Gathering Nisk's limp weight in one arm, he tried to stand, but his weak leg slipped in the muddy grass.

Still, the others moved so slowly that he was up again before they could react. Nisk's hand twitched and Heyoka knew he must be alive. Bracing, he balanced on the good leg and swept the other under an attacker who was closing in. It fell in slow motion as he turned for the ledge, planning to follow the yirn back down the hillside until he could catch it and ride them both out of here.

Lightning cracked again, this time very near, filling the air with an electricity that stood his fur on end. Pulling Nisk's arm over his shoulder, he saw a dark figure pursuing him, only a few strides away and moving at normal speed as though he finally had a companion in this lonely blue realm. The face was so similar to his, it was like looking at a doppleganger. He dropped Nisk and tried to counter the spear point descending at his head, but it was moving even faster than he could. His arm rose to block it, but he saw he would be too late. At the last instant, the attacker changed his angle and caught him with the shaft full across his skull.

Just as Beshha drifted off into a languorous sleep, something *squawked* like a zzil with its tail caught between two rocks. Ears flattened, she scrambled out of her cushions and retrieved the small black box from behind a tapestry depicting Jhii First-Mother, then punched the button to silence it. One of these days, she thought crossly, the stupid thing was going to wake the whole hold, not that it was going to matter much longer if it did. "What?" she demanded.

"I've done it!" a voice said.

Beshha picked at a front tooth with a clawtip. "Who is this?"

"Fik, Line Mother of Qartt."

Beshha's ears pricked. "Is that just more loose talk, or have you finally found the nerve to jump into this pattern and get your claws bloody?"

"I'll shred your ears for that, you old yirn!" Even distorted by the tinny tones of the box, Beshha could discern the cold fury in Fik's voice.

"So you always say." Beshha arched her neck and preened the fur on her throat. "But of course you would have to come all the way up here to Jhii to do it."

"Don't think I won't! Now that I hold Qartt, I have no intention of hiding behind my daughters. I'll do my own fighting."

What an idiot. Beshha's eyes crinkled with annoyance. No wonder it had taken that ginger-haired moron so long to do in old Chytt. Such crudities as teeth and claws were part of the past. Those lovely Outsider weapons signalled a new pattern, one that employed the mind, not the body, to achieve the good things in life. She set the speaking box down on the carpet and groomed her rib fur. "Well, if you're so keen for action, why didn't you take care of those two scruffy males before they got all the way up here?"

"What are you talking about?"

"That Black/on/black male showed up nosing around Jhii with old Nisk." Beshha leaned back against her cushions. "I thought you and that lop-eared bunch from Vvok were going to take care of him." She reached for a leftover joint of kikinti, sniffed it, then pushed it away. Something freshly killed would have to be brought up.

"He got away from us. Just hold him and we will deal with him as soon as we can."

"Surely you don't think I'm stupid enough to keep them here?" Beshha's lip curled with distaste. "I sent them on, then dispatched a party of four to finish them—well away from Jhii." Pulling the cord out of her mane, she shook the dark-brown mass out over her shoulders. "Unfortunately, only two of the incompetent idiots lived to return and tell me of their defeat."

"You should have killed him while you had the chance!"

"And have every female in the hold telling the most outrageous tales at the next Gathering? You know how such things get around." She lay back on cushions worked with looping designs in golden thread, blinking thoughtfully at the ceiling. "If they are stupid enough to come back, they deserve to die and we will kill them then. For now, we'll call a Council meeting and exercise our new majority." Beshha closed her eyes and snuggled down into the gynth-scented softness. "We are going to have our way at last and there is nothing Kendd, or Rebban, or any of those ridiculous males can do about it."

❖   ❖   ❖

When Khea returned, the sleeping Outsider cradled in her arms, she could see in Fitila's outraged posture that the scout had not agreed to the Restorer's demand. Her own ears sank and she felt unutterably foolish. Access to such power as Vexk possessed was part of an immense, never-ending pattern, intertwined with the sacred matters of life and death themselves, vastly beyond her ability to even perceive, much less be a part of. A cull-face like herself could never hope to be worthy of anything like that.

The waxy smell of burning torches filled the air as the flickering shadows danced across the sand, adding to the atmosphere of restless agitation. Fitila gestured at two Vvok servants waiting with a litter. Her bared teeth glimmered like raw bone through the dimness. "Take your place and be quick about it!"

Her tone was threaded with menace and she could see how Fitila detested her for not being of the top rank, grudged even the air she breathed. Trembling, Khea settled the Outsider on the litter, taking care with its head, then wished for a blanket to cover the poor furless creature against the chill of the night breeze, but none had been provided, and she was reluctant to ask. She took up one of the litter poles, while the scout snatched up the other and stalked beside her in bristling silence. Reading beyond the anger in the stiff carriage of the older female, Khea realized Fitila must have fallen under the Line Mother's displeasure. Even in the dark, she could distinguish fresh welts and scabs on the scout's arms and neck.

As they struggled up the twisting path back to the red-orange cliffs, Fitila maintained her angry silence, only snarling when one of the slight-bodied servants lost its footing and endangered the litter. It was well into the hollow quietness of night by the time they reached the top and their tethered mounts.

Fitila turned to Khea. "Can that thing ride?"

"Not in this condition." Khea glanced down at the small sleeping body, lying very still on the litter. "But it weighs very little. I can take it up in front of me."

Relief flashed across Fitila's face. Khea realized just a few days ago, she had felt the same reluctance to touch it herself, but Outsider skin was not disgusting, was in fact much the same as hrinnti, only softer, more like a newborn's. She mounted the yirn, then reached down for Mit-su. The two servants handed the fragile body up and she took it in her arms, settling it against the yirn's hump. It mumbled in its strange language and turned to regard her sleepily.

Khea tightened her arm around it, then took up the reins. "Fitila is very angry," she whispered. "You must be quiet." The Outsider murmured a little more as Khea urged the yirn after the others, then it relapsed back into sleep. It was still so weak, Khea thought uneasily, gazing down at the small flat face.

Riding across the evenness of the plateau, the remainder of the journey went much faster. Her mount trotted after the others without direction, while she balanced Mit-su's dead weight and attempted to process the new concepts she had seen and heard since leaving Vvok. She'd had no idea of the immense power Restorers wielded. To preserve life, to actually snatch it back from the Gates of Death—she shivered and studied Mit-su's still face. Without Vexk, this creature would now be dead.

Just as they were nearing Vvok, the party breasted a small rise and turned aside at the sight of several torches burning yellow-green in the darkness. "Does it yet live?" a voice demanded.

It was Seska. Khea ducked her head respectfully. "Yes."

"Then pass it to a servant and return to the hold." The dark gray of the Line Mother's face was barely visible in the shifting light as the breeze twisted the torch flames.

"It is very weak." Khea clutched the frail body closer as a servant reached up for it.

"I do not care if it dies before Ankt looks on it tomorrow as long as the disgusting thing tells me what I want to know now." The Line Mother prowled closer, her ears pinned. "Hand it down!"

Mit-su stirred as Khea passed it into the servant's hands. "Khea?"

"The Line Mother wants to—talk to you." Khea's mouth felt very dry. "You must tell her anything she asks."

"Now go back to Vvok!" Fitila urged her yirn between Khea and the Outsider. "Your duties with this thing are at an end!"

The two servants who had accompanied Fitila, as well as the two who had been waiting with the Line Mother, started off for Vvok, which was just visible as a black outline against the lighter night sky up ahead. Khea's mount, anxious for home, trotted after theirs eagerly. She glanced back over her shoulder, twisting the stiff harness in her hands. What did the Line Mother mean to do with Mit-su? And why had she come out here to do it under the cover of darkness?

As the path to the outlying buildings curved, she suddenly urged her mount to lengthen its stride and come abreast of the others. "Take my yirn back to the pen," she said to the startled servants as she slid down the yirn's side. "And say nothing of this to anyone, or I will claw your noses off!"

Amazed at her uncharacteristically severe tone, the servants glanced fearfully at her, but said nothing. Khea watched them ride on toward the pen driving the extra yirn before them, then turned back. Her ears trembled at the magnitude of her disobedience as she slipped through scrubby brush.

Whatever the Line Mother intended for Mit-su was surely dishonorable, or she would not have chosen to do it away from the eyes of the hold. This was a dark pattern, disturbing in its implications. Khea had no idea what part a lowly youngling like herself could play, but she knew even a Line Mother was not free to disgrace the Line.

Chapter Sixteen

The transition from exhausted, fitful sleep to fearful consciousness was abrupt. Mitsu blinked up at two sharp-toothed, obviously malign faces looming over her. It was night, she realized, heart pounding, the metallic taste of fear in her mouth. She sprawled outside on the cooling earth, pummeled by a brisk evening wind that carried the smell of sand and acrid vegetation. Several torches had been thrust into the ground nearby and cast shifting, nightmarish shadows. Neither of the two hrinn who had cared for her wounds were present now, and those who were here seemed bristling and angry. She had a flash of that terrifying moment outside the males' house when another hrinn, the same buff color as one of these, had struck her down.

A stream of guttural Hrinnti was being thrown at her; she tried to concentrate, but her head was still fogged and they were speaking so fast she couldn't make sense out of more than one word in every two or three.

"What —— male —— do?" The buff-colored beast kicked her ribs. "What —— do ——?"

The blow was restrained, but pain rocketed through her tender side and shoulder, stealing the breath from her lungs. She curled against it, wondering what in the name of the All-Father Above these sodding beasts wanted from her. Racking her brain for a few scraps of Hrinnti, she managed to gasp out, "Slow—talk slow!"

A dark-gray hrinn, scarred and whip-thin, wrapped its fluttering red robes around itself and squatted beside her on the barren, sand-littered earth. "The Black/on/black, what does —— want?" Its eyes glittered like obsidian ice in the torchlight.

Black/on/black? Mitsu stared up at it. "Not—understand."

The hrinn reached out and flexed sharp claws through Mitsu's loose robe into the flesh of her arm. "Why —— Black/on/black —— back to Anktan?"

Back . . . Black/on/black . . . Flinching from the punishing claws, Mitsu finally connected the questions with Blackeagle. "Find—Line." She felt ill and sweat broke out on her forehead despite the cold night air. "Right word—Line?"

The hrinn cast her aside as it resumed its feet. "Levv —— dead! Does this male —— who —— Levv?"

The stars expanded and contracted, as though she floated on the vast rolling surface of some alien sea, borne on a racing current toward an unknowable destination. She'd traveled to those stars. Blackeagle had done his best to convince her to stay there, but she hadn't wanted to, though now she could not remember why.

Another kick connected with her wounded shoulder and shattered her thoughts. Pain knifed through her chest, paralyzing her lungs. Through tearing eyes, she saw the buff-colored hrinn draw back its leg again as she fought to hold onto the last shreds of consciousness.

Claws scrabbled over the sandy ground, accompanied by a low snarl as a furred body, pale against the night sky, appeared over a rise and launched itself at her tormentor. Mitsu shuddered as the two grappled in the shifting torchlight, so close she could have touched them. Sand pelted her face as they roared and tore at each other. The dark-gray hrinn prowled restlessly just out of reach, then finally found an opening to claw the newcomer off the other's back.

Without a pause, the pale-furred hrinn scrambled up and attacked the dark-gray. With a great deal of effort, Mitsu rolled out of the way of the snarling, writhing pair, getting a good look at the newcomer and recognizing the coat pattern—pale gray spotted with white—Khea!

The fighting pair slid over the sandy ground, coming toward her again. She tried to crawl out of their way, but the earth swept around her in great dizzying loops. The buff-colored hrinn leaped onto Khea's back and she fell heavily to the ground as it went for her throat. Obviously dazed, she gave a strangled cry, fought the buff-colored one off and limped into the darkness, streaming blood.

Breathing hard, the dark-gray regained its feet and strode stiffly back to where Mitsu lay half-blinded by pain and gasping for breath. Its fur was streaked with dark blood. "What —— Black/on/black —— Levv?"

Mitsu flinched. "Talk—slow," she whispered, and the guttural words rattled inside her head.

The beast seized Mitsu's robe in both fists and shook her as though it were a cat tormenting a mouse. "What —— male —— Vvok?"

Somewhere in her mind there were words to plead ignorance, but they wouldn't come. Mitsu's head rolled loosely as the hrinn raised her closer to its bared teeth. She felt its steaming breath on her face. She didn't understand. What did it want to know? Her fingers fumbled at the hands knotted into her robes.

With a snarl, it flung her back to the ground. A soundless blackness reached up to swallow her as her temple struck something sharp and unyielding.

Missa gazed out at her charges as they gathered to hear her nightly story. She was no true Teller, of course, but she had heard the tales in her youth, and what she didn't remember, she could invent. The cave vibrated with the comforting sound of the breathing of the younglings and herself. The earthen floor was cozily dry, insulated by several turnings from the entrance and the fearful buffet of the mountain storms now raging outside. They were *safe*, she thought, *safe*. She had to remind herself of that often, even now, after so many seasons. No one knew they were here. No one would sweep through this secluded cave in the night to finish the carnage they had wrought so long ago at Levv.

She began the tale of the First Gathering, studying the circle of waiting faces, the daughters of Levv for whom there would never be any such thing as a true Gathering. She faltered; such thoughts made her feel old and useless, just the remnant from an earlier era of grace and order, as out of place as a fragile pot put to work hauling rock, or a delicately woven festival garment worn to shreds on the trail. The life and customs she remembered had no meaning in this rough, unstructured existence that was all Levv could provide for its children now.

"And then what happened, Line Mother?" Young Nin's eager black eyes were bright with reflected flame.

"Hush, Nin, and you might find out." Missa flicked a tolerant ear at this brash youngster, who was less than half the size of her age-mates. Old Kef, *her* indomitable Line Mother, would have culled such an undersized cubling at birth, either abandoning her to die on some hillside, or designating her an unnamed servant, but Levv could ill afford to waste any of its precious few births these days. She sighed through her nose, feeling her own inadequacies. A proper Line Mother would have struck Nin to the floor for speaking before being addressed, much less making direct eye contact, but what had such polite standards to do with Levv now?

She tried to remember the next part of the old story as Nin snuggled back against her plains-bred age-mates. "Now, as I was saying, Uwn and—"

The yellow flames bent double as damp night air rushed into the cave from the covered entrance several chambers away. Missa lurched to her feet, alarmed. Kei and the others were back from their nightly patrol early. Perhaps, in spite of the weather, they had brought down some game. "You two." She selected several of the larger young females. "Run ahead and see if they need any help." The two younglings leaped up and disappeared around the bend. Missa limped after them as fast as her sore old bones would allow.

Entering the large communal chamber, she caught the scent of sodden fur and something more . . . the unmistakable musk of another Line. Fur prickled along her shoulders and spine and the old fear yammered at her. The last time she had detected the scent of another Line, most of Levv had perished.

Levv's young Leader, Kei, glanced up from where he knelt beside two still, drenched bodies on the stone floor.

"How many more?" she asked fearfully.

"There were only these two," Kei said. "We checked thoroughly."

Gathering her coarse brown robes around her bony body, Missa stepped over several puddles. The strangers were full-grown males, both black-furred, one in the black robes of a servant, the other clad in the tattered green of . . . She tried to remember, but she wasn't sure if green indicated the Mish River Males' House, or the Inner Mountains. A whine rose in her throat. What would a pair from either of those places be doing this high in the mountains? Had they come back to finish Levv? Were there more behind them?

One of the males had the distinctive white throat as well as the scent of far Kendd, but the other . . . She looked closer, then motioned for Kei to turn him over. As far as she could tell, the other was black with no off-color markings at all, and exuded the familiar scent of *Levv*. She stretched out her hand and made herself check the male's drenched undercoat: black as well.

"Black/on/black," Kei's deep voice said.

"And Levv." The words were only a hoarse whisper in her throat.

Kei raked his dripping mane out of his eyes. His expression was grim and disbelieving. "He looks my age, perhaps a bit younger. Was such a one as this born before the end?"

Missa felt dizzy. Wiping her wet fingers on the rough brown of her robes, she stood up and backed away. Fear surged through her. "I don't know. That was too long ago."

Kei seized her shoulders and gazed down with disrespectful directness. "You can remember all sorts of nonsense to fill the cublings' heads, when they should be learning how to hunt and weave and gather. Now tell me—was one like this ever born?"

Missa whimpered as the memories of that last day tried to force their way back into her consciousness— the terror . . . the blood . . . cublings torn from her arms and dashed against the rocks as she fled. Her eyes squeezed shut and she hung trembling in his hands.

Kei snarled, then pushed her away. She stumbled back against the cold cavern wall and huddled against the unforgiving rock.

"Bind them." Kei's voice was hoarse with anger. "And then get some sleep. If they survive, we will question them at first light."

Missa kept her eyes closed until Kei stalked out of the chamber, his stride as distinctive to her ears as the stride of any other member of Levv would be. Because they were so few, they knew each other far too well.

She stayed long enough to watch buff-colored Ais and black-furred Bey tie the two unconscious males with tough mountain vines, then fled to her place two rooms back with the other females. Alarmed, the young daughters of Levv looked up from weaving baskets and mats to stare at her frightened face with wide black eyes. "Go to sleep!" she snapped at them, then turned away as they huddled together in a mass of varicolored fur back by the wall in the rough rags that were all that was left to Levv now.

She was a poor substitute for a Line Mother and she knew it, although fortunately these deprived younglings did not. Still . . . Missa picked up a stick and poked the fire back to life, letting the familiar scent of wood smoke soothe her nerves as she watched the fat sparks dance upward. Even an early cull like herself could serve in the Line Mother's place, if she were all that was left, and so Missa had been—the only adult female left in Levv after the attack so long ago.

Curling up beside the fire, she shivered and closed her eyes. She could feel the blood-soaked dreams—her old enemies—stacked up behind her eyes, waiting to torment her through the night. She shivered. Kei would be furious, if she woke him again, and it distressed the younglings to hear her scream.

Khea hid behind a stand of scrub, dazed, but retaining at least enough presence of mind to remain upwind of her two Vvok elders. The smell of her own blood dripping into the sand was overwhelming, and her mind reeled with the enormity of her actions. She'd had no intention of challenging the Line Mother, yet somehow that was exactly what she had done. It was as though something outside herself had taken over, making her do bizarre things she had never dreamed possible. Was this what it was like to blunder into an emerging *pattern/in/progress*? Younglings, like herself, heard tales of the great patterns, of course, but were told nothing of their make-up or names. That knowledge was reserved for those of her elders who had the courage, wit, and stamina to pass all their gleanings. Only they had any hope of recognizing the shape of seemingly random events and then riding their crest to attain control.

The Line Mother appeared to have given up questioning Mit-su. The Outsider had lain still and unmoving for quite some time now, despite their efforts to make it talk. Khea's heart pounded. Perhaps it was dead.

Seska's chest heaved with frustration as she stood over the crumpled body. Dark streaks of blood dampened her own tattered robes. She hobbled over to the remaining yirn, mounted laboriously, then clawed it into a frenzied run back toward the outlying buildings of Vvok. Khea watched her go, trembling as she realized she could never return home. Having bared tooth and claw on the Line Mother and lost, her blood was now forfeit.

Fitila snubbed out the last torch, then threw the Outsider across her yirn like a sack of grain and rode off. Khea followed, taking care to stay upwind. Already stiff from the gashes that crossed and recrossed her throat and shoulders, her pace was painfully slow and she had to trail the other by scent. Her hold on consciousness faded in and out. Several times, she came back to herself to find she was wandering aimlessly under the indifferent glare of the stars, her

open wounds matted with sand and her mouth tasting
of ashes.

The wind picked up, moaning against the rocks and
drowning the lesser night sounds, as the trail led
toward the southern end of the plateau. Was the scout
going to the Outsider hold? A trace of hope formed
in Khea's mind. If the Outsider were returned to its
own kind, then it might yet survive, despite the
beating it had just suffered, and Vexk's efforts would
not have been in vain. Her ears sagged as she thought
of the Restorer's pale-gray face. Once Vexk learned
of her disgrace, she would turn her away, perhaps
even kill her, as would any of the Lines. She was
outcast now, less than the meanest unnamed servant,
meat for anyone's teeth.

She straggled up to the edge of the plateau to find
Fitila seated on the ground, her yirn tethered a short
distance away, apparently waiting for something, the
Outsider dumped at her feet with no more care than
if it were a bundle of trade goods. A self-contained,
strangely steady light burned before her on the
ground, definitely not a torch or any sort of true fire,
because it never smoldered, or wavered, despite the
erratic wind.

Fitila looked up as the air began to throb. Khea
crept along a low stand of stubby gynth bushes as
close as she dared while the other raised the light
above her head. The throbbing grew louder until she
made out a sleek black shape soaring through the air
like an oversized jit. It landed with a heavy thump
just inside the circle of light and the air quieted.
Khea's heart pounded as she caught the now-familiar
scent of Outsiders, then saw two of the flat-faced
creatures emerge from the thing's maw. Ears trembling, she crept closer. Even if she died for it, she
had to hear.

The two Outsiders spoke in Hrinnti, but the wind
snatched away their words. One set a box down on

the ground, opened it, then handed a slim black cylinder up to Fitila. She turned it over as the other seemed to explain something, then pointed it out into the darkness. A line of fierce green fire blazed and a bush burst into flames.

An Outsider weapon! Khea flattened her shaking body to the ground and forced herself to remain still as smoke billowed into the wind, although common sense urged her to flee. She had seen this much; she must see the rest.

Fitila tossed the cylinder back into the box, then mounted her yirn. One of the Outsiders handed both light and box up to her. She extinguished the light, then balancing the box before her, she rode back into the darkness toward Vvok, leaving Mit-su sprawled in the sand.

One of the Outsiders picked up her limp body, then climbed back into the sleek black thing. A few breaths later, the throbbing began again and it leaped into the air. Khea rose from her hiding place, head spinning, and stared down at the scorched bushes. Smoke still curled up palely into the darkness. She crushed a blackened stalk between her fingers, then scrubbed the soot from her skin with clean sand. The shape of this pattern baffled her. What could the Line Mother want with Outsider weapons? And why had Mit-su somehow been the price?

The screen in Sanyha's room beeped insistently again, then subsided for another twenty seconds. Throwing an arm over her face, she turned over and tried to focus on the screen through eyes opened to the merest slits. Damnation, she wasn't on call. What time was it anyway? Two? Three? Her mouth tasted like a toxic waste dump. The pale-blue screen beeped again and she floundered out of bed to grope across the room in its dim light. When she was close enough to read the message though, her irritation dissolved.

It wasn't Sickbay beeping her; it was the automatic response she'd keyed into the outside lock.

She snatched up a pair of discarded coveralls from the floor and palmed the doorplate while she hitched them up. Fortunately, the halls were empty at this hour as she ran through the complex so there was no one to ask what was the emergency. Three breathless minutes later, she jogged up to Eldrich and Allenby as they cleared the inner lock, handling a bedraggled, slight body clad in hrinnti robes between them. Bruises and abrasions covered the face of the small-boned woman and her head lolled to one side.

Without speaking, she bent over the unconscious woman and peeled an eyelid back with professional concern. The pupil contracted normally and Sanyha nodded, more to herself than the others. "I've seen worse. Let's get her to Sickbay."

"Are you sure that's really necessary, Dr. Alvarez?" Eldrich's cool gray eyes bored into her.

Sanyha's stomach churned. The undertones of this situation were so damn odd. "You've got to be kidding."

Eldrich smiled thinly. "Of course." He turned to Allenby. "Help the good doctor take Corporal Jensen down to Sickbay."

Allenby nodded, anxiety written across his pale pinched face.

"How soon do you think she'll be able to talk?" Eldrich released the girl as Allenby took her full weight across his own shoulders.

Sanyha frowned and reached for the girl's wrist, then counted silently for ten seconds. "It's hard to say," she lied and released the wrist. "Does it matter?"

"I'm sure you realize Sergeant Blackeagle is still missing." Eldrich's voice was precise, smooth. "I was hoping she might know what had become of him."

"I thought you weren't going to authorize a search party."

The ghost of a smile flashed across his face. "I'm not. Still, I have to report. Keep me posted on her condition." He turned his back and walked down the passageway toward his own quarters.

Sanyha's jaw set as she watched him go. *What in the Thirty-eight Systems was that all about?* His aloofness sent a chill snaking down her spine. She looped one of the Jensen woman's arms around her shoulder, then motioned with her chin at Allenby. "Come on." Even without looking, she could feel him scuttling along beside her.

Chapter Seventeen

When Kei returned to the outer chamber in the morning, the older of the two intruders had regained consciousness. He was a well-formed black, highly muscled, just at the far edge of his prime. He had a jagged cut on one arm, another on the back of his head, but was not badly hurt. A familiar cast to his ears whispered Levv lay somewhere in his heritage, but the breadth of his chest and shoulders, as well as his scent, plainly stated his matrilineal descent was through another Line. That was all lowlanders counted, the distinctive scent-signature of male descent only being discernible at birth, fading after the first few days of life, and unacknowledged thereafter.

The other male, who so unaccountably smelled of Levv, had not moved even a hair from the spot where Kei had dumped him the night before. Surprised, Kei hunkered beside the still body. It was his blow that had felled the intruder and he had not struck that hard. Beneath the tattered green robes, he saw now an odd shiny black thing encased the male's right leg from knee to ankle. Kei prodded it with one finger; it was hard and cool to the touch with a tiny green light inset close to the knee. The fur behind his ears prickled—it was an Outsider device. The old males had spoken of such before the last of them died fighting to protect Levv. Remembering that day, he rubbed a twisted scar on his own muzzle.

A body-length away, the white-throated male followed Kei's movements with his eyes. "You are Levv."

Kei twitched an ear in acknowledgment. "Why have you come here?"

"He is also Levv." Indicating the Black/on/black with his nose, the male struggled against his bonds to sit up, but fell back against the rough rock floor. His eyes gleamed with desperation. "He is very ill."

Kei examined the unconscious male, seeing how shallow his pants were, how his tongue lolled out on the stone. Resisting the urge to touch that legendary Black/on/black fur, he rose. "Levv is dead."

"And yet you survived." Bunching his muscles, the male managed to flop awkwardly over onto his stomach. "He survived, too, because somehow he left this world for another, but he will not live much longer without aid."

"Another world?" Kei had heard vague rumors of such things. His lips curled back, baring his teeth in a fierce grimace as he thought of the years of scrounging and hiding that had been the lot of the remaining children of Levv. "How?"

"I do not know, and since he came to us looking for answers, I assume he does not know the whole story either." The male hunched up into a sitting position in which Kei knew the tightly knotted vines had to be cutting off his breath. "But he can answer none of your questions, if you allow him to die."

Kei leaned down and pressed his fingers to the Black/on/black's muzzle where the fur was thinner;

the other's skin temperature seemed dangerously low. "I did not strike him that hard."

"He is suffering from drawing power without proper preparation."

Kei sat back on his heels; that made sense. He remembered how, in the rain the night before, he'd been forced to use the Old Ways himself in order to capture this one. The Black/on/black had moved with the augmented speed that smelled of power and he had been obliged to do the same himself, or these two would have escaped to take word back to the Lines of their survival, assuring the extermination of Levv.

Kei stood up. "Ais will bring him food when he wakes."

"It has gone beyond that!" The other male tugged uselessly at the fibrous vines. "He has used power constantly through the last few days without preparation of any kind, and with little food or sleep after. He must replace the raw energy he used."

"What makes you think we even have a pool?" Kei's nose twitched at the thought of allowing a stranger into such a sacred place. "And why would we allow him to use it, if we did?"

"He is Levv! He is of your Line!"

"Males have no Line." Kei felt a muscle in his jaw jump. "Is that not what you teach down below in the males' houses?"

"Many things are taught there, including *honor/ among/ gender.*" The male stared up at him with angry eyes.

"What do you care?" Kei looked up as Bey entered the chamber, his dark-brown fur contrasting with the two black-coated males. "Whatever he is, he is not of your Line." Bey studied him expectantly, waiting for direction.

"I have sponsored him, because I believe long ago his life was spared for a reason. The attack on Levv was the beginning of a massive, unnamed pattern, unlike anything ever recorded, and he is at its center. He has something important to do. You cannot let him die now!"

Patterns! Kei's ears flattened in disgust. The five older ones who had come back, Nael and Sunet and the rest, had occasionally spoken of such things in an attempt to explain the forces that controlled the universe, from the growth of the smallest plant to the decision of their fellow hrinn to exterminate Levv.

He had never understood, though, how something without substance could supposedly make him act in any way other than what he'd originally intended. At every turn, from his earliest seasons, *he'd* had charge of his life, deciding where to go, what to kill, how to protect the others. In the end, he had discounted such stories as tales fit only for the smallest of cubs. He believed in what he could smell and see and touch, nothing more. With a snarl, he bent down and cut the damp, shredded robes from the motionless black body and cast them aside into a sodden heap.

The stranger was black from the tips of his feet-claws to the end of his nose. Kei sat back, thinking. He was Black/on/black himself, except for faint buff streaks behind his ears. Missa said Levv had always bred many fine black-coated hrinn, marked with only modest amounts of white or brown, but this one was more. Not even a single off-colored hair marred his perfection. To the eye, he did appear to be *the* Black/on/black straight out of legend, predestined for greatness . . . sacred.

Which, like patterns, was only more nonsense, but noses did not lie. Whatever else he might be, this one had been born of Levv, and so few were left that none could be spared.

He turned to Bey. "Release that one."

Bey reached for his knife as Kei bent over the Black/on/black and sawed through the tough vines with his own blade, salvaged long ago from the ruins of Levv. He could feel Bey's curiosity, but he had no intention of trying to explain any of this to the others now. He didn't even know how to explain it to himself.

The rich smell of coffee filtered through the muzziness of sleep and Mitsu stirred. Someone must have been down to the mess already. Time to roll out. She pried open her right eye, but her left one seemed swollen shut. Had she been fighting again? A woman's oval face framed in long dark hair moved into her field of vision. "Well, hello. I'm Dr. Alvarez. You're going to be all right, but you took some bad licks and have quite a shiner there." She touched Mitsu's left eye.

The gentle pressure hurt like hell, bringing back the pain of the last few terrifying days, her injuries, the hrinn. Her heart began to race. "Blackeagle?" she managed in a voice like rusty nails.

The doctor studied her with concerned brown eyes. "Sergeant Blackeagle went back out to find you, and no one has seen him since."

"Damnation!" The word came out in a hoarse half-whisper. "My fault! He told me—" She would not cry! With an effort, she took a steadying breath. "I would kill for a cup of that brew."

Dr. Alvarez poured a steaming mug of coffee, then raised the bed and loosened the blanket so she could sit up. "What happened to you?" She perched on a stool beside the bed as Mitsu sipped the strong dark liquid. "You've been out—what? Three or four days now?"

Mitsu tried to think back, but it was mostly all just a blur of cramped earthen rooms combined with pain and fever. "I don't know." The coffee warmed her throat, making words a little easier. "Someone jumped me outside the males' house, but then afterwards they tried to patch me up."

Dr. Alvarez sipped at her own mug. "Strange. Hrinn are very wary of humans. They don't like anything about us, especially the way we smell. I can't imagine why they would take care of you, instead of just abandoning you or bringing you back here."

"Yes, Doctor," a polished voice spoke from the doorway, "why *did* our furry friends insist on entertaining the young lady so long?"

Mitsu stared at the stubby silver-haired man entering the room, then finally put a name to his stony face: Eldrich.

"How nice that you're feeling better." He helped himself to a mug of coffee. "I need to talk with you a few minutes."

Dr. Alvarez glanced up, disapproval tightening her lips. "She's been through the wringer. She needs rest."

Eldrich's gray eyes drilled Mitsu over the top of his mug as he sipped his coffee. She felt unaccountably cold as he murmured, "We have to clear up a few matters."

"Five minutes then." Dr. Alvarez crossed her arms. "But try not to tire her out."

Eldrich sat on the edge of the counter. "Run along, Doctor."

Alvarez's head jerked up. "What?"

"If you wish to continue your employment here, you will give us some privacy." He glanced at the door. "Have I made myself understood?"

She hesitated, then palmed the doorplate and stalked out. Eldrich waited until the door slid closed behind her. "Now, Corporal Jensen, tell me again why you and the departed Sergeant Blackeagle came to Anktan, and this time I want the truth."

Unnerved, Mitsu drained the last of her coffee. Damn, her first impression of this glacial bastard hadn't done him justice. Blackeagle might well be dead, as a result of her stupidity, and he was just standing here, radiating cold interest like a monument chipped out of ice. "Sergeant Blackeagle wanted to search for his family."

"An interesting fiction." Eldrich moved from the counter to the edge of her bed. "But you and I both know this culture possesses nothing resembling family in the human sense of the word." His fingers drummed on the blanket. "I want to know your real mission here on Anktan."

A bead of sweat broke out on Mitsu's forehead. "I don't know what you're talking about."

He wrenched her wrist back. "What have you reported?"

With an oath, Mitsu twisted her arm free. "Don't touch me, unless you're ready to die!" A buzzing white mist sprang up behind her eyes. The breath rasped in her chest. The claustrophobic memory of her time underground swept back over her, a dark and airless universe of pain. She locked her hands to keep them from shaking. "Look, no one sent us. We came here for our own damnfool reasons, which you already know, so there's nothing to tell. What do you think we want?"

"Stop playing games. Either you level with me now, or you'll have to answer to someone higher up later."

The room began to swim. Mitsu lay back and pressed her fingers over her eyes. "This is stupid. I don't know anything. I just came here to back up my partner."

"Fine." Eldrich's voice became smooth again, like a wall with no doors. "Hold to that ridiculous fiction for now. We will continue this conversation later."

Ankt's red eye glared down balefully as Khea came back to herself. Head swimming, she sagged against the red-orange wall of rock towering over her, shivering, despite the mounting heat. Tiny black wind-nits buzzed around the clotted blood on her throat wound, but the effort to brush them away seemed too great.

She wasn't far enough from Vvok though. Someone might still come upon her, so she summoned her last shreds of energy and climbed the next boulder. Ahead, a low whitestone roof shimmered in the morning heat. Heart pounding, she ducked back into the shadows. After wandering all night, she had no idea where she was, but the best she could expect from any Line, especially Vvok, would be death, and it was much more honorable to seek that on her own terms.

Low voices echoed through the rocks; she saw red and brown fur appear as someone approached her through the maze of stone. Frantic, she turned and climbed back through the boulders, a scarlet mist rising behind her eyes.

"Khea!"

She had been recognized. A vast river of shame flooded through her; she could not bear for anyone she had known before to look upon her now. She was outcast, unclean, unfit to live.

Claws scritched over stone in pursuit. "Khea, wait!"

She looked back over her shoulder into a tricolored face. It was Cimmi, who had tended the Outsider alongside her just—yesterday? Frantic, she redoubled her pace, unwilling to face her, or anyone of the Restorers' Guild. She wanted only to hide in the rocks and wait for death.

As she tried to climb, the redness behind her eyes thickened until she couldn't see and her legs buckled. Warm wetness soaked her gashed throat as she fell backwards. She lay there panting.

Running feet padded up behind her, worried voices whispered. She caught Cimmi's scent again, this time mingled with another's. Raking her handclaws into the stone, she tried to rise. The scents behind her grew stronger, and she made out Vexk, the one person she could not bear to see now. With a convulsive effort, she rose to her knees, then wavered, unable to go farther.

"Youngling, wait!" Vexk called in a breathless voice.

"No!" Khea labored to say, but her voice was no more than the faintest whisper.

Vexk dropped to the ground and touched her clawed face. Khea dropped her head back to bare her slashed throat. "Take my worthless life so no one else can look upon my shame!"

"No, child, your death is not part of this pattern." Vexk ripped a piece of her own robes to staunch the blood from her throat, then drew her upright.

The redness behind Khea's eyes was spinning, pulling her down into an angry vortex of pain and despair. "You do not know what I have done!"

Vexk urged her onto her feet, then supported her as her legs almost gave way again. "By coming to us, you salvage Vvok's honor. Nothing else matters."

Unable to protest, Khea allowed herself to be led away, but she knew that later, when they understood what she had done, they would deal with her like the nameless thing she had become.

A hint of warmth crept back into the freezing universe of blue that imprisoned him on every side. Heyoka's nose and fingertips tingled, then he flexed his fingers and the circulation surged in an agonizing wave that convulsed his muscles and tied him into knots of pain.

"Lie still!" The words were spat in Hrinnti close to his ear. He relaxed and the pain ebbed, although the blood thrummed through his hands now, and he began to feel his arms again. The air was dank and vaguely sulfurous. Water lapped against stone somewhere close-by but he couldn't summon the strength to open his eyes.

"Black/on/black—I still don't know if I believe it." The words, spoken behind him, echoed as though in a large enclosed space.

"Black/on/black and *Levv*, think of that," said a

second, more distant, voice. "Do you believe what the other one said, that he was sent to us?"

"Don't be stupid. If the Voice meant to help us, why wait until now? It would have happened long ago."

The tips of Heyoka's ears hummed with returning circulation now. One of them twitched involuntarily, sending pain down through his neck and jaws. He convulsed, then choked on an unexpected noseful of water.

A hand braced his head back. "Idiot! I told you not to move."

The pain retreated, leaving in its place the slow advance of warmth into his toes and feet, which then seeped into his legs. He pried his eyes open and gazed blearily around. He was floating in a vast pool of some sort in a cavern hewn out of dark rock. Several torches had been wedged into holes high up on the walls and burned with a steady yellow-green light. The water was oven-hot, obviously a hot spring of some sort, enveloping him up to his neck and steaming into the cooler air. Stretching cautiously, he found he could move his fingers now with less pain.

And the world was colored normally. Somehow he had escaped the terrible blueness without dying, but where was he—and what had happened to Nisk? They had been camped on the side of the mountain, then the others had come upon them. He remembered being struck down, nothing after that. "Where—is this place?" He tried to twist around and see who held his head.

The hands released him, but the water was quite buoyant and he floated on his own. A black-furred hrinn with a wild, unbound mane and a scarred muzzle swam to the edge of the pool and heaved out, water streaming from his black fur. Another male, shorter, with dark-brown fur, sat on his heels by the wall, a spear in one hand, watching him with an avid expression.

Heyoka dug his handclaws into the rock at the pool's edge to keep from being washed under. His head felt stuffed with mud. He had no idea what he was doing in this pool, or who these hrinn were. "Why have you brought me here?" he asked. "What do you want?"

The black-furred male, much deeper than he was through the chest and more muscled, shook himself, sending drops of water flying through the air. His black eyes burned down at Heyoka like pools of molten obsidian. "Fool! We want nothing from you. We merely brought you here to save your life. Levv, or not, I should have left you to die out in the storm."

Levv. The scent of the other's wet fur permeated the air, oddly familiar. Images swept through his mind. *Angry, snarling voices . . . pain . . . sliding down steep inclines . . . falling, running until he thought his lungs would burst . . . falling again—*

The male stared down at him, nostrils flaring. "The other said you fled to another world. I find it hard to believe a Levv would disgrace himself by running away like a frightened yirn!"

"I did not—run away." Heyoka flopped up onto the rock shelf at the pool's edge, then lay there, trembling from the effort. The water, reflecting the black of the surrounding rock, washed over the ledge, then subsided into diminishing waves. "I was taken prisoner and made a—" He hesitated. There was no precise analog for slave in Hrinnti. "—an unnamed servant to another species."

The other's ears flattened. "Only the earliest culls become servants!"

Heyoka shivered as the cool air penetrated through his fur to his wet skin. The male scowled, then kicked him unceremoniously back into the water. "I did not spend half the day sweltering in that pool just so you could kill yourself now. Stay in there until I say you are fit to come out."

Heyoka choked as his head went under, then flailed for the side and hung by his clawtips. Through layers of exhaustion, the long-suppressed violent *other* in the back of his mind surfaced. How dare this hrinn, this savage, treat him so? He was their kinsman, unjustly forced into slavery, now—against all odds—returned from the vastness of space. They should be welcoming him, not abusing him. His lip curled in a silent snarl.

The male snatched a heap of discarded brown cloth off the floor. "I am Kei, Leader of what is left of Levv." His head brushed the top of the cave. He had to be the tallest male Heyoka had seen yet, a good nine inches taller than himself.

He pulled the shaggy, wet mane back from his face, revealing an ugly black scar that snaked across his muzzle from right eye to left jaw. "Stay in that pool, or I will shred your ears and feed them to the females." Ducking his head, he disappeared around a bend in the rock wall.

Heyoka stared after him as the significance of that twisted, shiny scar penetrated his brain. It matched the one he bore on his leg. He'd stake his life that Kei had suffered a laser burn across his face.

A flek laser burn.

Chapter Eighteen

Eeal Eldrich slid a compact laser pistol in his pocket, then checked his watch: thirty more seconds. He allowed himself a glimmer of satisfaction. The explosion in the motor pool would solve two problems at once, thus conserving energy. Matters were coming together nicely.

A muffled boom shook the station and he stepped out into the corridor. A smile tugged at his lips, but he dismissed it. It would not do to manifest an inappropriate response at this late stage. It grew more difficult every day to maintain his pretense. Soon, though, his kind would own this miserably frigid rock of a planet and then they would dispense altogether with the humans that infested this station. His job would be at an end and he could go back to his people. He smoothed the bulge in his pocket and set off toward Sickbay, two intersections away.

Off-duty personnel raced past him in answer to the alarm. Keeping his head down, Eldrich quickened his pace until he reached the door and slipped inside.

No sign of Dr. Alvarez. This time he did allow himself to smile.

The Jensen woman was sitting up in bed, her eyes on a screen filled with emergency instructions. He punched the console off. "Feeling better, Ms. Jensen?"

"Corporal Jensen." Her bruised face stared back at him from under a tangled mop of short black hair. "What's going on?"

Nasty stuff—hair, Eldrich thought. Fortunately, the body he now wore had little. Why didn't humans just depilate their whole bodies? "Only a small mishap." He edged closer to the bed. "Matters are already in hand."

Her unsettling blue eyes were fixed on him. Eldrich had always thought eyes were humans' most disgusting feature, so small and such a myriad of bizarre colors. No wonder his kind would never consent to live in the same universe with this loathsome looking lot. He was going to take great pleasure in annihilating this particular hive himself.

"Have you had any word on Blackeagle?" Her tone was low, tense.

The status board above the bed revealed that her heartbeat was accelerating. He made his voice soothing. "As a matter of fact, yes. He's in my office, being debriefed."

She blinked, then leaned forward. "That's great! Is he okay?"

"None the worse for wear, as they say. I'll send him to visit you as soon as the staff has finished questioning him. They're beside themselves with excitement. He's gained a wealth of information, so it may be several more hours, even longer, unless . . ." He paused. ". . . unless you feel up to coming along yourself."

"Of course I do." She slid her feet out of the bed, then swayed as she tried to stand. A bead of sweat broke out on her forehead. She brushed it away and pushed herself onto her feet. "I need some clothes."

"Oh, just slip on a robe." He waved his hand at the garment lying across the foot of her bed. "No need to be formal. Everyone here understands what you've been through."

She picked up the robe, then hesitated. "It would only take a minute for me to get dressed."

The skin between Eldrich's shoulders crawled. He had to get this miserable female out of the medical facility before casualties from the explosion began to arrive, and the stupid hiveless body which he was trapped inside could hardly carry her fast enough, if he was forced to subdue her, not to mention the attention that would likely attract. "Well, if you're not up to it—"

Her face drawn and pale, she sighed, then gingerly slid her bandaged arm through the loose blue robe. "No, I'm fine."

"Very well." He palmed the door. "If you're sure."

Flek! Just thinking of his old enemy made Heyoka's heartbeat quicken with years of ingrained battle reflexes. Flek remade the worlds they took with a vicious thoroughness so that the atmosphere became poisonous and nothing of the native ecosystem survived. From the beginning, they had ignored all efforts of other species to communicate with them, whether to parley, negotiate, or compromise. If there was even the slightest chance they had invaded Anktan, he had to know.

Bunching his shaky muscles, he heaved halfway out of the warm embrace of the water and lay there gasping like a beached fish on the black rock, fur plastered to his skin. The backwash lapped against the sides of the thermal pool and the warm, sulfurous smell intensified. After a moment, he summoned the strength to draw his legs out of the water too, then lay on the rock, dripping and exhausted. He felt burned somehow, as though fire had swept through his brain and left in its wake only ashes.

Muffled voices came from around the bend in the wall, then Kei reappeared, carrying an armful of brown cloth. His eyes glittered angrily in the torchlight. "I told you to stay in the pool!"

Bracing a hand against the wall, Heyoka levered himself onto his feet. "I have to know what happened to your face."

Kei bristled. "That is not your concern, *coward*."

"I did not run away!" Heyoka met Kei's feral gaze, finding nothing of himself in those hot black eyes, nothing he could relate to, or understand. Kei would obviously like nothing better than to tear his throat out, and his own instincts were advising the same, but he had no idea why. Both outcast, related by blood and similar in size and coloration, shouldn't they be allies?

Kei flung the garments he carried at Heyoka's chest, then stalked out of the chamber, fury written into every line of his body.

Heyoka unrolled a brown overtunic and tugged it over his wet shoulders. The fabric was coarse, but sturdy, and the warmth steadied him so that he was able to straggle after Kei through a series of irregularly shaped chambers until he emerged outside. Kei, his claws ready, his lip curled in a snarl, whirled upon him. He fell automatically into a defensive stance, his own ears flattened. *Attack!* the *other* insisted inside his head. *See how he brazenly stares you in the eye, bares his claws, shows his fangs—tear his throat out before he rends the flesh from your bones!*

They stood there, locked in each other's gaze. The red sun hung low in the western sky and the shadows were long and jagged. The breeze stirred, filled with the scents of sun-baked earth and stone, leaves crushed beneath their feet. A row of spears stood against the rock entrance. He longed to snatch one and thrust it deep into Kei's belly.

The bushes to the right crackled, then Nisk appeared, several small limp game animals tied at the feet and thrown over his shoulder. He gazed inquiringly at the two of them.

His heart racing, Heyoka pointed at Kei. "Look at his face!"

Nisk studied the thick scar twisting from eye to jaw. "An Outsider weapon?"

"Yes, but Outsiders are not all the same." His voice was strained. "That scar was made by a weapon used by only one kind of Outsiders, the kind I have fought against for most of my adult life."

Kei dropped his gaze and rubbed the scar self-consciously. "Why would Outsiders shelter you, if you fought them?"

Heyoka's legs threatened to buckle. He needed to sit down, but sensed he would lose what little credibility he had left, if he did. "I lived among *humans*, the Outsiders of the drylands. Your face was scarred by a *flek* weapon, the same kind that injured my leg. Flek don't study other lifeforms, as humans do. They simply take whatever they want and kill whoever gets in their way."

"Outsiders are Outsiders! Sometimes they are foolish enough to dare our mountains, but we always kill them all!" Kei picked up one of the spears and thrust it toward the slate-gray crags stretching above them.

Cold, gelid as the naked vacuum of space, swept over Heyoka. "*Outsiders* come into these mountains?"

"From the other side. There are many, more than I can count." Kei's nose wrinkled in disgust, then he bared his double rows of strong white teeth. "Let them come back a thousand times—we will kill them all!"

"If there are flek on Anktan, then all the hrinn on this planet together could not kill them." Heyoka ran a hand back over his sagging ears. Bone-deep weariness dragged at him until he couldn't think straight. "I must see these Outsiders for myself."

Kei's ears flattened at the implied order in his voice and for a second it seemed he would spring, but then he turned aside. "Tonight." He spat the word in a half-snarl. "We will go when Ankt sleeps."

The gray-and-white cubling whimpered and Vexk returned to her side. She had dosed Khea with a sleeping potion, but apparently not enough; the youngling's sleep was shallow and troubled. Vexk wondered again exactly what had taken place when Fitila and Khea had returned to Vvok. Why had Seska disciplined this cubling so severely? Was she at fault for demanding the youngster in payment, or was something larger at work here, some pattern for which she had no reference?

Khea's eyes flew open and she stared around the dimly lit chamber.

"You are safe here." Vexk made her voice low and soothing. "Go back to sleep."

"But the Outsider!" Khea's gaze was wide and fixed. "They will kill it!"

Vexk's ears flattened. Did this center around that poor weak creature?

Khea blinked as the herbs in her system began to take effect again and drag her back into sleep. "It—it does not even have claws." Her eyelids sagged.

Vexk pressed her back into the soft pile of cushions and the cubling lacked the strength to resist. "Who will kill it?"

"Fitila," Khea mumbled, ". . . and the Line Mother. They . . . they . . ."

"What, youngling?"

"Light . . . light that . . . burns." Khea's eyelids

fluttered. "The Outsiders brought light that . . . burns. I saw it."

A weapon of some sort? She touched Khea's shoulder. "Why did the Outsiders bring the light that burns? Was it to wrest the Outsider from Vvok?"

"Fitila . . . took the light." Khea's head tossed on the pillows. "Burned . . ." Her voice trailed off into senseless mumbling.

Disturbed, Vexk soaked the cloth again in the herbal infusion and squeezed a few more drops into the cubling's mouth. Perhaps now she would rest more peacefully. For herself though, there would be no sleep tonight. If she understood even a little of what Khea had seen, something was definitely out of balance.

The Outsiders had always been very careful with their weapons. She had heard of lights-that-kill, but in all the time since Outsiders had been a presence on this world, they had steadfastly refused to share them with the hrinn. Yet now Khea had seen Fitila with one. A new pattern was arising, something dark and furtive, full of teeth and claws and death. She feared to see the shape of it complete.

Someone had tossed a branch of gynth leaves onto the fire just inside the cave. Nisk savored the soothing scent as he studied the Black/on/black, outlined against the early evening darkness near the cave entrance, head bowed. His limp was more pronounced and he had obviously lost weight from his ordeal.

The males and females of Levv, coming and going from the cave, passed him without comment, but Nisk saw the way they looked at him, the unspoken deference written into their posture. He himself had difficulty approaching Heyoka now, which irritated him, but it was one thing to speculate that a figure out of legend had reappeared to join an emerging pattern and quite another to actually witness him accomplishing feats no hrinn should be able to even attempt, much less survive. The only one who seemed unaffected by the implications was Kei.

In the ordinary way of things, those who could absorb enough old power to attain blueshift speed could sustain it only for brief bursts, the length of a fight, perhaps, or a hunt, at most part of a day; but the Black/on/Black had gone on in that manner for nearly two days without drawing power first, or replenishing it after. He *was* more than other hrinn, as the legends had promised, however little he appeared to understand such things himself.

Kei emerged from the cave and handed Nisk a huge curving longbow. He fingered the smooth length of polished wood, noting the careful work down to the protective glyphs carved into the grip, then drew the string and sighted along his arm at the dark outline of a tree. The balance was true. "A fine weapon."

"It belonged to Seill, one of those who renounced his males' house and came back to us after Levv was destroyed." Kei sank to his haunches on the grass and stared out into the night sky. His black eyes reflected the starlight. "We were only a few frightened cublings in the days after. We didn't know where to go, what to do. Without them, we would have died."

Nisk had known Seill, a raw-boned dark-gray from the Inner Mountains Males' House. "He is dead?"

"All those who came back died in the first battle we fought in the valley against the Outsiders. I smelled death that day myself." Kei touched his scarred muzzle. "Since then, I have been oldest, so I have had to decide everything."

"What of the females?"

Kei's eyes narrowed. "I decide for them too."

Nisk shifted uneasily. "Grown males do not concern themselves with such things."

"The oldest surviving female, Missa, was an early

cull, hardly better than an unnamed servant." Kei
stared into the darkness. "We can trust her to do little
more than tell ridiculous tales and watch after the
youngest cublings."

Males and females living together as one big hold!
Nisk's nose twitched with indignation. "It isn't proper
for grown males to live with females."

Taking out a bit of rough brown cloth, Kei took
the bow back and began to rub an aromatic herbal
paste into the dark wood. The scent filled the air. "Do
not speak to me of things that are proper!" His voice
was gruff. "Was it *proper* for the Lines to slaughter
females and cublings who had never committed any
wrong?"

Nisk glanced uneasily at the big black-furred male.
What choice had been left to this ragged bunch of
survivors, he asked himself, except to live as they
could? But still—! He couldn't imagine how Kei
managed such an odd and unhealthy arrangement. He
must help them sort themselves out as soon as
possible. The madness had been declared to run
through the female line, after all, not the male, so
perhaps he could sponsor Kei and some of the more
promising others and get them accepted into a males'
house where they could learn how to conduct themselves.

"What would you have had me do?" Kei kept his
eyes on his hands as he polished the beautiful old
bow. "Go off, as was 'proper,' and leave the females
in the care of a witless, half-crazy old *servant*?"

Nisk kept silent, remembering the tawny striped
Line Mother who had ruled Kendd in his far behind
cubhood, stern Satta, whose claws had been quick but
fair. He tried to imagine an early cull in her place
and failed.

Kei handed the longbow back to him and stood,
his well-muscled body tall and straight as the trees
on this hillside. Nisk felt a surge of respect for this

indomitable young male. He was rough at the edges, and clearly knew nothing of the accommodations between males which allowed them to interact without tearing each other's throats out, such as the subtle dropping of gaze, or giving way without seeming to notice the other's presence, but he had faced unimaginable disaster and made far more of it than anyone would have ever expected.

"We will go now." Kei glanced over at the silent Black/on/black.

Nisk slung the bow over his shoulder, then accepted a leather pouch full of arrows. The Black/on/black fell in behind them as Kei led, as silent and impenetrable as the night itself. The path leading up to the pass wound above them, long and steep. Kei ghosted ahead in the darkness, seeming to touch nothing as he passed, leaving no sign. Behind, Nisk could hear the Black/on/black's uneven gait as he trudged wearily after them, favoring his weak leg.

Suddenly Kei froze, looking above them into the sky. Nisk gazed up too and sighted a strangely bright light, no bigger than the tip of a claw, moving as though it had purpose, as no proper star could. The Black/on/black threw his head back and watched, ears flattened, hackles bristling, until Kei moved on into the darkness and they had to follow, trying to keep their footing on the loose chaff that had eroded down from the pass up ahead. When the angle became too steep, Nisk followed Kei's example and dropped to all fours, digging in with his claws to keep from slipping.

The Black/on/black fell further and further behind, unable to match their pace with only one sound leg. Pebbles rattled back down the slope as Kei surged up to the opening between the crags first, then wedged himself there, waiting silently until Nisk joined him. Even though the night air was cool and sweet, he detected a faint, nose-burning stench as he scrabbled up the last body-length of bare rock. The wind sang against his face as he balanced on the knife-thin edge and gazed down upon an immense array of intersecting curves of light, white and gold and pink and green and blue, stretched out over the plains like the claws of a great slumbering beast. His throat closed—it was true then. He realized he had not really credited the Black/on/black's fears until now.

The jagged rock bit into his legs and he shifted to a more comfortable position. "Why did the plains hrinn allow Outsiders to build here?"

Kei's ears flattened. "The Outsiders burned them to ashes, along with the trees and the grasses and the kikinti they followed. We used to mate with the plains hrinn, who had no opinion about the fitness of Levv to exist, so cublings would be born and the Line would continue," Kei answered. "But then one season, when the time of Gathering arrived, we found only blackened husks lying scattered around the beginnings of this thing instead. When we got too close, Outsiders poured out and drove us back into the mountains with their terrible burning lights. The older males held them off long enough for the rest of us to escape, then died screaming as we ran." He turned his head as something scritched behind them in the darkness, but it was only the claws of the climbing Black/on/black.

Nisk reached down for his wrist and a blue spark jumped between them, as though, in spite of everything, he still held so much power, he couldn't contain it. Bracing himself against Nisk's weight, Heyoka swung up and settled heavily between the two of them. His head swiveled as he took in long curving tubes of light stretched over the dark floor of the valley, the smaller colored lights dancing back and forth, the unnerving stench which had grown stronger with a shift in the wind. Faint sounds reached them too, squeals, pounding, grinding. The creatures below, whatever they were, seemed very busy, even though it was dark. The Black/on/black's eyes were wide, his breathing rapid. He said something in that other, slippery language, shook his head and switched to Hrinnti. "This is much worse than I thought."

The bubble of light they had seen before in the sky descended to the ground with a shrill whine that carried back up into the mountains. Kei unlooped the longbow from over his shoulder and reached for an arrow. "You have fought these creatures before, so you know how to kill them. They are almost impossible to approach. Teach us how to drive them away."

"They cannot be stopped with a bow, or a spear, or claws." The Black/on/black fell silent, ears flattened in thought. "That thing down there is a *transfer grid* which will bring thousands and thousands of them here."

Kei snarled. "Why do they not stay in their own place?"

"It is not their nature." The Black/on/black stared down at the plains as the small light leaped up into the sky again. "We must go to the Outsiders on the other side of the river and get help as soon as possible. The *grid* looks almost complete, and once it is, no one will be able to save this world."

Chapter Nineteen

The last of the three worst burn victims died just after dawn. Staring at the body, still swathed in tubes beneath the portable Med, Sanyha longed to just lay her head down and weep with anger. It infuriated her to have to sit by a patient's side and watch him slip away when she knew a fully equipped Med could have saved his life, but no one had foreseen that a burn unit might be necessary here.

The smell of unguent and disinfectant filled the air as her temporary assistant, Alice, tended another patient. Sighing, Sanyha went through the motions necessary to consign the body to the crematory, then sat down before her screen to file the report. Halfway through the details, she sipped at her stale coffee and wondered again where Mitsu Jensen had gone. Obviously someone had transferred her out of Sickbay in order to make room for the incoming casualties, but she really ought to be checked daily. Those claw marks had been wicked.

Punching up the personnel roll, taken after the explosion, she scanned the list: no Jensen. Had someone forgotten to log her in, or—Sanyha grimaced—had she used the emergency to slip back outside to search for Sergeant Blackeagle? If all soldiers were as tough as she was, Sanyha was amazed the Confederation hadn't already won the war. She double-checked the lists, hoping she was wrong. If Mitsu Jensen took another bad mauling, she wouldn't survive.

This time she noticed a second name missing, Eldrich, and put in a call for Security.

A familiar face still smudged with black appeared on her screen. "Security here. Cuppertino speaking."

"Scott, it's Sanyha Alvarez."

"I think we've got all the casualties out now, Doc. How are they doing at your end?"

She paused, trying to control her voice. "I lost the three worst, but I think the rest will make it."

"Damnation!" He rubbed a burned hand over his face. "This was deliberate, you know."

"What?"

"Someone set this explosion." His smoke-reddened eyes narrowed. "Used something like a goddamned grenade. Either someone on staff, or—"

One of the visitors. Mitsu Jensen had been in the station yesterday and now she had disappeared. "You're sure, Scott? It's not an accident?"

"Accident, my—!" He broke off. "Sorry, Doc, but those guys were good buddies of mine."

Sanyha glanced over her shoulder at the remaining five patients who still needed her. "Mitsu Jensen is missing. Have you seen her?"

"No." Scott leaned up against the wall and pulled his singed hat off to wipe his brow. "She and this Blackeagle guy, they're both combat vets, aren't they?"

Sanyha nodded, hearing his unspoken words as well: not only were they both veterans, they were Rangers and therefore trained in demolitions.

"Well, if she lit out, she must have been on foot. Every vehicle we had went up with the garage."

"I can't find Eldrich either." She realized she was twining a strand of her hair around her finger and stopped.

"That cold bastard!" An expression of disgust passed over his seamed face. "I wouldn't put anything past him."

"Scott, do me a favor." Behind her, she could hear one of her patients groaning and knew she would have to get off the circuit. "Take an inventory of the motor pool. See if any of the equipment was out when the explosion went off."

"Nothing was signed out."

Sanyha bit her lip. "I know, but I have a hunch that maybe a hopper was out anyway. Just check it for me."

Scott snugged the dirty, blackened hat back over his hair. "Sure thing, Doc. Let you know in an hour or two."

She nodded and punched the connection off, hoping what she feared was not true.

Then, somewhere in the station, she heard the *whump* of another explosion.

A thriving hive of flek burrowed into the surface of Anktan: of all the things Heyoka had thought to find on his native planet, surely that had been the last. Still overwhelmed by what he had seen up there from the mountain pass, he accepted a steaming wooden bowl of dark tealike liquid offered by a cubling and made himself drink. It tasted, as well as smelled, of ashes, as did everything else now, since he had emerged from blueshift. And wherever he turned, things seemed hollowed out, as though they lacked a center, but whether that was a lingering side effect of the strain his body had endured, or simple culture shock, he could not say.

The loss of Mitsu was a dull ache relegated to the back of his mind now. She was most likely dead, and he had much, much more to think about now than the problems of one or two individuals. This whole world was at risk, if it weren't already too late to save it. He had to get back, alert the station as to what he had observed and summon troops. If the flek established a viable transfer point here, this entire quadrant of space was in danger as well. A dozen inhabited worlds existed within easy reach of Anktan. He had to go back *now*.

Kei emerged out of the darkness, shadow-silent, eyes bright with reflected starlight. He had not spoken since their return, but his smoldering presence set Heyoka's teeth on edge and his personal scent, overlaid with the pheromone signature of Levv, had intensified somehow, saturating the mountain air until he found it hard to think of anything else. Heyoka tasted iron in the back of his throat, as though lightning were about to strike.

"I have decided." Kei loomed over him, blocking out the stars. "Tomorrow, you will lead us against the Outsiders."

Heyoka squinted at the arrogant face. Kei's black-furred features were barely discernible against the background of night, as difficult to see as he was to understand. What relation would he be to Heyoka in human terms—brother . . . cousin . . . uncle? None of those relationships seemed to exist between hrinn. They had no word for "son," and certainly none for the nebulous concept of "friend." Here, there were only the males' houses and the Lines, nothing else. A hrinn's association with one or the other defined him to all he encountered as either family or foe, with nothing in between.

He set the empty bowl aside with exaggerated care. "I told you before—their weapons are so powerful, we would die before we even got close enough to see them." Weary of Kei's brash, tireless ignorance, he stood, planning to seek out Nisk and return to the river valley.

Kei's massive body moved to block his way. "*You* fought them and lived."

The other's pheromones beat at him, overwhelming his senses, awakening aspects of his nature he had not experienced before. He swallowed hard, trying to think past the primal images of blood and torn flesh surfacing in his mind. "It would take seasons upon seasons to teach you how to fight the flek, even if we had the proper weapons, which we don't and never will. I have to go back and get help!" He stepped around him, then staggered as pain shot through his lame right leg. Balancing precariously on his left, he leaned over and checked the brace: the green light had failed, meaning its power was exhausted, and he had no way to replace the power cell until he returned to the research station.

"I am Leader, so it is for me, not you, to decide how we will fight." Kei's scarred muzzle wrinkled in a fierce scowl. "We will lure them up into the mountains, perhaps dig a trench, then cover it and trap them that way."

Heyoka saw the ruined worlds again in his mind, the fused wreckage of ash and bone and glass that was all the flek ever left behind, and the savage *other* within him broke free. "We can't take chances!" His claws sprang open. "These particular Outsiders will kill everyone on Anktan," he said through gritted teeth, "not just Levv." Breathing hard, he glanced around for Nisk, hoping to use him to divert Kei. "This is far more important than any one Line."

Kei bristled. "Nothing is more important than Levv!"

"Even for a *male*?" Struggling for control, Heyoka

limped painfully toward the cave. "I thought the matter of Line was beneath the notice of a *mature male*."

With a snarl, Kei seized a handful of Heyoka's loose mane, jerked his head back and slashed at his exposed throat. Heyoka blocked his arm, then countered with an elbow to the breathing nerve centered in Kei's chest. Kei doubled over, struggling for breath.

Jaws clenched, Heyoka backed out of reach. "Once they finish that grid, they will arrive here in the thousand-thousands to raise the surface temperature of this world until your blood boils and change the air until it burns your lungs to bloody shreds and when they are done, not one hrinn will be left alive anywhere!"

"You are afraid!" Kei's eyes were icy black holes into a desolate wasteland Heyoka could not fathom.

"I *am* afraid, because I understand this enemy," he said, "as you do not."

"Fool! You only understand how to fail!" Kei's nose twitched. "If we follow you, we will all die!" He stretched a finger at Heyoka's chest and discharged a bolt of agonizing blue fire.

The world whited out, taking all sight and sound with it. When he came to himself again, lying on his back in the grass, every cell in his body throbbed. He put a hand to his ringing ears. A few feet away, Kei studied him with a feral expression.

Heyoka tried to regain his feet, but he'd wrenched his bad leg when he fell and the pain flooded the damaged nerves until he couldn't think. He fumbled for the pressure point and, with shaking fingers, applied acupressure to the sciatic nerve until the pain backed off, a temporary measure at best, which could buy him a few more minutes of mobility. Breathing raggedly, he lurched back up onto his good leg, the other, dangling uselessly.

"So, *Black/on/black*." Kei circled to the left, forcing

Heyoka to hop awkwardly to face him. "Tell me I'm wrong. Show us that you are fit to lead. Take my life if you can!" He leaped, his hands thick with crackling blue flame as he seized Heyoka's shoulders.

"No, I—" Heyoka hung transfixed in his grip, his consciousness fragmented by the bolt of lightning exploding through him. His vision fuzzed; he couldn't draw air into his lungs, couldn't move so much as a fingertip, the agony building until he thought his tongue and eyeballs and brain would melt. The stench of burned fur filtered through the air, but then, as his heart stuttered, he caught a faint glimmering of the nature of the energy coursing through him in an unending river of pain. There were places in his battered body that did not feel the pain, pathways of a sort. He struggled to channel the power through those and felt it charge him somehow, flowing through his abused nerves, aiding instead of destroying him. He quit fighting and instead opened himself to the wild blue fire, drawing it like a magnet. Startled, Kei thrust him away.

Energy crackled through Heyoka's body, running along his nerves now in the same way blood flowed through his veins. He was vibrantly alive . . . empowered in a way he'd never known before. He stretched a hand toward Kei's chest and blue fire snaked from his fingers to the other's fur. Kei staggered backwards, then crumpled with telltale slowness to the scintillating blue ground. Glancing around the clearing, he saw everything was blue again, bluer than the skies had been back on Enjas Two, as blue as the clearest day on Old Earth.

In slow motion, Nisk drifted through the scrubby trees around the mouth of the cave, met his gaze languidly, then abruptly approached him at what seemed like normal speed. "You must shut it off," he said, his words ungarbled. "You have to control it, or you will die. Think of silence . . . darkness . . . sleep."

Blue fire sizzled through his brain as he tried to concentrate on what Nisk was saying. This episode of blueshift was different; he had more energy available, and so could spend more time accelerated like this, but he already sensed on the cellular level, the price would also be greater, and the last episode had nearly cost his life. Closing his eyes, he reached for the remembered feel of space on the long hops between missions, deep and cold, empty as silence itself. When he felt it at his core, still and vast, he opened his eyes to Nisk's grave face, now returned to its normal black.

Nisk sagged to his knees, drained. "I did not draw power first."

A few feet away, Kei sprawled in the grass, his breathing shallow, singed fur still smoking. How long had they fought, Heyoka wondered numbly, minutes . . . hours . . . days? He took a deep breath and realized the sun was just edging up over the horizon. He thought again of the flek entrenched out on the plains, the transfer grid almost completed. "I have to go."

"I will get the yirn." Ears lowered, Nisk rose.

"No!" Kei hoisted up to one elbow, his eyes glazed with pain. "He is Levv. The Lines will kill him if he goes back!"

Heyoka squatted beside the black-furred male who represented the family he had crossed light-years to find, the only family he would ever have. "And the flek will destroy this world, if I do not."

The red-eyed flek chittered at Mitsu, then paused as the voder it clutched in its spidery digits translated. "For being here you investigating."

Mitsu stuffed her knuckles between her teeth to keep a hysterical laugh from bubbling up. She realized it was only exhaustion compounded with adrenaline, but she couldn't allow herself the luxury of weakness,

not that she understood what these sodding things
wanted from her anyway.

She braced her bound wrists on her knees and stared
up at the stomach-churning creature. Her skin crawled
to be so near it. "Vacation! You smush-faces savvy that?
I'm here on a goddamned, stinking vacation!"

The flek's feathery ear stalks trembled as the voder
twisted her words into flek chitter. Then it tucked the
voder box under a thin white arm and walked through
the seemingly solid wall of her cell. Mitsu wedged
herself into the corner and tried to stop shaking. If
she could only figure out how they triggered the wall's
permeability, then maybe she could get out of this
place.

She was too goddamned angry with herself to be
as afraid as she ought to be. Why had she let that
worm, Eldrich, trick her into leaving the station? She
was a combat vet, not some naive weak-kneed civilian
with mud for brains! She should have seen through
his ruse.

As for the fact flek were on Anktan—that was a
good one. She'd bet a year's pay no one in Confederated space had the slightest suspicion about this
setup. She raised her wrists and eyed the slick white
fiber which bound her hands. Her teeth hadn't made
a dent; it was, no doubt, fabricated in some particularly nasty flek sort of way.

Eldrich's head appeared through the slick surface
of the wall with a faint pop. He stepped aside and
made room for several flek who followed him. The
air they brought with them was strong and acrid.

She coughed. "Disgusting company you keep these
days, Director."

"Preferable to that of previous days," he answered
smoothly. "Soon, however, I will shed this vile shell
and return to my previous state."

The butterfly flutters in her stomach turned to lead.
"What are you talking about? Are you brainburned?"

The two flek chittered about something, but the voder they carried remained silent.

Eldrich smiled thinly. "How much does the Confederation know about our work here?"

That again. She hunched farther back in the corner and tried to think past the thud of her heart. No wonder Eldrich had been after her at the station about "missions" and "irregularities." He suspected she and Heyoka were here because of the flek.

"How much do they know?" Eldrich's cold gray eyes pierced her.

No matter what he said, he couldn't be a flek, she thought. The biotechnology didn't exist to turn one of those things into the semblance of a human. But if he were human, why was he working for them? "I don't get it. Are they paying you, Eldrich?"

The voder chittered out a translation. Eldrich scowled, then gestured. The two emaciated-looking creatures seized her sore shoulder and dug fingers into the tender, half-healed skin. "How much have you told your superiors?" he demanded. "And where has Blackeagle gone?"

"All-Father blast your hide, get these sodding things off me!" She screwed her eyes shut against the pain.

"Then tell us what you know."

But she knew nothing, could tell them nothing! And yet the truth would not suffice. "Everything!" she lied. "They know it all!"

The fleks released her. She opened her eyes, sweating and heaving as though she were going to be sick. Eldrich watched her, tapping a slender silver tube against the palm of his hand. "I surmised you could be of some use, and naturally, I prefer to be right." He pointed the tube at her head and smiled.

Once the sun's red disk dropped behind the peak overlooking the flek, Kei and Nisk insisted the three of them stop for the night. Heyoka maintained too

much was at stake; they had to ride on, but Nisk and
Kei overruled him, arguing that yirn did not see as
well at night as hrinn. Pushed on after dark, the beasts
would mostly likely take a critical misstep and break
their necks, as well as those of their riders.

But Nisk and Kei had no concept of the carnage
flek would wreak on a defenseless world like this one,
could not possibly imagine what lay in store for all
of them, hrinn and human alike, should the grid be
completed, and Heyoka knew it was his fault for not
making them understand. Urgency beat through him
as he paced the clearing they had chosen on the side
of the mountain, unable to settle and rest, though
every step wrung another jolt of pain from his bad
leg.

They were surrounded by striated gray boulders,
protected not only from the winds, but the eyes of
the flek, he hoped. A leathery winged flyer soared
on the updrafts overhead, hunting, and its thin cries
echoed against the mountain. For the first time since
awakening in the thermal pool, he could smell the
dozens of varieties of plants that grew in the damp
earth and sun-heated stone. Long-buried memories
stirred as he paced, fragments of conversation,
frustrating glimpses of nameless faces, all of which
slipped away even as he tried to grasp them. He had
stood in these mountains as a child, breathed this
same air. He could almost remember . . .

"Sit down," Nisk said as he struck a spark from
his flint. "Wearing yourself out will not help after
using Old Power."

Heyoka squatted beside the older black-furred
male. "Just exactly what is this 'power'? You never
really explained."

Nisk fed a handful of twigs, one at a time, into
the tiny yellow flames he'd kindled, then added a
scattering of tiny blue leaves from his pocket. They
gave off a soothing scent as they curled into flame.

His ears waggled as he considered. "Many males are born with the ability to draw power. It is an ancient discipline which allows them to move with such speed that the eye cannot follow, and also to wield the sacred blue fire. Some are made with a small talent for this, others more." He met Heyoka's eyes, his face impassive over his white throat. "The Black/on/black receives this ability in the greatest measure."

Back to that Black/on/black nonsense again. Heyoka rubbed his ears in frustration. It was just a myth based upon a kernel of truth. His particular coloration must be a genetic tag for a certain type of mitochondria in his cells, nothing "sacred" about it. "Where does this power come from?" he asked.

"The warmth of Ankt will provide it, if you bask long enough." Nisk gestured with his muzzle at the ruddy glow along the western horizon. "But it is easier to draw the heat from a pool." He sat back on his haunches, gaze trained on the flames. "In the last few days, you have proven the legends about the Black/on/black to be true. Even in my prime, I would have been dead long before now, if I had even attempted what you have done since we left the males' house."

Uncomfortable, Heyoka lurched to his feet again, but Nisk continued, not seeming to notice. "It is taught that the Black/on/black comes among us when the immense *patterns/in/motion* that shape all of existence decree such strength is needed. Now that I have seen that monstrous thing defiling our plains, I know why you were born into these days. You have come, not to see this extraordinary pattern, or to name it, as ordinary hrinn must, but because you are part of the pattern itself."

Nisk looked up as Kei came back from watering the yirn. "In the beginning, I thought this pattern might be *patience/in/illusion*, which obscures the true nature of things, but that has arisen before, and has therefore been described, and is reportedly nothing

like this. We are in the midst of something far larger
and more powerful than any pattern ever detected.
Seeking out patterns is the most sacred act a hrinn
can perform; it orients us in the stream of life, gives
us direction, puts us in balance with the rest of
creation. We must name this particular pattern which
has brought you back among us, so we know what
we are supposed to do, or chaos will destroy us all."

Superstition piled upon superstition, Heyoka
thought, yet as good an explanation for the outrageous
presence of flek on Anktan as any he might come up
with. "Can females draw power?"

"A few, but it is a much rarer gift, and wielded
only in order to *restore/to/balance*, not to fight." Nisk's
nose twitched as Kei threw a handful of silvery fishlike
creatures onto the grass, then sank to his haunches.
Beyond insisting he would accompany them, the big
Levv male had said almost nothing since Heyoka had
bested him that morning.

"You spoke to me of Restorers before." Heyoka
looked down at his aching leg, encased in the now
useless power brace.

Nisk followed his gaze. "When we reach the valley,
we shall seek them out."

That is, Heyoka amended to himself, if there were
any Restorers, or anything else left by the time they
reached the valley at this rate. He turned his eyes
to the early evening sky and searched for the telltale
lights of flek transport while Kei tore into a raw fish.

Chapter Twenty

Heyoka passed the remainder of the three days it took to travel back across the low mountains in a feverish haze. Every time he thought he had come to terms with the situation, the reality of it surged back over him: *flek were entrenched on Anktan.* In the entire history of confrontation between the two species, Confederated forces had never wrested a world back from the flek that was more than poisoned slag and ashes, if even that much. If he'd had a com-unit, he would have warned the station, then set up a command post and dug in to observe while he waited for a coordinated response from the military. As it was, he was forced to ride every rock-strewn inch back across the mountains astride a maddeningly slow yirn.

When they passed another males' house, Nisk directed them to wait outside while he went in to seek supplies. Minutes later, he returned, eyes glittering with rage, ears strangely askant, a body posture Heyoka could not interpret.

"They are dead," was all he would say, but Heyoka

caught an acrid whiff of flek from Nisk's fur and pieced together the rest. Like Levv, this house was situated fairly close to the plains. After Kei and his siblings had blundered upon the grid and were routed, the flek must have searched this area. Unlike the persecuted remnants of Levv, these males had not expected an attack, and so, caught unaware, had all died. The memory of that torrid green beach on Enjas Two swept back over him, the coppery salt reek of the ocean, the crackle of flek fire as it altered the direction of his life forever.

At twilight, the three of them emerged from the rolling hills onto the fertile side of the river valley, guiding their weary yirn in silence until they reached a ford. Just above the flood plain, Heyoka saw circular fields of what Nisk identified as ripening Qartt grain, now bending before the gentle dusk breeze. The air was mellow, filled with the fresh, wet scent of running water and the rich earthiness of tilled land, wonderfully familiar. Relief flooded through him to be so close to the station and civilization again. Human thoughts coursed through his mind, human considerations. Once he alerted Confederated forces, this problem would no longer be his responsibility alone. That was how humans did things, worked in concert to multiply individual strengths and knowledge, relying on reasoning and training, rather than the aggressive, individualistic chest beating and bared teeth that characterized hrinn.

Twisting around on his yirn, he caught Nisk's eye. "The Outsiders aren't far from here. Why don't you both go back to Levv and wait until I can return?"

Nisk stiffened. His usually mobile ears did not betray his agitation, but his eyes burned like black coals. "Have you understood nothing of what is happening?" He sat his fidgety yirn like a statue, an impenetrable dark silhouette against the graying sky, staring out at the vast sweep of wasteland beyond the river. "This pattern has been emerging since the day you left this world as a cubling. Even as we stand here, it is shaping our future. Everything we are, everything we will become, is bound up into it. We cannot leave it unnamed."

Exhausted and battered, Heyoka found himself unutterably weary of hrinnti ways and hidebound hrinnti thinking. He couldn't wait to be among humans again, to eat cooked food, read a book, to talk things out rather than be forced to fight for the right to make even the smallest decision on his own. "This has nothing to do with patterns!"

"Fool!" Nisk leaned closer, ivory teeth catching the fading light. "Do you think I don't know a pattern when I smell one? This one has swept me away from my fellow males so that I am houseless, then pushed me beyond the bounds of reasoning to confront creatures no hrinn has ever seen and then continued to draw breath. If we do not learn how to flow with it, rather than stand against it, it will destroy us all, and chaos will once again rule. For reasons known only to the Voice, you stand in its center, so in order to name it, I must follow you."

Heyoka scowled and turned to Kei, who professed not to believe in such supernatural nonsense as hrinnti patterns, but the big male met his eyes only for a brief glowering instant, then looked to the ground. Having gone from brash anger to resentful deference in the space of one savage skirmish, he now maintained an almost unbroken stony silence.

At the station, he knew these two would be regarded as illiterate savages, but the cant of their ears and the set of their heads warned him it would do no good to protest further, so he urged his mount into the rushing green water. Less than a mile beyond the river, they passed out of the flood plain up into a different landscape of tough desert pavement pocked with occasional sweeps of red-orange sand.

At their backs, the sun sank behind the mountains and Heyoka worried they would not reach the station before dark. Finally he caught a glimpse of the gray tarmac where he and Mitsu had stepped off the shuttle . . . how many days ago?

He wished she would be there to razz him about the appallingly inept way he had handled this whole miserable business, but knowing his kind much better now, he had no illusions that she'd survived. One unguarded slash from a hrinn's claws would have torn her throat out, and the natives never pulled their blows.

Nisk and Kei rode up to the long low station compound with him, silent as two shadows. Their glittering black eyes watched as he slipped down the yirn's shaggy side and limped over to the outer lock's monitor. He'd lost his yellow security pass somewhere in that first day out so he punched the call button. "This is Sergeant Blackeagle. I need access."

Static burst from the speaker embedded in the door. He keyed it again. "Blackeagle here. Open up." Minutes trickled past. He raised his fist to bang on the outer lock. "Blast it, let me in!" Finally he propped himself against the rough sand-scoured wall to ease his leg. Although he'd been on it for barely ten minutes, he might have been standing knee-deep in hot coals. His lips curled back from his teeth at the thought of the months of physical therapy ahead to make walking merely endurable again.

The door grated open, a few inches at a time, then a slender dark-haired woman peered around the edge at him, brown eyes reddened from weariness, or lack of sleep.

"It is you!" She tucked a straggling lock of long dark hair behind her ear. "My god, Blackeagle, you look terrible."

For a baffling second, he couldn't place her, then caught her scent: Dr. Alvarez, who, only days ago, had tricked him with a sedative while precious hours were passing, hours in which he might have had a chance to find Mitsu before it was too late. She was one of the last people he wanted to see now.

His nose twitched as he realized how *small* she was. He'd already forgotten how much more frail in every way humans were compared to hrinn. He caught a whiff of something in the station's conditioned air, familiar, yet out of place. His hackles rose. "What the—?" He darted past her into the lock. With an air of grim disapproval, Kei and Nisk followed.

"Hey," she protested as the pair pushed past her, "they can't come in here!"

Inside, Heyoka smelled the telltale odor more clearly. Nostrils flaring, he identified the acrid signature of at least three different kinds of explosives. He turned back to Alvarez. "What's your situation?"

Giving his companions a wide berth, she caught up with him. Her long hair straggled around her face and there were smears of dirt on her cheeks. She looked like she hadn't slept in days. "We've had a series of explosions." Her brown eyes were bleak. "Security thinks they were set. There have been eight deaths so far, and more are missing."

Two blue-uniformed men sprinted around the corner and slid to a wary stop on the tiled floor, weapons ready. Kei threw back his head and roared as Nisk sank into a fighting crouch, his claws flexed. The guards flinched and Heyoka hastily interposed himself, empty hands raised and turned palms out. "Be still!" he called over his shoulder in Hrinnti.

The guards gripped their rifles until their knuckles shone white. Alvarez waved them back. "It's all right. This is Sergeant Blackeagle. I know him."

"But what about the other two?" The first guard, swarthy and middle-aged, motioned with the muzzle of his gun. "That one may be tame, but the other two are as wild as they come."

"I'll handle it, Scott!" She passed a hand over her sweat-grimed face. "Please."

The guard hesitated, then nodded. "All right, Doc, it's your funeral." He lowered the rifle.

Tame . . . Heyoka felt a snarl rumbling in his own throat at the implications of that word. He realized his handclaws were flexed and forced them sheathed again; he had to sound sane, reasonable. "I have to get word to the authorities. I've found a *flek* installation on the other side of the mountains."

Alvarez went alabaster beneath her smudges and scrapes. "Our communications center is nothing but smoke and ashes."

Heyoka tried to jolt his mind back into the military mode in which he'd functioned for so many years. "I need transport and arms."

"Every bit of transport we had went in the first explosion." Her eyes moved past him into the gathering darkness outside. "And the armory went up too. All the firepower we have left is what Security had checked out that day."

"Damn!" The human word felt good on his tongue, like scratching an itch that couldn't even be acknowledged in Hrinnti. Options, he told himself, there had to be alternatives. There had to be something he could do. "When is the next ship due in?"

"Seventy-eight days from now. I checked." Arms hugged to her body, she dug at the wall with the heel of her shoe. "I thought we could make it until then, but now . . ."

No communications, no transport . . . His head whirled. Someone had done a surgical job of rendering the station helpless. He called the shining lines of the flek grid back into his mind, comparing the unfinished structure to holos of finished units he'd seen. "I don't think we have seventy-eight days left."

The fear in her eyes confirmed that she had followed the progress of the war and knew all too well what the flek would do to this world. "Isn't there anything we can do to stop them?"

Stop a transport grid without trained troops? In his mind, he saw the line of chitinous dead-white warrior-drones again as they swarmed down the beach, laying an impenetrable shield of green laser fire before them. "I don't know." His eyes slid to the black-furred forms of Kei and Nisk standing behind him.

She brushed at her hair again with a gesture that reminded him so much of Mitsu that guilt stabbed through him. "Have you had any word of my partner?"

Alverez looked stricken. "She came in with Eldrich a few days ago, but disappeared again the next morning."

"With Eldrich?" Heyoka's ears flattened. "He sent a team out after all?"

"No, he brought her in himself." Her face was hollow-cheeked and drawn. "After his initial refusal to allow anyone to look for her, I thought it doubly strange when he and Allenby showed up with her in the middle of the night, all very hush-hush, and then the three of them disappeared the next day."

"Eldrich is gone too?" Heyoka prowled restlessly to the other side of the doorway, the pain in his leg eating at him with each step.

"And Allenby. They might have died in the explosion, but . . ." She bit her lip.

"What?"

"One of the airhoppers is missing, although none were signed out."

But Mitsu had survived. He made himself hold onto that. If only he'd come back sooner.

Three more men, their blue uniforms stained with soot and sweat, joined the others, wearily staring at the hrinn. Heyoka's nose twitched as Kei flexed his handclaws. "Tell them to give us weapons so we can leave." Kei's tone was close to a low snarl. "Hrinn cannot live in this stench."

"They have no weapons." Heyoka's nose wrinkled; the station did smell terrible, reeked in fact of humans and sweat and explosives and plastics and a hundred other things he'd almost forgotten in just a few days' time.

Nisk shook himself. "It is as I have been telling you—this pattern does not involve the Outsiders. We must find this shape alone."

Heyoka hesitated, then decided to check the communications center for himself. "I must look at something before we leave. Wait for me outside." He headed down the dimly lit station corridor. After a moment, he heard the pad of hrinnti feet behind him.

Vexk waited on the low roof of the Restorers' Hold, chin propped on her bent knees, while Cimmi and Khea dug medicinal roots up on the ridge. Twilight had descended and the growing dimness to the east possessed a dense, clotted consistency, denoting, she thought, a rare convergence of patterns. Everywhere, new shapes were arising unexpectedly within the bounds of those already extant, grinding each other into furious chaos, then spinning away into nothingness. Most hrinn experienced but six or seven recognizable patterns in a lifetime, but these days had lately proved themselves of an altogether different quality, crowded with too many possibilities and therefore fraught with danger.

The wind carried the heady promise of rain out of the west, rare this late in the season. She had tasted the same damp edge in the air on the night she had severed her own ties with Vvok. Watching Khea, it swept back over her now, the anguish and loss of identity, the intense period of mourning that followed. Leaving one's Line was devastating enough, but in addition Khea had witnessed Vvok's disgrace, something

new, even to Vexk, who had thought by now nothing
Seska did could surprise her.

No word had come to her from Vvok, not even
an imperious demand for the return of this surprising
cubling over whom they had imperiled their honor.
But then, if old Seska were dealing with the Outsiders
for weapons, a disobedient cubling was likely to be
the last thing on her mind.

The two cublings walked back through the gathering darkness toward the hold, the tube-shaped collect-
ing baskets slung low across their shoulders. Khea
lagged behind, silent and weary, although she had
insisted upon making herself useful. Her wounds were
healing well, but she carried herself stiffly, as though
something deep within pained her still. There was
more to this matter than she had yet revealed. Vexk
jumped to the ground as the two approached.

She gave Cimmi's red, white and black head a
playful rub as the cubling passed, then waited for
Khea to catch up. She could see the deep gash on
the cubling's throat was still scabbed over, but looked
as though it would heal cleanly. One of her own ears,
notched with old scars, twitched as she remembered
Seska's punishing claws in her long-ago cubhood. Vvok
was indeed a harsh mistress, but no different of course
than any other Line. This business of trading for
Outsider weapons though, *that* was different. "Stay,
youngling," she said.

Khea sank into the prototypical posture of respect,
eyes down, head bowed. The next thing she knew,
Vexk thought sourly, the child would hide her face
against the sandy ground. Reaching down with both
hands, she pulled the cubling up until she could look
into her startled eyes.

"*This*," she said firmly, "is our way. We are equals
here, with no Line Mother to demand obedience or
shred our ears. We are in balance, within and without.
We come because we fit no pattern followed by the

Lines, and we stay because we are one with the sacredness of *restoration/to/balance* itself." The young body trembled in her hands. "I knew you felt its shape when I first saw you with the Outsider."

She loosed her fingers and Khea stumbled back until she fetched up against the hold wall. She looked over Vexk's shoulder to the red-orange cliffs leading up to the plateau—and Vvok. Her eyes were shadowed with overwhelming grief.

"We must be in balance ourselves, before we can restore others," Vexk said.

"I—" Khea's voice was low, strained. "I have brought great shame upon myself, so I have no place anywhere, most of all not here where such sacred work is done."

Vexk waited as Khea's healing chest heaved.

"I—challenged the Line Mother," Khea managed finally, her face averted. "When she struck the Outsider, I lost my head and attacked her, before Fitila pulled me down from behind."

Vexk was amazed Khea had taken on old Seska herself, as well as Fitila. "Lawful challenge forbids onlookers to intervene," she said, considering Khea's dilemma. The demands of restoration sometimes conflicted with the need to conduct one's self honorably in the eyes of other hrinn, so it was important to always seek the balance point, where as many aspects were fulfilled as possible. "It was Fitila who dishonored herself, not you," she said. "And you must realize it was not really you who protected the Outsider, but the pattern itself. You were drawn into the sacred process of *restoration/to/balance*, so that you could do nothing else but take whatever steps were necessary to preserve its life."

Khea stared at her dumbly.

Vexk closed her eyes, reliving the exhilaration of being caught up in something so much larger than herself, that heady, dizzying sense of power and purpose which made everything else seem vague and petty. "One does not decide to become a Restorer," she said. "The pattern takes its own. You were destined for us from the blink in which you perceived its sacred shape. Tomorrow, we will go before the Council of Lines and settle this matter officially."

The corners of Mitsu's lips were split and bloodied from chewing at the fiber binding her wrists, but she thought that if she gave up, she would go crazy. After repeated rounds under the conditioning device Eldrich was using on her, flek thoughts skittered through her brain like tiny insects. During her clearer moments, she'd pieced together that this must have been what had happened to Eldrich, too. They had twisted his mind into knots until he believed he was a flek serving them in a temporary human body. No wonder he worked for their cause.

If she could manage to become flek enough to understand how that damned permeable wall worked, she could escape, but sometimes now it seemed she remembered what it was like to have four arms and to serve the hive from the instant of her birth. It was fortunate she didn't possess the information Eldrich was working so hard to extract from her, because she had the gut-wrenching feeling that very soon she was going to slip over the edge.

It was beyond Kei how any sane creature could live amidst the putrid smells and sharp-angled objects Outsiders crowded into their cramped hold. He'd heard a few vague tales of the bizarre way they lived, but experiencing it for himself was far more unsettling than he had anticipated. The ceilings brushed the tops of his ears and there was no room to turn around, and certainly no sign of sand or pool or rock. How did they clean themselves? Where did they rest? His nerves crawled with the need to be away. On the other side of the chamber, the Black/on/black, who had shed his tattered brown robes for fresh black ones, sorted through a heap of incomprehensible items, ears laid back, expression grim.

A fierce emotion swelled within Kei's chest whenever he looked upon him now. Puzzling and altogether unfamiliar, it dominated his mind as surely as the Black/on/black had bested his body. He felt prickly as a thorn about it, yet knew that for as long as he continued to draw breath, wherever the Black/on/black walked, there he would have to walk too. Was this what it was like to be caught up in a *pattern/in/progress*?

He approached the door, then flinched as it slid open again, revealing the gleaming silver passage beyond. His ears flattened as he sniffed cautiously at the smooth slab of metal. How did it move by itself like that—had they imprisoned some unfortunate early-culled servant inside? It was far too thin to contain even the smallest of hrinnti cublings, but the biggest Outsider he'd seen was paltry in size. He backed away and the door closed with a faint whoosh.

The Black/on/black glanced up, lips wrinkled back in irritation. "Quit playing with that thing!" He picked up a round gray cylinder the length of his hand and tucked it into the waist of the black trousers.

Kei caught the musty scent peculiar to the pale flat-muzzled creatures of this hold and looked back to the door as two of them edged into view. A low snarl escaped his throat. The Black/on/black flattened his ears and spoke to the intruders in a short string of the high-pitched alien gabble.

One answered and gestured with the gleaming gray stick in its hands at Kei and Nisk.

Casting aside the bag in his hands, the Black/on/black replied sharply.

Kei could see the fur on the other's neck standing

straight up. Were they threatening him? He bared his own teeth.

The Black/on/black glanced at him. "Stay back!"

"Why are they here?" Kei prowled restlessly from wall to wall. "Do they wish to go and fight these flek creatures with us? Or do they mean to challenge you?"

"They want you and Nisk to leave," the Black/on/black replied, never taking his eyes from the two at the door.

"Good!" Kei shook himself. "This is no place for hrinn."

"No, you don't understand. They want you to go"—the Black/on/black's expression was grim—"and for me to stay."

Chapter Twenty-one

The security guards were demanding he stay, but ordering the natives, the hrinn, out. Before Heyoka could think, the dark *other* within him surfaced and gave voice to a deep-throated roar that reverberated until the small room rang like the interior of a bronze bell. Macabre visions raced through his mind, throats torn out, blood splattered across the walls like paint, fragile human flesh rent from ivory bone until there remained only him and the blessed silence.

Both guards backed into the wall, faces gone white as newly cast plas, fingers convulsively clutching their weapons. Heyoka saw his fearsome image reflected in their staring eyes and fought for control. Rage pumped through his veins, both at himself and these shortsighted idiots. Whatever their personal feelings, they had to think beyond them now. With flek dug in on the other side of the mountains, they were all on the same side.

The taller of the two stepped forward, the stubble of his beard clearly visible beneath translucent skin. He cleared his throat. "Be r-reasonable. We can't have *savages* roaming this facility. Security is already badly compromised as it is."

Heyoka leaned down and read the name off the man's badge. "Listen to me, S. Cuppertino. If you don't get your sorry butt down to Communications and do everything within your obviously limited ability to make repairs so we can get a message out, you people will have a flek hive located *in* this facility."

Cuppertino swallowed. "The staff is afraid to come out of their quarters as long as these two are here. They have to leave so we can make repairs."

"Hey, no problem." Heyoka snatched up the backpack he'd thrown down in disgust and jammed in a packet of concentrated rations. "They think you stink. They can't wait to get out of this place, and frankly neither can I."

"But *you* can't go!" Cuppertino fingered the long black barrel of the laser rifle nervously. "You're the only one in-station with combat experience."

A snarl rattled in Heyoka's throat and he realized he'd flexed his handclaws. Glancing down at the wicked three-inch points, he was suddenly amused. All his life he had fought to control his temper and seem as much one of these fragile, soft-spoken creatures as possible, but it was pointless. He was not human, and never could be. Bit by bit, his carefully cultivated veneer of humanity was being pared away, revealing someone else beneath, a stranger he had yet to comprehend.

He turned his back on them. "I'm not going to sit around here, holding your hands, while you try to piece that com-link back together." Shouldering the pack, he limped toward them. The two guards fell back well out of reach as he lowered his head to squeeze through the human-sized door. Kei and Nisk pushed through close behind, bristling, ears pinned back, eyes grim and wary.

This place did reek, he thought. He felt like he

would never get the smell out of his fur. Would he ever be able to bring himself to live like this again?

Just before he reached the outside lock, Sanyha Alvarez hurried around the corner. "Sergeant Blackeagle, wait! I brought a power pack—for the brace. I noticed yours was exhausted."

He stared at the tiny bright metal disk in her hand. With it, he could short circuit most of the pain for a few more days, but then it would be depleted and he would be as bad off as ever. Even as he stood there, considering, the pain simmered like liquid fire along the nerves of his leg, a constant reminder that he was not whole.

Nisk pushed ahead of him and peered out the door. "That strange light is in the sky again."

Heyoka thrust his muzzle outside into the cooling evening air. High overhead, a spark raced in a linear path across the darkened sky, one shimmering point of light among stationary stars. Exposing themselves like this indicated the enemy's high level of confidence. Time was most likely even shorter than he'd thought. It was so infuriating! He'd spent years fighting the flek wherever they showed their disgusting bone-white faces, feeling at least marginally in control of his fate, but now here he was, stuck on an undeveloped planet far off the shipping lanes where they could entrench themselves until it was too late for the forces responsible for this quadrant to respond. And all he had to fight them off with was a sonic blade, a half-charged laser pistol, and his bare hands.

He flexed his claws again, seeing how the deadly black curves caught the artificial light spilling out from the hallway. *His* bare hands were not as limited as a human's though . . . and a whole planetful of like hands were scattered out there in the darkness, ignorant for the moment of the growing danger. What if they knew?

He studied Kei and Nisk as they followed the ship's trajectory. Perhaps, if he could convince the Lines and the males' houses of the threat at hand, with experienced direction, the hrinn could damage the grid enough to prevent its completion until the Confederation could be alerted. He pushed past Kei into the evening air and looked around for the yirn they had left outside. "We have to go back to the males' house. I think there might be something we could do to protect ourselves."

Nisk's ears slanted back. "I have been lawfully vanquished, and Rakshal will use the opportunity to challenge you again."

Once again, Heyoka found himself amused. He brushed absentmindedly at the long strands of mane blowing around his face in the night wind. "I have much more important game than my worthless hide to lay before Rakshal's claws."

No matter how many times Seska pressed the button, the gleaming metal box remained stubbornly silent. She did not like the smell of this, not one bit. Now that their long-sought goal was so close she could almost pin it under her claws, it boded badly for the Outsider to fall silent.

Thrusting the small box back under her cushions, she curled up and ran an idle clawtip over the engraved silver armlet circling her upper arm. It was a Jhii working of the old story of Dsuffa First-Hunter and very fine, yet surely they would all have an abundance of such things once the Council of Lines met tomorrow and approved the opening of full relations with the Outsiders. There would be fine cloth and machines to labor in the fields and medicines to cure every ill. No one would ever have to grovel to those miserable Restorers again. She would be free to tear out that traitorous Vexk's throat herself. Her eager handclaws sprang free at the thought.

Her head turned at a perfunctory scratch at the door, but Fitila's buff-colored nose was already halfway across her quarters before she could even grant permission. "Since when do you approach the Line Mother before you are bid?" Her voice was edged with anger.

Fitila hastily prostrated her lean, scarred body on the carpet. "I was concerned for your safety. I have not been able to find that wretched outcast, Khea, anywhere."

Seska sat up on her cushions, snarling a little with the pain in her stiff hip joints. "That cubling was always a pathetic, weak thing. No doubt, she crawled off into the rocks to die of her wounds."

"If that were so, then I would have found her dead body." Fitila sat up, her gaze trained on the floor. "I have been able to track her only as far as the northeastern edge of the plateau."

Seska flicked an ear. So the whelp had crawled off toward the Restorers.

"Tomorrow the Council will meet, and I am still uneasy. What if the wretch tries to speak before the Council about what she saw?"

"Do not be stupid." Easing back against the red cushions again, Seska looked at the thick carpet, remembering how the Outsider had lain right here in this chamber in a tangled bloodied heap at her feet. "The young idiot saw little and understood even less. Thinking back, I cannot understand why the cub-trainer did not cull her long ago. She certainly would not have passed the next gleaning. Even if she did survive, no one will pay the slightest attention to her."

She preened at the dark-gray fur along her arm. "I am more concerned that the Outsider does not answer us now."

"Have Beshha or Fik spoken with it recently?" Fitila moved closer and picked up the bowl of oil which was always warming close by, then poured a bit on Seska's fingers and began to massage them.

"That is an interesting thought." Closing her eyes, Seska gave herself up to the easing of the ache in her joints that always plagued her in the cooling evening air. "Call them on the little box and find out."

Then, as Fitila fumbled beneath the cushions for the device, Seska's lip curled back with another thought. "And send a jit to the Restorers. Command Vexk to attend me tonight."

"She will not come. We refused their price."

Seska considered for a moment. "Tell her that we wish to discuss this trifling matter of payment. That should bring her. She has no way of knowing the cubling is dead."

Her eyes drifted closed, her claws tingling at the thought of tearing that pale-gray throat. It would be prudent, as well as pleasant, to remove Vexk from the world. Even though Restorers had no vote in Council, Vexk often attended to speak her mind. It would be much safer to eliminate her now so no loose tongues would be left when she took control of the Council tomorrow.

Nisk halted his yirn at the bottom of the path that threaded down from the plateau.

Heyoka roused and squinted into the velvet darkness, disoriented. For hours it seemed, he had followed the older male, trusting Nisk's sense of direction. Weariness had soaked through him, settling on the back of his throat like a bitter draught. A faint scent of sulfur hung in the cooling night air. "Why are we stopping here?" He rubbed his aching eyes with one hand.

"To use the pool in this cave." Nisk slid down. "We should draw power before confronting Rakshal."

Kei sampled the air before dismounting. "Someone has passed by here quite recently—a female."

"Restorers sometimes use this pool, but no one should be here this late." Nisk hobbled his mount.

Heyoka swung his leg over the yirn's hump, then eased down to the ground. The moment his right foot took weight, pain knifed through his leg and it threatened to buckle. He dug his fingers into the yirn's shaggy wool and held on until the initial wave of agony receded, then limped after Nisk, trying not to give into it more than he had to. No doubt, he should have taken the power pack offered by the doctor, but he had been too proud and angry at that point to accept help, and it was too late now.

Kei flicked an ear as he passed, then stalked after them as they entered the cave. Heyoka leaned against the rough wall inside and fumbled in his pack for a coldlight. Nisk sniffed the cool cavern air, then wordlessly led the way, navigating each turning, following the faint, twinned scent of sulfur and water. The sharp shadows cast by the coldlight dodged before them over the twisted formations of rock.

Each step was worse than the one before. The pain ate at his nerves, grinding his reserves down until he was overheated and panting, unable to think any further ahead than getting through the next step, and then the next. Finally, they ducked under several low-hanging stalactites and stood before a heavy gold-worked tapestry hung across the passage. The air was noticeably warmer here, and moist. Droplets trickled down the glistening walls and pooled at their feet.

Nisk picked up the corner of the tapestry. On the other side, under the golden light of a flickering torch, a wet-furred female knelt beside a vast steaming pool, a set of yellow robes clasped in her hands. Despite the lateness of the hour, she did not seem startled to see them.

"Patterns within patterns," she murmured and her dark eyes glittered with the mellow gold of reflected torchlight.

Nisk lowered his ears. "Vexk, we did not mean to disturb you."

She must be one of the fabled Restorers, Heyoka realized. Her fur was a pale, luminescent gray, and her dripping mane fanned across her shoulders. She rose to her feet and drew on her outer robe, radiating a vast quiet that seemed to swallow all questions, smooth away concerns. Heyoka had a sudden vague sense he had walked in this cavern before, had seen her and stood here speechless in exactly the same fashion. Each breath he took, each blink, seemed a repetition of what he done before, as though he were caught up in a loop that he could not break.

She studied him, then her dark eyes widened and she looked to Nisk. "He is Black/on/black?"

"Yes," Nisk said simply. "He has come at last."

Heyoka bristled. That nonsense again! Didn't these people have anything better to think about? The spell broken, he limped back toward the chamber's entrance.

Vexk's ears pricked at his halting gait. "You are injured?"

"A long time ago." Heyoka reached for the embroidered fabric.

She blocked his way and peered down at his bad leg, concealed beneath the loose trousers. "How were you hurt?"

"It doesn't matter." His tone was gruff. "It will never be any better than it is right now."

"A Restorer told you that?" The set of her ears clearly indicated her disbelief.

"Outsider restorers," he said. "They were quite learned."

"I do not know how their craft compares with ours," she said. "But perhaps I can still help." She indicated a stone ledge beside the pool.

Heyoka scowled. "We do not have time—"

"You must make time for this, Black/on/black." Nisk

turned on him. "It was not chance that Vexk is here tonight. This meeting is part of the great unnamed *something/in/motion* which is making itself felt more and more each day. You cannot stand against it."

Vexk met his gaze. "You feel it too," she said softly. "A huge pattern, different from any other, gathering us in until we are one with its intertwined curves and arcs, making something entirely new."

Nisk stared over her head as though he could see something in the air. "I did not want to say this before, but among us, those with injuries or weakness, as well as any sort of ugliness or imperfection, are culled—not permitted to hold high rank or breed." His gaze dropped to Heyoka's damaged leg. "Few will be willing to listen to you—as you are now."

Heyoka felt the final crack in the wall of his already badly eroded self-confidence. The Hrinn—his people—would not listen to him unless he were physically perfect, the one thing that, no matter how hard he tried, he could never remedy. He ran a dry tongue over his lips. "The damage is permanent."

Vexk bent her pale-gray head over his leg and eased the cloth up over his knee in order to lay her supple fingers on the scars. "Sit here . . . think of nothing."

Feeling somewhat awkward, he complied and stared up at the ceiling where strangely convoluted whirls and circles had been carved into the red-orange rock of the cave. They seemed to dance and spin, combine with each other in unsuspected ways. The Restorer's strong hands slid along his throbbing leg . . . curiously warm. The heat felt good, seeping into the ache that had become so much a part of him in the last few days, he hardly knew where it ended and he began.

The warmth increased, simmering along the twisted flesh, almost equal in intensity with the pain that gnawed at him night and day. His mind drifted, following the heat as it drove away the pain, feeling it reestablish normal pathways for sensation to come and go from his leg. Slowly, micron by micron, the heat advanced, forcing the pain to retreat before it.

Then suddenly the advance was balked by a black knot of pain, so intense nothing could pass. He felt Vexk strain, pouring all her strength into the fight, but the damage was too great. He sensed that she would soon exhaust herself without finishing what she had begun.

She lacked the power, he thought. The special cells of her body could only hold so much extra energy and she had expended nearly all of it now. Much more was needed. The struggle with Kei floated back into his mind, the memory of power channeled. It had been different and yet in some ways it seemed to him this was essentially the same process.

His leg began to cool, allowing the pain to resurge, not as intensely, but still present. He opened the channels in his own body, as he had learned from Kei, then tried to direct his own energy to the internal struggle under Vexk's fingers. He closed his eyes and concentrated, trying to sense the pathways Vexk had used. Her hands loosened, then she paused. Warmth crept back into his muscles and nerves. Her damp mane brushed his fur as heat flowed against the pain again, inching down his leg with agonizing slowness.

He lost all sense of time, knowing only that he channeled the power stored in his own body to fuel the fight directed by Vexk's touch. Much later, he dimly realized the pain was gone, truly absent for the first time he could remember since Enjas Two. Even under the influence of the most advanced drugs and power brace technology, he'd always had the sense pain was merely lying in wait, ready to leap out and sear his nerves again at the first opportunity. Now it was *gone*.

Voices murmured over him. He opened his eyes and tried to sit up.

Vexk's firm hands pushed him back against rock now warmed by his body heat. "Sleep, Black/on/black."

"But the males' house—"

"They will be at the Council meeting tomorrow, along with everyone else." She blinked down at him with enormous black eyes set at an angle in her face. "Sleep."

Weariness spun over him. His eyes sagged shut again and he let himself be pulled down into the darkness.

An infestation of flek just over the mountains! Sanyha hesitated in front of the wreckage of the communications center and longed not to believe it. The acrid stink of smoke still clogged the air. She accepted the box of scavengeable parts Scott Cuppertino held out to her and stared numbly down at the assorted unfamiliar shapes. "This is all you could find? What about Stores? Can we get any usable parts from there?"

"Maybe." He ran a hand over his sooty hair and sighed. "This is not my area. Saunderson was the only one with the training to put together a subspace comlink from scratch."

And Saunderson was dead.

Neither one of them wanted to voice that fact, but it lay between them and any possibility of success like a vast chasm. Her fingers tightened around the box. "The flek obviously know we're here. Wouldn't we be safer if we just evacuated and hid out in the hills until the ship comes? I mean, it's crazy to sit here so they can pick us off any time they want."

"I don't know, Doc." Scott's smudged face contorted into a weary grimace. "Seems like they've already put us out of commission. I don't see why they'd think a little place like this will be worth bothering with now. We're all goners anyway as soon as they start fiddling with the atmosphere."

She sighed. "Let's call a meeting of the remaining Section heads and—" A loud boom thundered through the station, staggering her shoulder-first against the wall. "My god!" She glanced up at Scott. Her own panic was mirrored in his smoke-reddened eyes.

He grabbed her arm and yanked her into the hallway. A second explosion, closer this time, threw them both to their knees. Head spinning, she struggled to her feet, then tried to gather up the com parts she had dropped.

Scott hauled roughly at her arm. "Forget that junk! We've got to get out of the building!"

"We'd better take some medical supplies!" She tried to twist out of his grip and go back. "There'll be injuries!"

Another *whump* shook the building right over their heads and chunks of debris showered them. For a moment, she couldn't think past the ringing in her ears, then she saw Scott stagger to his feet, blood streaming from a dozen cuts and his right arm dangling. The lights flickered and died. "We'll all be dead if we don't get outside!" he said.

She felt his hand pull her out of the wreckage. Stumbling after him over unseen obstacles, she held her other arm out and felt her way through the blackness. She couldn't remember the station ever being totally dark before, not even at midnight. She realized she was disoriented.

"Move it, Doc!" Scott's fingers anchored in the material of her uniform.

Another explosion shook the floor beneath them, but it seemed farther away, probably down at the other end. A load of ceiling tiles crashed on her head as part of the roof caved in. She pitched onto her knees with a lungful of dust, coughing.

"Come on, Doc!" His voice was determined. "Not much farther now."

How could he be sure? she asked herself, trying to wipe the cough tears out of her eyes. Then a crack of dark blue appeared against the blackness overhead.

Chapter Twenty-two

In the morning, Vexk returned to the pool chamber with Khea at her heels. She raised the sheltering tapestry, hung to trap the heat of the thermal pool within. Warm, moist air swept over her as she glimpsed an ebony-furred figure emerging from the water. At first glance, she thought it was the Black/on/black, then detected the faint beige patches just behind the ears; it was the other Levv, called Kei.

The Black/on/black was still stretched out, asleep on the rocky ledge where she had left him. He was not as large as some males, or as muscled, and yet, she had glimpsed a presence in his eyes last night that tantalized her, an air of having seen and understood things beyond ordinary knowing, of standing at the center of events as they unfolded into something wondrous and new. Her nose twitched as she considered again the impossibility secreted here in this cave: two *Levv* males, one grown up wild as a kikinti in the mountains without even a proper Line Mother or males' house to mold his behavior, and the other raised off-world among an altogether alien breed . . . two more oddly shaped pieces to fit with the unsettling news Khea had brought back from Vvok. If only she could perceive the pattern that wove these disparate elements together, she would know what to do.

She stepped inside, then held up the tapestry so Khea, her arms loaded down with bundles, could squeeze past. Nisk, also wet from the pool, tied back his dripping mane and sniffed appreciatively at the aroma of the food and drink they had brought.

"Freshly steeped taif." Vexk set out the steaming jug. "And yellow-cake with mizb paste."

Nose quivering, Kei approached. His wet fur clung to his body, revealing him to be even more massive than she had thought. He would create quite a stir at a Gathering, she mused, then wondered at herself, thinking about such things out of season.

Kei sat on his haunches. "The old ones used to speak of such foods."

Vexk was touched by the starved look on his scarred face. He was obviously hungry for everything long denied him—acceptance, tradition, ritual. Of *what* had Levv actually been guilty all those seasons ago? Had they committed wanton slaughter without challenge, or blood-debt, or any other acceptable reason? She had to admit now she really did not know, but the Council of Lines had been out of balance since that terrible day. The odd number of Lines allowed three of them to dominate the other two, and no good would ever come of that. The ancient patterns called for six Lines, evenly balanced in power, as in the Beginning.

"Khea and I leave for the Meeting Ground soon." She broke a loaf of moist yellow-cake into smaller pieces.

Nisk's battle-notched ears raised as he squatted beside the jug of dark-gold taif and poured out a portion for himself. "The Black/on/black needs to speak to as many hrinn as possible about the creatures beyond the mountains. The Council of Lines would be the perfect time and place."

"But will they believe him?" Kei's massive shoulders bristled. "He is Levv."

His tone was edged with bitterness, and he had a right to it, Vexk thought. She met his gaze with a Restorer's frankness, which made most hrinn uncomfortable, and was impressed with how well he withstood her inspection. Not a hair stirred and the cant of his ears was quite indifferent. "It may well be that the attack on Levv was one aspect of the pattern now emerging. I have followed it most of my life, and although I do not yet know its name, I can say with certainty it is large and very involved, so that it disrupts any other smaller patterns that try to arise."

She crossed to the sleeping Black/on/black and stared down at him. "His very existence implies that it began with him." She brushed the ebony fur with her fingertips, marveling at the perfection of the sacred pattern, not an off-color speck anywhere. His eyes darted back and forth beneath closed eyelids. He shifted, cried out, then sprang, snarling and angry, and knocked her backwards. Her head cracked against the opposite wall of the cavern. A star of black light exploded behind her eyes and she only distantly felt the powerful hands constricting her neck, the claws ripping.

"No!" Dimly, she heard Nisk's voice as the other two males struggled to drag off the Black/on/black. Her head rang and her vision tunneled down to a narrow coruscating field of red. Blood thundered in her ears as though a fierce storm raged within her head. The thought flickered through her mind that Levvs *were* mad as the other Lines had said all along. Nisk had made a terrible mistake bringing this one here.

Then the cruel claws piercing her neck fell away, and she could breathe again. The Black/on/black hung

limp in the other two males' grasp. She slid down
the wall, gasping, her head pounding. Khea dashed
to her side and blotted the gashes with her sleeve.
Just like a fully trained Restorer, Vexk thought
distractedly and clung to Khea's arm for support.

Over on the other side of the chamber, the Black/
on/black's gaze was misted and strange. She thought
again of the reputed madness carried in his Line, then
looked deeper. It wasn't that at all, she realized. The
bleakness in his eyes was raw, naked fear. Fur rose
on her shoulders as she contemplated an enemy that
inspired that kind of fear in a hrinn such as the Black/
on/black himself, who was born to master all patterns.

With a convulsive shudder, he looked away. "I was
dreaming of . . . them, the flek." He raked trembling
fingers back through the disheveled mane hanging in
his face. "You don't know what they can do to a world
once they take it."

She had not really understood the night before,
when Nisk had tried to explain about the off-world
creatures beyond the mountains, but she saw the
deadly truth now—in the set of his ears, the disorder
of his fur, the bleakness of his eyes. This danger was
much larger than anything he could explain, far beyond
her limited experience. "Nisk spoke to me of this while
you were sleeping." She hesitated. "They sound—very
strange, but everything about this pattern is new."

"I—" He stepped toward her, then glanced down
at his leg. "The pain is gone!" The bottomless black
eyes were wide now, surprised. "I thought perhaps
I had dreamed that too."

"Then you should be able to walk whole into the
Council meeting." Nisk pushed a piece of yellow-cake
into his hand. "There you will tell the Lines of
these—flek—who think they can steal the very earth
from under our feet. Then they will follow you back
across the mountains and wipe them from the face
of our world."

The Black/on/black stared at the yellow-cake crumbling in his palm. "If they can be made to listen to a Levv."

The circle of six gray monoliths on the crest of the hill had kept watch over the Lines down through untold generations. Beshha breasted the top of the hill, her daughters trailing a discrete and respectful distance behind, and stood gazing up at the striated stone of Jhii. It loomed over them all, intricately carved to memorialize great *patterns/in/motion* detected in the past, many of which had made Jhii preeminent in its day among the other Lines. In the center, just above her head, was her favorite, the sinuous swirl of *death/in/longing*, which had precipitated the downfall of Levv and set in motion the series of events that would culminate in today's victory.

Above it was incised *stars/over/fire*, the ancient pattern which ruled all business conducted up here on top of the hill and had brought the boon of measured discourse to her kind. She felt its powerful presence already threading through her thoughts, seeking to calm ambition, soothe edginess, but she fought it. A daring new pattern was being summoned, one that would both suit her far better and bring a new way of life to the Lines.

She eased onto the uncomfortable stone seat, worn hollow by previous Jhii Line Mothers and sniffed the scent-glyphs behind her, then crooked a claw at her daughter standing just outside the great circle. "What is this—*retreat/Line/disappointment*?"

"Surely not!" Syll darted forward. "Who would dare write such a thing here?"

In spite of her dislike of exertion, Beshha raked her gold-tipped handclaws across Syll's ears. "Well, it might as well be! Have these glyphs redone immediately before anyone else notices, or I will tear your throat out!"

Ears bright with blood, Syll lowered her gaze and stalked over to the bundle of supplies they'd brought. Beshha settled back against the cold damp stone, seething. She hated being wrong, but it was clear she had been too lax. Perhaps she should raise another hungry young breeder up in Syll's place. That would teach—

Orange robes fluttered at the periphery of her vision. "I never thought to see your bloated presence lolling in the Great Circle again."

Beshha's own ears flattened as she recognized the hoarse voice of Kendd's broken-toothed Line Mother, Yikan.

Yikan's yellow-and-white face was aloof. "What calamity pried you out of Jhii's warm tunnels? Have you finally killed Syll?"

"Oh, it *is* you, Yikan." Beshha ran an idle clawtip over the intricate scrollwork carved into the side support. "I'd heard you were dead."

"Not yet." Yikan pushed one of the silver bracelets dangling around her whip-thin arm back into place. "Unless you would care to attempt to send me through the Gates yourself?"

"Are you suggesting Line should fight Line?" Beshha tried to look shocked.

"Do not play the innocent with me, you young rag-ear." Yikan settled in the great Kendd seat directly across the circle from Jhii. "It has been done, as you very well know."

"Ah, but those days were very dark." Beshha twitched at a fold in her robes. "I dislike speaking of them."

"I have a long list of things I dislike." Yikan bared her worn teeth. "Shall I name them?"

"I doubt we have the time." Beshha flicked an ear as a line of light-blue-robed females approached the circle of stones from the northwest. "Why not list the things you can still do—at your age."

"Enough time remains for me to see a few more wet-ears like you come and go at Jhii." Yikan's gaze across the open circle was uncomfortably direct. Beshha resisted the impulse to look away. "Which is sad—some of us still remember when Jhii was an honorable Line."

She was spared having to answer by the arrival of Rebban's Line Mother, Aan, and her sturdy contingent of daughters, all wearing their manes in long plaits down their backs. She watched as the dark-brown old female greeted Yikan, then took Rebban's ancient seat, next to Kendd.

Rebban and Kendd. Beshha narrowed her eyes. They were the last of the conservatives who dictated little or no contact with the Outsiders, and today, for the first time, she was going to have the satisfaction of watching them overruled. That was what had drawn her out of the comfort of Jhii's compound. The pattern she and the others had been courting for so many seasons was nearly complete. With Fik's ascension to the head of Qartt, the Council lay beneath the claws of those who were not afraid to try patterns never before followed.

Qartt and Vvok had not arrived yet, but red-eyed Ankt still rode low in the sky. Soon, Beshha promised herself, her time would come. From this day on, nothing would ever be the same.

Heyoka's body hummed with stored power as the yirn carrying him plodded toward the river. Until Nisk had finally persuaded him to soak in the thermal pool, he had not understood the difference between *drawing* power and merely using what his body had already stored. The energy he had used in blueshift before had come from the ordinary workings of his own cells, and therefore had left him dazed and drained afterward.

But when he immersed himself in the steaming pool, he had felt the cells of his body accumulating thermal energy and converting it into something potent, frightening in its intensity. He felt larger somehow, too big for his skin and too full, as though if anyone touched him, he would lose this tremendous charge of energy in one gigantic burst.

The two Restorers passed them, riding double on a single scrawny yirn. It balked at the edge of the water, then waded reluctantly into the shallow ford. Vexk wore a makeshift bandage around her neck torn from the younger female's robe and he felt guilty every time he saw her. He might easily have killed her in that terrible dream-addled moment back in the cave and he wanted badly to apologize, but could find no words in Hrinnti for such an emotion. It was possible to express that one had made a slight error in judgement, or to convey probable inappropriateness of an action, but references for accepting guilt simply did not exist in the vocabulary he had so far acquired. He wondered if hrinn were so obsessed with the outside influence of "patterns," they had no need to take responsibility for wrongful actions.

Nisk's mount hesitated at the river bank, snorting at the swirling green water, so he leaned over and snarled into its ear. It lashed its tail and splashed on into the river. Heyoka's stolid beast followed without protest, and he heard the muffled splash of Kei's yirn to the rear. From the opposite bank, they angled up into the hills, following a worn trail through scrub that soon became denser and more leafy. As they climbed, Heyoka noticed a circle of huge stones set into the ground like monstrous doors into another reality.

Nisk turned back to him. "When you are ready, you must wait for the Council to notice you. Males, even Leaders of the males' houses, have no rights here and must be invited to speak."

"This is too serious a matter for games of protocol." Heyoka glanced aside at the sheltering mountains, all that stood between them and the flek. "This world has very little time left."

"For countless generations, the pattern which rules the Meeting Ground has allowed us to come together without killing one another unnecessarily," Nisk said stiffly. "We do not consider it on a par with a sport for untried cublings."

Patterns again. Heyoka rolled his eyes wearily.

Nisk rode on, gaze solidly ahead. "Expect nothing from the Council. Do not even think of what you want, when you tell them what lies beyond Levv. Line Mothers care little for other voices than their own, but if you remember that you are only a male and know nothing of our ways, they may listen."

The narrow track led up onto the broad top of the hill. The four yirn fell into single file, horned heads bobbing as they plodded up the incline. The great stones loomed, now close enough for even the incised patterns that covered them to be visible.

Just before the top of the rise, they dismounted and left the yirn in the care of bright-eyed cublings robed in an assortment of colors. As they moved downwind, the scents of assembled hrinn assaulted Heyoka, a tidal wave of Jhii and Vvok pheromones blended with a multitude of unidentified males and females. He stumbled, the taste of brass on the back of his throat. Heat surged through his body as his capillaries dilated in unison and a glimmer of blueness leaped from one set of handclaws to the other. The savage *other* within him surfaced and clamored to make itself heard.

The hilltop seemed to seethe with energy, as though each blade of grass, each clod of earth, every molecule of air had a life all its own. He felt an indefinable presence, hovering just at the edges of his vision, as though, if he could turn around fast enough, he would catch sight of it. Was this a side effect of so many hrinn gathered in one place, and if so, why didn't it affect everyone else in the same way? Was he just overly sensitive because he'd had so little experience mingling with his own kind?

Vexk turned to them, her pale-gray face solemn. "Khea and I will go first, but you should hear what she has to say. It involves the Outsider who accompanied the Black/on/black to this world."

Still overwhelmed, Heyoka stared numbly at the gray-and-white cubling. "Mitsu? What do you know about her?"

Khea flinched at the mention of that name and then shrank behind Vexk, who calmly smoothed a fold of the youngster's yellow robe. "Told once, this tale will be difficult enough, Black/on/black," she said, then took the cubling's arm and walked her past the onlooking daughters of five Lines down a crushed-gravel path between two of the huge stones and into the apparent hurricane's eye of the inner circle.

He followed them, Nisk and Kei at his heels, and stopped just short of the stones, peering around the edge of the closest. Lesser-ranked females drew back from the three males, ears pinned, to give them a wide, but grudging, berth. Snarls rattled in the backs of their throats. This was clearly not a place for males.

Before each of the six monoliths stood a smaller stone, carved into a huge ornate seat, each different from the rest, and in five of these sat a Line Mother. Three were lanky and scarred, one young and well-muscled, and the fifth, whom he recognized to be Beshha, was plump and sleek. Heyoka realized with a jolt that the empty sixth seat must have belonged to Levv.

A dark-gray female seated on the far right jerked to her feet at the sight of Khea. "How dare you bring that wretch *here*? Her blood is forfeit to Vvok!"

"Is that so, Seska?" Vexk's tone remained cool. "Then how will you pay for the restoration you requested?" She stood before the old female, tall, straight, proud—and fearless.

Seska bristled. "The guild must name another price—this cubling challenged me and lost!"

"Khea has admitted as much." Vexk's tone was leisurely. "But was that not strange behavior for a cubling as retiring as this one? She has not even passed her final gleaning."

"Knew she would not pass, no doubt." The numerous silver and gold bracelets around Seska's withered arms and ankles clinked as she shifted restlessly.

"Was it that?" Vexk turned her pale-gray face back to Khea. "Or did she offer challenge because she could not bear to watch you rip Vvok's honor to shreds before her very nose?"

The old female's lips wrinkled back over broken teeth in an angry snarl. "This matter is for Vvok to decide!" She motioned for a tawny-furred daughter to seize Khea.

"No!" To her right, a yellow-and-white-spotted female rose and stared around the circle imperiously. "This smells of Council business."

The crowd of watching hrinn milled, mumbling low asides to one another as the yellow-and-white sank back on her seat, her eyes still on Khea. "Speak, youngling. What matter endangered Vvok's honor so greatly that you risked a challenge you were too far young to win?"

Khea glanced from the yellow-and-white face back to the dark-gray one. "One of the Vvok scouts wounded an Outsider, then brought it back to the hold. The Line Mother charged me—at the cost of my own life—not to let it die. It grew so weak and ill, I took it to the Restorers. But when it recovered and Fitila came to take it back to Vvok, she said the Line Mother no longer cared if it lived or died—" The young voice faltered, then went on. "Seska met us on the path and ordered me back to the hold.

But—I was concerned—the Outsider was still so weak—and crept back in the darkness. I did not understand why the Line Mother had bid me save it, or forfeit my life, then . . .''

She stared down at the ground, fringed ears trembling.

"And what did you see when you went back, youngling?" Yikan's tone was patient.

"They were . . . beating it."

Less than twenty paces away, Heyoka's handclaws scraped over the great stone.

Khea's voice was so low, he had to strain to hear her. "They demanded that it tell all it knew about Levv's end . . . and the Levv male who had come back from the stars."

Kei burst past Heyoka to enter the circle, every hair on his huge body bristling, making him seem even larger and more savage. He stared hotly around the circle of stones, then stalked to the empty stone seat and sat down. "Yes," he said, his voice underlaid with a deep, rattling growl, "let us speak finally about Levv!"

Chapter Twenty-three

Kei's scarred face glared with brazen directness at the dark-gray Line Mother and her outrage crackled through the air. The clusters of onlooking lesser-ranked females were stunned to silence, while Heyoka, half hidden by the monolith, could not decide whether he wanted to charge out there to stand by Kei's side, or tear his throat out for interfering.

On the one hand, he knew all too well what Levv's disgrace had cost its few survivors, including himself. He flashed back to the burn of the slaver's whip, and the difficult years afterward, trying to be something he was not and never could be. But then too he thought of the flek infesting the plains, making ready to lay waste to this world while the Hrinn dallied here, arguing about events that had happened over thirty Standard years ago. This was not supposed to be about Levv, but the flek, and he could not let Kei spoil the only chance he had to rally the Hrinn against them.

Seska prowled across the inlaid stone into the center area of finely crushed gravel. Gold and silver jangled around her ankle at each step. There was death in the set of her jaw, and cold naked fury in the wicked line of her claws. "Get out of that seat, you miserable excuse for a male!" Her eyes glittered like chunks of black diamond. "No male has ever been allowed to desecrate this circle since the Beginning!"

"You dare to speak to me of desecration?" Kei sprang back onto his feet, his black fur contrasting starkly with the striated gray of the surrounding stones. "After what you, all of you, committed against Levv?"

"Fool, why bother to speak of Levv now?" Beshha's voice was smooth and lazy. "There is no Levv. A few of the lower ranked females might have escaped to breed brats with plains hrinn, but such progeny could never be considered truly *Levv*."

Kei raised his muzzle high, proud and fierce in his coarse brown robes. "I bear only the blood of old Levv! Your noses know the truth of that!"

"Evidently he bears the same madness that brought Levv down." A snub-nosed pale-ginger female spoke from the Qartt seat. Much younger and more muscled than her counterparts, she leaned forward, eyes fever-bright. "It was said none of the males carried it, but apparently that is not true."

"The penalty for madness is death!" Seska wrenched the shocked eyes of the crowd back to her. "Long ago, the Council acted to prevent this scourge from spreading to the other Lines. How can we allow this diseased male to live, knowing he could breed with our unsuspecting daughters and taint our Lines?"

Almost forgotten in the center of the circle, Vexk slipped between Seska and Kei. Her eyes were luminous, as though she saw far beyond that particular moment. "If we are speaking of madness, Seska, then make us understand why you concerned yourself with an *Outsider*. Your actions make no sense."

This was of no help either, Heyoka thought,

debating how to interrupt. Over on the far edge of the circle, a dark-gray figure skulked through the crowd, a male, watching him with fervid black eyes. His hackles raised.

"Why," Vexk continued, "bring the Outsider back to Vvok in the first place, and then, if you wished to preserve its life, why not send it back to its own kind? Why, instead, contract for a restoration, for which you were obligated to pay, and then afterwards beat the poor creature for information about Levv until it was senseless, before trading it for lights-that-kill?"

Next to Vvok on the great circle, a brown-furred Line Mother sprang to her feet, ears flattened to her skull. "Lights-that-kill?"

Seska hobbled back to her seat and eased down onto the carved stone. "In exchange for the return of the wounded one. Outsiders trade with all of us from time to time. They might give you something of value too, if you were more clever at bargaining."

Unable to wait any longer, Heyoka entered the circle. "Among Outsiders, the penalty for giving you weapons would be death." He was suddenly overwhelmed with the sobering knowledge of the identity of those who must have dealt with Vvok. "It was not *humans* from the station who traded you those lights, but *flek* from the other side of the mountains, the same flek who intend to steal the land from under your feet and the air out of your lungs!"

"Another Levv heard from." Seska's face contorted into a bare-toothed sneer. "It seems we did a poor job of it when we sought to put an end to Levv's madness, but we can rectify that now!" She motioned to those waiting behind her and a double handful of tawny and dark shapes streaked toward Heyoka and Kei.

The suppressed *other* in his subconscious shook itself like an awakening wolf, then gazed out through

Heyoka's startled eyes. Blood! it whispered all too eagerly. It was the pheromones, he realized, appalled. The females were almost upon him as he groped within for the power he had stored and for the first time purposefully shifted the faces around him into blueness.

It was easy.

The racing females slowed until they might have been stop-action tapes, advancing one leisurely frame at a time. He extended his arm and loosed a bolt of raw blue energy, bathing each attacker in turn. They drifted to the stone-inlaid ground like autumn leaves. He glanced behind him at Nisk, where the older male stood, a pillar of blue. He could feel his heart whizzing in his chest . . . the blood pounding in his ears like an overworked engine . . .

Control it . . . if he couldn't drop back out, he would die, and then this entire world would be lost, along with the proud, savage hrinn who ruled it. He held his breath, willed his heart to slow, color to return to the world, the garbled drawn-out sounds around him to make sense again . . .

"—him!" Seska shouted, then gaped at the seven females sprawled in a heap, fur still smoking. Snarls and growls continued as Kei battled the three who had come at him.

The savage *other* within him woke again and, caught by surprise, Heyoka spun and roared, a full-throated thundering which carried something of the blue power within it. His extended claws caught the sun and reflected it around the stone circle. The three remaining females, hard-pressed and bloodied, froze, staring at him with stunned black eyes. A shower of blue sparks burst from the tips of his handclaws.

The *other* glimmered behind his eyes, a brilliant, overpowering light shining through the cracks of his conscious mind. It longed for the taste of blood, but knew he could not give into it. "The matter of Levv

must be settled later." His words rang out in the
brittle silence. "Right now, death lies in wait for all
of us on the other side of the mountains. We have
a chance, one small opportunity, to stop the flek
before they change Anktan into a death world where
neither human nor hrinn can live." He turned to the
multitude of sharp-nosed hrinnti faces pressing in
around him. "And if you let them steal this world,
a hundred others will die soon after."

"Black/on/black!" The whispers built into a crescendo, a rising tide deep enough to drown him.
"Black/on/black! Black/on/black!"

"No!" he tried to shout over the chant, but Nisk
fought through the excited crowd to his side.

"Without the Voice's protection, this one would
have died with the rest when Levv fell." Nisk's earnest
black gaze bored into the milling, expectant crowd
of hrinn until there was silence again. "A pattern arose
in the midst of that chaos to shape his life, and he
has walked at its heart ever since." He stepped away
from Heyoka and lowered his eyes in a pointed
gesture of submission. "He is not merely directed by
it, but at its center, so that all events flow from him.
He is the guiding force!"

"He is not!" The dark-gray male he had noticed
earlier, shouldered through the throng of females,
striking with his handclaws at those who would not
give way. "Since when have *you* heard the Voice,
banished one? I remember nothing in my seasons at
the Mish River Males' House about you hearing the
Voice."

"I have never claimed to hear it, Priest." Nisk met
the newcomer's eyes squarely. "But that does not
prevent me from recognizing patterns, or him from
being the Black/on/black."

It was Rakshal, Heyoka realized, who had challenged him that night back at the river when Nisk
had fought in his place.

"He is the Outsiders' creation." Rakshal's gray muzzle swept around in a wide arc as he stared the crowd down. "Just as they make boxes that fly and talk, they have made this thing which only looks like a Black/on/black to fool us."

"No one made me!" The *other's* rage boiled through Heyoka until he thought that it would sear his brain. "You and I can settle this later, anytime you want, in any way. For now we must all work together and fight the flek!"

"You would like that, would you not, false one?" Rakshal bared his teeth and glided closer, balancing on the balls of his feet. "Do the Outsiders want our land so badly that they have to trick us into leaving it? What waits beyond the mountains? I say that any hrinn who follows this creature there will never hunt again!"

Rakshal's smell this close was overpowering, male pheromones full of acrid overtones that Heyoka suddenly recognized as the by-product of power. No doubt, he smelled much the same at that moment. Staring into the other's glittering eyes, the *other's* desire to kill built into a burning ache.

"*Black/on/black!*" Rakshal's tone was mocking. "If you really are a legend, then try to kill me, but beware, I have the power of the Voice in my claws!" He sprang, already moving faster than any normal hrinn could have moved.

A split second later, Heyoka dropped into blueshift too, fighting for his life against this male, who was both taller and heavier than he was, and whose muscles and bones had the advantage of developing in this gravity. Rakshal's charge carried him backwards and he struck his head against the stone-inlaid ground. Dazed, he struggled against the wicked double rows of teeth at his throat, then managed to thrust his feet into the pit of Rakshal's stomach and send the other male flying over his head.

He scrambled back onto his feet as, a few feet away, Rakshal faced him again. All around them, the onlookers, still in normal time, were as motionless as the great circle of stones. Then he rushed Rakshal again, fighting on in their private universe of silent, electric blue.

Rakshal's claws slashed at his throat, but this time he was ready and snatched his gray robes, using the priest's momentum to trip him. For a moment, the gray-furred male sprawled at his feet and Heyoka circled him warily. If he had any chance to win, it lay in his combat training and experience, although, perhaps, in the end, it would just come down to which one of them could hold blueshift longer.

Raising an arm, the priest suddenly blasted him with a bolt of sizzling blue fire. Heyoka staggered and sat down hard, the world fuzzing out around the periphery of his vision. The power sizzled through his body, then grounded out into the rock beneath him, leaving him weakened and confused.

"Black/on/black!" Rakshal sneered, moving in. He lifted his arm and seared another shaft of burning blueness into Heyoka's chest.

Heyoka fought the colors invading his vision. He had to hold on; if he dropped out of blueshift, even for a second, the priest would have him, then the flek would rule Anktan, and it would all be his fault.

Rakshal snarled. "Die, false one!"

Each breath bore the agony of a million gees, but then the dark-gray priest stumbled, and Heyoka sensed the attacks were draining him too. If only he could use the energy Rakshal was throwing at him instead of letting it drain back into the ground. Rakshal stretched his arm out for the final blow. Heyoka braced himself, heart leaden in his chest. Another such blow might well kill him. What he needed was additional power of his own . . .

The bolt of blue fire snaked out towards his chest.

On impulse, he embraced it, opening the channels within and trying to draw it into his nearly depleted reserves as he had drawn the heat of the pool. A fierce burning shuddered through him, a molten red-eyed pain that faded to a tingle. He took a tentative breath, which came more easily, then another.

Rakshal blinked in surprise, then hit him with another bolt, weaker than the last. Heyoka took it more quickly this time and sublimated it into his own cells. He rose from the ground.

Rakshal backed away, moving more slowly with each step until he seemed not to be moving at all. *He had lost the blueshift.* Reaching within, Heyoka found the key faster this time and dropped back into normal speed. "We should not fight each other like this." Humanlike, he held his hand out. "Stand beside me to save this world."

Instead, Rakshal leaped, fastening his teeth into Heyoka's throat. Driven back with the force of his attack, Heyoka replied with a savage surge of blue fire, discharging as much as he could channel in one burst as they fell. Jaws convulsed into his throat, bringing blackness even closer, then relaxed and slipped away.

He heaved the priest aside and stumbled back to his feet, staggering with weariness. Nisk leaned over the priest's limp body. "He still breathes. Finish him while you can."

"No!" Heyoka's head hung wearily as he dabbed at the streaming gashes on his throat with the back of his hand. "I have beaten him fairly. He cannot stop us now."

Nisk's ears flattened. "Are you one of us?" His eyes reflected the morning light of the red sun, more alien than he had ever seen them. "Or are you just an Outsider that walks like a hrinn? You have to decide. He will never be beaten until he is dead!"

Heyoka paused, remembering. "But he let you live

when he defeated you for Leadership of the males'
house."

"Because he had not the strength left to kill me.
And now, because I lived to be your sponsor, *you* will
finish him."

Heyoka realized Nisk's logic was valid; Rakshal
would only interpret mercy as weakness and attack
him again the first moment he regained his strength.
And they had no more time to waste in this futile
infighting. It might already be too late to save this
world. They could not delay a moment longer, but
the overlay of more than thirty Standard years of
human culture bound him. Revulsion swept through
him as he gazed around the crowd of expectant sharp-
muzzled faces, knowing what they wanted.

At his feet, Rakshal's body shuddered, then the
angry dark eyes slitted open, glimmering up at him
like wells of black ice. His lips wrinkled back in a
weak snarl. "False hrinn! I knew you were not the
Black/on/black! I knew—"

As though it belonged to someone else, Heyoka's
arm rose, then discharged blue fire into the priest's
body until his stored energy was gone and he was
drawing from the energy needed for normal cellular
function. At his feet, Rakshal writhed and twisted,
blackening into a blasted, lifeless thing until Heyoka's
vision grayed out and he had to admit he had nothing
more.

"Black/on/black!" All around him, the chant began
again, softly at first, then louder, building into an ear-
splitting litany he could not shout down. "Black/on/
black! Black/on/black!"

Heyoka stared at the people he had crossed a
galaxy to find. The fire of fanaticism was written
across their furred faces, yet he was painfully aware
there was very little truth to this Black/on/black
mythology. At the most, he had only a slight edge in
the number of certain power-absorbing cells in his

body which obviously all hrinn must have to some
degree. He wanted them to stand against the flek
because they understood the danger, not because of
a chance-generated genetic combination that made
him resemble an old legend.

But moments before, they had been ready to tear
out his throat because he was born of Levv. Now that
they had caught him up high on the wave of their
expectations, they were his because he had taken
command in the only way they understood.

A few feet away, Nisk lifted his gaze briefly from
the charred form of the priest, speaking to Heyoka
with searing ebony eyes: the Black/on/black was a
weapon forged to their own hands. If he would be
what they expected, the Hrinn would follow him and
fight the flek with every life and resource they
possessed. But if he insisted on being merely Heyoka
Blackeagle, an outcast Levv male, he would share
Levv's, as well as Anktan's, death. It was not a choice
he faced, but a certainty.

He threw back his head, and with a roar that shook
him down to the depths of his soul, thrust his fist
high into the air.

The ear-splitting feedback from the testing of the
transfer grid would deafen her in time—if she lived
that long. Mitsu thought the latter unlikely, though,
in those few moments left to her now when she could
still think like a human. There weren't many.

Although she'd told the truth about her reasons for
coming to this forsaken rock and then made up more,
the flek seemed to be waiting for something—she
wasn't sure what, no doubt something particularly
flekish which her thinking processes weren't quite
perverted enough yet to comprehend. Maybe tomorrow.

Hunching in the corner of her white-walled room,
she beat out a flekish song of which she had become

fond, though she lacked the necessary chitinous covering on her fingers to do it well. For some reason she could no longer remember, she'd resisted at first when Eldrich insisted she learn it, but now the tune was soothing when the human part of her was sad and worried.

As it almost always was.

Eldrich thrust his head through the slick whitish wall and stared at her impatiently. A bit of the special gas mixture needed for the hive to remain fertile slipped through and she sniffed appreciatively.

Soon she would be sufficiently flek in her thoughts to satisfy her captors and they would let her out. She would be able to investigate this base and find out if her human half retained enough control to do any damage.

Stepping into the small room, Eldrich drew the wretched silver tube out of his pocket and pointed it at her head. Closing her eyes, she braced herself for the wrenching dislocation and alien thought patterns to come. If she were strong enough, she would get her chance, if—

As the light faded, the main body of the crowd drifted down to the river to watch the supposed Black/on/black bathe his wounds, leaving three of the Line Mothers behind in the great circle. Seska dismissed her attendants in order to speak freely to Beshha and Fik, and they did the same. The mingled scents of the six Lines lingered on the grass and permeated the air, both heady and nerve-wracking at the same time. It might almost have been a Gathering, she thought. She prowled restlessly across the inlaid stone, cursing the pain in her joints that made her limp and seem less potent than she was. "Black/on/black, my ears and nose too!"

"But what if he really is?" Fik played with a strand of polished bluestones, staring moodily.

For one so newly ascended, Seska thought, her stance was overconfident, a fault that could be exploited.

Fik gazed at the distant figures at the river. "A powerful pattern is at work here. You saw what he did."

Seska eased onto the red cushions piled over the great stone seat of Vvok. Her lip curled in a silent snarl. What a pair of limp-eared idiots! If it were possible to do what had to be done alone, she would rip both of their hearts out just to have the blessing of silence once more.

Beshha selected a handful of ripe mottled-green mizb fruits from Seska's dish and popped them neatly into her mouth. "We may have been mistaken about the nature of this pattern." The cant of her ears was uncertain and her scent had an erotic edge to it.

Seska realized the Line Mother of Jhii was more than a little attracted to the Black/on/black. "Shut up!" She relaxed against the plush cushions. "You're making my head ache with all this whining!" She stretched an arm above her head, listening to the bracelets clink together. "It is not we, but they who mistake the nature of this pattern. It has been ours from the start. We have only to step into the center."

"But the Outsider does not answer the box anymore." Beshha fussed at her mane, tangled by the breeze on top of the hill. "What if it has gone away? What if it is *dead*?"

"Those creatures never die unless someone kills them." Seska studied the other two, who apparently could not smell beyond the ends of their dull noses. "You haven't done something stupid, have you?"

"No!" Beshha looked horrified. "I have not even seen one for seasons now."

"Nor I." Fik sneezed twice in quick succession. "Fitila is the only one who has crossed trails with an Outsider in recent memory. Perhaps she killed it."

"You have only to listen to that disgraceful gray-and-white cubling to know better than that." Beshha's eyes crinkled slyly. "How could you let that happen, Seska?" Extending her handclaws, she worked at a snarl. "Really, Jhii has not lost a youngling to that barren bunch of thieves for seasons now."

"Only because Jhii has not bred a cubling with a single scrap of talent since long before I was born!" Seska pinned her ears back. "Which is a great deal longer ago than either of you two lackwits is equipped to understand." She gazed down at the crowd wading in the river, the figures so tiny at this distance, so vulnerable looking. "Tomorrow, we will rally our daughters and follow this supposed Black/on/black across the mountains with the others." She flexed her handclaws. The last of Ankt's gaze reflected redly along the curved edges. "This part of the pattern is not yet clear to me, but he speaks of a battle. If there is fighting, stay close to his back."

Her eyes sagged closed, but the red afterimage of Ankt lingered on the inside of her eyelids. "You know how dreadfully easy it is to make a mistake in the heat of battle."

Chapter Twenty-four

With the first ginger streaks of dawn, hrinn, both on yirnback and on foot, filtered through the Meeting Ground into the green-carpeted hills and on toward the mountains. Heyoka could almost feel the disapproval of the ancient standing stones as they presided over what had to be a doomed exodus. The scents of the six Lines were so mingled at this point, he could not separate one from the other, and the wildness that engendered beat through his blood. He understood now why hrinn did not often assemble in large groups. Immersion in so many pheromones called the savage within each of them to the surface, made challenge and then senseless death almost inevitable, yet they had no chance at all unless they faced the flek as a unit.

He wished he believed in patterns so all of this would make sense, but he saw nothing ahead of them but almost certain failure and death. He tried one more time to calculate the chances of success and shuddered at the thought of arrows against lasers . . . spears against aircraft . . . teeth and claws against armor. If he dwelled on it, he knew he would lose his nerve. However slim their chances, they could not cower here and allow the flek to proceed unimpeded. They would all simply have to do their best.

The evening before, the assembled Line Mothers had dispatched small leathery messenger jits to every hold and house up and down the Mish River Valley. Now hrinn trickled in, answering his summons without any real concept of what they were up against, coming solely because he was the reputed Black/on/black, and in every face, in the multitude of ice-bright midnight eyes, he saw a reverence that made his skin crawl. He was not what they thought, most certainly not the one for whom they had been waiting. He was only a sham, and a very poor one at that.

The only person who understood even the smallest part of what facing the flek meant was Kei, with his scarred face and angry, arrogant manner. Unfortunately, he was consumed with the past, still far too concerned with the fate of Levv, and his every word reeked of challenge. Even if Kei had crossed the mountains years ago with this news, they would never have followed him. They rallied now only for the Black/on/black and would stay until he stumbled and proved the legend hollow after all.

Behind him, hrinnti footpads whispered against the inlaid stones; he caught Kei's scent, a broad masculine base note, underlaid with the specific pheromone that said "Levv." He flicked an ear back, acknowledging his relative.

"Something approaches from the south," Kei's deep voice said. "It stinks too much to be hrinnti."

Heyoka's heart jumped. "Human or flek?" he asked, praying it would prove to be humans from the station.

"It does not matter!" Kei's massive outline was dark against the fading night. He seemed larger than

Heyoka remembered, more brutish. "Outsiders are all the same! We should kill all of them!"

"They are *not* the same." Exasperated, Heyoka shouldered his backpack and headed toward the edge of the bluff. His cuts and scrapes from last night's duel still ached and his temper was short. "And if you have any desire to live through the next few days, you had best learn the difference."

Khea's graceful gray-and-white form appeared out of the half-darkness, ghost-pale, except that, he reminded himself, hrinnti imaginations had never conceived of anything so fanciful as spirits. She cast her eyes down. "Black/on/black, Vexk asks your assistance."

If he lived here a thousand years, he thought irritably, he would not become accustomed to the way these creatures never looked you in the eye unless they intended to kill you. He touched her shoulder. "What does she need?"

The cubling shrank from his fingers without seeming to move. "Outsiders are approaching from the south. She hopes you will speak with them."

Absentmindedly, he nodded, then realized the gesture was meaningless. "Show me," he amended, then followed her slender yellow-robed form back through the rapidly growing light.

At the edge of the gentle bluff leading up to the Meeting Ground, Vexk waited beside the trail. "Outsiders," she said and wrinkled her nose in frustration. "I mean *humans*. I found them close to the river, but only one speaks our language and that very badly. I could not understand what it wanted."

Boots scraped against the rocky path that led up from the flood plain. Ten . . . perhaps fifteen, Heyoka estimated. A dark-haired head emerged from the trail's cleft and stopped.

Heyoka stepped closer. "Are you from the station?"

"Yes." The figure edged forward. "Sergeant Blackeagle?"

Then he caught her scent. "Dr. Alvarez! What are you doing up here?"

"I—" She sagged against the rock, legs buckling. "I'm sorry." She rubbed at a scabbed cut on her forehead. "We've been walking all night." One by one, a line of weary, grime-encrusted figures appeared behind her and waited in dogged silence.

He studied her face. Lines of strain outlined her mouth and her eyes were bleak. "Did you contact the nearest base?"

"The—the flek blasted the station again after you left." Her voice shook. "You were right. There isn't much time left. We—" She glanced back at the exhausted men and women braced against the rocks. "We brought you what supplies and weapons we could salvage from our stores. I'm sorry it isn't more. We should have given you everything when you first came to us with the news about the flek. Anyway, whatever you have in mind, we've come to help."

A man stepped forward, his right arm a thick white bundle bandaged tightly against his body. "We never stocked explosives, but we did scrounge eleven undamaged laser rifles and some extra power clips."

"This is Security Chief Cuppertino." Alvarez pushed a lock of dark hair out of her face. "Scott, that is. And I'm Sanyha."

Heyoka looked over the tattered, but determined men and women, trying to evaluate them as recruits. They were soft, as well as untrained, and worn out, but he understood the measure of the human spirit much better than he did that of the Hrinn. Once humans got their teeth into something, they rarely let go, no matter what the cost. He held out his hand.

Scott Cuppertino stared at his fur-covered hand, then gripped it awkwardly with his undamaged left. "I just want a chance at those bastards, Blackeagle. Just give me a chance." His dark-shadowed eyes blinked convulsively.

Another few minutes on his feet and this one was going to collapse. Heyoka turned to Vexk. "Can you arrange for some food—*cooked* food—for them?"

"Cooked?" Vexk blinked at him. "Are they ill?"

Heyoka felt amusement welling up in him again. "Just cook it. I will explain later." Dammit, he told himself, why did he feel most human when he was among hrinn? He pulled the doctor back onto her feet. "Go with Vexk. She'll see you get food and rest before we leave."

The doctor's fragile human fingers closed around his wrist. Then, nodding, she and the rest of the humans straggled after Vexk's pale form.

"You are not letting those creatures stay?" Kei glared at the small band.

Fur bristled along Heyoka's spine. He was too tired for this, he told himself. He should have gotten some sleep last night instead of trying to plan for the coming march. "Those *humans* have come to fight at our side, and they brought weapons, which may give us an edge."

"Lights-that-kill?" A fierce eagerness came into Kei's tone and his nostrils flared as he tilted his scarred nose up into the breeze. "I will take one then!"

"No, it's better that they keep the weapons." Heyoka watched Kei's eyes narrow. "They already know how to use them, and it's hard for hrinn to learn. Our hands are too different, and you do not have enough time to learn."

"You cannot trust those creatures at our backs! You can never know what they are thinking!"

"Them? I understand them perfectly!" Heyoka flattened his ears. "It's you that I never understand!"

The other male, taller and burlier than himself, snarled as he struggled for self-control, plainly burning for yet another fight. No more fighting, Heyoka thought wearily, not now when he was too tired to go on and too frightened to give up. Why did everything on this goddammed planet have to be settled by violence? Couldn't these creatures ever *talk* things out?

Bruised and aching, he stood his ground, staring into his mirror image's furious eyes. *This* is what he would have become, if he had not been stolen away by the flek, an unthinking brute who lusted for blood, no matter whose. He realized he would not trade places with Kei and forego the sequence of events, terrible as they had been, which had made him what he was today.

Kei's black gaze glittered in the dim early morning light. He seemed poised on the edge of a charge, then whirled and disappeared down the rocky trail. Heyoka stared after him, hands balled into fists. That was stupid! he told himself. What was wrong with him? He'd led men into battle before. He should have placated Kei, made him understand he was too valuable a fighter to be burdened with a weapon he didn't understand. He should have . . .

Numbly, he wondered how many more times he would say that before the end.

After her second rib-crunching fall, Sanyha abandoned her yirn. They were just too damn big and ornery, and she lacked the strength in her legs to hold on. She watched as her nasty-tempered mount tossed its horned head, then trotted off down the narrow track ahead of her. She didn't care if she had to crawl across these mountains on her hands and knees, she wasn't getting on one of those things again.

Ahead, to the west, the red sun hung low over the mountains. She brushed the dirt off her elbows, then followed the yirn's rump down the hillside. The procession of hrinn was strung out across the mountain trails and she had to keep checking over her shoulder to make sure no one ran over her.

"Problems, Doctor?"

She glanced up to see Sergeant Blackeagle speaking from a switchback higher up the hill. She dabbed at a bloody scratch on her hand. "It's not the first time."

"Stay there. I'll catch it for you." He leaned over his mount's shaggy neck.

"Don't—" she began, but he'd already disappeared around the bend before she could finish. "—bother."

A moment later, she flagged him down as he approached. "I really don't want to see that misbegotten beast again." She tried to smile up at him, but the expression wouldn't quite fit on her lips. "I might feel obliged to shoot it and that would be a waste of good ammunition."

He stared down at her, sharp-muzzled face and black eyes unfathomable, then reached down, grasping her arm with his five inhumanly strong fingers and two thumbs, and swung her effortlessly up behind him onto the beast's backbone.

"Thanks!" she gasped. The yirn fell into its rough gait before she could get her balance and she had to clutch Blackeagle's waist to keep from falling off. Each stride reverberated all the way up her aching spine. Yirn-riding reminded her of one of those purposefully jolting rides at amusement areas—without the safety harness.

They rode in silence, the yirn setting its own wild pace up and down the hillsides as they traveled toward the flek base on the other side of the mountains. After a while, her eyes sagged closed and she found herself leaning against the warm, plush-furred back in front of her, the tied-up plume of his mane flowing down and tickling her face. Even through the overtunic, his fur smelled clean and musky, a little like an expensive purebred dog her father had once bought for her, imported all the way from Earth.

"Did you ever find her body?"

The question came from nowhere, startling her. Sanyha realized she must have been dozing.

"Body?" She loosened one arm and rubbed her eyes with the back of her hand.

"Mitsu's."

She could feel his voice resonating in her fingers where she touched him. So strange to hear those deep rumbly undertones in Standard without an accent, and stranger still to be riding through the mountains in the company of the same primitive creatures whom she had been studying for years now as impersonally as if they'd been germs under a microscope.

"No, I'm sorry." She paused, trying to get her thoughts together. "We never found Allenby or Eldrich either."

"Eldrich!" The black-furred face looked back at her. "Could he be working for the flek?"

"I guess it's possible, but why would he?" The yirn bunched its muscles to climb a rough spot in the trail and she tightened her grip on Blackeagle. "I mean, how would they pay him? Flek don't deal in anything we recognize as valuable, except slaves, and humans don't believe in slavery."

His body swayed with the yirn, effortless and confident even in the short amount of time he'd had to learn. "Still, she might be alive, since you didn't find her body."

Sanyha didn't know what to say. The images of the bodies she had found floated again into her mind, all the friends and colleagues. Three quarters of the station personnel had died, some in the preliminary explosions, and then more later, in the secondary attacks. She thought of the wounded she had left to be cared for as best they could by the few who had stayed behind. She thought of the years of work to understand this unique species and culture that were now in ashes.

And of course, there was the loss of this entire

quadrant of human-colonized space if the flek got their transport grid up and running. Hundreds of planets lay within striking distance of Anktan, once the flek had been allowed to remodel it to their tastes.

Against all of that, the life of one woman should seem almost insignificant, and yet as a doctor, she'd never been able to weigh lives in that way. She leaned her head against his furred back again and sighed. "Yes," she said, letting the words come out softly, "she may still be alive."

The ear-splitting squeal had almost a pleasant quality about it now, like a flek working song. Mitsu stood beside Eldrich, with the cool evening breeze on her face, looking down from one of the high corner towers into the multicolored center of the grid, seeing the indistinct outlines of a diamond-bright—something—shimmering there. For a second, it seemed the huge object would make it through and solidify, then the tech-drones lost the pattern. Once again, the atoms materialized in random sequences and a heap of smoking rubble scattered across the grid floor.

She beat her fingers together, playing an appropriate dirge to mourn the failure, knowing Eldrich watched her all the time for unflekish behavior. One slip and he would shut her up again for more conditioning, and then perhaps it would take completely, and she would have nothing of herself left.

At the present, she had managed to retain some portion of her humanity, though how much, even she was not really sure. For a few more minutes, she watched the tech-drones scurrying about below, cleaning up the mess so they could make their adjustments and try again; then Eldrich snagged her arm and pulled her inside through the slick wall.

She held her breath as they passed through the semipermeable wall, then emerged with a thankful *pop* on the opposite side. Eldrich steered her over to the screen wall and pushed her down on the floor before it.

"Begin again." His voice was pitched almost as high as flek chitter. "Estimate the troop strength of all enemy bases on this side of the quadrant."

The room darkened as the star map came to life in front of her, the human bases glowing with a smooth, even, blue light. Enemy bases . . . she hunched down on the floor, trying to remember those details from another time, a vaguely distasteful life she had lived among doughy-skinned creatures covered with unsanitary hair who had almost no talent for song. For a second, she saw a dark face in her mind, sharp-nosed, confident. A feeling came over her, she wanted to see that face again, wanted to talk to . . .

Then the feeling ebbed, replacing itself with a strong revulsion for all that hideous fur.

Almost unconsciously, she beat out a mournful rhythm with her forefingers, then fixed her eyes on the map. Although it was painful to remember, her duty lay to the hive. Beginning with the closest system, Bala Cithni, she began to recite her best estimates.

By the time they reached the peak overlooking the flek grid, Kei had still not reappeared. Heyoka had cursed himself repeatedly over that blunder. Not only would Kei have been a great help, since he surely knew the region by heart, but he and the rest of the Levv survivors deserved to fight at their side.

As he and Nisk climbed up to the high notch above the flek installation, he heard a scuffle in the bushes below as several young males sniffed out a long-legged kikinti and dashed after it. On the first night out, he'd tried to organize a foraging system to allow the main body to travel quickly while a few of the more skilled hunted for the rest. That arrangement had fallen to pieces with the first argument between hrinn of different Lines and Houses, as had every other provisioning scheme he'd since tried to implement.

Finally, he'd been forced to realize his fellow hrinn lacked the elemental cultural referents for a march like this that even the greenest human boot camp recruit would have comprehended. They simply could not be organized in the same way as humans. They understood single combat for advancement in rank, or defense of honor, but they were not capable of taking orders from anyone who hadn't demonstrated the ability to tear out their throats.

For the moment, they would do as *he* directed, because he was the so-called Black/on/black and had Rakshal's blood on his hands to prove it, but he could not be everywhere, supervising everything, so his "army" of hrinn trickled across the mountains, a process as frustrating as herding cats. No wonder they worshipped "patterns," he told himself. The ability to impose order on this world looked like a god-given gift to them.

Nisk motioned at the garishly lit grid. "It looks much the same."

Heyoka braced his back against the outcropping of gray, large-grained stone and studied the scene below. Long curving lines of electric pink and blue and green met at the center of the grid, and colored bubbles of light danced in and out. "After dark, I will go down there and look around."

He heard a muffled curse, then boots sliding in the loose chaff that covered the rock face leading up to their vantage point. Glancing back, he saw Sanyha Alvarez sprawled on her stomach at the bottom. She muttered, then began to work her way up to the top again, using the cracks and crevices for finger holds. When she was within reach, he pulled her the rest of the way.

Cradling skinned forearms, she balanced on the

rocky crest between the two of them and stared down
at the grid in the center of the broad russet-and-gold
plain. "My god! It's so beautiful, like a fairy castle
made out of light, and so—big! I had no idea." She
hugged her arms to her chest. "How long do you
think it's been down there? Could it have had anything to do with your disappearance?"

And then, it all clicked . . . the flek grid . . . the
location of Levv just on the other side of this last
mountain, the Line closest to the flek . . . his
abduction and surfacing in a *flek* slave market . . .
they all fit together in a nice neat package, perhaps
even a pattern, as a hrinn would say.

The flek had required a secure area to build their
grid, with no observers, or at least none that anyone
would listen to—and suddenly Levv had stood accused
of terrible crimes never before committed by any
Line. Someone had framed them and used the
Council to do his—or her—dirty work. But he was
puzzled—how had the flek found a way to influence
the Council, and even more mysterious, how could
flek and hrinn ever have had enough in common to
work toward a common goal?

He made a mental note to investigate the Council
meeting that had condemned Levv. Who had brought
the allegations to the Line Mothers and borne witness
against Levv? Was it possible some of the same hrinn
were working with the flek?

If so, then all the danger wasn't down there in
front of them. Some of it could be hiding in their
midst.

Chapter Twenty-five

The illuminated grid stretched across the plains more than half a mile in a stumpy, irregular pentagon. As Heyoka prowled the low brush surrounding it, the night was filled with the smell of rich black earth and greenery, comfortingly familiar, but overlaid by the pervasive alien stink of flek technology and the nose-burning stench of the flek themselves. His nerves were afire; despite years of combat, he had never been this close to an actual flek installation and every instinct told him to flee. Standard Confederation strategy was to bomb such grids from armored air transports or, when feasible, fire upon them from the safety of orbit. As far as he knew, no one had ever successfully conducted a ground assault on one.

He emerged from a stand of prickly blue-leafed bushes and the air snapped with a faint redness, barely visible in the dark, even to his hrinnti eyes. He froze, pulse thundering, his fur standing on end as he took in the flat, acrid odor of a high-energy field. Beneath his feet were several small hard lumps, seared bodies of small rodentlike creatures that bore mute testimony to the nearness of death. He'd been trained to nullify energy fields, but had none of the necessary equipment, so he faded back into the untrimmed scrub and circled north, monitoring the night sounds which had finally returned, soft and hesitant, after the grid's earlier wrenching noise.

The structure loomed above him, impossibly massive, ablaze with garish pinks, greens, purples, and blues that no doubt had some function or meaning in flekish terms. Although he saw movement occasionally on the tall, irregular lattices that formed the sides and the high towers at each of the five oddly spaced points, he could discern no details. Five hundred flek could lurk within. Or five thousand. Or more.

He was panting by the time he reached the next corner, even in the cooling night air, when an agonizing squeal began, a noise like two engine parts that had never known lubrication and were scraping each other to slivers. He dropped into the stiff grass and covered his sensitive ears, gritting his teeth. Over on the far side of the grid, a vehicle of some sort launched into the star-dotted night.

After a moment, the sound receded enough to be bearable. He hunched there, ears pinned, watching the vehicle dwindle until it was only a point of light. Did this mean the flek were still limited to conventional transport? If so, then perhaps the grid wasn't as close to being operational as he had feared and time wasn't as short.

The bushes rustled behind him. He eased around, trying to sniff out who, or what, might be back there, but the wind was out of the wrong quarter. He wished for Kei's more experienced nose, but heard nothing more, and continued working his way around the grid, lattice by lattice, searching for a place where the energy field was weak, or where they could perhaps dig under it.

From somewhere inside the huge grid came a series of great clacks and groans, then the ear-splitting whine began again, vibrating through him until his bones resonated and he felt like howling with pain and frustration. An unheard snarl burst out of his throat as he sprinted toward the next tower.

Out of the corner of his eye, he caught another flicker of movement and spun around. The twisting branches quivered as pale fur slipped past. His snarl became a full growl. He had left orders for everyone, human and hrinn alike, to stay back in camp on the mountain. Not one of them had any idea of how to conduct a military reconnaissance, but of course, hrinn were all so bloody independent. They always did exactly what they pleased.

The din from the grid ascended in pitch as he dove back into the brushy cover. Casting about, he sniffed not one, but several, perhaps as many as five hrinn in the low bushes. What had possessed them to follow him down here? They were jeopardizing everything.

Ebony eyes glittered to his right, and then a stocky pale-ginger female leaped for his throat with feverish eagerness, knocking him backwards. He rolled as her claws ripped his clothing to shreds and gashed his unprotected throat and chest.

He scrambled away and gasped for breath, dangerously close to the energy field protecting the grid's shining latticework. She followed, joined a second later by three more. Handclaws flexed, they fenced him in a rough half-circle, stiff and proud, eyes reflecting the green and pink and electric blue of the garish lights overhead. He recognized all of them: three were the Line Mothers who had spoken against him at the Council of Lines, the other had attacked him at the foot of the plateau when he was searching for Mitsu. This was no overeager bunch trying to help. They had been trying to stop him from the first moment he'd set foot on this world.

His savage *other* surfaced with a rage that made the previous tempers of his life seem like the mildest of moods. He was Leader—him! He had earned that title with tooth and claw and blood, and now none should stand in his way! How dare they challenge him yet again when so much was at stake! He would tear their ears off and feed them to the yirn, gouge their stupid short-sighted eyes out and trample what was left into the ground!

With a snarl, he drew the laser pistol holstered at his side and fired at the nearest, an old dark-gray female wearing the red of Vvok. As she threw herself aside, fur singed, the other three closed and carried him back into the searing bite of the flek's energy field.

His muscles convulsed into painful, unresponding knots and his entire nervous system exploded with pain. The laser pistol slipped from his fingers into the grass. He dimly sensed the other three tumbling around him, writhing in agony, clawing great clods out of the turf. From training, he knew they had scant seconds before the high-energy field cooked their brains, but he could see nothing, feel nothing, but the terrifying electric redness sizzling through him. He smelled the stench of his smoking fur; in another second his body would be incinerated . . . *by the field*, a faint voice insisted somewhere in the back of his mind, *by energy*.

Even as the pain drove white-hot sparks through his brain, he tried to get his claws into that thought . . . what was it . . . about energy . . . ? His hands convulsed, claws flexed and useless, then a blue spark jumped from one to the other . . . energy . . . *power*! Suddenly he understood. Unlike humans, or flek, he had channels for handling outside energy within his body. And although he didn't know the consequences if he laid himself open to so much power, he was dying anyway. He quit fighting and embraced the raw redness, letting it surge through him as though he were a living wire. For an instant, he thought he would explode, then the field snapped out and took him with it . . .

He sprawled stunned and dry-mouthed in the wiry grass, the indifferent stars winking down, someone's twitching arm tumbled against him. Vaguely, he realized the field had been disrupted. The pain had stopped, but his thoughts darted first one way and then another, like a pool of frightened fish, and comprehended little beyond that one essential fact.

An alarm blared high up in the grid. He heard frantic chittering, the rattle of exoskeletons against plastic. He was in danger. The energy field could come back on any second, so he had to move out of range. His muscles were still spasming, and he couldn't seem to make his nerves carry the messages necessary to move. He felt hot and sick, unable to focus. A few feet away, he saw a dark-furred hrinn limping back into the brush. One of his attackers still lived! If he died, she could still betray the rest of his force on the mountain to the flek!

"No!" Had he said that in Standard or Hrinnti? He couldn't tell. Somehow, he made his hands and arms work together enough to crawl forward, inch by precious inch, on his stomach. One of his legs tingled, then cramped, the muscles contracting into a hot knot of agony. He lurched forward on hands and knees, then collapsed on his face. Was he far enough? He suddenly realized total silence had fallen. Even the alarm had ceased its mind-numbing blare.

Then the power sprang back into life, the red field snapping just inches behind his left foot and the air choked with the stench of burning fur. Rolling over on his side, he stared at the three hrinnti bodies inside the force field lying next to his laser pistol.

"Damnation!" He couldn't afford to lose that pistol.

They had so few modern weapons as it was. Forcing himself back onto his hands and knees, he hung there trying to regain his balance while the brush swooped around him in great stomach-churning circles. If he could just find a long stick, perhaps he could hook the gun and pull it out, although the flek would be here any second, checking the perimeter for the source of disruption.

"So, *Levv*, there must be some truth to the old legends after all." The dark-gray female hobbled into his field of vision. "No ordinary hrinn could have taken that and lived." She limped closer and he saw the many silver and gold bracelets catching the crazed flek colors as they clinked down her thin old arm. "But fortunately, nothing in the legend suggests a Black/on/black cannot die."

He caught the gleam of purple and green and pink on something metallic held awkwardly in her hand. With a shock, he realized it was a laser pistol. "Whe-where did y-you get that!" he demanded, struggling with his continuing lack of coordination.

"Not everyone is as stuffy and conservative as Levv, *Outsider*." Holding the gun steady, she leaned over, fitting her digits with difficulty to the grip designed for four fingers and a single thumb. Her tongue flicked out around her muzzle. "Of course, Levv is not anything at all these days, is it? Just a few nit-infested culls left, and soon those will be finished too."

The noise from the grid rose again, but this time the tones were different, more frenzied, dissonant. They were probably testing, searching for the disruption, he thought. "We can settle this later. We have to get out of here."

"Of course, we have only your word that these creatures mean us harm." She bared her broken, yellowed teeth down at him. "Perhaps they have come to give us all the devices and knowledge the humans would not and our Outsider was one of them. If so, he was remarkably free with his gifts." She wrinkled her nose and leaned closer. "Perhaps we should welcome them."

"You don't know what you're saying!" Heyoka tried to gather his muscles for a single great leap. "You have not seen what they do to a world once they steal it, but I have."

"Fool!" She steadied the pistol. "You are not wanted here—"

Heyoka launched himself at her, but landed short, his handclaws just grazing the silver circlets around her ankle. A laser bolt scorched his right shoulder. He fell heavily as a massive blackness burst the low tangled brush and crushed her to the ground just beyond his nose.

Suddenly, the scrubby blue-leafed bushes seemed alive with hrinn, whispered with their passage, the garish lights gleaming in their black eyes. Several pairs of strong hands scooped him up from the ground and supported him as a huge black-furred hrinn struggled with the smaller dark-gray. He caught a glimpse of the pale-beige patches behind the big black's ears—Kei. "Don't kill her!" He struggled against the hands supporting him. "She knows the truth about Levv, about all of this! If you kill her, we will never—"

Glancing up, Kei hesitated, his bared double rows of white teeth strangely pink and green in the light of the grid. The old Line Mother fastened her broken fangs into the young male's throat. Enraged, he broke her back like a stick of firewood and dashed the twitching body to the ground.

Heyoka didn't realize he was still struggling until a tawny young female flexed claws into his arm. He stopped, but the ground reeled beneath his feet, and he saw lights bobbing down the grid's lattices. "We have—to get out of here!" His voice was hoarse. "If the flek find us here, everything is lost!"

Kei met his gaze, muzzle slicked with blood, eyes huge and so very, very black.

Blacker than the deepest space where stars had yet to be born, Heyoka thought wearily, trying to force his reluctant legs to hold him up, blacker than anything a human could have understood or named. The big Levv male flicked an ear, and the hrinn melted back into the brush, dragging Heyoka along with them.

Sanyha leaned over and sniffed the haunch of kikinti meat roasting on the makeshift spit. Even though she felt too bone-crushingly weary to eat, her mouth was watering. She rotated the spit a quarter turn, then sat back and watched the sparks dance skyward on the hot updraft. If this march hadn't had such a desperate purpose, she could have enjoyed eating outdoors and sleeping under the stars. It had been years since she had enjoyed such simple pleasures.

The breeze shifted and the head of every hrinn in camp suddenly swiveled to look downslope. Then a huge black-furred male dressed in brown strode into the firelight, followed by a whole host of brown-robed hrinn, two of whom were supporting the limp form of Sergeant Blackeagle between them.

"What happened?" She jumped to her feet and dusted her hands on her ragged station pants. "Are you hurt?"

Blackeagle raised his head and blinked dully at her. He looked shocky to her experienced eye and his muscles were spasming. "No." He ran a trembling hand over his face, then flinched and stared at it. "I'm—I'm all right."

Scott hurried up. "Well, you look like hell." He reached for Blackeagle's arm, but the two hrinn holding him laid their ears back and snarled.

"We not—hurt—" Sanyha began in broken Hrinnti,

then stopped. By the fierceness in those faces, they would just as soon tear her heart out as look at her.

Blackeagle raised his head, eyes glazed, then snarled something short and sharp that she couldn't make out. The two hesitated and the big black-furred male stalked over to add his voice. They eased Blackeagle to the ground beside the fire and retreated from the light. His robes were soaked with blood and burned in several places. She could see now that the palms of his hands were scorched, as well as the bottoms of his feet. He must have tangled with the flek.

"It—" His eyes closed, and he just sat there in the shifting firelight, panting, shaking. "It means— *something*."

Sanyha knelt at his side and gingerly peeled away the bloody black fabric that had been cut to shreds over his chest. Red-orange blood oozed from a dozen gashes, and one slash near his throat pulsed with bright blood at every breath. "I think you've nicked an artery. Sit still while I get my supplies."

Leaving the golden circle of light, she hurried through the darkness to the meager medical supplies they had salvaged from the bombed-out station. She could taste the bitterness of panic in the back of her throat though. She was not an expert on hrinnti physiology and body chemistry, as her earlier attempt to treat Blackeagle had aptly demonstrated, and she had so little with which to work.

Fumbling with the straps of a half-charred backpack, she sorted out a few items that might be of use, then dashed back to the fireside, pushing her way through a circle of watching hrinn. She wondered what would happen to their small company of humans if Blackeagle died. He was the only link between the humans and the natives—as well as the only trained soldier among them. What had happened down there? Were the flek trailing him back here right this very minute?

Kneeling at his side, she checked his eyes again. They were glassy and his skin was too cold. He was definitely slipping into shock. She looked down at the drugs she'd brought, a chill running through her because she had no idea what effect they would have on him. Trembling, she finally made herself choose a disinfectant. Surely that would be all—

A gentle double-thumbed hand grasped her arm. Startled, Sanyha looked up into a pale-gray face, the same female who had met them back at the river and brought them to Blackeagle. The female spoke to her in the low growly tongue that, even after all these years, Sanyha could only half-translate and barely speak.

"What?" Sanyha glanced aside at Blackeagle who was staring into the fire. "Not—understand."

Without being rough, the female moved her aside, then squatted down in her place. Hands gripped her shoulders and Sanyha looked around into Scott Cuppertino's concerned face. "I think they want to take care of him themselves." He kept his voice pitched low, quiet. "They probably see injuries like this all the time."

But they were savages! Sanyha wanted to shout. She was a trained doctor with centuries of civilized research in medicine behind her. She couldn't just stand by and watch them chant a few spells over him while their only chance for survival died of shock and blood loss.

"When I—they lost—power." Blackeagle looked up from the fire and tried to focus on her face. "That's it! That's how—we'll—how we'll do it!"

The tall, graceful gray-furred female motioned to the huge black hrinn and he reached down from behind to pin Blackeagle's shoulders. Then the female traced her finger along the terrible gaping gash that ran from the side of his neck down onto his chest.

Sanyha forgot to breathe as she watched the hrinn's moving finger mark a line of coruscating *blue fire* over the bloody wound. Blackeagle stiffened, then the inner nictitating membranes spasmed shut over his black eyes and he slumped against the large male holding him. The pale-gray never stopped, tracing the length of the deep slash until she had reached its end.

When she had finished, she sat there, head bowed, breathing in great heavy pants as though she had run a marathon. Sanyha edged closer to examine the wound. Although a few bright beads of blood still dotted the jagged line, the gash was closed.

Mitsu could hear the angry chittering songs echoing through the interior of the great transfer grid. A storm of distress swept the hive, uniting the castes. Security had been breached. Even now warrior-drones were searching the perimeter, tracing the cause.

Unfortunately, the temporal point at which the grid had gone dark had been most critical. Piles of ash smoldered in the center of the transfer platform where the incoming shipment had been just about to coalesce when the power had failed. The tech-drones had lost several of their number who had been too certain that this time they would succeed and rushed forward to view the materialization.

As soon as their bodies had been consumed, work would continue. The hive never mourned and certainly never wasted time in sleep. Mitsu shrank back against the slick white wall as several replacement techs, newly hatched, rushed to take the fallen drones' places. As soon as they had ingested their instructions by consuming the dead drones' bodies, preparations would continue. Very soon now, this freezing rock heap would be completely theirs.

Had the humans caused this? She started to scratch the itchy spot just behind her third arm, then realized she had none anymore. She glanced down in dismay at the soft disgusting pink of her hands, then, sickened, looked away.

Unbidden, a memory of a time when those same hands had held a rifle seeped back into her mind, a time when she had fought chittering dead-white creatures that swept against Confederation troops in the millions once they had broken through to a planet. Once, she had laid her life on the line to fight those creatures.

But now she was here.

An egg-matron stalked along the high passageway where Mitsu stood, then paused to glare at her with smoldering red eyes. For a second, she dared to stare back, then it struck her to the floor with both pairs of arms.

Huddling against the wall at the creature's feet, Mitsu shut her eyes and beat out a tune of despair on her fingers. She understood, of course; she was disgusting.

Chapter Twenty-six

Waking was hard and sharp, as though someone had snapped off a command in his ear, ordering his Ranger unit back out on the front line with the flek just beyond the next hill.

Which, of course, they were.

His eyes flew open and, for a moment, staring up into the cold gray fringes of dawn, he couldn't remember how he had come to be on this rocky, windblown hillside, then his scorched hands and feet began to throb, and the desperate fight down in the shadow of the flek grid swept back over him. He found himself surprised to be alive.

He tried to sit up and failed, having been, at some point, securely tucked into the heavy folds of a striped fur. He sank back, light-headed and drained by even that small effort. Beside him, a pale, curled-up form stirred inside a nest of leaves, then blinked at him with sleepy black eyes. "Be careful, or you will open those gashes again." Unbound mane fell across her shoulders as she leaned over to loosen the fur constricting his movements.

311

His nose twitched at Vexk's familiar scent. "Kei?" he rasped, his breath a white fog in the frigid predawn air as he sat up.

"Still here, as well as the others who came in with him."

Heyoka held his head in his hands and tried to think. "I—need to talk to him."

Rising in one effortless movement, she brushed the leaves out of her fur and robes, then arched her back in a long sinuous stretch. "Stay here and I will bring him."

He huddled before the ashes of the previous night's fire as her tall pale-gray form disappeared into the early morning dimness. Every inch of his body ached, from the tip of his nose down to the pads of his feet, and his thoughts seemed to barely ooze toward completion, but something, some critically important notion, lurked down in the murky depths of his mind, waiting to be noticed. He closed his eyes, reaching, then found it—that moment when he had opened himself and the whole grid had lost power. He couldn't make an accurate estimate of how long the blackout had lasted, since he had lost consciousness, but it *had* happened. If *one* hrinn acting alone and unprepared could accomplish that, what could ten do . . . or twenty . . . or fifty?

He studied the dark heaps of hrinn curled up asleep all around him on the mountainside. How many of them could use their bodies to channel power? Nisk had once commented that most hrinn had the ability to a greater or lesser degree, but how many of these could broach a high-energy field, as he had, and live? Surely Kei, and perhaps Vexk, but how many more?

Vexk reappeared with a burning brand and an armful of wood. Dwarfing even her sleek height, Kei's ebony form stalked after her, mane already neatly tied with a length of brown cord. Heyoka stared up at the big male, wondering if *he* would have been that tall, had he grown up on this world.

She added fresh branches, rekindled the fire, then faded out of earshot. Heyoka leaned close as the yellow flames fed on the wood, feeling the warmth ease his aches. Kei squatted beside him and dribbled a handful of tiny blue leaves into the fire. His averted gaze was smoldering obsidian as the leaves burned with a pleasing menthol odor. He seemed to want something, but Heyoka could not tell what it was. "Gynth." Kei indicated the leaves, then rubbed at a newly scabbed-over scratch on his already scarred face. His eyes met Heyoka's for just a second. "Good for strength after blood loss."

Heyoka noticed the silver gleam of a laser pistol tucked into Kei's waistband. He must have recovered the old female's weapon after the fight. Well . . . Heyoka flicked an ear. Kei had earned it, whether he would ever be able to fit his alien hand to its human-tailored grip or not. "I have a plan to break into the grid."

Kei's black nose wrinkled appreciatively. "Then we will kill the Outsiders!"

"All of the flek," Heyoka agreed solemnly. "But first we must surround the grid with hrinn who can absorb power from the pools. How many of those with us can do that?"

Tilting his muzzle skyward, Kei considered. "Perhaps one in every three or four, maybe more, maybe less. It depends on those who came across the mountains with you, and I know nothing of these lowlanders."

And then, Heyoka thought, there was always the question of whether there were any more traitors biding their time among the hrinnti force. They couldn't afford another disaster like the night before. He stared at his scorched palms. "You saved my life last night." He didn't look at Kei. "I will not forget that."

Kei jerked to his feet, massively dark against the gray dawn. His ears were flattened against his skull and the savage *other* that lived within every hrinn shone diamond-bright through his eyes. "You are the Black/on/black, as well as Levv. How could I have done any less and still served my honor?"

Heyoka realized why he had never encountered any Hrinnti words for "thank you"; there were none. To thank Kei was to imply he'd had a choice, and to the hrinnti way of thinking, there had been no choice, only the right thing to do and the wrong, and Kei, being honorable, could only have acted as he had.

"You could not." Heyoka suppressed a sigh and pulled the striped fur around his aching chest. "Find Nisk, as well as the remaining Line Mothers and those who can speak for the other Lines and males' houses. We have much to plan before tonight and very little time."

Without speaking, Kei strode off into the grayness. Heyoka turned his head to watch the beginnings of color creep into the eastern sky, thinking that, if his plan failed, few of the hrinn on this mountainside would live to appreciate another dawn.

As the day wore on, they sorted themselves into three rough groups: those who could blueshift for any amount of time at all, those who could not, but could channel power in their bodies, such as Restorers, and those who could do neither, but were able-bodied and ready to fight. For his plan to work, each group was critical, and if any one of the three failed, then all of them—humans and hrinn alike—would die.

In the afternoon, as the ominous racket from the grid set their teeth on edge again, he outlined each group's part in what was to come later that night. The first group would penetrate the red energy field that protected the grid and lay themselves open to the power, thereby hopefully shorting it out as he had the night before, only for a longer period of time.

The blueshift group would make up the second wave. He had counted Nisk among them, but the older male warned him that many males, especially older ones such as himself, were capable of only very short bursts of blueshift speed. So, without really believing they would obey him, Heyoka sorted the older males out and instructed them to stay in the rear of the front wave where they could still be effective if they dropped to normal speed. Then he sent them all off to the Levv caverns to take turns drawing power in the same thermal pool Kei had once used to save his life.

Lastly, he instructed the rest of their force, made up of both hrinn and humans, and armed with whatever was available. Even though they could not attack with the stunning speed of blueshift, they would be valuable through their sheer force of numbers and ferocity. Studying the human and hrinnti faces before him, he wondered what chance they would have against flek lasers and armor. Even with the most modern of weapons, he had not fared very well back on Enjas Two.

But then, as Nisk had once pointed out, he had survived to fight again—and perhaps that would prove to be the flek's fatal mistake.

The dissonant wail from the grid ran up and down the scale, standing every hair on Heyoka's body on end. The alien stink was nauseating this close and his scabbed-over cuts throbbed in time with the awful racket. He turned his eyes away from the garish greens and pinks and blues that illuminated the grid on all sides and concentrated on threading through the tangled brush. Showers of bright purple sparks fountained up from the center of the grid into the dark night sky. The activity seemed different from the night before and he was worried. Just how close was this monster to being operational? Had they come too late after all?

Up ahead, he saw the edge of the brushy cover just short of the grid and its protecting energy field. Although he had decided his place would be in the second assault group with the other blueshifters, he wanted to supervise those who would attempt to short the energy field. Levv had contributed a handful of younglings, both male and female, to this group, which also included the two remaining Line Mothers, many of the adult females, and all of the fully trained Restorers. Watching Vexk's pale form stride forward, he suffered another round of misgivings. He had tried to persuade the Restorers to hold back a portion of their number with the argument that they would be needed later to help with the wounded, but they had all insisted on taking their place beside the rest.

Flattening his ears, he satisfied himself finally that everyone was in place and nothing further could be done, then threw back his head and gave a great, deep-throated roar that seemed to come from the very bottom of his soul. Without hesitation, the assembled hrinn, male and female, Levv and Jhii and Vvok and Qartt and Kendd and Rebban and Restorers alike, leaped into the faintly shimmering redness, then toppled in the protective field, limbs thrashing in agony.

"Control it!" he called to them, knowing even as he spoke they would have to find their own way just as he had, or die trying. His breath came hard and heavy and his chest ached as the smell of burning hide and fur filled the air.

They would not be able to do it, he thought anxiously, pacing up and down before the barrier, handclaws fully flexed with nothing to rip. Perhaps he was stronger somehow; perhaps there was more to this Black/on/black nonsense than he had credited.

He should have thought of something else, some other way. All of this would be on his head and they would all die—

Then Vexk's contorted body eased inside the angry redness, as did the hrinn's next to her, and then another's four body-lengths down. The field crackled and sparked, and—disappeared, taking with it the terrible green/purple/blue/pinkness of the grid. A wrenching silence fell.

Heyoka raised his arm. "Now!" Waving like a madman, he reached within for the feel of blueshift and entered the universe of *blue*. Leaping onto the slick-sided latticework of the grid, he climbed swiftly, clinging to the crevices with both handclaws and feetclaws until he was high enough to see down inside the grid.

Below him, the flek stood like shiny white statues with the faint form of a huge—something, half-materialized in the middle of the whole structure. Hooking his leg over the edge of the lattice, he dropped down inside on a high, narrow walkway, then raced toward the far end, which was thick with flek. He carried no laser pistol, having lost his the night before and not having the heart to ask someone else to give up theirs. Although he was undoubtedly the best shot they had, he had accepted only Kei's spear and, beyond that, would use tooth and claw and fist like the rest.

His path took him near a pair of flek who had half-turned toward the outside, reacting to the blackout. With a savage open-clawed swipe, he knocked them both from the catwalk, then ran on. Just as he reached the far end, he saw the dark spill of hrinn into the grid below. He paused to watch, shocked to see several had already slowed so much that they were almost out of blueshift. Worry washed over him; how many would be strong enough to last until this attack was over? Suddenly he wished he had thought to have

them conserve their strength by dropping in and out
of blueshift as danger warranted.

Taking his own advice, he phased out of blueshift,
then glanced around the alien structure. Long shiny
beams were constructed at every conceivable angle,
making the structure appear crazy and unstable to his
human-educated eyes. Picking a direction, he raced
on, scattering flek before him like ants fleeing a fire.
The grid was still dark, but a number of small lights
sprang into life, and he heard the sizzle of lasers
somewhere down below. He dropped to his knees,
making himself as small a target as possible, and
scanned the massive structure for the likely location
of their central energy source.

The power came back on, flickering, then holding
steady. Heyoka found himself cursing in a stream of
Standard. What had happened to his first force?
Sliding back into blueshift, he raced down the walkway and dodged the silent, unseeing flek to check the
area for entrances. But although the walls seemed to
front rooms of some sort, he could find no doors or
windows. Was the only access somewhere below? He
hesitated, looking for a way down to the lower levels.

Then he noticed the familiar shape of a *human*,
stuck somehow in a slick white wall, face and hands
half-visible. He reached out and touched one of the
hands; the skin was still warm. He dropped out of
blueshift and stood open-jawed as a man emerged
from the wall in front of him.

It was Eldrich, the director from the research
station. He would never forget that thatch of silvery
hair, or the cloying sweet scent of too much cologne.
The man's gray eyes widened at the sight of him.
Heyoka gripped his throat and shoved him back
against the white wall, flexing handclaws into the
tender human skin so that tiny streams of bright-red
blood trickled down. "Don't even think about twitching, or you're dead!"

Eldrich's eyes rolled, but he said nothing.

"Where is the power plant?" Heyoka shifted position to crush his forearm against the other's windpipe. "Answer me, or I'll throw your worthless carcass down there with the rest of your buddies!"

Eldrich flailed his arm toward the wall he had just come through.

"Where's the door?"

"There—is no—door!" Eldrich squeaked out. "You—have to go—through."

Heyoka pulled the human around in front of him as a shield as he saw the green shafts of laserfire splitting the air below. He reached behind and rapped the wall with his knuckles—hard as nails. "Where?"

"Hold—on," the man wheezed. "I can take—you."

Heyoka allowed him just enough slack to walk on his toes and then followed him through what looked like a solid wall. It parted around their bodies like hot sticky taffy. Once inside, he immediately sneezed, then sneezed again, eyes burning in the noxious gaseous mixture that was the future of this world if the flek prevailed. He shoved his hostage toward a bank of controls glittering with lurid pink and green indicator lights, then froze. In the farthest corner, a dirt-encrusted human face, topped with matted short dark hair, blinked up at him. Pale enough to be an apparition, Mitsu cringed as though she expected him to attack and tear her apart, and he saw not the least light of recognition in her wild blue gaze.

"My god!" His stunned mind tried to make sense of this. He had never expected to find her here, but it all fit. Eldrich must have kidnapped Mitsu when he fled the station and held her ever since. She looked emaciated and crazed; the veins under her skin stood out like roads on a map to someplace no human should ever travel. What in the name of all that was holy had they been doing to her? "Mitsu—" His voice cracked. "Are—are you hurt?"

Her eyes did not meet his and her broken-nailed fingers danced over each other in a macabre, senseless pattern that went on and on.

He swallowed hard. "Never mind. It's all right now. I'll get you out of here." With his free hand, he reached for her matchstick-thin arm, but she bolted past him and dove headfirst through the white wall as though it were water. Dismayed, he shoved Eldrich around. "Take me back through!"

With a sneer, the human stepped back into the malleable white substance. Heyoka followed, but just as his muzzle broached the opposite side, Eldrich twisted out of his grip and left him stranded in midstride less than halfway through. The wall instantly solidified and trapped him within. Frantic, Heyoka tried to claw his way out, but the damn stuff was tough as plasticrete now. If his nose hadn't penetrated the other side, he would already be suffocating.

Think! he berated himself. Mitsu was slipping beyond his reach—again—and, in addition, he had to return to direct the attack. He was an idiot to let himself be sidetracked like the rawest of recruits, adding yet one more blundering failure to his list of faults. He—

With a flash that was almost visible, the savage *other* within him escaped with a swiftness that brooked no intervention. The primal anger simmering in the back of his mind for as long as he could remember surged through his veins like molten iron, a source of strength he had always denied, but which now became a lever he could use to move the world. Furious with the flek and himself, he strained, grunted, flexed his claws and threw his not-inconsiderable might into trying to move just a hair, but the damn wall was so solid, he doubted even a laser would make a dent.

Then, with a terrible fierce clarity, he saw that he had been a fool. He had the body of a hrinn, but still didn't think like one. There wasn't a laser at hand, but he did have access to a certain amount of sheer *power*. Reaching inside, he summoned the energy stored for blueshift from the special cells of his body, then discharged all of it in one massive bolt.

The resulting blast shattered the wall and threw him across the narrow walkway outside. He caught the edge of the slick white floor with his handclaws just as his legs skidded over, then dangled there, trying to get his bearings. His skin crawled as several small, lower-caste flek skittered over his hands and disappeared around the corner.

He swung one leg up, then the other, and sprawled there, half-stunned, blinking in the noise and smoke. He could hear the mixed din of hrinn and human and flek fighting below and the power—their main objective—still blazed, so nothing was settled yet. He groped his way upright, using the remains of the wall for support. His muscles were trembling and drained. Releasing himself had taken every bit of his stored energy.

Down in the heart of the grid, a human body topped with silver hair sprawled crookedly; he must have caught Eldrich in his blast. Green lasers crackled overhead, close enough to singe his ears. He ducked and saw the distinctive black of Mitsu's hair as she dashed into one of the oddly angled towers that stood on each of the five corners.

Dizzy and shaken, he climbed over the rail and wearily descended the lattice. Halfway down, his foot slipped and he fell, landing with a numbing jolt on his chest. A hot nauseating blackness swirled over him, but he fought it off and struggled to his feet. His ribs throbbed with each breath and a sticky warmth saturated the fur on his chest. Evidently he had reopened one of last night's gashes. Well, he told himself, by the time he lost enough blood to make any difference, the battle would be either won, or lost.

A laser bolt sizzled into the lattice just above his

left ear, boiling the plas into white slag. He hit the floor again, searching for the source. After a second, the warrior-drone fired again, and he realized the damn thing had the angle on him. He would have to work his way around to the other side to get past it. Flexing his handclaws, he prowled toward the flek's unsuspecting rear.

The grid was crawling with filthy, fur-covered animals! Mitsu shivered convulsively as she plunged through wall after wall, looking for something to fight back with, anything! The stupid egg-matrons retreated as she searched, chittering angrily in High-Flek, refusing to help or direct her in any way.

"Fools!" She pushed two aside, hearing the crack of their chitinous bodies against the wall. Couldn't they tell her loathsome pink body was just a temporary shell for one of their own kind? The Deciders had promised to return her flek body to her once the grid was finished.

She slid through another wall, this time into a storage room filled with strangely shaped packages wrapped in glistening white. Dropping to her knees, she tore at the slick packages, but the tough coverings resisted her nails. Then she realized they were the same substance as the walls and activated the porosity-field generator on her belt, rendering the coverings a soft, puttylike consistency that she could tear off.

The first package, vaguely circular, yielded only starter mold for the main food source, the second was a block of dormant wall compound which could not be grown until it was exposed to the proper wavelengths of radiation. The next, however, was a full lot of small stick lasers, all primed and ready to fire.

Gathering as many as she could carry under her arm, she activated one and plunged back through the wall, traveling toward the central loading platform.

Each time she passed a frightened tech, or egg-matron, she shouted and beat at its hard body until it ran before her toward the center.

As long as they did not allow the smelly verminous beasts born to this planet to penetrate the main power crystals at the heart of the great grid, the natives could not possibly win.

Chapter Twenty-seven

To his relief, Heyoka found, as he worked around the flek fire, most of his hrinn-and-human force had battered its way inside the grid during the critical minutes when the power had been disrupted. He caught glimpses of them above on the strangely angled walkways and silhouetted against gleaming white walls as they fought savagely in small groups, pressing toward the interior of the grid itself.

His *other* approved the flek's ferocity. Its own savageness was now an integral part of him, threaded through his every aspect, almost indistinguishable from the portions of his personality he had always accepted. He sensed it would never again be a distinct and separate part of him, never again suppressed, and that would have worried him, if he'd expected to live beyond the next ten minutes.

The ear-splitting noise climbed toward an agonizing crescendo that ate at his nerves. Striving to rejoin his forces, he slipped in and out of the harshly delineated shadows, slashing at flek with handclaws when he had the chance. Many of those he cut down were workers and, therefore by nature, not efficient fighters, but he sensed something altering the nature of the battle. The flek were falling back to form a living shield around the great open space in the middle of the grid, and even the non-warring castes, who should have been fleeing, were fighting with increased purposefulness.

Sliding his back along a disgustingly warm, slick wall, he paused as lasers sizzled just out of sight. The stench of burned fur filled the air, and he glanced reflexively down at his own scarred leg, before peering around the corner. Two smoking dark-furred hrinnti bodies lay tangled a few feet away, but the way was clear. He grimaced as the grid's screech rose another few agonizing notes. It was definitely in operation, no doubt to bring through a few thousand armed warrior-drones.

Black fur flickered, then Kei dropped out of blueshift beside him, materializing as though he had come from another dimension.

Over his shoulder, Heyoka saw the vague, ominously huge outlines of—something—forming down behind the seemingly solid veil of flek fire. His hackles raised as he pointed. "They're protecting the center, so it must be their vulnerable point. We have to get in there and destroy either their controls, or their power source before they bring in more warriors."

Kei's black eyes glittered as he turned to look. His robes were torn and spattered with blood, and the top of his left ear was badly singed. Then, without a word, he was—gone, as suddenly as if he'd been lasered into atoms. Heyoka reached for the energy to blueshift and follow, but felt only hollowness within; if he tried, this time he probably would die, as Nisk had been so direly predicting all along. It was too bad, he told himself as he jogged wearily toward the middle of the grid, that there hadn't been more truth to the Black/on/black myth after all.

The outer levels were empty of flek now and the warrior-drones were laying down their customary impenetrable firing pattern to protect the grid's core. He and the other hrinn, along with a handful of humans, assembled around the glowing center. Then he saw her, small and pale, dressed in a ragged blue shift, running between one group of flek and the next, shouting and beating at their white bodies with her fists when their attention flagged. For a moment, he forgot to breathe with the shock of seeing that familiar snub-nosed face. *Mitsu*—his friend and partner—was holding the flek defense together with non-warrior drones in a last-ditch effort to preserve the incoming transport.

The other males fought out of blueshift, picking the enemy off one at a time, slowly increasing the odds in their favor, but, being unfamiliar with technology, they were aiming for the flek and ignoring the controls. The outlines of the incoming shipment were firming up now, shimmering with the garish rainbow of flekish colors. He calculated that by the time his hrinn cleared the way to the center of the grid, it would be too late.

Inside the huge box-shape, he could see shiny white chitinous bodies equipped with the heavier body armor of warriors, ready to emerge and crisp the attackers. He shouted at the blueshifting males to break through the flek lines and destroy the controls, but it was no use. Blueshift was almost a silent universe; within it, normal speech sounded so garbled and drawn out that they could not understand him.

His handclaws flexed in frustration. Another few seconds and it would be too late. The new warriors would be here, armed and fresh. Human and hrinn alike would be wiped from the face of this planet and the flek would possess a new stronghold from which to infest this quadrant of human-held space.

Someone had to get inside and stop the transmission. Dodging a laser bolt, he reached for the cool feeling of otherness and again found only a curious lassitude. The *other* snarled, thwarted and enraged. He had to stop them, whatever the cost—there were much worse things than an honorable death. He threw back his head, roared with furious frustration, then *shifted*. Weariness dragged at him, but the gaps in the flek laserfire were apparent now and it was a relatively simple matter to step between the bolts into the center area where an almost motionless small human stood with her fist upraised.

With him, in the awesome silence of blueshift, he saw males on the other side, killing flek with gruesome efficiency. He shouted to them, but they didn't seem to hear, so he pressed on, stumbling. He was so tired, putting one foot in front of the other seemed more than he could possibly do, and yet the *other*'s anger kept him moving. The early days that he had spent in the flek slave pens came back to him again, the pain and the stink, the fear. He would not let that come to Anktan. These were his people and he would not let the flek have them!

The blueness wavered and, for a second, normal colors bled into his vision. Gritting his teeth, he wrenched himself back into blueness. He had to hold blueshift; if he slowed to normal speed, they would have him in a flash.

A glittering crystal array behind Mitsu caught his eye, molded as though it had grown out of the grid floor. Perhaps it had; reports said flek did not construct things in the same fashion that humans did. If he could take this grid relatively undamaged, the Confederation might learn a great deal about flek technology and how to fight it . . . if . . .

He passed Mitsu, nearing the crystals, picking up his feet with an agonizing deliberateness and laying them down as though they were part of some machine he was operating and not feet at all. The huge transport cube had nearly solidified. Inside it, he could see the flek readying their weapons, firing short test bursts of green laserfire over their smooth white heads.

He focused on the gleaming crystals, which were as beautiful as delicate stalagmites spun from the purest water ice and shining with the same breathtaking frigid blueness that surrounded him. He brought his claws down and smashed the first pillar. It drifted apart in glittering splinters. His vision blurred as he raised his arm for a second blow and he had to swing blindly, but he felt his claws bite into the crystals and send them spinning toward the grid floor. Then he slid out of blueshift, the normal colors of life jerking him back into crushing decibels of noise.

A few feet away, the huge transport vehicle blackened, then shivered into a million charred and smoking pieces. A multitude of flek incinerated between one breath and the next, he thought giddily, then found his nose pressing painfully into the floor. Somehow he had fallen without noticing. He struggled to turn over, then stared up at the grid looming over him at strangely canted angles.

Behind him, the flek whirled to face the disaster as the grid's wail wound down and down into a gut-wrenching squawk. Hrinn dropped out of blueshift all around him, intent on finishing the job he'd begun, smashing the fairy-tale crystals until they were only a sifting of crystalline dust scattered across the grid floor.

With a cry of anguish, Mitsu rushed him, laser stick extended in her hand, her face alien and twisted with hate. Blinking mistily up at her, Heyoka tried to call her name, but his tongue refused to form the words.

Then Kei was beside him, massive and black,

stepping between them as Mitsu approached, fitting his alien thumbs to the laser pistol's grip and calmly taking aim.

"No!" Heyoka got the word out, but Kei did not even flick an ear. Enraged, his *other* gave him the strength to struggle to his knees as his vision hazed in and out. "It's not—her fault!"

Dead-on, Kei fired at the approaching small figure.

Without even realizing what he had done, Heyoka found the world *blue* again as he tried to outrun a laser bolt. His handclaws reached . . . caught at the edges of her shapeless garment and toppled her to the floor. As her small body fell slowly against him, he enfolded her in his arms as he had so many times before, friend to friend. The *other*, woven through him now in a thousand parts, agreed; no one was going to kill his partner, the only one besides Ben Blackeagle who had ever looked at him and seen a *person*, not while he was still kicking! Achingly cold blueness took him as he clasped her to his chest, mixing itself with an ominous blackness the exact shade of Kei's fur. "No one," he whispered hoarsely. "No one—"

A frigid blue hole had been punched through the fabric of space/time and was sucking the life out of his bones at an astonishing rate. Even the thoughts that tried to form in his head were stolen by the arctic blueness before they could gel. He would not escape this time, but Anktan was surely safe; the flek would never use that grid to travel between planets now. And Mitsu . . .

But that half-formed thought troubled him even as it slipped away. He'd had Mitsu in his arms. She should be safe, yet Kei had been there with the killing lust upon him, Kei who thought all Outsiders to be of a piece and that humans were the same as flek, Kei who would protect the Black/on/black at all costs . . .

Someone spoke close to his ear. He couldn't make the words out, but strained toward them, using them as a beacon to lead him out of the frozen blueness.

The words came again, harsh and angry.

The *other* bristled. What right did anyone have to be angry with him? He had done his best and if that was not enough, he could do no more. Angry now, himself, he struggled toward the universe of sound, the realm of light and warmth and . . .

"—still or I will tear your ears off, not that they were ever much to look at anyway!"

The voice was hrinnti, making him even more worried for Mitsu. If he could only feel his arms and know if he still held her.

"He—live?"

That voice was human, speaking in halting broken Hrinnti. He tried to speak but managed only a slight groan.

"He will live, no doubt, a great deal longer than he deserves!"

Was that Kei? As he listened, he became aware of a distant warmth, working against the awful draining blueness. He tried to phrase a question, then shivered, sending painful spasms all through the body that only seconds ago he had not felt at all.

"Let me take him now," a soft hrinnti voice said. "You should get some rest. He will recover."

"No!" It was Kei. Suddenly Heyoka felt sure of that. "He is Levv and it is for *me* to do this."

"It will not benefit him if you make yourself ill too," the other hrinn chided.

And that was Vexk, Heyoka thought, so she had survived the battle. It reassured him to know that, with everything else he had bungled since coming to Anktan, at least he wasn't going to be responsible for the loss of her craft to his people. He heard the lap of water against stone, smelled a hint of sulfur.

"Let me or, perhaps, Nisk watch over him. We can call you if he awakens."

I'm all right, Heyoka wanted to say, but the connections to make his mouth respond just didn't seem to be there. The voices dissolved into a hazy blur as sleep dragged at him, a soft, welcoming normal sleep that whispered of refreshment and ease. He quit resisting and drifted away into the warm darkness.

Two lives danced in her mind, flames from two fires fed on vastly different fuel: she was Mitsu Jensen, a Ranger in the Confederation Forces, and she was a flek spy-drone, temporarily transferred into a miserable soft-skinned body. The humans in this place kept insisting such a transformation was not possible and she was one of them, but of course, they were supposed to think that. And, anyway, what did they, undifferentiated creatures that they were, really understand about the universe and the way it worked? In trying to know a little about everything, humans knew practically nothing at all, unlike the flek, masters of specialization.

Perched atop a large rock outcropping, her fingers skittered over each other almost unconsciously, beating out a sad little dirge for the ruined transfer grid down on the plains. The savage fur-covered beasts had smashed the crystals and slaughtered the tech-drones who were the only ones with the knowledge to grow replacements. Even if the drones had lived to start again the next day, the grid had been over thirty years in the making. It would never again have been functional in her lifetime.

Strong fingers grasped her shoulder and she looked around. It was the gray-and-white beast that had been set to follow her everywhere. For some reason, it continually spoke to her in low guttural syllables she did not understand.

"Go away!" she chittered at the creature in pure High-Flek, but, paying her no heed, it tugged at her arm and kept saying the same beast words over and over again. Knowing from the experience of the past few days that it would simply drag her off if she did not comply, she stood and picked her way down the rocky jumble. One of the humans came up to join them, a female, if she remembered correctly, with long dark hair and a puckered laser burn that stretched across her right arm.

The woman began speaking to her, and after a moment, she was surprised to find she understood. "—wouldn't you like to see him, Mitsu? He is asking for you."

For a second, an answer was on the tip of her tongue, then flek chitter rose in her mind, the derisive tones of the Deciders when she had made another mistake. "Spent too much time among them, did you? Damaged, are you? Never again will you be one of us?"

The woman shook her head and spoke to the gray-and-white beast. It urged her toward the dark opening leading into a system of natural caves. She hated the caves; they were dank and smelly and full of even more of the hairy beasts, but these creatures imprisoned her inside every night anyway. One evening, she promised herself, they would forget to bind her and then, before she escaped, she would find a laser and burn them all for what they had done to her people.

She dug her heels in as they passed under the overhanging rock of the cave entrance, but the beast didn't even seem to notice. Continuing on, it pulled her around a series of twistings and turnings that Mitsu could have sworn they had never taken before. Finally, they entered a well-lit gallery with a high ceiling and a steaming pool in the center. Torchlight danced on the water, yellow and somehow inviting.

In the pool floated a black-furred beast, its head

propped against the rocky ledge and its sunken eyes closed. Something stirred in her at the sight of him; it *was* a him, suddenly she was quite sure of that. Kneeling, the woman touched his shoulder and spoke. The creature's eyes opened and looked up at Mitsu, strange luminous black eyes that held a bit of the vastness of deep space.

He spoke to her in a halting deep-throated voice that was cracked and strained. Her skin flushed cold and then hot in rapid succession, and a vision burst upon her of a black-furred face telling jokes under a clear green sky. Even though she was just a dirt-behind-the-ears kid, raw and untrained, she laughed with him. Just that day, she had saved his furry black hide from being burned into cinders, and they both knew it.

The double rows of white teeth glittered at her in the harsh light of the camp torch. "Think you're pretty smart, don't you?"

"Smart enough to save your ass anyway." Laying her laser rifle on the grassy ground, she plunked down beside him and began to ease her boots off.

"Not so fast!" Flexing his claws, he scratched behind one of his sharp-pointed ears. "This side is reserved for officers. The noncom flop is clear over on the other side of that grove."

"Sleep here?" She made a face at him. "I wouldn't sleep in the middle of a bunch of cross-eyed stiffs like you guys if you advanced me three months' pay." Tugging at her boot until it finally gave, she wriggled her hot, aching toes with a satisfied sigh. "A girl's got her reputation to think of, you know."

"A girl?" He shook his head in a curiously human-like gesture. "Damn, and here I bet Danelli that you were some kind of Jernigan asexual replication!"

"Very funny, Blackeagle." She began working on the other boot. "It's not like you've got a lot of room to talk, you know."

"Well, I suppose you could stay over here in officers' country." His nose wrinkled, displaying that gruesome double set of four-inch fangs. "If I booted your ass upward."

"You wouldn't dare." The second boot slid off and allowed the cooling evening air to reach her aching foot.

"As of seventeen hundred today, local time, Short-stuff."

"You're kidding." She gathered the two boots up and stared at the sharp-muzzled face suspiciously.

"I expect your orders will be cut by this time tomorrow, that is, if you manage to live that long." He lay back against the grass-covered ground. "Though you're so goddammed green that I don't know why I even offered to train you. Guess I just felt sorry for you."

"*You*—train *me*?" She stood up and glared down at his relaxed form. "As a sodding officer? That'll be the day!"

"Tomorrow *will* be the day, as a matter of fact." He closed his eyes. "Oh-four hundred and don't be late. I hate that in a partner."

Partner . . . the word echoed in her mind, through the barren white chambers erected by the flek . . . *partner . . . partner . . .*

Tears were streaming down her face. The black-furred form stirred in the pool, then heaved up onto the rocky ledge. "You took . . . your time . . . in coming . . . Shortstuff."

Her hands started to beat out a quick tune of distress. She stared at them, startled by the paleness of the skin and the bones showing white through it, then thrust them into her pockets.

"Don't you . . . think you've had . . . enough time off?" The words came out very slowly, as though each were more valuable than gold.

The bones protruded through his hide too, all the

more evident now as his wet fur clung to the outlines of his emaciated body. He'd lost so much weight that she hardly knew him. "Given—up—eating?" she asked finally, each word forced to thread a confusing maze in her head before she could force it out.

"The chow . . . here is . . . terrible." His black eye closed in a very humanlike wink. "But I'll . . . eat it . . . if you will."

She started to answer him, but flek chitter rose again in her mind, overriding the other voices, drowning out everything to keep her inside the warm, smooth-walled prison they had built for her. Then wet fingers closed around her arm, double-thumbed and strong, fingers to pull her away from the flek, back into the cave with him. For a second, they felt alien, strange, out-of-kilter, then her vision shifted and she suddenly knew it was going to be all right. She was safe at last.

Epilogue

At official request, Heyoka escorted the Confederation major down to the remains of the flek grid within hours of his arrival. It had taken weeks for the research station's communication lapse to be noted, and then more weeks to divert the nearest military ship in that quadrant to investigate what appeared to be a low priority communications anomaly. Once a ship had arrived and learned the true state of affairs, its commanding major had been sorely disappointed over the destruction of the facility. Heyoka had expected that, but for many days after the attack, he'd been too near death to stop the hrinn from carrying through their mission to obliterate the flek. The loss of a relatively intact installation to study was not inconsequential, but the only real alternative had been a functional flek grid, and no one was foolish enough to desire that.

The major opted to examine the grid alone initially. As he explained, his techs would be all over it soon enough, and then no one would be allowed to casually roam it for fear of contaminating the already minimal evidence. Together, the two of them hiked down the side of the mountain toward the blackened, twisted stubs on the plains, all that remained of the five towers. Crystalline shards scattered throughout the ruins ahead of them shone like droplets of fire in the afternoon sun.

Heyoka had not returned since the day of the attack, nor had Mitsu, and the somber scene was so altered from the arena of smoke and terror and desperation he remembered, he had trouble orienting himself. He stopped just outside the breached outer walls and studied the broken structure through narrowed eyes. *There* he had climbed the outer lattice and found Mitsu; *there* Eldrich had fallen to his death, and in the broad center of the transport pad, *there*, he had smashed the crystals with his own claws and brought the potential invasion to an end.

He breathed deeply, trying to detect the acrid flek stink that had to be lingering in this shattered, abandoned place—and failed. Roughly a hundred days had passed since the destruction of the grid and still his vision had a bluish cast to it, while everything tasted, as well as smelled, of ashes. Although he'd had a taste of blueshift burnout once before, traveling across the mountains with Nisk, it had been only the palest whisper of this. Vexk however predicted that continued soaks in the thermal pool would enable his cells to eventually replace all the energy he had lost and the symptoms would pass.

He trailed after the major through the broken latticework and thought of the newly proclaimed pattern, *stars/over/stars*, which not coincidentally bore the shape of his life, beginning with the arrival of the flek before his birth, encompassing his enslavement, education off-world, the wrongful downfall of Levv, and the final extermination of the flek on this planet. For a long time, he had discredited Nisk's preoccupation with the supposedly sacred *patterns/in/*

progress, but now it seemed he could almost make out the shape of this one, immense convoluted whirls and loops that literally spanned worlds and had brought them all to this place and time, this altered condition.

During his convalescence, he'd had a great deal of time to think and had come to realize that humans recognized patterns too, though of a more generalized nature, naming them "commerce" and "religion," "education" and "war," but their patterns shaped lives just as surely as such perennial hrinnti favorites as *balance/in/flow*, *wisdom/through/silence*, and *death/in/longing*. It took skill to sniff out emerging patterns and he doubted he would ever be proficient, but he seemed to sense several unnamed ones now, just beyond the edges of perception, waiting to be discovered and give new form to hrinnti life.

Several feet away, the major nudged back his combat-gray hat, then leaned against the stubby remains of a half-melted flek wall. "Well, those hrinn of yours didn't leave much for us to study, Black-eagle." He hooked his thumbs through his belt. "Or have you taken a native name?"

Suddenly, Heyoka couldn't remember the man's name, another one of those frustrating glitches in his brain that plagued him these days. He covered by pretending to examine a flattened flek laser tube. "The hrinn call me 'Black/on/black,' but that's not a personal name." The heavy gravity began to cramp his legs and he sat in the shade of one of the few still-standing slick white walls. "I prefer Heyoka Blackeagle."

"Black/on/black?" The man nodded. "Well, that suits you. It was a turn of luck you happened to come back here just at the right moment. Right man in the right place at the right time, I guess you could say."

Man . . . no human had ever called him that before. Heyoka tried to imagine how shocked the major would have been if he had seen him try to tear out the priest's throat with teeth and claws in a ritual fight to the death while the rest of the hrinn looked on in approval. His *other*, integrated now throughout his being, radiated grim amusement. No *man* could have done what he'd had to do.

The major swept his gaze around the shattered grid. "Now, are you going to explain to me how you managed this with almost no modern weapons, or do you and I have to dance another few rounds together?"

He'd left the Hrinn's ability to blueshift out of the story initially, but too many humans had seen the final battle. The secret was out, and once known, that genie could never be forced back into the bottle.

"Dr. Alvarez has some bizarre story about hrinn moving so fast that you can't even see them." The major settled in the shade beside Heyoka. "And, in a universe where a band of primitives can destroy an armed flek base, I suppose anything is possible."

If he shared the secret with these Outsiders, hrinn could be trained as formidable soldiers, especially if they were armed with modern weapons. Even without lasers and armor, their own natural advantages made them fearsome fighters, but did he want that role for his own people? He thought back to the numerous unnamed servants toiling in the deepest burrows of the five Lines, as well as the excess males living in males' houses. Many of them might like to have alternatives.

Also sobering was the thought that if he had never been kidnapped, and then later trained as a soldier, the flek would hold Anktan this very moment and the hrinn would be no more. Soldiering was not a dishonorable occupation, no matter how personally weary he was of fighting and killing.

"We want to learn from them and work alongside them." The major stared into the amber sky. "Just as we learned from you, son, and fought at your side now for years. And don't forget human and hrinn alike died here together to stop the flek. Your people can bring a great gift into the Confederation, and we can offer them much in return."

"They don't understand what's involved." Heyoka ground the heels of his hands against his aching eyes, trying to press his ever-present weariness away. "If you're going to expose them to your culture, it has to be done right. You can't just make them second-class citizens fit for the battlefield, but not for polite company. They are a proud people and deserve better."

"Well, son." The major gripped his shoulder. "I'm afraid that will be out of my hands. Doing right by these people is going to be entirely up to you."

"Me?"

"As a new Adjunct to the Confederation Office of Admissions, I expect you to see that these people are eased into Confederation culture at their own pace, and that only those who are ready leave Anktan for study and training."

"Since when am I an 'Adjunct' to anything?"

"Since the moment I got here and sized everything up." The major eyed him critically. "Of course, I did confer with my superiors. They stipulate that you'll have to retain your Confederation commission and your citizenship, as well as travel off-world when necessary to oversee matters. You have any strong objections?"

All these years, Heyoka mused, he had wanted to find his own kind and be one of them, and now that he finally had, he knew he would never really be able to think their thoughts, or live as one of them. Perhaps, he thought with a twinge, in his deepest places, he had really only wanted to be human. Perhaps he had believed that if he came here, he would find hrinn to be the same as humans and then claim his own humanity, but they were not the same and it was not possible for him to ever be wholly human or hrinn; he would always be an amalgamation of both the human culture that had raised him and his hrinnti physiology.

And he had already had the unfortunate experience of overhearing some broken-toothed old Teller in a males' house spinning out the new legend of "H-oo-kka Lost-Male and the Flek" to eager-eyed cublings. He hated being reduced to a living shrine almost as much as he hated the thought of leaving Anktan's red-orange soil and never coming back.

"Well, son, don't say you're going to turn me down."

But maybe there was a way out, a middle path that took advantage of his dual nature. "No, sir." He pulled himself to his feet and, for the first time since Confederation forces had landed, saluted. "I think you might just have yourself a deal."

PRAISE FOR
LOIS MCMASTER BUJOLD

What the critics say:

The Warrior's Apprentice: "Now here's a fun romp through the spaceways—not so much a space opera as space ballet.... it has all the 'right stuff.' A lot of thought and thoughtfulness stand behind the all-too-human characters. Enjoy this one, and look forward to the next."   —Dean Lambe, *SF Reviews*

"The pace is breathless, the characterization thoughtful and emotionally powerful, and the author's narrative technique and command of language compelling. Highly recommended."   —*Booklist*

Brothers in Arms: "... she gives it a geniune depth of character, while reveling in the wild turnings of her tale. ... Bujold is as audacious as her favorite hero, and as brilliantly (if sneakily) successful."   —*Locus*

"Miles Vorkosigan is such a great character that I'll read anything Lois wants to write about him.... a book to re-read on cold rainy days." —Robert Coulson, *Comics Buyer's Guide*

Borders of Infinity: "Bujold's series hero Miles Vorkosigan may be a lord by birth and an admiral by rank, but a bone disease that has left him hobbled and in frequent pain has sensitized him to the suffering of outcasts in his very hierarchical era.... Playing off Miles's reserve and cleverness, Bujold draws outrageous and outlandish foils to color her high-minded adventures."   —*Publishers Weekly*

Falling Free: "In *Falling Free* Lois McMaster Bujold has written her fourth straight superb novel. ... How to break down a talent like Bujold's into analyzable components? Best not to try. Best to say 'Read, or you will be missing something extraordinary.' " —Roland Green, *Chicago Sun-Times*

The Vor Game: "The chronicles of Miles Vorkosigan are far too witty to be literary junk food, but they rouse the kind of craving that makes popcorn magically vanish during a double feature."   —Faren Miller, *Locus*

What Do *You* Say?

Send me these books!

Shards of Honor	72087-2 ◆ $5.99	☐
Barrayar	72083-X ◆ $5.99	☐
Cordelia's Honor (trade)	87749-6 ◆ $15.00	☐
The Warrior's Apprentice	72066-X ◆ $5.99	☐
The Vor Game	72014-7 ◆ $5.99	☐
Young Miles (trade)	87782-8 ◆ $15.00	☐
Cetaganda (hardcover)	87701-1 ◆ $21.00	☐
Cetaganda (paperback)	87744-5 ◆ $5.99	☐
Ethan of Athos	65604-X ◆ $5.99	☐
Borders of Infinity	72093-7 ◆ $5.99	☐
Brothers in Arms	69799-4 ◆ $5.99	☐
Mirror Dance (paperback)	87646-5 ◆ $6.99	☐
Memory (paperback)	87845-X ◆ $6.99	☐
The Spirit Ring (paperback)	72188-7 ◆ $5.99	☐

 LOIS MCMASTER BUJOLD
Only from Baen Books

continued 🐾

DAVID WEBER

continued 🕿

DAVID WEBER

On Basilisk Station
0-671-72163-1 ◆ $6.99   (available May, 1999)

Honor of the Queen
0-671-72172-0 ◆ $6.99   ☐

The Short Victorious War
0-671-87596-5 ◆ $5.99   ☐

Field of Dishonor
0-671-87624-4 ◆ $5.99   ☐

Flag in Exile
0-671-87681-3 ◆ $5.99   ☐

Honor Among Enemies(HC)
0-671-87723-2 ◆ $21.00   ☐

Honor Among Enemies(PB)
0-671-87783-6◆ $6.99   ☐

In Enemy Hands(HC)
0-671-87793-3 ◆$22.00   ☐

In Enemy Hands (PB)
0-671-57770-0 ◆ $6.99   ☐

For more books by David Weber,
ask for a copy of our free catalog   ☐